THE CAPTURED GIRL

A Novel of Survival during the Great Sioux War

By Tom Reppert

ISBN: 0692668845
ISBN 13: 9780692668849
Library of Congress Control Number: 2016904495
Helen's Son's Publishing
Sagle, ID

CHAPTER ONE

July 15th, 1875

Before the attack, they killed all the dogs. Several of them, mostly troop mascots, had followed the regiment from Camp Harrison in the Dakotas as it pursued a hostile raiding party deep into Wyoming Territory. Now, within two miles of Running Hawk's Cheyenne village on Crazy Woman Creek, Colonel Gannon wanted to ensure absolute silence. He put 2nd Lieutenant William Raines, two months out of West Point, in charge of the gruesome task.

With the surrounding mesas faintly visible in the darkness, the young officer gathered a detachment of fifteen troopers and set to work. They muzzled the dogs with ropes and then either silently strangled them or knifed them. Some men grumbled when they learned Colonel Gannon spared his two staghounds from the executions.

The task proved more difficult than expected for Raines' troop when their own mascot, a big wolf-like mongrel named Bob, wouldn't die. He was first strangled but five minutes later stumbled back into the troop area. Sergeant Reardon cursed, grabbed the dog and plunged a knife into its belly.

Then, because he had loved the mutt as much as any man, he gently carried him to a dry creek bed and laid him to rest atop a grassy mound in the center. Several troopers wanted to bury him, but the sergeant said angrily they didn't have the time.

"Get back to your horses," he snapped.

A few minutes later, Bob wobbled back among them, wagging his tail and bleeding out of his belly. That's when Colonel Gannon marched up, furious. Every bit the dandy, he wore a red plume in the band of his slouch hat and a fringed, buckskin jacket with no insignia or rank. Even after weeks in the field, he still smelled heavily of lilac water.

"Lieutenant Raines, why is this animal still alive?" he demanded.

Raines sputtered, "The dog seems… he seems not to want to die, sir. Perhaps—."

Impatiently, Sergeant Reardon stepped up. "Colonel, sir, Old Bob's a quiet one. He won't make a sound."

Gannon cut him off with an abrupt wave of his hand. "This is not a debating society, Sergeant. Can't anybody in this damn army follow orders? Finish off that dog."

"I'll do it," Frank Nash, the Chief of Scouts, said as he appeared out of the darkness. From his belt, he drew out a long, thin picket pin and grinned. "I have just the ticket."

His unkempt brown hair fell from under an old flop hat like filthy spigot water. Shriveled human ears dangled on rawhide from his buckskin shirt, trophies he bragged taken off Indians. Ironic then that his own left ear was missing, lopped off he claimed in a stand up fight with a Sioux warrior, but word around camp was a woman had cut him. Raines didn't like the man, despite his frontier fame. He was essentially a bully.

Stamping his boot impatiently, Colonel Gannon said, "Then, for God's sake, do it. We move out in five minutes and woe be damned the man who is not ready."

While Gannon marched off, the men watched in frustration and anger as Nash held Old Bob down with his knee, the rope muzzle still in place, and with a rock quickly hammered the picket pin into his skull. The dog's muffled yelp was cut off, and he finally went limp. Standing up and brushing his hands off, Nash said, "There. Now that's how you kill a goddamn dog, boys."

Raines swore under his breath. After an instant's silence, Reardon cursed at the men, "Move, damn you! Don't stand there like mules. Get to your mounts."

Moments later, the regiment rode out toward the Cheyenne village, leaving Old Bob lying in the buffalo grass.

As the regiment neared the encampment, Gannon split his men, sending two companies around to the rear to block any escape, while the main body moved up to the ridgeline ahead. Approaching his first battle, Raines's bowels felt watery. He had never been so frightened in his life. Having prepared for this moment seemingly all his life, now that it was here, he'd rather be anywhere else on God's earth.

Unusually tall and lean, he appeared anything but a cavalry officer. His campaign cap askew, a shock of unruly blond hair poking out, he seemed more the bumpkin than the scion of a wealthy New York City family. When he reported to Camp Harrison, Colonel Gannon seemed affronted that he'd been sent such a useless officer and assigned him to a company of Irish malcontents, the regiment's most hopeless troop, where they called him *Billy Boy*, not *lieutenant* or *sir*. They saw him as a laughing stock who would get them killed, and Raines feared one of them might take it upon himself to dispatch their new lieutenant.

As a joke, the furrier assigned Raines an ancient, broken down nag as his cavalry mount, one so old it had actually served in the Civil War. Everyone had a hearty laugh about it. He had to admit he and the horse did make a comical pair looking like Don Quixote and Rocinante. Like that great mount, this poor beast's fastest gait was a creaking walk, her head bobbing like a chicken.

Now, aboard his Rocinante the Second and a couple hundred yards from a massive Cheyenne village of murderous hostiles,
he saw his lifelong desire for an army career as a foolish adolescent dream. He'd give anything if he could be back safe in New York with his family. Instead, it was his lot to die on a grassy field in Wyoming Territory.

Moving cautiously, the regiment spread out along the ridge overlooking the sleeping encampment and waited for the colonel's order. It was still too dark, but on the eastern horizon the sky glowed faintly gold. It would not be long. There were at least a hundred tipis stretching across the narrow valley. Raines could do the math. A hundred tipis meant around four hundred warriors. This would be bloody. Too many would die. He thought the colonel insane to attack them with only two hundred and eighty men.

Below lay not only the great chief Running Hawk but also the vicious Cheyenne war leader Spotted Horse, who had been making settlers cringe throughout Wyoming, Montana and the Dakotas. To bag both of them today would be too much for Gannon to resist, even if he had only five companies in his command.

In the morning quiet, the dread of imminent battle sat in Raines's stomach like a sponge soaking up his courage and he belched. Beside him, Sergeant Reardon glanced his way but said nothing. His hand shaking, the lieutenant drew his sword in a sweeping movement, forcing Reardon to duck. "Jesus, Billy Boy, careful with that thing," the sergeant whispered harshly. "Put it away. Use your damn sidearm. That blade will get you killed. Got to get in too close to use it."

Reardon was no friend but the advice made sense. He sheathed the sword, drew his pistol and sat his horse, waiting as each interminable second passed. He glanced at the colonel twenty yards to the left, talking in hushed whispers with one of the newspaper correspondents accompanying the expedition, James Howard of the Chicago Tribune most likely. Gannon loved the press and they loved him.

Behind them were the Crow scouts, Frank Nash among them, their horses stamping about excitedly. Then, mounted on greys, stood the brass band, ready when the attack began to break into the regimental song "Pat Murphy of the Irish Brigade." Raines thought it an odd battle hymn since it sounded more like a sad Irish drinking song than anything martial, but then most of his men were Irish and all of them drank.

Reardon leaned toward him. "Steady, Billy Boy."

Flustered, he gripped the reins of his nag. "I am steady, Sergeant."

"You're passing gas like you was trumpeting the charge, lad. Colonel Gannon's going to be putting you in the band."

At that moment, dogs began barking in the Indian encampment and a shot rang out from somewhere distant. They had been spotted. The colonel cursed and ordered the charge.

At the first blast of the bugle, Raines's old nag snapped up her head and bolted forward like a cannon shot, racing far out in front of the regiment. Frantically, the lieutenant pulled on the horse, but it had no effect. In seconds, he was already thirty yards in front, widening the distance rapidly and heading straight for the Indian village.

CHAPTER TWO

In his blind panic, Raines considered leaping free, but that would likely break his neck. If he was lucky enough to survive the fall, it would make him look the fool. They'd say he fell off his horse or worse that he was a coward. As scared as he was, he preferred death to ridicule. So, he clung for dear life and made himself as small a target as he could.

Behind him, the regiment screamed *huzzahs*, the bugler kept blowing the charge and the band played "Pat Murphy." The clamor spurred the crazed mount on more wildly. In a terrifying few seconds, it carried him splashing across Crazy Woman Creek and into the heart of the Indian camp itself. Warriors were pouring from their lodges and firing a hail of bullets and arrows at him. He would have died there but the horse kept running right on through them so quickly they could not get a clear shot. It took him on out the other end of the encampment, rose up on its hind legs and swung back on another run through camp, back through a rain of arrows. Finally, she drew to a halt right in the middle of the village, bucked once, then sagged, spent, her head nestling close to the ground, gasping for breath.

By then the place had turned into Dante's Inferno.

The regiment had come and people were dying. Mostly Indians. Men, women and children alike. The soldiers fired at anything that moved while the Crow and white scouts set upon the Indians and scalped them dead or alive. Raines's fear turned to nausea.

That's when the oddest thing he'd ever seen in his life took place. Old Bob showed up. The spike still sticking out of his head, he loped across open ground toward the Indians as if knowing exactly where he wanted to go. Astonishingly, the line of Cheyenne ceased firing and allowed him to pass through. He kept going right on up into the hills behind the village.

Then, like a thunder clap, the firing commenced again.

As a great haze of gunpowder drifted over the village, an unarmed Cheyenne with long grey braids stepped out of his tipi near Raines, planted an American flag in the ground, and folding his arms stood in front of it. Raines thought it the bravest thing he'd ever seen. For about ten seconds, cavalrymen galloped past the Indian without noticing. Then Colonel Gannon rode up and shot him in the head.

At that moment Raines's childhood dreams ended. All his life he had believed war was about glory and heroes. There was nothing glorious or heroic in this. It was slaughter.

Gannon reined his horse up next to him and shouted excitedly, "That was Running Hawk. I killed Running Hawk." Raines stared at him with a mixture of confusion and horror.

"Well, get after them, man." The colonel gestured with his pistol.

"Sir?"

"That's your troop, isn't it?" He pointed to the hills where several cavalrymen were pursuing a group of Indians up a coulee. "Go after them. Lead them. Don't let a single one of the bastards escape."

"Yes, sir," he said halfheartedly and turned the old nag toward the hills. The horse managed a lumbering gallop.

As he left the village, a dense black cloud of gun smoke engulfed him. The acrid smell singed the hairs in his nostrils and made it hard to breathe, and the poor visibility sent renewed panic through him. He imagined warriors coming out of the mist in every direction.

"Ride, you dumb beast, ride," he shouted angrily and spurred the horse on. She shot forward, the bitter smell or his growing terror seemingly giving her renewed energy.

When he finally escaped the mist, he found himself far up a narrow coulee but the wrong one. His men were not here; he was alone. He thought that just as well since his first battle had been an utter disaster. He had found himself wanting in every way as a soldier. The images of women and children cut down in volley after volley made him feel sick, and he feared he might actually vomit.

He heard the pounding of a horse's hooves and turned to face an Indian boy, thirteen or fourteen, with a drawn pistol trying to ride by him. Raines had his own pistol in his hand and realized he'd not fired a shot yet. In an instant, he made the decision to let the boy pass.

Desperately, he tried signing to him his intention, but the boy fired at him from only a few feet. The lieutenant heard the bullet whine passed his ear. The boy fired again before Raines snapped off a shot but missed also. Wildly for several seconds, they kept shooting at each other, hitting nothing.

Finally, a shot caught the old nag in the head, splattering blood and grit onto Raines's face. The horse dropped instantly and the lieutenant rolled away. The boy shrieked a war cry and rode right at him. The lieutenant fired twice more, the second time hitting the boy in the chest, toppling him from his pony.

Raines stared at the body, at the tiny hole in the chest and the vacant eyes. This was supposed to be a rite of passage, killing your first Indian. It did not feel like a rite of passage. Instead, a vast emptiness spread inside him.

Disgusted, he started walking back toward the village. He had had enough. They would court-martial him, drum him out of the army if he was lucky, put him in front of a firing squad for desertion if he was not.
Right now, he didn't care. He wanted no more of it.

The sun had come up and burned off the morning chill. He sat on a fallen log, as tired as he had ever been in his life, and waited for whatever was to come. He listened to the staccato sound of distant gunfire, the shouts and commands and screams of battle as if he were the lone person in the audience at the Academy of Music Opera House watching Tristan in hell without his Isolde. He pushed the tumult from his mind and thought of his own Isolde, his fiancée Nancy. The glorious Nancy Merchant. He pictured her beautiful face framed by golden ringlets, saw the coy smile that so entranced him. Odd, she came to mind now. Missing her at this exact moment, he felt a palpable ache.

He was reaching into his pocket for the locket with her picture when an Indian bounded on foot over the crest of the coulee, darting right at him. He jumped up fumbling for his gun, then froze. It was a girl, maybe seventeen or eighteen, with wild terrified eyes. At sight of him, she shrieked in alarm but kept coming. A moment later, Nash sprinted over the top after her.

"Stop the little bitch, Lieutenant," the scout yelled.

She dodged past him, but Raines did not attempt to stop her. Something in her eyes shocked him, her terror, yes, but something more. In the numbing fog of battle, he couldn't fix on it.

"Damn it, Lieutenant," Nash cursed, rushing past, firing a shot at the girl.

She fell but quickly scrambled up, trying to limp away. By then Nash was on her, viciously clubbing her once with his pistol, knocking her to the ground. In no hurry now, he began unbuckling his belt.

Raines took a couple steps forward. "What are you doing?"

"She's a quick one, she is," he said, glancing back at him with a hideous grin. "I owe her this. Stay out of it."

She was on her belly, one arm pinned under her, the fingers of the other groping in the dirt. Nash dropped his pants and stood bare-assed over her and said as if he knew her, "You know you got this coming, girl. You know you do."

Falling to his knees, he violently jerked her onto her back. As she spun, she lashed out with a knife, slicing his thigh open. He stumbled back, screaming, "Bitch!"

She struggled up once more and tried to escape. From his sitting position, Nash aimed carefully and fired. She fell hard this time, blood seeping quickly into the side of her calico dress.

Calmly, Nash tied a kerchief over the wound on his leg, pulled up his pants and hobbled over to her. He drew his knife and clutched her hair, yanking her into a sitting position. She stared up at him with a mixture of terror, rage and hatred. He was going to scalp her while she was still alive.

Raines shouted, "Stop! That's an order, Nash."

Nash's eyes darkened. "You got no say over me, Billy Boy." He put the knife to her forehead and began cutting. Blood flooded out.

Raines's sudden fury overwhelmed his fear. He jammed his gun hard into the man's temple and cocked it. "This says I do. I'll scatter your pea brain all over this ground if you cut one more whit. Do you understand me, you bastard?" His voice was high pitched and frenzied as if he'd gone mad.

Nash stopped. "No you won't, Billy Boy." But his tone indicated he was not so sure.

"I swear on my soul I will."

The cut across the girl's forehead was barely an inch long but it bled profusely. When Nash released her, she fell back onto the ground, gasping for breath, wiping blood from her eyes. They were frozen in that tableau, her on the ground, Raines pistol pressed against Nash's temple, when Sergeant Reardon and two soldiers rode up. "What's going on here, Billy Boy?"

Raines didn't answer immediately, but Nash did. Brushing the lieutenant's gun aside, he said, "Damn, Reardon, glad you're here. Do something about this lieutenant of yours. I'm trying to kill myself an Injun, but the boy here don't seem to get the purpose of this day."

The sergeant glanced at Raines. "Lieutenant?"

Raines didn't know what to answer. To say he was not going to allow anymore killing of women and children might not work with men caught in bloodlust, though he had to admit Reardon seemed in control of himself. He had not seen the sergeant shoot anyone. Still, the colonel seemed to want every Cheyenne dead. He would back Nash. But, Raines was not going to let anyone kill this Indian girl, not even Reardon.

Before he could speak, the girl struggled into a sitting position, holding one hand on her forehead and one at her side as if trying to stop all the blood from escaping her body.Then, he realized what was so strange about her. Her eyes were pale grey, the color of river ice. She spoke to Reardon in a sharp voice that carried a distinct Irish lilt. "Are ye blind, man? I am Morgan O'Connor, and I am no Indian."

CHAPTER THREE

The aftermath of the battle at Crazy Woman Creek couldn't have been more surprising to Raines if he had been promoted to general on the spot. He thought he would be court-martialed and drummed out of the army, but instead was heralded as a hero. Colonel Gannon and the rest of the regiment assumed his mad dash into the village had been on purpose. Though dumbfounded, Raines was not foolish enough to set the record straight. He accepted the unwarranted plaudits and the new respect with a forced smile, a little guilt, and the repeated lie, "I was only doing my duty."

His men still called him *Billy Boy* but now with some friendliness and even pride behind it, and a few even addressed him as *sir.* The biggest shock of all came when James Howard, the reporter from the Chicago Tribune, told him he was now famous. As the regiment made its way back to Camp Harrison with their prisoners—all women and children—the Tribune reporter and two other newspapermen had sent in stories with dispatches telling of the victory and his brave charge. The absurd, tragic fight with the Indian boy he had killed turned into a stirring account of single combat against a great war chief named Fighting Bull, who, as far as Raines knew, didn't exist.

They did not mention the gut-pissing fear, the baptism of fire shattering every illusion he'd possessed or his walking away from the battle. Clearly, a good story trumped truth in the newspapers.

When Howard saw his expression of incredulity, he laughed. "If you are so indisposed to the public eye, think of poor Miss O'Connor. We have dubbed her *The Captured Girl,* and in all my years in the news business, I have never seen such a plum of a story. People already crave any information we can glean about the girl. After all, she survived four years among the savages." He waved a hand dismissing Raines's concerns. "Don't fret so. She will be far more famous than you, Billy Boy."

Raines blanched at the name. Howard had already turned and hurried off to catch up with Colonel Gannon. The lieutenant remembered two days ago when there was so much blood on Miss O'Connor he thought she would die. He had carried her from the battlefield as she slipped in and out of consciousness, while all around them gunshots rang from the hills where Colonel Gannon pursued the Indians. At West Point, they told him all battle was chaos. He had found it so.

Inside the hospital tent, disorder reigned. Wounded men groaned and screamed; orderlies rushed about trying to help them. Doc Whalen stood over an operating table, drawing an arrow from a man's leg. Held down by two orderlies, the man on the table wailed in pain. The doctor gave a final pull and the arrow came loose. He held it up, studying it a moment, then noticed Raines. "Get that squaw out of here," he yelled, glaring. "I will not be treating any damn Indians in here till these men are attended to."

That took Raines by surprise and he stood for a moment uncertain what to do.

"Get out, Lieutenant!" he said. "Can you not hear a plain order?"

"She's white, sir. A prisoner among the Indians. She's wounded."

The doctor stared at her for several seconds. "All right. How bad is it?"

"Well, she's been shot."

He snapped angrily, "Is she about to die, Lieutenant?"

"No, I don't know, sir. I don't think so, but she's bleeding."

"Then, stop the damn bleeding. Put her on the cot over there. Use one of those clean bandages. I'll get to her when I can."

Raines did as he was told, laying her down and pressing a clean cloth against the cut just below her scalp line that was still bleeding profusely. She woke, and alarmed, drew her knife.

Raines held up his hands. "I'm trying to help you. I need to stop the bleeding."

She stared at him a moment, then slid the knife back in its sheath. She watched him warily as he worked. Raines told her to hold the head bandage in place, and she did. Tossing aside propriety, he searched for more wounds on her body, and she made no attempt to stop him. One of Nash's bullets had torn open her calico dress over her ribs, revealing chalk white skin and a bloody gouge. He ripped the dress open further and pressed a bandage against the wound. He found the last wound on her hip, barely a nick but it still bled. With his other hand he placed a bandage over it.

"Thank you," she said just above a whisper.

He nodded. After another few minutes, the doctor made his way to her and told Raines he'd done enough damage and to leave. An hour later, while the last remnants of battle continued off in the hills, the doctor found Raines waiting outside the tent and told him, "As I suspected, her wounds are not serious. One bullet clipped her hip, leaving a nasty welt, and the other struck her side, bruising her ribs and gouging a long furrow out of her skin. Her head wound bled quite a bit and she's had a significant loss of blood, but she'll heal. That girl's a tough one.

I sewed up the head wound and the one on her ribs while she was conscious. It had to hurt like hell, but she didn't make a sound. We just need to keep the wounds clean."

Later that day, the fighting ended and Gannon returned, prancing into camp on his big grey gelding, like a man leading a parade. He addressed his men and told them it had been a great victory. All the Cheyenne warriors had either been killed, or driven into the hills. Sickening to Raines, though, several women and children had also been killed. He had never thought to see that. It was not battle as he had imagined it would be.

The regiment burned the village, everything that wasn't taken as souvenirs. Each man, including Raines, chose a fresh mount or two from the Indian horse herd before slaughtering the rest. The bodies of nearly five hundred horses were left to rot on the prairie. The idea he knew was to eliminate the Indians ability to travel quickly. Destroy their way of life and leave only the reservation for them to go. With the smoke of the burning lodges still fresh in his nostrils, the regiment started back for Camp Harrison.

Now, two days later, they were riding through the dry country of eastern Wyoming with its rolling prairie, short grass, sage and occasional high bluff. And instead of being under arrest, he was being lauded by one and all. Raines and his troop were assigned to guard the captives and the pack train at the rear of the column, where they ate dust.

"Not a very glorious way to treat a hero," he said ruefully to Reardon, who stared at him a moment, then laughed.

"No, it ain't, Billy Boy."

The captives walked just ahead, no threat to escape. Sergeant Reardon had said with a cynical smirk that they wouldn't even consider it. They knew they'd eventually be reunited with their men when everyone turned up at the Tall Bull Agency on the reservation.

"These hostiles," he said, "become reservation Indians pretty damn quick when the weather turns cold."

Raines spotted Miss O'Connor just behind a hospital ambulance thirty yards ahead, walking with a pronounced limp. Even from where he was, he could see dried blood stuck to her calico dress. He had to admire her determination. If he had her wounds, he would have been laid up in the wagon for days, but she insisted on walking.

A boy around three years old rode on the back of the ambulance just in front of her, his feet dangling in a gentle kicking motion. Bare-chested in the heat, he wore but a simple breechcloth and moccasins. He had brown hair that hung loose to his shoulders. He was jabbering to Miss O'Connor, which she encouraged, laughing and even placing her hand over her mouth once in mock astonishment at something he said. A clear bond existed between them. Abruptly, the boy jumped down and held his arms up to her to be carried. When she shook her head firmly, he ran back to another woman, an older one, who lifted him up onto her back.

Raines urged his mount forward, and eased in beside her, touching his campaign cap. "Morning, Miss O'Connor."

She glanced up at him. "Good morning, Lieutenant." The word *lieutenant* rolled out slowly like a large pebble. *Lutenant.*

He was surprised by the force of her, just a small, thin girl with grey eyes, but one with an intensity and self-assurance unusual among someone so young. Surely near his age—he guessed eighteen—she clearly had far more belief in herself than he did in himself. She was pretty, though her coppery skin a bit too baked by the sun. Her auburn hair was pulled back in a single braid, looking every bit the Indian, and he indeed wondered after more than four years with the savages if she was not more Indian than white.

A faint ghost of desire shot through him, then a shift in the soft breeze brought the smell of her to his nostrils. She stunk and that held no allure.

With long days out on the march, he had become used to the fierce odors of so many unwashed people, but this girl was particularly in need of a bath. In the turmoil of battle the other day, he had not noticed, but now the odor was like an overwhelming fog. All the Indians bore it, a choking smell of rancid meat mixed with thick smoke.

The brief seedlings of romantic interest died quickly in embarrassment. He had a fiancée he loved. And, indeed, a poor, uneducated Irish girl could hold no attraction for him, even if she had not lived four years with the Cheyenne. "Miss O'Connor, you should be resting inside the wagon. Your injuries, surely."

When she answered, the words came haltingly as if she struggled to get at them. "Ah, Lieutenant…no, I think not. These…wounds are bare…barely scratches as me da would say."

He guessed not using English in the last four years she was straining to pick it up again. "But surely painful, he said." She shrugged, conceding the point. "Aye, some."

"But it has not been two days. If your wounds are to heal—"

As if speaking to a schoolboy, she said, exasperated, "Not in that wagon, sir. Too hard on my ribs."

Of course. He felt foolish and nodded.

She took a step closer to his horse. "Lieutenant, there…there was another white woman in camp. She had a boy, maybe a year old. Did you find them?"

His expression grew hard. "Yes. Her name was Mrs. Granger. She and her boy had been taken the week before from a Colorado ranch. It was these Indians we tracked back to Running Hawk's camp."

"Are they safe?" she asked.

"No, they are not safe, Miss O'Connor," he said more heatedly than he intended as if she were partially to blame. "The savages murdered them. The child was no older than one year."

She exhaled sharply and looked away. Nothing else was said for another minute. He saw an eagle circling above a high bluff and felt a gentle breeze that did little to cool the already growing heat. He was upset, plagued by the last two days. The Granger woman and her baby murdered. How could anyone think of these Indians as anything but ignorant savages? But their own women and children killed, driven off or taken prisoner, was that war or retribution? The level of barbarism he'd found in the West had shocked the marrow of his being. For the first time, he wondered if he belonged out here.

He glanced down at Miss O'Connor. A muscle in her face twitched from pain. In an instant, he felt overwhelming sympathy for her. She had been at the sharp end of all that savagery. Her ordeal must have been horrendous. Stories proliferated about captive white women, what happened to them, the unspeakable degradation. It was called the *fate worse than death*. And she so young.

Against her will, she would have been used by Indian men over and over for four years, a terrible brutality to endure. White society expected its women to kill themselves before submitting to such degradation. This one did not. It was easy enough to think such homilies from the safe distance of one's parlor, but not this close. Surviving must have been what drove her, and she had done that when few had. So long among them, though, she should have been half mad. Yet, her mind was clearly intact, which made him wonder.

Giving way to his curiosity, he asked, "If I may, Miss O'Connor, how did you manage to survive four years of captivity among the savages?"

Her eyes went cold, and she made no effort to answer. The saddle creaked as he leaned forward. "I'm sorry. I had no right to ask."

"You are…" she hesitated, her eyes shifting back and forth as if searching for the exact word, "…entitled, Lieutenant. I owe you my life. Simply, it's something about which I do not wish to talk."

"I understand," he said.

"I'm sure you do not."

He had been reprimanded, and it bothered him that she could make him feel that way. "I suppose I don't." He doffed his cap again. "Colonel Gannon extends his compliments and asks that when we camp tonight, you attend the evening briefing in his tent. He wishes to speak with you." He expected an answer, but when she made none, he added, "I will come for you when it's time."

As he rode back to Reardon, he couldn't shake the feeling his exchange with Miss O'Connor had been another kind of combat in which he had been found wanting.

CHAPTER FOUR

In the twilight that evening, after the regiment made camp, Raines escorted Miss O'Connor to the colonel's tent. She had a determined set to her jaw, as if a fighter being led into the ring.

"I assure you it's not an interrogation, Miss O'Connor," he said. "You have nothing to fear."

She ignored him, making no acknowledgement that he'd even spoken.

Inside the tent, several men had assembled, Colonel Gannon and his second-in-command, Major Collins, who leaned over a map on the camp table. The three newsmen accompanying the regiment were seated nearby in camp chairs as if a small jury. Under the illumination of a lantern that hung suspended from the center pole, James Howard was drawing a martial pose of the colonel on a sketchpad.

Frank Nash stood beside Gannon, pointing to something on the map. At sight of the scout, Miss O'Connor stiffened. The hair on her arms actually rose, and her grey eyes burned hatred.

"Sir," Raines said announcing himself. "Miss O'Connor is here."

Glancing over, the colonel forced a smile and stepped forward, taking her hand. "Ah, Miss O'Connor, you're feeling better, I see. Speaks well for your constitution." His black hair was slicked back and his thick eyebrows almost knitted together.

She snapped a nod toward Nash. "What is that man doing here?"

"Mr. Nash scouts for me. There still may be hostiles about. I assure you he did not realize you were white when he came upon you."

"He certainly knew I…I was a woman," she said sharply, her speech coming at that awkward gait. "While you…and your brave men were doing battle with Cheyenne warriors, that, that man was busy fighting women. I am lucky he is not a better shot."

Gannon made a gruff laugh, then indicated a chair in the center of the tent. "Please, sit down, Miss O'Connor." When she did, he took a chair behind the map table while Major Collins and Nash sat flanking him, giving the appearance of a tribunal. "I know you've endured a great ordeal," the colonel began. "I can only imagine how difficult it has been for you."

He waited for her to respond but she said nothing, watching him, her eyes remote and emotionless. After a moment, he cleared his throat and went on. "I have a few questions to ask you, Miss O'Connor, if you don't mind." He paused, his eye brows knitting together as if in deep concentration. "What can you tell us about Spotted Horse?"

Raines was watching Morgan closely, and at the mention of the name *Spotted Horse,* he saw her flinch imperceptibly. He wondered if anyone else saw it, or if they did, they interpreted it like he had. Spotted Horse was someone she knew.

"I can tell you nothing about him," she said."

Disappointed, Gannon tapped his finger impatiently on the table. After a few seconds, he said calmly, "As you know, we decisively routed the redskins to save you, and I myself killed Running Hawk. But unfortunately, Spotted Horse escaped. He was our main objective. This is why—."

"Colonel Gannon, you are mistaken," she interrupted him. "Spotted Horse did not escape. He was not there. He hasn't lived in Running Hawk's camp for three years."

Gannon exchanged disbelieving looks with Major Collins and Nash. Then, he nodded. "Are you certain of this?"

"Of course, I'm sure."

"Then is there anything at all you can tell us? Places he might be? Chiefs with whom he may try to find refuge?"

She gave a slight shake of the head. "Nothing."

This visibly disappointed him. Quickly, the three men whispered among themselves and another officer leaned over the table to listen. Finally, Gannon sat back and spoke to her again, his voice softening, "I know you must be wondering what will happen to you now. Let me reassure you, after what you've been through, we will not abandon you. The army will provide transportation to your family, wherever that is."

"I have no family but my brother."

Raines noticed the drawing Howard was making of the new scene, accurate in every detail but one. In the drawing, he showed Miss O'Connor standing with her head bowed as if ashamed of her four years with the Cheyenne. In reality, she sat in the chair, her head unbowed and looked directly at Gannon.

"Do you have elbow relations?" Gannon asked. "Aunts, uncles, grandparents?"

She nodded. "In New York. I haven't seen any of them in more than ten years."

Gannon's hand shot up emphatically. "There. You see, a start. I will assign Lieutenant Raines to assist you in finding them. He is from New York and has his contacts. Till we locate your relatives, you will be staying with my wife and me. The ladies of Camp Harrison will take care of you. They are a resourceful lot and will see to your needs."

"I thank you, Colonel, but I don't intend to leave the territories."

This took Gannon by surprise. "From my understanding, those people in New York are the only family you have left."

"No, they aren't, sir. I will go to them some day. They have a right to know what happened to my parents. But my younger brother is alive, a prisoner of Big Crow and the Cheyenne. I intend to find him. I will not leave until he is returned to me."

Major Collins shook his head, shifting a shock of white hair. "Dear girl, that is unsupportable. You must think rationally about these things. You have no family to support you here. You are female, barely more than a child yourself. How will you live? No, no, a young girl staying alone on the frontier will not do. At a time such as this, I assure you, you must be with family. Now, if we can—."

Her face hardened. "I will not leave without my brother."

Collins sighed and looked to Gannon for help. Frowning, the colonel shrugged. "So be it." He turned to Raines. "Lieutenant, you now have an added duty. Locate Miss O'Connor's brother, and we will attempt to reunite them. After all, Big Crow will need to be subdued sooner or later. If there is nothing else, gentleman, this meeting is ended. Lieutenant, see Miss O'Connor back to her tent."

In the darkness, as Morgan walked with the young lieutenant back to her tent, she seethed at having been so close to Nash.

The man had raped her and attempted to kill her more than once. The army would surely like to know he sold guns and whiskey to Indians. But Nash knew she'd been married to Spotted Horse and had his son.

If Colonel Gannon or any of his fine officers, including this young lieutenant beside her found out, she would be immediately cast out of white society before she had even re-entered it, and her chances of locating her brother would fall to nothing.

As she was about to go in her tent, the Lieutenant Raines said, "Miss O'Connor, are you tired? If not, then I thought we might talk a bit. I need to ask you a few questions about your

family if I am to find them. And your brother. That is if you're feeling well enough."

"All right."

Her nearness made him uneasy. He flinched when she brushed against him accidently, and he stared for a brief moment into her mercurial grey eyes before looking away. The heat still hung on as they ambled silently among the scattered pines and cottonwoods. The night was clear and moonless, the stars so bright that they cast faint shadows off the trees. He had to admit that even though she still didn't smell any better, a good measure of desire settled on him, which was troubling. He desperately hoped she wouldn't become aware of it. Because of his feelings for the golden-haired Nancy Merchant waiting for him in New York, his sudden romantic feelings troubled him. This Irish girl was not on the same plane as his Nancy.

He turned his mind to the tasks the colonel had given him. Daunting as they were, he had an idea how to proceed. Miss O'Connor had a kind of fame that would help. Women and children taken by Indians—men were never captured—became known even back East because of the lurid newspaper accounts of such things.

Raines even remembered reading four years ago while at West Point about Morgan O'Connor in the *New York World*. His family's New York attorney, the estimable Aaron Greenblatt, could use her fame to search giving them a chance for success.

Seeing one of the guards on the picket line ahead, he said, "We should not go farther. Indians might be about."

She spoke quickly in a language he couldn't understand. He guessed Cheyenne. A shimmer of embarrassment settled in her eyes. "Sorry. There are no Indians about, Lieutenant, except the ones you have captured."

"I wouldn't want to be shot by a nervous picket then," he said. "We can talk here."

"All right." Folding her arms in front of her, she leaned her back against a cottonwood.

A hundred feet off, the river flowed by gently with only the occasional glint of starlight off the water. The slope on the far side was sparsely studded with trees, isolated stands amid the tall grass. He said nothing for several moments, taking in the scent of pine. "Beautiful, isn't it?"

She said nothing, her face blank.

"Morgan is an unusual name for an Irish girl," he said. "It's English, isn't it?"

"Welsh. It's not really my name. My real name is Morrigan. Now that is Irish. Morgan seems to be what my family ended up calling me."

"Morrigan, the Irish Goddess of Strife."

She glanced up at him, surprised. "Well, now, Lieutenant. You do know your Irish—" she struggled for the next word.

"Legends?" he suggested.

"Legends. Yes." Then, she added with irritation. "I'm not an imbecile. I can speak English. Mam taught us, and she could speak it better than a Philadelphia lawyer."

"It will come back to you," he said.

She shrugged, still annoyed. She was such an uncomfortable girl to talk with, he thought, ready to bite his head off at any perceived slight. She knelt and began scratching tiny circles in the dirt with a stick.

After a few moments of silence, he asked, "How is it you have relatives in New York?"

She did not look up. "I was born there. We came west eleven years ago. My aunt, uncle and cousins still live there."

"Do you have an address for them?"

"No. We used to receive letters twice a year, but I long ago forgot the address. He's a shoemaker or was. His name is Kevin O'Connor. I played with my cousins, two girls about my age and a teenage boy named Finn. Finn took care of us during the day, if you could call it that, kept us out of trouble."

"What neighborhood was that?"

Morgan glanced up at him, hesitant, and turned the question. "The colonel said you're from New York. What neighborhood are *you* from, Lieutenant?"

He thought of his family and missed them instantly. His father and mother and three sisters. Along with Nancy, he wrote them all constantly like a boy sent off for the summer who is homesick. "I grew up in Manhattanville," he said without emotion. "We now live on Fifth Avenue."

Dropping the stick, she stood, hands on hips, and the Irish came out. "Do you now? The hoity toity." Her tone was not altogether joking, and for the first time the language was fluid.

"My father has been successful," he said almost defensively.

"What is a Fifth Avenue lad doing in the cavalry?"

"That's what my family want to know," he said. "It's a long story. Let's save it for another day." He pressed again. "Where are you from?"

She stayed in her brogue. "Not Fifth Avenue, t'is sure. I was born in Five Points. Are we not the pair?"

It surprised Raines that she came from Five Points. If any place in New York City had the fame of Fifth Avenue, it was Five Points. More accurately, infamy. It had a reputation for being the worst slum in the country, in the world; murder and mayhem stood as a way of life and poverty the touchstone. Surely, a vile place to live. But she showed no embarrassment whatsoever by the station of her birth.

"Then that's where I shall commence the search for your uncle. There is an attorney in New York who has done work for my family. I'll set him on the task."

"That's kind of you, Lieutenant, but I said I will not be leaving this country for New York, and I meant it."

"I understand." He nodded and asked her to tell him everything she could about Conor. She talked for several minutes with an edge in her voice alternating between concern for her brother and hatred for the Indian chief Big Crow. The boy must surely be all Indian by now, Raines thought. Getting him back into the white world would be infinitely more difficult than she seemed to think.

"Where was the last place you knew him to be?" he asked.

She shook her head. "That will do little good. The Cheyenne move too often. Big Crow is a well-known chief though. Someone will know where he is. It might be that easy. Find Big Crow, find Conor." She turned on him, aggressively. "Get him back for me, Lieutenant. Please. I will be forever in your debt. I will give you anything you ask in my power to give."

"That's not necessary," he said uncomfortably. "I promise you I'll do my best. We are a week out from Camp Harrison. When we get back, I'll telegraph every army post in the territories looking for Big Crow and your brother."

She closed her eyes for a long moment. "Thank you, Lieutenant."

They stood together silently for nearly a minute listening to the sounds of the camp fade as the men were turning in. A laugh came from somewhere nearby and then the rattle of a pan from a cook wagon. A coyote howled far off and Raines wondered if it might be an Indian signaling, but Miss O'Connor seemed unconcerned.

"It's getting late," she said abruptly. "I'd best get some sleep."

Raines escorted her back to her tent.

When she went in, he started for his troop area. But after thirty yards, he stopped and glanced back, troubled. He couldn't say exactly why he did, perhaps the sense she had been hiding something, or perhaps her abrupt goodnight. Moments later, Miss O'Connor appeared outside the tent and slipped silently into the trees.

CHAPTER FIVE

On the wide patch of grass where his troop bivouacked, Raines lay down on his bedroll with an uneasy sigh. Curious, he had followed Miss O'Connor, but lost her immediately in the trees. Guessing where she might be going, he went directly to the prisoners, and from a stand of pines, watched for her. He did not see her come. One moment, she wasn't there, and the next she was, sitting beside a stout woman near the fire. A young boy jumped into her lap. It was the boy he'd seen with her that morning. He saw her wince from pain, then she ruffled his hair. Seeing her among these Indians bothered him. They were murderers, savages. They killed Mrs. Granger and her boy. They killed Miss O'Connor's family, and here she was being friendly towards them. Why would she want anything to do with them?

He returned to his troop area and tried to sleep, but he couldn't shut his mind down. Confused and unsettled about the mysterious Morgan O'Connor and about his recent baptism of battle, he lay awake for hours trying to make sense of it all. Nothing seemed to fit into his preconceived notions, and he squirmed uneasily till finally he fell into a troubled sleep.

***

Morgan moved quickly through the trees. In a minute, she came to where the soldiers kept the prisoners, many of whom were already sleeping, sprawled out on the ground near the dying embers of a single fire. Two soldiers stood guard but they gave little attention to them, instead chatting quietly between themselves and trading a silver flask back and forth.

Morgan slipped among the thirty or so prisoners, moving quickly in beside Lame Deer. "He'e, Daughter," the older woman said.

"He'e, Mother," Morgan answered.

At her sudden appearance, little Ho'nehe leapt into her lap. Morgan sucked in a breath at the shock of pain and then ruffled his hair and gave him a fierce hug. She could feel blood anew seeping from her wounds, but she welcomed it. It took her mind from the anguish of losing both Running Hawk and Owl Woman when the white cavalry attacked. "You are still awake," she whispered in Cheyenne to the boy in a mock scolding tone. "You should be asleep. Warriors need rest."

"I wait for you, Mother," he said.

Lame Deer leaned in close as if to shield her words from the two sentries, though it didn't matter since neither spoke the language of the People. "He has run around all evening like his moccasins were on fire, waiting for you."

Morgan was relaxed here, holding her son and sitting next to her friend Lame Deer, her new mother, and the rest of the Cheyenne women that had been her friends for the last four years. No, almost five now. Five years since her white family had been killed. She was from the white world. She wanted to go back to it now. Knew she had to if she was ever to bring Conor home.

Morgan placed a hand on Lame Deer's shoulder, feeling a wave of warmth for her. When the soldiers had come two days ago, it was Lame Deer who saved Ho'nehe's life. Almost too vividly, Morgan remembered that morning in Running Hawk's lodge.

They were just rising for the day. Then, they heard a few sporadic gunshots, and she looked out the flap, seeing the lone rider cross Crazy Woman Creek. She screamed, "Soldiers!"

Without waiting, she grabbed Ho'nehe, the Sharps and a pouch of provisions, and fled from the lodge. She knew Running Hawk would stay behind. He had spoken about it often enough before. For him it was a matter of honor. He had promised never to fight the whites again, and he would not go back on his word. Owl Woman stayed with him. Morgan never saw her Cheyenne parents again.

Outside the lodge, morning had turned to chaos. The oncoming soldiers fired relentlessly into the village. Morgan fell in with several other women fleeing with their children. Bullets kicked up dirt around them, and two women fell. By now, warriors were fighting back, shouting for the women and children to make for the hills. When she was almost out of the village, a soldier on horseback with a drawn saber surged at her, and she ducked the swipe of the blade. As he swung around to come at her again, she set Ho'nehe down, lifted the Sharps and shot him from the horse.

Morgan picked out another soldier running down a brave and aimed. This time the rifle jammed. Leaving it behind, she lifted Ho'nehe and the pouch of food, and seeing Lame Deer ahead, sprinted after her. They rushed out of the village behind several others, climbing up a ravine and after a hundred yards hid behind a few boulders. Besides Morgan, Ho'nehe and Lame Deer, there were five other women and seven children. To be safe they would have to get much farther away.

"We must wait till the children have strength," Lame Deer said. She was sweating profusely, glistening off her broad forehead.

Morgan nodded, staring down the ravine a quarter of a mile, praying no soldiers appeared. But in the next moment, a single figure guided his horse up the slope.

She recognized him instantly. Frank Nash. Her heart withered to utter despair. They'd known each other for years. Hate for him seared into her more powerfully than a grizzly's claws. She knew his hate for her filled his black heart. If she'd had the Sharps…but she didn't. They couldn't outrun him. He would soon catch up. And he would kill her and Ho'nehe to be sure, and the others if he could. She had no doubt.

Lame Deer and the women saw him and rose, a few already scrambling farther up the ravine. Morgan clutched Lame Deer's shoulder. "You must take Ho'nehe. It is the only way. I know this man. He will follow me."

Staring hard at her for a second, Lame Deer nodded.

"I will find you," Morgan said. "If I don't, make him your son."

Lame Deer nodded again. She took Ho'nehe's hand, but he resisted, cried out.

"Go!" Morgan shouted at him. "I will come later. You must go now!" And he did.

On horseback, Nash would run her down soon enough, but maybe she could delay him enough for her son to escape. She ran in another direction and Nash followed, shouting in a rage. At a steep, rocky hill, she climbed on all fours to the crest. Nash leapt from his horse and began clawing his way up after her.

As Morgan bounded over the crest, she saw a soldier sitting on a downed log as if he resting during a Sunday walk. Upon seeing her, he jerked to his feet and drew his gun. She could not turn back. She ran straight at him.

CHAPTER SIX

On the day the Cheyenne raided her family's ranch, fourteen-year-old Morgan O'Connor awoke long before dawn, excited about this morning's hunt. Her mother was not yet tinkering in the kitchen, so as cold as it was, she decided to stay a little longer under the quilt next to her younger sister Fiona.

Morgan loved to hunt more than anything in life. Mostly, she shot sage hen, rabbits and wild turkey to augment the family larder and to sell in the nearby town of Lone Tree for cash. Two or three times a month, she went out with an adult for larger game, deer or elk, or even a lone, wandering buffalo. When the game became scarce in winter, families could starve. She took pride in providing meat for hers.

Morgan had been hunting for years. At seven, she began tagging along with her father Seamus and older brother Patrick. By age nine, her father allowed her to use a rifle for birds and small game, and to everyone's amazement, she soon began hitting them. By eleven, her marksmanship had become something of a legend even as far away as Bozeman and Bannack, the little hawk-eyed girl from Lone Tree. No one could quite explain it, a girl shooting so well, but she could knock the eye out of a rabbit at one hundred yards.

Eventually, just after her thirteenth birthday, her father decided to let her do all the hunting, leaving him and Patrick more time to work the ranch. He told her never to go farther than a mile from the house unless one of the adults came along. On her horse Rhiannon, she broke that rule the first day, ranging as far out as five miles in her new-found freedom and pridefulness.

Laying in the dark of the bedroom that March morning, she could see the frost where it had crept in along the window shutters and shivered, nestling closer to her sister. Ten-year-old Fi dozed, snoring with a soft wheeze, her vibrant red hair splayed out on the pillow.

Fi opened her eyes in blinking slits and groaned, "Why are you awake? It's the middle of the night. Let me sleep."

"I'm hunting this morning."

One of Fi's eyes went wide. "Well, for lord's sake, shoot something we can eat this time. No more porcupines and raccoons."

"Shut up," Morgan snapped. Her sister was a trial to her.

Fi turned away and fell quickly back to sleep. Morgan heard the rattle of a pan in the kitchen and swung her feet to the cold floorboards.

An hour later, after filling buckets of water from the well and stocking wood by the fireplace, Morgan gathered with her family around the breakfast table. Still dark outside, three oil lamps illuminated the room. Her mother Glenna signaled for all to grasp hands while she said a prayer praising the Lord for their bounty.

A short woman with brown hair, Glenna's lined, pretty face and startling grey eyes mirrored her ardent determination. Though the O'Connor children had less than six months of formal schooling, they proved better educated than most because their mother insisted on taking hours out of each work day to pound learning into them. All of them were steeped in Irish history and could tell a good story.

When the *amens* sounded, everyone went for the food, all talking at once.

"I like that prayer, Mam," Conor said.

He had bright red hair with a permanent colic, playful green eyes and the O'Connor freckles across his face. A jagged scar he received last fall at school traced along his cheekbone.

Glenna nodded to him. "Thank you, son. I knew if the prayer pertained to food, you would like it."

Fi laughed, and Conor scowled at her. "What are you laughing at?"

"That wasn't a prayer so you could stuff your gob, dummy."

"What do you know? You're just a girl with frog hair."

With a toss of her hand, Fiona flipped her hair back as if dismissing his comment as too childish to consider. On one side, she wore her hair pinned back with her favorite hair comb, revealing a delicate little ear. The ivory comb was small and distinct with two prongs and a design of three tiny fleur-da-lis across the curved top. It had been passed down to Mam from her own mam. That Fi had gotten it made Morgan a little jealous, but then she had been given a rifle by Da, a much better gift.

Their father Seamus frowned severely at his two youngest children. "Fi, do not call your brother *dummy* and, Conor, you know better than that."

"Yes, Da," both replied chagrined, but shot out their tongues at each other when Seamus turned to pass a platter of eggs to Patrick, who was grinning at the two of them. "What time will you be leaving for the Templeton Ranch?"

Patrick scooped several eggs onto his plate. "Mid-morning, I figure. I still need to bring three more head in before I start out."

"Take the Spencer rifle along this morning."

Patrick nodded. Glenna glanced over at her husband, briefly concerned, but said nothing.

Morgan smiled to herself. She had spent enough nights with girlfriends on their ranches to know her family was different. Eating meals, especially breakfasts, were somber, silent affairs, but with her family, even breakfast took on the characteristics of a raucous meeting. Over biscuits and gravy, everyone including eight-year-old Conor fought for his say. Their parents encouraged them to express themselves on any topic just so long as it held a coherent thought. If not, the comeback would be merciless. Wit was highly prized.

The conversation this morning turned to Patrick's sparking of Sarah Templeton at the Cross T ranch five miles away. With a bit of a cruel streak, Morgan teased him relentlessly about his using any lame excuse to visit her. Today, he was driving ten head of cattle there to join up with the Templeton's small herd and together take them on to the cavalry at Fort Ellis, a five or six day excursion, which Sarah, herself a good horsewoman, would accompany.

"Come hunting with me, Patrick," Morgan said, trying to make her suggestion sound serious. She knew he wouldn't but pestered him. "Oscar can drive the cattle to Fort Ellis."

Oscar Fernandez was the old hired hand who often accompanied her on the hunts to protect her—though so inept and lazy he could hardly protect himself—and to carve up and haul back bigger kills like today. Today she was going after elk or deer.

"Aye, and me ears would fall off with your constant jabber," Patrick retorted.

"I'll go with you," Conor said to Morgan excitedly. "It's about time I took up hunting."

She patted his arm. "Oh, I wish you could, but Da needs you this morning, don't you, Da?" She looked pleadingly at her father. She did not want Conor tagging along.

"Aye. I have to help Patrick cut out the stock," Seamus said. "You'll be the only man at home, son. You've got to look after your mam and Fi."

Morgan could see his disappointment. He'll just have to get over it, she thought. Hunting was hers, and she was not going to share it.

"Well, I've got a bit of news," her mother announced. "Ada Templeton sent word that a young school teacher is to arrive in Lone Tree next week. In fact, it's her niece all the way from Philadelphia. We will have school again."

Fiona said to Morgan, "Jesus, Mary and Joseph, I hope you don't kill this one, too." Morgan scowled at her, but everyone laughed.

They had no schoolmaster because Morgan had nearly beaten the previous one to death. Just after the new year began, a young Illinois Normal School graduate named Jacob Hartnett had stopped in the tiny hamlet of Lone Tree, which consisted of a saloon, a church, a sawmill and several roughhewn log cabins with hide doors, and signed on with Pastor Burleigh to teach the area's children their three Rs. To the valley people, a teacher was welcome. All the O'Connor young attended except for Patrick, as did twenty other children.

Morgan hated going because it reduced her hunting time, but her mother insisted. Short and stocky, Hartnett was a dandy, dressed with a department store suit he bragged of buying at Marshall Fields in Chicago. The stiff collar matched his personality. In a growing ritual, each morning he placed his foot on a stool and had one of the younger children wipe the dust off his polished shoes.

While not paying any attention to the lessons, Morgan still received good grades by using her smiles and charm. Each day about a half hour into the lessons, the need to escape his droning voice became overwhelming, and she would ask to fetch wood outside for the potbellied stove. Clearly smitten with her, he always grinned and allowed it.

When Harnett had been in Lone Tree seven weeks, the incident occurred that ended his stay.

Morgan had gone out after wood, and after a half hour later—stretching the time as long as she dared—she returned with an armload and saw her brother Conor standing in front of the class, holding out both hands, and Harnett, his eyes alight with fury, viciously striking them with a stout switch.

"You do not tell me, little man, that conjugating verbs 'ain't' going to help you brand a calf," he was screaming.

Conor did not move, wincing at each strike but fiercely standing his ground. One wild blow struck the cheekbone, opening up a long, bloody gash.

Morgan's temper exploded. The other children that day would swear her eyes shot fire and her hair flew about like writhing snakes, appearing like her namesake Morrigan, the mad Irish goddess of strife.

"You bloody bastard," she screamed. She hurled cordwood, striking him in the chest, knocking him back against his desk. Squealing in terror, he streaked for the door, bursting out onto Lone Tree's single street, the hellish Irish witch after him, hurling her missiles. Running out of ammunition, she snatched up an axe handle leaning against the sawmill without breaking stride, shouting over and over that she was going to kill him. When he fell, she tried to do just that. In a frenzy, she bludgeoned the man into unconsciousness and kept right on till Pastor Burleigh dragged her off.

"Nobody hits my brother!" she screamed.

After he regained consciousness, Hartnett wanted to press charges against her for attempted murder, but the pastor, the sawmill owner and the saloonkeeper told him there was no one to press charges to. A week later, hobbled, he left Lone tree and never came back.

After that, people around the small town looked at Morgan differently. At least none of the boys dared pull on her pigtails anymore. Or give Conor a hard time. No one wanted to run afoul of the O'Connors. Morgan had been switched by her da for the violence and given extra chores, but maybe she saw a spark of pride in him, at least she thought she did.

The memory slipped away, and Morgan came back to the family breakfast table. Everyone was laughing and joking about Fiona's primping herself constantly in front of the mirror. Seeing her family's faces caught in the flickering lamplight, Morgan could not help but be taken by this moment with them, wanting it to last forever. It was how she would always remember them.

CHAPTER SEVEN

"Should be game aplenty at the Horseshoe, lass," her father said as he gave her a leg up into the saddle. She wore a split calico skirt so she could ride Rhiannon astride and Patrick's old checkered winter coat against the cold. "Don't go beyond Horseshoe this morning. A deer would do us fine and get you and Oscar back before too long."

Above the high peaks to the east, the sky had lightened to an orange hue, only a few of the brighter stars remained visible. Patches of snow still clung to the ground as cold days now mingled with a few warmer ones. As always before the hunt, excitement shot through her. She slid the prized Winchester 66, her cherished birthday gift from last year, into the scabbard and looked down at his earnest face. There was worry in his expression.

"What is it, Da?" she asked.

He hesitated frowning for a moment, then said, "Nothing. Soon as you bring one down, you and Oscar come on back. We'll carve it here." His eyes flickered off to the north as if spotting something in the distance. She looked but saw only the valley in morning shadows.

She nodded and he gave Rhiannon a gentle slap on his rump. "Shoot straight, Morgan," he called after her.

"Always, Da," she replied.

As Morgan rode out, she settled in beside the wagon driven by Oscar Fernandez and headed down the miles-wide valley, flanked on both sides by steep, forested foothills. A carpet of wild flowers was already pushing up in the meadow and in a few weeks would be in bloom. A half-mile ahead, Lone Tree Creek glistened, winding like a snake. Beyond, rising up like leviathans, stood the snow-covered peaks of the Absaroka Mountains. She loved this land, and breathed it in as if the air contained its soul. It was more beautiful than all paradise in the Bible, and infinitely more so than the cramped wood and brick buildings of Five Points in the New York of fading memories.

Fernandez blew his nose in a handkerchief and hacked phlegm onto the ground. "Too damn early for beast or man."

He was a dour man and, to her way of thinking, a lazy one. Why her father kept him on, she couldn't guess. He snuck off from his work to sleep, and what he did do, he did with the speed of a snail. Worse yet, he seldom bathed and never in winter. His black beard housed a neighborhood of crawly things, or so she imagined in her disgust. Since she had gone to her father to complain about him, he had bristled around her, treating her with undisguised dislike.

In his raspy voice, he said, "Shoot fast today, señorita, so we can get the hell home. There are Indians about."

"What?" She couldn't keep the alarm out of her voice.

He chuckled. "They say big war party of Cheyenne near Bozeman Pass couple days ago. Old Sam Templeton says they go back east two days past, back where they belong, but who knows with Injuns." When he saw her alarm, he laughed. "Yes, sir, girlie, Cheyenne this far west is something, aint it? They'd surely take a liking to your pretty hair. You won't scare them off with no firewood."

This was the first she'd heard anything about Indians in the area. Maybe that was what worried her father. They caused trouble farther east but seldom this far west. She remembered the Indian scares just after the O'Connor family arrived in Bozeman several years ago; isolated ranches had been attacked and families slaughtered. She had huddled with Fi under the covers each night as if that would protect them. John Bozeman himself had been killed, but that had been Blackfeet, not Cheyenne.

"You're teasing," she accused angrily.

He crossed himself. "I swear it, señorita. You know Oscar. He always tell truth, no?"

"No," she retorted sharply. "You can swear all you want, you lying bastard. You lie about everything."

He laughed hysterically. "Maybe I tell your ma how you curse like a Mexican bandito."

She glanced warily at the nearby ridge expecting thousands of Indians to pour over it at any second. She fought the urge to turn Rhiannon around and race back for the house. Sensing another presence, her initial fright gave way to joy when Bran, the half wolf, half dog loped up alongside Rhiannon. She guessed him to be about two or three years old. He was her family's dog, kind of, his own master mostly. She was the only one he allowed to pet him. He came and went when he pleased, hunted his own food and had adopted the O'Connors more than they him. One white sock on his front right paw gave him a distinct look.

They had formed a good hunting team. The wolf dog searched out the prey quicker than she, but with her Winchester she brought it down quicker. When Fernandez carved it up, he always gave the beast his share, but today they'd have to haul it back to the ranch house first.

"Hey, Bran," she said to him in soft greeting.

He sneezed, shaking his head, gave a bark and streaked out ahead of her.

When they reached Lone Tree Creek, the day had begun to warm slightly though the sun, still hung below the mountains. For a little distance, the valley lay open before her, cut by the winding course of the creek around the rise of a grassy hill a half-mile off. The place appeared barren of wildlife, but she knew all manner of beasts big and small lived out there and up into the mountains. Up ahead, Bran moved cautiously in among the trees.

"Where's the game?" she muttered. "They should be at the water."

"The Indians scare them off," Fernandez said with a shrug. When he saw her worry, he added, "They catch a little niña like you, they roast you over fire."

"Shut up," she snapped.

She looked out onto the valley where a gentle slope rose to a low crest. Nothing in that direction either. Odd. She might have to range farther afield after all, she thought with little enthusiasm. If Indians were about, she wanted no truck with them.

"I'm going into the woods on foot," she said to Fernandez as she hopped down from Rhiannon and tied him to the wagon. "You can stay here. I don't want you scaring the game off."

"See, jefe," he said, his idea of a sarcastic joke.

Her irritation at his comment vanished quickly as the hunting fever that always took hold set in, and she started off in an easy lope up into the trees after Bran. She followed moving slowly and soundlessly like him. Surprisingly, even in the forest, no hint of life could be found this morning, no animals, not even a bird in a tree, nothing. The silence was unsettling. Something had scared them from the area. It unnerved her. She hoped Bran could latch onto prey soon.

They thread their way through the trees for nearly a half mile before the dog caught a scent it wanted to follow. Morgan could see his body tense and his nose sniff the air; a low growl rumbled in his chest, and he set off at a rush. She broke into a jog to keep up, careful to step on clear ground to make no sound.

Then, she saw it about fifty yards away in a clearing, a lone doe alternately nibbling in the tall grass and raising her head, sniffing the air, flicking her ears about searching for predators. Morgan imitated a fawn's bleat and the animal visibly relaxed. It was a beautiful animal. That baleful look struck Morgan with an urge to pet it. She lifted the rifle and fired. The deer collapsed instantly.

She approached the animal to make sure it was dead, though she knew it was. Bran sniffed at its carcass. He would protect it from scavengers and predators for the few minutes it took to jog back for Fernandez. When she reached the wagon, he lay asleep curled up on the seat. Not even the shot had awakened him. Morgan slipped up to him and yelled in his ear. "Wake up, you lazy bastard! I got a doe."

He jumped up and rubbed his eyes. "El diablo! Your padre know you have such filthy mouth?"

Ignoring him, Morgan untied Rhiannon from the back and leapt aboard. "Take the wagon to the Bend. That will be closer. I'll drag it down."

"See, jefe," he growled.

But, abruptly, reins in hand, he froze, staring into the distance. Frowning at first, she then glanced back over her shoulder to follow his gaze toward the far hill. She heard the sudden pounding of hooves, first like a buffalo stampede. Then, with a squeal of terror, she saw them racing over the crest, a sight that locked her in panic so deep her heart felt sealed in ice. Indians, twenty at least, were galloping down the slope and across the creek toward her home. Three split off and with wild war cries came at her and Fernandez.

Frantically, the hired man snapped the reins, screaming at the horses, but they had just started when an arrow caught him in the back of the neck, and he slumped writhing onto the seat.

Moaning, frozen in her panic, Morgan did not move. But Rhiannon was smarter. The horse bolted up the slope and ridge that led back to her house. The three Indians swept passed Fernandez, coming straight for her.

It penetrated through her paralysis that she had to somehow warn her family. She drew the carbine and fired off a couple shots in the air. Would that give them time to barricade themselves inside the house? Then she realized if they heard at all, they'd think she was hunting. The Indians would swarm on them before they could defend themselves. She dug her spurs into Rhiannon savagely, trying to gain the ridgeline and get home.

Then, Rhiannon went down.

Morgan slammed hard on the ground and lay stunned. A shrill screeching pierced her sluggish mind. She sat up and realized it was her horse. In agony, his head flopped back and forth; an arrow stuck out of his hind leg and a front leg was bent at a terrible angle. The horse was done.

Her heart exploding, her body shaking, she saw the first Indian leap from his horse and run at her, his axe raised. Then, streaking out of the trees, Bran surged at him, taking him down in a tangle of fur, claws and teeth. The Indian screamed, waving his arms frantically and trying to stand. A sudden shot struck the dog and he spun off his prey, yelped and flopped on the ground.

Bloody, the Indian staggered to his feet.

Like a knife slashing her mind, the comprehension hit her she must act or die. She must act or her family would die. The blood-soaked Indian stumbled at her like a living nightmare. The other two warriors, their horses laboring up the slope, closed on her, less than ten yards away. The thought that they had come to kill her family overwhelmed her. As if a dam burst, rage surged in her. She still held the Winchester, and in one quick motion, she brought it up, shot the nearest Indian in the face, aimed at the next and shot him center chest, levered another shell and shot the last in exactly the same spot. Both toppled to the ground as their horses swept past her.

With a snap glance at Rhiannon, she chambered a cartridge and shot the screaming horse in the head, then instantly sprinted up the ridge for home. Weaving in and out of the trees, she heard shooting and distant war cries. Over a slight rise, her home appeared a few hundred yards away. At the sight, dread flooded through her. Indians milled in front of her house, firing into it with bows and rifles. She saw two men lying on the ground, one next to the well and the other by the corral. Too far to see detail, she knew she was looking at the bodies of her father and brother Patrick.

Her mother, Fi and Conor must still be inside. Finally, several Indians rushed the house, crashing through the door. One flew back out, and, a second later, Morgan heard the sound of the shotgun blast, then screams. More Indians swarmed into the house. Her heart was dying.

As she ran home, her chest began to burn, her breath came like bellows, but she pushed on. A hundred yards farther, she fell hard to the ground, gasping for air, and crawled out onto a stone ledge. Her legs had the strength of putty. Below, she could make out more clearly the bodies of her father and brother Patrick, stripped naked, mutilated and scalped. Seeing them sent waves of nausea through her and she retched up her breakfast.

Moments later, Conor and Fi were dragged out of the house. Morgan whispered, "Don't struggle. Don't struggle. Let them take you. I will find you."

Conor was lifted up to an Indian on horseback, but Fi still stood in the grip of the oddest man Morgan had ever seen, an Indian so massive across the shoulders that he looked like the side of a house with a head on it. Amid the crowd of men around her sister, the man drew his club up and swung.

Morgan screamed, "No!" and buried her head.

They hadn't heard her in the cacophony of slaughter. When she looked up again, the broad-shouldered Indian was lifting Fi's beautiful hair into the air and screaming a war cry. The other Indians closed in around him, whooping as if he'd just brought down a fierce warrior, not a ten-year-old girl. He leapt on his horse and Conor was shifted to him.

She realized she couldn't shoot now. If she did, they would catch her and Conor would be lost. She eased the rifle down and swore she would get her brother back and kill them all.

Quickly, they gathered the horses from the corral and rode back up the valley toward Lone Tree Creek, screaming their chilling war cries again.

Before they were a hundred yards away, Morgan dropped from the ledge and bounded down the slope toward her home. Patrick, her father and Fi lay in the yard dead; she couldn't look at them right now. She rushed past and into the house and at first, in the dimness, couldn't see anything. When her eyes adjusted, she saw her mother lying naked, scalped, blood staining the floor below her head.

Morgan's knees gave way and she collapsed, finally dropping the rifle. She couldn't hold back her tears.

"Morgan," the voice was faint. Seconds later, it came again. "Daughter. Take this."

Morgan raised up and wiped her eyes again to look at her mother holding out her fist, and Morgan placed her hand under it. Inside was her mother's blood soaked gold cross. Her voice struggling, barely audible. "Take it. You must save Fi and Conor. They will be…they will be taken." It was several more seconds before she said her last. "You must save them. Promise me, daughter."

Fi was already dead. She couldn't save her. Barely able to speak, Morgan said, "I promise, Mam. You just…" But her mother's eyes had glazed into lifelessness.

Morgan screamed in anguish. In a flick of time, except for Conor, her entire family was dead. They'd awakened this morning, each with plans for the day, for their life, and then in an instant they were gone. She would never see them again. Conor, all she had left. Sitting beside her mother, holding her knees, she rocked back and forth, unaware of the passage of time.

Minutes or hours went by, she didn't know which, till she became aware of something moving behind her. When she looked back, an Indian was staring at her. The monster who had killed Fi. He was something out of a child's nightmare, powerful shoulders, a jagged scar running across his cheek and merciless, flat eyes.

With a scream, Morgan jumped up and stumbled back against the wall. Her body trembled as a dribble of pee run down her leg. Picking up her rifle, he studied it with curiosity. Just then, several other Indians squeezed through the door and stared at her as she had the deer that morning. Knowing she was about to die, she closed her eyes and thought of her family.

CHAPTER EIGHT

Francis Gannon stood on the edge of the parade ground with the officers' wives, waiting for the regiment's return. Her husband's adjutant had ridden in twenty minutes before to report they were a few miles away. All of Camp Harrison turned out to greet their returning heroes. Besides the wives, two companies had formed in the parade ground; merchants, traders and other civilians crowded onto the boardwalks.

A hot gust lifted a dust devil into the air. Mrs. Gannon knew you either got used to the constant dust and heat or went mad. Barely thirty, she was slender with grey streaks already in her hair. Her soft hazel eyes reflected her reputation for compassion but belied her toughness. As the commander's wife, she ran the social life of the post with as much firmness as her husband did the military side.

She'd married Natty just after the War of Rebellion and had not regretted a moment since. She loved the smells and sounds of an army post and Camp Harrison was one of her favorites. No balustrade, it lay open to the land, its buildings scattered haphazardly like children's blocks. Long, narrow enlisted barracks, the sutler's store, granary, guardhouse, quartermasters, adjutant's office, billiard room, barbershop, photographer's studio and Suds Row where clothes flapped on lines.

The sun glinted off the Cheyenne tipis of the Tall Bull Agency a half-mile away, and on the low hills and buttes nearby where numerous scaffolds on which the Indians placed their dead stood.

When the first riders of the regiment crested the grassy ridge a mile off, a cheer went up around the post and several women clapped. Mrs. Gannon's chest swelled with pride when she recognized the figure in front, her Natty, saw him striding on his magnificent grey stallion.

"Can she even speak English anymore?" Mrs. Collins, the major's wife, said making no attempt to hide her scorn for the Captured Girl.

Curious, the wives had been talking about her for nearly a week since word had come with the dispatch rider that she had been rescued. Few if any captives survived among the savages as long as this one and came back white. Mrs. Collins wondered if the girl would even be sane.

"Of course, she can speak English," Mrs. Gannon insisted.

"She has lived with them far too long," Mrs. Collins persisted, as if the girl had had a choice. In her late forties, she was a heavy, bosomy woman with a puffy, square face. "She is not fit for decent society I tell you. Any respectable woman would have taken her own life."

Mrs. Gannon chided her, "Mary, we must extend the hand of Christian charity."

The older woman grumbled but did not reply.

The distant strains of the regiment's brass band could be heard playing "When Johnny Comes Marching Home Again." It grew louder as the soldiers drew closer and finally marched into post.

A few seconds later, the band fell silent, and Colonel Gannon reined up in front of his wife and the other ladies, sweeping off his slouch hat in an expansive bow.

"Dear wife, ladies, you are a sight to fire the heart of any warrior." He swung his mount around and called, Lieutenant Raines, bring the O'Connor girl up. She should meet the ladies of the post immediately."

Raines rode back and returned moments later with the Captured Girl walking beside his mount. The civilians craned their necks to get a glimpse of her, and the officers' wives stared with unabashed curiosity. When she was brought up, Mrs. Gannon's heart tugged at how young she was. The poor child. In her squaw garb, she appeared more savage than civilized.

"Look how dark she is," Mrs. Collins exclaimed derisively, her voice loud enough for everyone to hear. "Like she is actually one of them."

Mrs. Gannon chuckled. "Really, Mary, with that swath of freckles and those grey eyes?" She went forward and took Morgan's hands. "Welcome, dear. Welcome to Camp Harrison."

Gannon's saddle creaked as he nudged his horse closer to the women. "Francis, I know you and the other ladies will be able to see to her needs."

"We will, indeed, Natty." As Mrs. Gannon led her toward the other women, the girl looked every bit as wary as a wolf with its paw caught in a trap.

***

After the regiment had been dismissed, Raines hurried over to the camp adjutant's office to send a telegram to Aaron Greenblatt, his father's lawyer in New York, asking for his help in locating the O'Connor family in Five Points.
Then, using Colonel Gannon's name, he had the telegrapher send messages to the commanding officers at every post in Montana, Wyoming, Colorado, Nebraska and the Dakotas, requesting the location of the Cheyenne chief Big Crow and

any information about a captive white boy named Conor O'Connor. He gave the boy's description, including the distinctive scar on his left cheek. If any information is known, the respondent should notify Lieutenant William Raines at Camp Harrison, Dakota Territory.

As Raines was leaving, the mail clerk caught up with him. "A letter for you, sir," the private said, handing him the envelope. His heart thrilled. It smelled of lilacs and rosewater, and he knew instantly who it was from. Nancy, his beloved. All the anxiety and confusion of the last weeks drained away. All was well now. He hurried back to his small, log quarters and quickly opened the letter.

Kind sir,

I received your letter of the 12th. Glad to hear from you. We have been corresponding for some time together. Now, we will have to quit corresponding as I have pledged my affections to another and will soon be joined in wedlock. I shall have to say farewell to you, and my dread of being tied to military camps is now assuaged. As there was no date set between us, I feel at liberty.
In way of further explanation, I would just say to you that I was also afraid you would meet your death out there and not return; you are far away in the West, exposed to savage Indians, terrible winters and deadly diseases. If I had joined you, I too would have faced such perils. Besides, I did not relish the idea of cracking my teeth on those hard crackers, which are so much your daily fare. I wish you good sailing.

Your friend,

Nancy Merchant
PS. Write and tell me what you thought when you received this letter.

"What he thought!" Raines barked aloud. She had taken a sewing needle to his eye. That was what he thought. The pain could not have been greater. His breathing grew more rapid for several seconds. He had to persuade her to reconsider. In desperation, he slammed up the roll top desk and drew paper out of his drawer, dipping his pen hurriedly in the inkwell. Then, before he could write a word, he sat for nearly two minutes, the pen dripping onto the paper. He could think of nothing to say. No thoughts came to mind. Just terrible emotions at being so cruelly disposed of. Finally, he set the pen slowly on the desk and closed the desktop.

***

Upstairs in a small bedroom in the colonel's house, Morgan stood naked in front of a long mirror, studying her recent wounds. None of them had healed completely. All had thick black stitches, including the one on her forehead where Nash had tried to take her scalp. She allowed a fold of hair to cover it. The doctor said he'd remove the stitches in a couple more days. The seven cuts from the time she took part in the Sun Dance on the light skin of her upper arm stood out like rows of furrowed ground, the nub of her small finger looked ugly but reminded her of her son.

She fingered her rawhide, amulet necklace, touched each sacred part, the bear claws, ancient stone arrowhead, and gold cross. This last reminded her how much her family loved her. The first two that Owl Woman and Running Hawk had loved her as well. Both killed at Crazy Woman Creek. They wanted to be her parents, and they weren't. They couldn't be. No one could replace her real parents. But she loved them back. The necklace also told her everyone she loved was now dead but Conor and Ho'nehe. These two were all that was left of her life.

Morgan turned from the mirror to the dresser and ran her hand over the folded change of hand-me-down clothes the women gave her, a worn green dress, patched petticoats, white cotton stockings and a stiff corset. It had been a long time since she wore such clothes. She had bathed and been told to take a nap, but she couldn't sleep. What Indian woman ever napped? She sighed at the fine touch of the fabric. So smooth. Clothing for the coming inquisition.

When the women had escorted her from the parade ground, they couldn't contain their curiosity and began peppering her with questions. She answered none of them, remaining silent, stoic. Mrs. Gannon held up a hand for them to stop. "Ladies, ladies, let's leave the poor girl alone. Come at four for tea. I'm sure she will be well rested by then and will answer all your questions."

She took Morgan's arm and led her off. "I won't impose on you, but a word of advice. Lord knows you are entitled to your privacy, but you must be aware people are curious and will never stop pestering you till you tell your story." She looked at her with an expression of sympathy. "Or at least a story. You must rejoin white civilization, Miss O'Connor. Be a part of it again, for your own good. And this is the first step."

Mrs. Gannon was right, Morgan decided. She must rejoin white society, and to do so, she had to tell the women something. To have any chance of getting Conor away from Big Crow, she needed these women's good will. Colonel Gannon and his officers would control any hunt for her brother, and their wives controlled them. Simple as that. Same thing in a Cheyenne camp. The women always controlled the men though the men never knew it.

She threw on a petticoat and picked up the corset. An odd-looking thing. Beautifully decorated with lace trim, it was robin's egg blue with striped yellow and red stays. Thirty unbending stays, all to lock the body into a perfect hourglass figure.

It was heavy, and Morgan resisted putting it on. Her hand trembled, and she realized she was nervous, as if going into battle against the Crow or Blackfeet. She swallowed hard, looked out the window into the afternoon sunlight, then in one motion pulled it over her head and onto her waist. Her fingers fumbling, she worked at the fastening busks over the stomach, sucking in her breath several times. One by one she got them latched.

Breathing heavily, from both the constriction and foreignness of the garment, she stared at herself in the mirror, studying her hourglass figure. White society. Eyes locked on her corseted image, she did not move for a full two minutes. Then, swiftly, she ripped open the busks, let out a gasp of air and drew corset back over her head, tossing it aside. She couldn't do it. She couldn't wear that thing.

After a moment, she donned the cotton dress without undergarments. "Time to face the enemy," she muttered and headed downstairs.

CHAPTER NINE

In the hallway on the first floor, Morgan approached the parlor, pausing when she heard the hushed murmur of voices. She was nervous, even a bit fearful. These women were a different breed of enemy. Behind smiles and good intentions, pretend or otherwise, they did not have her interest at heart. Some hated her and did not want her among them. She trusted no one.

One terrible apprehension burrowed inside her. She could not tell these wasicus about her son. They must never know she willingly married a Cheyenne man and bore his baby. And not just any Cheyenne, but Spotted Horse. If they learned that, Colonel Gannon would have her unceremoniously escorted off the post to the Indian camp and leave her there to fend for herself. Conor would be as far away as ever. So, she would tell most of the story truthfully and lie about the rest. She would certainly not tell them her son was now less than a half-mile away in the Cheyenne camp.

"I don't understand you, Francis," Morgan recognized the high-pitched voice of the flat-faced woman rising above the rest. "Four years among the savages doing…well, we all know what she was doing. I can't express how disgusting to proper womanhood—."

"Then don't, Mary," Mrs. Gannon said sharply. "No matter what she did, we must treat her with the love and compassion for which our Lord is noted."

Mrs. Collins made a loud harrumph as another woman began to speak. Morgan continued the rest of the way down the hall and stood in the parlor door. After having known her own homestead and the inside of Cheyenne lodges, this room shocked her. So many things. Every square inch was cluttered with paintings, portraits and knickknacks. A large fireplace took up most of a wall. Morgan noticed a tiny piano and a grandfather clock by the far entrance that led directly into the living room.

Mrs. Gannon and the flat-face one sat on a divan and three other, younger women flanked them in cushioned, hardwood chairs, all with teacups and saucers in their hands, chattering like hens. At first, no one saw her. One of them, the youngest of the group, glanced her way and gasped as if seeing a wild Indian at the door. Perhaps, she had.

Smiling broadly, Mrs. Gannon set her cup down and went to her. "Come in, my dear."

She guided Morgan to a chair near the open window, which caught a warm breeze that shifted the curtains. Mrs. Gannon handed her a cup of tea and introduced the others, all young women from good families, except for the flat-faced one Mrs. Collins, who was older and from Chicago.

Morgan remembered not to slurp the tea and watched the others to see how to hold the cup and saucer. At first, they engaged in small talk about the opportunity of putting on a play now that the regiment was back and the officers could fill the male roles.

"Do you like plays?" one of the young women asked.

"Never seen one," Morgan said, meeting their collective gazes. "My family used to put on our own sometimes, but I don't think that's what you meant."

"How delightful," Mrs. Gannon said. "Then, you'll be just perfect for one of our theatricals." She set her teacup aside and paused, smiling as she studied Morgan. "Miss O'Connor, I now how difficult it must be, remembering your time with the Indians. You see, we want to assist you in settling back into civilization in any way we can, and it might help us if we knew something about your terrible ordeal."

When Morgan did not respond, she went on, "You were with the Cheyenne for such a long time. It must have been dreadful. You're safe now with us. We do not wish to pry, but—."

Of course, you do.

"—would you mind telling us something about what happened in the last four years? It might help us understand the nature of our own situation here at Camp Harrison."

Morgan sat silent for so long staring with unfocused eyes in their direction that the women began glancing at each other. Then, in a restrained voice, she said, "Four years this past March, I was taken. I was fourteen."

As she told her story, the women listened in horror and fascination. Morgan told them of her family's murder, the savagery of the sexual assaults on her, and the slavery of the next six months. She spoke without emotion or shame. Whenever she paused in the telling, the silence became so pronounced that the ticking of the grandfather clock by the door could be heard. She left out any mention of Frank Nash.

She shifted to her life with Running Hawk's band, in which her hardships were no more than what any Indian woman faced. Though she tried to hide the love between her and her adoptive Indian parents, she knew that when she spoke of them it was unmistakable. She finished her story by telling them about how their brave husbands rescued her and how she would be forever grateful, hoping that would be enough for them to push their husbands to help her. It had taken her a half hour to tell four years. When they saw she was going to say no more, disappointment etched itself on each of their faces.

Mrs. Collins asked bluntly what all the women wanted to know. "We are quite aware what these savages are like. We know what they want from white women. You said you were despoiled."

"I was."

Mrs. Collins's face held an expression of both distaste and satisfaction. The room fell silent, waiting for Morgan to go on. When she didn't, the major's wife said. "You did not think of, well, to put it bluntly, taking your own life instead of suffering such indignity? Any decent woman would have."

Mrs. Gannon said hastily, "Mary, I do not think it necessary to—."

Morgan cut them both off, her voice icy. "In the four years I was captive, I knew white women the Cheyenne had taken. Not one took her own life." She stared at Mrs. Collins. "Until you are faced with that choice, actually faced with it, you have no right to judge me."

Mrs. Collins blustered for several seconds, but said nothing.

Mrs. Gannon gave a firm nod. "You are absolutely right, Miss O'Connor. No one can possibly know what they would do in such a situation."

Upset, Mrs. Collins mumbled something and looked away. Morgan added no more. In fact, with her anger simmering, she decided not to say another word. As silence pervaded the room, she wondered if she could have been like these women if her life had gone differently. She supposed she could, and her anger eased. She told herself again she needed them, so she forced a smile. With her part done, the conversation drifted into other topics, and she was left out. Soon after, the afternoon tea ended, and she was grateful for it.

That evening, with Colonel Gannon and his wife, Morgan ate her first meal among white people in more than four years. The small dining table was set with a bouquet of colorful flowers in the center, a white, laced tablecloth and three plates set with knives, forks and spoons. When Mrs. Gannon filled Morgan's plate with meat, potatoes and green beans, she stared down at it, uncertain what to do. Precise etiquette governed even the simplest of meals. The forks and spoons were to be used in a specific way, but she'd forgotten all of it. For the first time, she was embarrassed by her situation.

Beside the plate, her hands clinched and released several times.

"What is it, dear?" Mrs. Gannon asked kindly.

Morgan's eyes were glazed when she lifted her head. The colonel and his wife could see the little girl that she had once been. Her voice quavered, "Me da and mam taught us manners. They expected us to be ladies and gentlemen. I've forgotten what to do." Then Morgan's jaw set and the glaze left her eyes and fierce wariness entered them as if she'd attack anyone who made fun of her.

Mrs. Gannon gave a friendly smile. "Don't worry, Morgan." She glanced at her husband. "Natty brings his field manners to the table all the time. I'll show you what to use for what course. You'll remember quickly enough."

Morgan sat straight as she could. She remembered that much. As they ate, Mrs. Gannon guided her through the correct utensils for the food dishes, praising her on her upright posture. Morgan grew more comfortable as her table manner came back.

Toward the end of the meal, though, when she unthinkingly belched, a sign of good manners among the Cheyenne, she knew she had made a serious blunder. As if a cannon had gone off, the dining room fell silent. After several seconds, Mrs. Gannon released a small burp, placing a hand to her mouth. When she started laughing, Morgan joined in.

"I'm eating with mad women," Colonel Gannon said with mock disapproval.

Mrs. Gannon placed a hand on Morgan's shoulder. "When Natty is away on his duties, you and I will belch to our hearts content."

Morgan was beginning to like this woman. What struck her as strange was that Mrs. Gannon reminded her of Owl Woman, the same innate kindness, the same outgoing affability.

After dinner, pleading exhaustion, Morgan went upstairs to her small bedroom, put on her moccasins and waited till nightfall. When she heard the Gannons turning in, she slipped

out of the house. In the dark, she hurried through the post and out past the log building of the Tall Bull Agency into the reservation encampment. There, she went directly to Lame Deer's lodge where Ho'nehe was sleeping, bundled in an old buffalo robe.

"He knew you were coming," Lame Deer said quietly. "He's been trying to stay awake."

At the disturbance, Ho'nehe woke and, seeing his mother, squealed with delight and ran to her.

CHAPTER TEN

For the next few days after his fiancée summarily discarded him, Raines drifted through the ether. Everything he saw or heard had a jaundiced, repugnant sheen to it. The lilting voice of one of the laundresses singing as she worked struck him as horridly strident. The warm summer mornings with songbirds fluttering was a discordant racket, and the daily work details with his men, which had always given him a feeling of satisfaction, was an ordeal to get through. But, he was thankful for the constant work and training. It was during the nights that his insides bled out through open sores, and he could think of nothing else but Nancy and being jilted by her.

Pleading illness, he begged out of any social activities the officers' wives planned, and they were numerous. Almost nightly, some entertainment was going on. Card parties, dances, dinner parties, theatricals and any countless number of gatherings. In his state, Raines had no desire for the demands of one of the wives' social evenings. If he went and languished in his misery at the back of a parlor, which was likely, he would be asked relentlessly what was wrong, and his broken engagement was the last topic about which he wanted to discuss at a dinner party.

One evening after Retreat, the walls of his small quarters closed oppressively in on him, and he had to get out, even for just a few minutes. He left for the sutler's store to buy coffee.When he entered, he saw Frank Nash sitting by the unlit pot-bellied stove with a couple post hangers-on, all well drunk. Raines ignored them, walking directly to the counter.

"Well, lookee here, gentleman," Nash said with a tone of amusement. "If it ain't the hero of Crazy Woman Creek hisself, Billy Boy Raines."

Raines did not look his way. "Coffee," he said to the clerk, pointing to the shelves behind him. "One of those bags will due."

"I know you done raced out ahead of the rest of us," Nash said, glancing at his fellows for support. They were all grinning. "But it seemed like you saw the error of your ways mighty quick like and stayed out of the fighting. Now, you can tell us, Billy Boy. We're all friends here. Did you shit your pants cause it sure smelled like it when I run into you?"

The men laughed uproariously. Raines stiffened his back. The clerk handed him the coffee, his hands trembling. Raines set the coin on the counter.

"Let's have no trouble in here, Frank," the clerk said.

Nash's face contorted in rage. "You shut your pan, Barnett." After a moment, the twisted grin returned though the rage remained in his eyes. "I said someday we would have a reckoning, Billy Boy. Now's as good a time as any." His hand slid to the pistol stuck in his belt.

This was madness, Raines thought, and pointless. To him, Nash was one of those western types whose penchant for violence and utter lack of moral restraint used to shoot fear through him. But it didn't this time. Calmly, he studied the infuriating leer on the man's face. It surprised him that he was not afraid. Instead, fury burned in his chest. He shifted his hand to his army sidearm. He longed to draw it and kill the man. The urge was overwhelming. His whole being focused narrowly on killing Frank Nash, should the man draw his weapon.

That's when the door opened and Mrs. Gannon and Mrs. Collins came in. Sighing, Raines's focus crumbled. He said good evening to the women and left. As he was going out the door, he heard the laughter of the men around the stove, Nash's high cackle above the rest and then the man's voice. "Someday I'm going to have to kill that boy."

It had not been a couple of good days.

On Saturday morning after his troop fed and groomed their horses, Raines swung by the adjutant's office to drop off the letter he had finally written Nancy. In the last few days, he'd written and torn up several responses—all of them bad-tempered—but in the end, he wrote a friendly letter, wishing her the best of good fortune, and then tried to forget her.

As he dropped off the envelope, the adjutant's clerk handed him a telegram.

"It came in a half hour ago, sir," the clerk said.

"Thank you, Bauer."

Lieutenant Wm. Raines

Camp Harrison, Dakota Territory

Sent men to Five Points. One roughed up. Barely escaped with life. Contacted all known O'Connors in that rag slum and elsewhere in city. No trace. Finally, learned from informant, couple matching names of your girl's aunt and uncle once lived in Bowery. Have Pinkerton attempting to locate current residence. Have you any more specific information that may help?

Greenblatt

Raines took the telegram to Colonel Gannon who stood outside his office on the boardwalk, watching the Changing of the Guard. A few feet away, 1st Lieutenant Walter Percy, an officer in his early forties, was reviewing the twenty-man detachment about to go on guard duty, checking carefully their uniforms and rifles.

The colonel glanced quickly at the telegram and handed it back, lit a cigar and focused back on the ceremony. "Wife won't let me smoke these in the house. I have commanded armies, Lieutenant, but Mrs. Gannon commands me. Find a good woman to take care of you and entertain you in these wilds, young man. It's worth all the tea in China."

Raines wasn't sure what response to make, so said nothing.

Gannon placed his hands behind his back in a casual stance. "Finish this business with Miss O'Connor, Lieutenant," he said firmly. "Speak to her. She must know something more of value, especially about Big Crow. Do it quickly so we can send the poor girl on her way. I feel sorry for her, but having a young, unattached female on post, especially one with her past, causes problems."

"Yes, sir," Raines said. He didn't mention that half the laundresses were young and unattached.

CHAPTER ELEVEN

Raines was not able to see Morgan till later that evening after Retreat. Mrs. Gannon said she was around at the back of the house. When he found her, she was sitting on a solid wood bench under a shade tree, staring engrossed up at the hills and high bluffs a half-mile away where the scaffolds the Cheyenne buried their dead stood out starkly in the evening sunlight. The commander's house was at the edge of the post closest to the buttes. It had been a warm day, scalding in fact, and a slight evening breeze had begun to cool it down. Still, sweat drenched his blue uniform shirt.

He was afraid he would startle her and, removing his army hat, said lightly, "Good evening, Miss O'Connor."

She wasn't startled. Not turning around, she said, "Good evening, Lieutenant Raines."

"May I join you?"

"Of course."

Placing his hat beside him, Raines sat down next to her, making sure that at least a foot separated them for propriety's sake. In the waning sunlight her freckles stood out, making her appear like an innocent schoolgirl. He thought her pretty. He could say that to himself. She was a pretty girl, but that meant nothing to him. To break the long silence, he asked her what she had been doing today.

Drawn back from whatever she'd been thinking, she smoothed her dress patiently, then raised her head and looked at him. "What have I been doing today? Ah, in many ways, the same things I did with the Cheyenne. Spent time with women doing women things. This morning Mrs. Gannon and I went to Mrs. Lawson for a sewing bee. Or a quilting bee. I'm not sure which it was. I spent many a morning among the Cheyenne women sewing shirts, dresses, moccasins and any number of other things. Then, after lunch we all met again at Mrs. Collins to plan a theatrical the ladies are putting on in a few weeks."

He noticed her usage with the language had come back. She spent the next several minutes explaining the play, a farce about mistaken identity, and how the officers, including him, would be rehearsing and performing it in the amusement hall. As she was talking, his thoughts drifted away to Nancy Merchant. He saw that golden hair of hers fluffed high on her head and the ringlets framing her lovely face. He saw her coy smile, saw her tapping his chest with her closed fan, watching him with her flirting eyes, heard the lilting laugh. *Jilted!* He'd been jilted. Someday he would find her and tell her he'd forgotten her. He realized Miss O'Connor was staring at him.

"Is anything wrong, Lieutenant?" she asked.

"No, no, I'm sorry. Please, go on," he said hastily.

She laughed abruptly, something he hadn't seen her do before. It lit up her face. Her grey eyes sparkled with real amusement. "Well, sir, I suppose that only proves I'm not a very entrancing female, something I already knew."

Frantically, he held his hands up, as if to hold back such a terrible assertion. "No, not at all. You are, indeed, entrancing." He sputtered another second. Saying that word flustered him. "I mean you are—."

"It's all right, Lieutenant. I don't care whether you find me entrancing or not."

That was abrupt, he thought. He took out his kerchief and dabbed his sweating forehead. "I'll be happy to see the sun go down, though."

"Then why don't we get right to the purpose of your visit, sir?" The spark of amusement was gone from her eyes.

"Yes, I suppose we should."

He told her about the telegrams he'd sent to all the posts throughout the territories, and that he'd heard nothing back yet. "Can you give me anything that might help us locate Big Crow's band? Anything that might narrow the search area."

"There's nothing to give."

He frowned. "Please try. You might remember where they live during the summer? There must be favorite locations Big Crow prefers to camp."

She sighed and spoke like his childhood schoolteacher explaining a difficult concept. "Like all Cheyenne, Big Crow moves his people to follow the buffalo. In the winter, he camps in a river valley, only leaving if the food runs out. When spring comes, he moves out into the grasslands to hunt buffalo again. He could be anywhere within a thousand square miles."

"Perhaps we shall soon hear something from one of the army posts," he offered, keeping a tone of optimism in his voice, then fell silent. He noticed several scavenger birds circling far off in the distance. An animal of some sort had met its end. Such a violent country.

As for Morgan, silences never bothered her. Out of the corner of her eye, she actually studied him for the first time. Quite an odd fellow. At first sight, there was nothing impressive or imposing about him. Several inches over six feet, he was tall, angular and sometimes comically awkward—his knees now rose inches above the bench with his hands resting on them.

He wore his blue cavalry pants stuffed into polished boots and suspenders over a light blue shirt with his rank on the shoulders. The large hands and feet protruded out of his clothes like animals escaping. His shock of blond hair seemed to have a mind of its own, a cowlick standing sentry at the back of his gaunt head.

There was something about her rescuer that she couldn't quite pinpoint but liked. Perhaps, a clear sense of himself despite his awkwardness, or a keen understanding of people. Of all the white people she'd met since his rescue, he was the only one who hadn't judged her in some way. Today, his deep-set blue eyes, usually lively with a hint of amusement, were sad and anxious. Something clearly troubled him.

"Have you received bad news," she asked him.

Startled, he said, "No, why would you ask that? Not at all. Not at all."

She shrugged. She would not pursue it. It was his business. She rose. "Let's go down to the creek." He followed her.

As they approached the water, a few frogs and insects rose in chorus from the creek and meadows across the way. Small fish darted back and forth in the shallows below. A couple trees hugged the bank and they stood under them. A drowsy sultriness from the day's heat hung in the air. After more than a week back in the white world, she could find no solid ground on which to stand. She had been rescued from Nash, but she couldn't say she'd been rescued from the Cheyenne. She did not know how she felt about that. Unsettled. Uneasy. Confused. She was lost. But she couldn't allow that. She had a son to care for and a brother to find.

"I need to ask you more questions about Five Points," he said, interrupting her thoughts. He showed her a telegram from a fellow in New York named Greenblatt.

Morgan read it and handed it back. "Thank you, Lieutenant. I appreciate what you're doing for me."

"Tell me something about Five Points," he said. "I know it's difficult to remember specifics from so long ago. Let's try this. Tell me the first thing about Five Points that comes to mind."

She thought a second. "The smells."

"What about them?"

"They were not pleasant."

When Morgan began talking about her early childhood, memories flooded back, mostly about her cousins, Brianna and Anya, and Big Finn. Finn was their guardian, if a sometime bullying one. They all lived in a tenement house, both families, hers and Finn's, ten people crammed into a single bedroom apartment.

"Everyone was always out and about, especially in the summer when the rooms were so hot you could bake bread in them," she said, paused and sighed. "Dear Lord it was hot. When it wasn't raining, we slept on the roof with most of the other families. Outside during the day, everyone made a go of it the best way they could. Hucksters and peddlers. They used wagons and planks on ash barrels to create their shops, selling anything. Even the front doors of the tenement houses were used for shops."

Morgan made a face as if she'd stepped on a skunk. "I remember a smelly fish stand full of slimy, odd-looking creatures. In one doorway hung big sausages of god knows what kind of meat knocking against the customers' heads as they entered. When the sun would shine, Papa and Uncle Kevin sold and repaired shoes from our tenement doorway." She glanced over at him. "It was not much like your upbringing. But it seemed normal to me." She spoke without embarrassment.

"Who can say what is normal?"

She stared at her hands folded in her lap, a slight smile touching her lips. "One day Sadie the Goat stole me mam's stockings from the clothes line out our window. Don't know how she got them down. I caught up with her in Bandit's Roost, pushing her wheelbarrow of second-hand stockings and cotton yarn. She had her big son Calvin with her. That boy was dumb and mean as they come. Every one of us was afraid of him. I pretended I was interested in buying a pair of stockings and we began bargaining. I really put on the show, twisting innocently the knot of my hair like a little girl lost. She thought she had a sucker. She set the wheelbarrow down, took her stool out of it and sat right there on the crowded street. As we negotiated, she began darning holes in the stockings. 'You got money, lass?' she says. 'Some,' I say."

Raines grinned, engrossed in her little story as she shifted in and out of her Irish brogue, animatedly using her hands.

"My cousin Finn was talking with a group of teenage boys in front of a dive, the Bucket of Blood. He catches on immediately to what I'm doing and comes over, pretending he doesn't know me. He begins to bargain for the ugliest pair of stockings. While he's distracting Sadie and Calvin, I snatch up handfuls of stockings and yarn and dash off. When the old woman notices, she screams and her son gives chase, but I'm already at the next alley and lost in the squeeze of the crowd. I laughed all the way home. Later, Finn takes everything I stole except mam's stockings and cuffs me hard on the head for not getting away with more."

"You stole back what she took?"

"And more." She looked straight at him, not a hint of shame in her eyes. "I did steal sometimes. I wish I could say I felt guilty then, but I didn't. I don't now if that's what you're getting at." She glared at him. "Sadie the Goat stole from me family, and that I won't abide from anyone."

He met her three more times the next week, finding himself looking forward to seeing her. Surprisingly, he discovered she was bright and well spoken. He wondered why that would surprise him.

He supposed he had not expected it from a poor Irish girl, and he realized he had incorrectly prejudged her. She said she had been fairly well-educated by her mother, but during her few days in a school house, she'd learned nothing of consequence beyond the perfidy of the male species. *Perfidy*. She'd actually used that word.

She could talk with the perfect King's English, then switch instantly to her Irish brogue, especially with Sergeant Reardon or any of the men from Raines's company, which she did often enough on her frequent treks about post. He did not think of Nancy Merchant once all week.

The third time the two met was on Friday evening after the single officers had been invited to the Gannons for dinner. Raines requested he and Miss O'Connor take the opportunity to speak again before he left and she agreed. Under the star-filled sky, they sat in the swing out on the side porch.

The remained silent for nearly ten minutes, not saying a word. Raines thought it odd. With any other woman, she or he or both would be expected to make conversation, but neither did, and it didn't make him feel awkward at all. It seemed normal, comfortable even. He listened to the creak of the swing. The sound of conversation drifting over from Major Collins' house fifty yards away where a card party was breaking up and couples were heading home. From farther away on post, some men were singing, likely his Irish troop well into their cups by now and ready to bark at the moon. He hoped there were no fights tonight.

Abruptly, a thought struck him, and he chuckled. "It's like we are an old couple in our dotage, married half a century, sitting on our porch, taking in the night."

Morgan laughed. "Is that a proposal, Lieutenant?"

"No, no, not that I wouldn't…I mean, of course you…what I'm trying to say, Miss O'Connor—."

She laughed again. "Don't worry. I won't hold you to it. But in lieu, you must do me one favor."

He was relieved. "Certainly. Ask it."

"We are seeing much of each other these days. This Miss O'Connor business is becoming quite cumbersome. Any time we are in public, we can refer to each other formally if that's what you want. But when we are alone like this, you must call me Morgan and I shall call you Will. Is that an acceptable alternative to marriage?"

The thought of such familiarity delighted him. Turning toward her, he said, "It is…Morgan." He caught the starlight reflecting in her eyes, magical, beautiful, and took a shallow breath. His heart swelled and an overwhelming longing consumed him. As he was about to speak, she stayed him with a gentle hand on his chest.

Just then Mrs. Gannon came around the side of the house. "Lieutenant, it's getting late. Perhaps this is a good time to say your good nights."

He rose as did she. "If you are available tomorrow, Miss O'Connor…" he began.

Mrs. Gannon interrupted him. "You must postpone tomorrow, Lieutenant. I'm afraid she will be unavailable. A very important visitor is coming all the way from Chicago just to see her. He is due tomorrow before noon. I know you will understand."

Disappointed, Raines said, of course, told both women good night and made his way back toward his quarters. As he went, he could not help wondering who was coming all that way from Chicago just to see Miss O'Connor…Morgan.

CHAPTER TWELVE

"Miss O'Connor, may I introduce Colonel E. Z. Judson," Gannon said. "Colonel Judson, this is the young lady herself, Miss Morgan O'Connor."

Standing beside Gannon in the drawing room of the house was a short, portly, middle-aged man wearing a brightly colored vest and flat red hat set askance. He removed the hat and bowed to Morgan. With a pudgy face and walrus mustache, he looked in no way military, and she could not guess his purpose for visiting her.

He extended his hand to Morgan, "Ah, the Captured Girl. When I read in the Tribune that you had been rescued, why, I hopped on the first train west to find you and now I have. You will delight them all."

She shook his hand, which had a light touch. Mrs. Gannon rushed in patting her hair and beamed at the portly man as if President Grant had entered her house. "Sorry, I'm late. Mrs. Lawson's child was sick."

Gannon introduced his wife, and taking her hand, Judson bowed. "Delighted, Mrs. Gannon. Such a lovely home you have here."

"We do our best," she said nervously.

He turned to Morgan. "I'm so glad to find you, well, in one piece, Miss O'Connor."

She could not begin to understand what was going on. "Colonel Judson? Are you in the army?"

"No, no, it's an honorary title," he said. "You may know me better by my sobriquet, Ned Buntline."

She didn't. The name baffled her but clearly everyone else knew it. "Sorry, sir. I do not know that name either."

He chuckled. "Well, I suppose my theatrical productions have yet to play in Cheyenne villages.

"Shall we sit, Colonel?" Gannon said, and they sat down while Mrs. Gannon served tea and biscuits. "This is my own blend, Colonel," she said as she poured Buntline's cup. "Just a hint of peppermint."

He sipped and smiled. "Ah, yes. Now that just caps the climax, madam. Simply caps the climax."

Pleased, she sat down beside her husband. Buntline set his cup and saucer down. "Shall we get to the pinch, Miss O'Connor? You must be wondering what this is all about. I produce theatrical plays that have become popular throughout the country and even in Europe. Right now, *Scouts of the Prairie* is playing before sold-out crowds in Chicago. The players are those of which you must have heard. Buffalo Bill Cody, Texas Jack Omohundro and the Peerless Morlacchi. It is quite the show. I want you to join us."

She wasn't sure she heard right. He wanted her to do what? Her look of astonishment prompted him to add, "You will be performing each evening to packed houses I can assure you."

"You want me to go on stage? You want me to act?" she said it as if he were mad.

"No, no, you would be yourself. You wouldn't be acting. Just telling your story, and I will embellish it with actors portraying Indians and an actor playing the colonel here. It will have the audience screaming wildly. Of course, there are others who have been taken by the wild red men before, but you seemed to have captured the imagination of the country. You are quite famous, you see."

Morgan momentarily shivered with disgust at the thought of portraying her life on stage. No audience deserved to gawk at pale imitations of her mother or father, at Patrick or sweet, ornery Fiona's spirited short life. And none had the right to mock her life among the Cheyenne or judge her or her beautiful baby Ho'nehe.

His grin widened. "And the earnings are quite good. As much as a thousand dollars."

"A year?" Mrs. Gannon blurted out. She turned to Morgan. "That would be excellent money."

Buntline laughed. "No, madam, a month."

In the stunned silence that followed, a loud knock came at the door, and Mrs. Gannon hurried to answer it. Moments later, she returned with Frank Nash. A bolt of fury shot through Morgan, and reflexively she slipped her hand in her pocket, grasping the bone handle of her knife. She said coldly, "What's he doing here?"

At first, shocked by the force of her question, no one answered her. Nash wore a clean muslin shirt and checkered pants. His long brown hair was slicked back falling to his shoulders, hiding the gnarled hole where she had cut off his ear. Nervously, he fumbled with the beat-up hat in his hands.

Finally, Buntline said, "Why, Mr. Nash has accepted my offer to join our combination troupe." He grinned at Gannon. "From your troop to our troupe, eh, Colonel? After all, the title of our play is *Scouts of the Prairie.* Except for Buffalo Bill, is there a more famous scout than Frank Nash?"

Nash's eyes shifted from Morgan to Buntline. "I can meet you in Chicago, Colonel."

"Splendid. And you, miss?" Buntline asked Morgan.

"Sir, your offer is generous, but as I've explained to Colonel and Mrs. Gannon, I will not be leaving the territories till I find my brother. He is still among the Cheyenne. When I free him, we will travel to New York to find the last of our family. I will not be going to Chicago."

"Perhaps, if you gave it some thought—." Buntline began.

She cut him off sharply, "I will not change my mind, sir."

"I am disappointed." He sighed, glancing at Nash. "Then you're it, my boy. But first, we must do something about that name. You see, Frank Nash is too plain. No, it just won't do. We have Buffalo Bill, Texas Jack, Wild Bill, and, of course, the Peerless Morlachi. What shall we call you?"

Morgan chimed in, "How about *Earless* Frank?"

As their eyes met, an understanding sped between them like fired gunshots, carrying hatred so strong it had physical presence. And a sense of unfinished business.

CHAPTER THIRTEEN

When Morgan had been a captive for six months, Frank Nash and another white trader came to Big Crow's camp. Morgan was out gathering loose firewood along the river at the time, part of her endless days in which the women of the village worked her from before dawn to long after sunset, carrying water and wood, stretching hides on racks, tending horses and drying meat on racks. If she was slow, she'd be beaten. A woman she called Buffalo Face often struck her out of spite.

She was not the only white woman in camp—there were two others—but she seldom had a chance to speak to any of them. They suffered the same drudgery and beatings. The captive white children, five that she knew of including her little brother Conor, were adopted by families and taught Cheyenne ways. She desperately wanted to prevent that. She desperately did not want him to forget his real family. But he was a little boy, and already, browned by the sun, he looked more Indian than white. Conor lived with Big Crow and his wife, who called him hee'haho, *son*. They called her Vehoka, *White Girl.*

One month after they had been taken, she'd tried to escape. A severe rain storm struck. In the barrage of thunder and lightning, she stole into Big Crow's lodge while he and his wife slept beside Conor. For an instant she thought to draw a knife and cut his throat, but then she'd be killed, and Conor would never get away. With a gentle hand over his mouth, she awakened him. Silently, they went out into the terrible rain, found two ponies in the horse herd and slipped away into the fierce storm.

They were free for twelve hours.

Big Crow and twenty of his warriors ran them down and brought them back to camp. He allowed the women to beat her so savagely she was laid up for three days. Why he didn't have her killed she could not imagine.

As Morgan listlessly picked up loose branches for firewood that day Frank Nash came, she was losing hope that she would ever get her brother away. That's when she heard the rattle of wagon wheels. She knew instantly what it was and knew it must be white men. She dropped the wood and ran into camp. The wagon rolled in and stopped. White men. New hope surged into her soul, and she rushed toward them.

When she reached them, the Cheyenne had gathered in a large crowd. Piled haphazardly in the back of the wagon were guns, bolts of calico cloth, barrels of whiskey and junk trinkets of all kinds. In exchange, the white men asked for buffalo robes and American money. That was what gave her hope. Big Crow knew the value of American money, as did seemingly most chiefs, and like them he had clumps of it about his lodge to use to purchase goods from traders like these or at trading posts. Morgan thought they had a lucrative dodge going. Capture white women and children, use some as slaves while raising a few children as their own, sell the rest back to anyone who would pay, usually family members. But Morgan's family was dead. Maybe, they were here for someone else.

A tall and broad shouldered man with long, unkempt brown hair stood up on the wagon seat and looked over the crowd. Abruptly, he announced in English, "Morgan O'Connor, you here?"

The sound of her name shocked her, and she took a moment to respond. "Here. I'm here," she shouted and pushed her way forward. "I'm Morgan O'Connor. Are you here to rescue me?"

"An old prairie bum told me you was here," he said, looking down on her from his great height on the wagon. "Thought I'd come take a look."

The man in the back of the wagon was showing an old rifle to a brave. He glanced at her and grinned, reveling in his yellow and black teeth. No warmth came from him, but something else, something rotten and fetid. Disconcertingly, he had a glass eye.

"That there's my pard Axil Grimm," the man standing on the wagon seat said, gesturing with his thumb. "I'm Frank Nash. Nice to make your acquaintance. You look mighty thin. Looks like them braves been wearing you out some. But we'll fatten you up just fine."

She stepped closer and put a hand on the wagon. "Can you help me? My brother is in camp. I won't leave without him."

"Now, maybe I can. You got anyone to pay ransom for you?"

"Our folks were killed. We've got relatives in New York."

"New York!" He laughed. "New York! That's a good one."

She held her hands together in a begging gesture. "Can you help me, sir? Please?"

"Sure, I can. Don't you worry your pretty little head. That's why I'm here. I'm going to take care of you."

Her heart raced. They were going to be rescued. "My brother is with Big Crow. It might be harder to get him away."

Nash rubbed his jaw in thought, then nodded firmly. "We'll take care of him. It might take a bit of negotiation."

"Thank God."

He grinned again but there was no warmth in his expression. Morgan stared up at him, the last of the sunlight framing his tall body. He had flat, emotionless eyes that seemed to give off
no light. For an instant, she sensed a flicker of warning, then dismissed it. She had no choice. What had she imagined, a Sir Galahad here on the plains to rescue her and Conor? It would be hard men like these, or not at all.

"Now, you go on about your business," he said. "I'll be negotiating for your release soon as I can see Big Crow. These things take time. Maybe tomorrow morning. Maybe later."

That evening, the camp celebrated, new guns firing in the air, men including the white men sitting about large fires and exchanging jugs of whiskey. Eventually, Buffalo Face took Morgan back to the lodge. For whatever reason, she was not even angry Morgan had not brought in firewood. After the Indian woman left, she lay down on her blankets to wait through the night for her and Conor's fate to be decided. Though she thought she wouldn't sleep, she was exhausted, as she always was, and soon dozed off.

The threads of a disjoined dream scattered in pieces through her mind. Big Crow locked her in chains and dropped her into a placid blue lake when she struggled to escape before she drowned. She couldn't break loose; she couldn't breathe. The crush of something heavy pressed on her as if a giant boulder had followed her into the water and landed on her chest.

She woke up, struggling, gasping for air. Someone smelling of dead things and whiskey lay heavy on top of her, his hand pressed over her mouth. He pushed her dress above her waist, then grunted and fumbled at his trousers. Overwhelmed by terror, she fought wildly, but he punched her twice in the face, sending shocks of pain through her body. Still, she struggled, twisting and slamming her fists into him.

He slapped her twice more. "Easy now, missy. You just ease off there you want to get yourself free of this place." It was Nash. "I done paid Big Crow for you and this is the thanks I get. You, me and Grimm will be riding out in the morning. So I got you free. Or maybe you want me to sell you back to Big Crow? I can do that, you know."

"Bastard," she breathed out harshly.

"Relax and enjoy the ride, little girl." he said with a nasty laugh like the stuttering screech of a hawk.

He grunted and thrust roughly but gratefully finished quickly. Pants still around his ankles, he rolled off her, and sighed. "There now. That wasn't so bad, was it? Frank Nash knows how to treat his women. And make no mistake. You are now my woman."

Within her, something broke. She had never been the sweet, girlish kind like Fiona, but she had been a decent, moral girl, someone her da was proud of. The last of that girl died this night.

"I'm not your woman," she said without emotion. "I will never be your woman."

He rose to a kneeling position above her and said with a harsh snort, "Don't kid yourself. I done bought you. You got no choice." He grinned. "Axil and me, we like a good spirited white woman."

He had never intended to rescue Conor. The betrayal tore into her, ripped away whatever made her human. Her rage erupted. Fumbling for the knife by the cooking pot, she clutched it and in a motion so quick he barely saw it, she stabbed at his head.

Too late, he twisted away. Screaming, she hit his ear and sliced down hard, lopping it off completely. Blood spewed in a torrent. He howled wildly, holding to the side of his head.

She came at him with her knife again. Fighting her off, he scrambled on his butt away from her.

"Stop. I can't see! I can't see!" he screamed.

Drawing his pistol, he snapped off two wild shots that went through the tent flap, then clubbed at her with the barrel, striking her head. She stumbled back and he hit her again. She collapsed on the floor. He fired off another shot blindly and missed again, then grabbed his pants still about his ankles and stumbled from the lodge, screaming, "The bitch cut my ear off! The bitch cut my ear off!"

In a haze, Morgan saw him disappear through the flap then passed into unconsciousness. With turns of fog-filled waking throughout the night, she grasped moments of lucidity, and in each one wondered when they would come for her, resigned herself to being killed. She had failed her mother; she had failed Conor. They would tie her to a post and probably the women would beat her to death. It seemed to her several people came into the lodge. As a blacksmith's hammer pounded inside her skull, they stood over her talking, but she was too groggy to understand what was said. She did not care about them. She would soon die. She would give them no more of herself. Regrettably, she had not killed Nash. His betrayal left her filled with hatred so powerful it brought bile to her throat.

In the morning, she awakened with the worst headache of her life. Immediately stepping outside, she found everything had changed. Nash and Grimm were gone, and she was not to be killed. Instead, she had been sold to a Cheyenne chief named Running Hawk from another band for seven horses.

Outside the lodge, her head throbbing, Morgan was met by a Cheyenne girl, who told her Nash had become the laughing stock of the village, the wasicus who ran screaming from Vehoka, his pants around his ankles and his manhood shriveled in fear. He had sprawled out in the back of the wagon while Grimm drove away, ranting and cursing her as evil. Promising he would kill her someday. To Morgan's surprise, for the next hour or so, she was almost treated in a humane manner, people offering greetings and congratulations, laughing immediately when they saw her. One woman even traded a bagful of berries for Nash's bloody ear.

Soon after, Buffalo Face and several others approached while she squatted before a deer hide, trying to skin it but unable to focus. The woman who had been her chief tormenter for the last six months told her she belonged to Running Hawk, the famous warrior chief. Even she had heard of him. He was a tall, regal looking man in his fifties with grey hair tied in a single braid to his shoulders.
His beak-nosed face carried an air of calm. When she was brought to him, he smiled at her. She looked away to hide the hatred in her eyes.

An hour later, walking among the travois as her new band left Big Crow's camp, Morgan cast a last glance at Conor dressed like a little savage and standing with several other boys watching them go. His face wore an expression of distress as if she were abandoning him. She wanted to scream and run to him and comfort him, but that would accomplish nothing.

"I will come back for you," she said in English.

He gave an imperceptible nod. At least, that was what she thought she saw.

CHAPTER FOURTEEN

On a perfect Sunday, the sky fierce in its blue emptiness, the temperature warm but not unpleasant, Raines rode with Morgan up North Butte, a picnic basket attached to her saddle. Riding over grassy meadows toward the summit, he imagined for a moment that he was on a society outing in New York's Central Park, instead of in the wilds of the frontier, a lovely young lady by his side. Unquestionably, Morgan fit the bill as the lovely young lady. But astride, her dress tucked under her, she broke the illusion of society. No lady rode a horse astride. He doubted Morgan cared about the distinction.

In his imagination, he played out how this day would go. He saw himself on the picnic blanket kissing her, and her swooning with passion, him slipping a hand into her blouse and cupping a breast in his hand and feeling the softness of her skin on his fingertips.

"You're the quiet one, Lieutenant," she said, startling him and interrupting his dreamings.

It took him several seconds to reclaim his military bearing, to calm himself and to focus on the ostensible reason for the outing. "You must not laugh, Miss O'Connor, er, Morgan."

In mock earnestness, she said, "Why, Lieutenant, I must. Laughing at you is one of my favorite pastimes."

A hand over his heart, he said with playful sarcasm, "It is my honor to serve you, milady."

"At least you don't take yourself so seriously like the rest of your fellows."

"Oh, I take myself seriously. It's just that no one else does."

They both laughed and she said, "Don't be silly. I do."

Once on top of the butte, they spread out the blanket under a ponderosa pine looking out over the breathtaking view miles across the sweep of rolling prairie, the fort and the tipis of the Cheyenne beyond, glowing white in the noonday sun. From the basket, Morgan withdrew items and announced each as if presenting the precious objects of a treasure chest, egg sandwiches, cornbread, vegetable salad with a sweet liquor dressing, Graham bread and cheese and strawberries.

She handed him one of the egg sandwiches. "You said once you would tell me how a Fifth Avenue swell became a cavalry officer out here in my country. It's time to confess all."

"If you want. It's hardly remarkable. I guess you could say the War of the Rebellion did it." He started talking about his childhood and the coming of the war and about his father, who had been the owner of a textile factory on the northern end of Manhattan Island. At the beginning of the Civil War, Pierce Raines garnered a contract from the War Department to make uniforms, and this started the family's success on an upward spiral. In the fall of 1863, he formed a New York company and was elected its captain, leaving the running of the factory to his manager.

"My father's record in battle got him promoted to colonel, and he landed on General Grant's staff. When they were in camp, mother and I visited him as often as we could. For weeks at a time. I found myself playing soldier with Freddie, the general's son." Raines grinned, remembering, using his hands then to describe what happened. "He had a little lieutenant's uniform, and he marched me up and down the rows of tents to the delight of the soldiers. Some men even fell in with me and paraded about to form little Freddie's command. The general was delighted."

Morgan laughed. "I can just see you marching with all those men."

"I was the good little soldier. One day General Grant gave me a lieutenant's uniform, too. I don't know why he did that, but it made me feel like I had just won the war. I put it on right there in front of everyone, then stood tall and saluted him. The general returned my salute and laughed that deep, throaty laugh of his." Pausing, he looked at her, gauging whether to trust her. "At that moment, Morgan, I decided all I wanted in life was to be an army officer. I told that to Grant, and he said to contact him when I got older and he would see I got an appointment to West Point."

"I guess he did," Morgan concluded with a questioning raise of her eyebrows.

"To my surprise. Though president, he remembered. When I was sixteen, I got the appointment, a little young, but no one knew my true age, and four years later, here I am."

"And I'm glad you are, Will." Her voice was soft, almost serene.

He liked her saying his name. They passed an awkward moment of silence in which it seemed he should say something but couldn't think of what it should be. Instead, he took another bite of his egg sandwich.

When they finished lunch, she repacked the basket and leaned back against the tree, her knees pulled up close to her chest. He studied her. Her slender figure. The high, laced boots disappearing under the green, cotton frock. The swell of breasts pushing against the white blouse. The lovely slope of her neck and smoothness of her cheek. The swathe of freckles across the bridge of her nose.

Morgan was certainly different, more so than any female he'd ever met, a contradiction in every way. He wanted to be with her. Indeed, he wanted her in every way. With the impact of an artillery shell, the thought struck him that he was falling in love, and he was not ready yet to accept that. Not so soon after Nancy. But that was not the main reason. It was a leap with giant barriers. As the lone son of a prominent New York family, it had been drilled into him from an early age that he must marry well, a responsibility, a sworn duty.

Before he went off to West Point, he had been seeing their factory manager's daughter. There was talk of engagement. His father had put an arm on his shoulder and even though they were alone whispered, "Your mother has worked hard to achieve prominence for this family. Don't ruin it, Will, by telling this poor girl you will marry her. That will be the ruin of us. Son, she is not our kind of people. You're young yet. Go to West Point. There will be other, more suitable girls."

He first reacted with fury. He wanted to say that they themselves were not "our kind of people" not so long ago. But he said nothing. A few months after he went off to West Point, she married a deacon twice her age and it all was settled. He had not stood up to his father for the girl with whom he loved. Shame clung to him like a poisonous fog.

Morgan would be infinitely more unsuitable than the manager's daughter.

"My, you are pensive," she said. "You look like the weight of the world is on your shoulders."

"Not the weight of the world."

"What then?"

"Enjoying the breeze. And the view." He declared it, staring straight at her, making it clear she was the view. She brushed a curl back from her cheek and smiled with a dismissive shake of the head.

"Ah, sir, you do give a girl the vapors." Her tone was lighthearted and he laughed.

She closed her eyes and took in a deep breath. He scooted over to sit next to her, twisting a blade of grass around his finger. Their shoulders touched, sending a jolt through him.

With her knees up, her dress hiked high, revealing the smooth sheen of down on the coppery skin of one calf. It took his breath away. He swallowed hard as if downing a mouthful of pebbles, looked away, then back again. He stared fixated at the bare skin, his mouth going dry.

She opened her eyes and saw him staring. She made no move to cover up.

"You're beautiful," he whispered.

"Am I?" she said softly, her face openly pale.

"Yes." Gently, Raines took her face in both hands, kissed her eyelids and cheeks, and then seeing her startled look, kissed her gently on the mouth. Urgently, she lifted into him, and he wrapped her in his arms, feeling the warmth of her body against his, pressing his sudden hardness against her thigh. He could smell her woman scent. They kissed again and again. He wanted her. He would die if he didn't have her.

He caressed her breasts through the white blouse, realizing instantly that she was wearing no undergarments. His desire exploded. He was groping now, nearly out of control, fumbling for the buttons of her blouse when, abruptly, she took his hand and moved it away.

"I think it's time we return," she said firmly, but not unkindly.

He sat up blinking. His body roiled and it took him several seconds for his breathing to level and longer for his arousal to fade.

Finally, flustered, he said, "I'm sorry. I got carried away."

She pulled him to her and kissed him again, then gently shoved him back. "Don't be. If I'm sorry about it, I'll tell you."

When they started back, riding in silence, they took a different route, a longer path across the top of the butte. Desperately, Raines wanted to prolong the day, make it endless. He could not get the image of her in his arms out of his mind. He didn't want to. For him, the afternoon took on great clarity. A thousand separate scents floating in the air; the sound of small animals tracking through the nearby trees. Abruptly, he laughed, and she glanced at him with a smile.

A few minutes later, as they rode across a meadow with yellow flowers growing amid the tall grass, they saw a scaffold ahead. On top lay a body wrapped in a tattered blanket. Raines guessed it must have been there a long time because a skeletal arm and skull were visible. Underneath the structure were the scattered bones of a horse.

Morgan seemed gripped in an intense emotion, her back rigid, her jaw clinched. Finally, he asked, "Was he someone important?"

After a long moment, she gave the barest hint of a shrug. He was about to ask if she was all right when she spoke in a low voice, "His family thought he was. They dressed him in his best clothes and buried him here with his weapons and pipe and tobacco. They shot his favorite horse so he could quickly ride the trail to Seyan."

"Seyan?"

"The Place of the Dead." She gestured toward the sky. "The trail leads along the Hanging Road, the Milky Way, to where he will find his loved ones, his old friends. All those who died before him. They will live there as they always had, talking and singing and dancing around the campfires, hunting buffalo, making war on their enemies."

Staring up at the scaffold, he said, "Odd how beliefs about life and death develop in primitive people. The belief in an afterlife." Raines was genuinely curious and had already begun taking notes of his observations of Cheyenne ways.

She misunderstood his intent. "Their beliefs are just as valid as ours," she said with annoyance. "Who's to say which one has the right of it? You, Lieutenant?"

"I didn't mean to make a judgment," he said evenly. "The way I view it, many religions looking at the same thing from different angles."

She studied him for several seconds as a long silence followed. After a while, she nodded and her shoulders relaxed. When she spoke again, her voice was barely audible. "I have seen my family there. I see them in our old home in Lone Tree, gathered around the dinner table or working outside. They are all there. All but Conor and me. They are waiting for us."

His heart went out to her, but she must have misread his expression.

"You think it's not real. It is real. It is Seyan. Not the Cheyenne one but my Seyan." Her face took on a desperate determination. She touched her chest. "In here. They live in here, and that's real. They cannot die in here. I must get Conor back before he loses our family. Before he no longer even remembers them. If I can get Conor back, Will, then, as long as I breathe, as long as he breathes, we have our family."

***

That night, after visiting Ho'nehe and Lame Deer in the Cheyenne village, Morgan returned to the Gannon house and snuck in silently, slipping up to her room. She lay on the floor on her blanket, unable to sleep. She could not get used to the bed yet. Will Raines dominated her thoughts. This afternoon had complicated her life. She had enjoyed the moment when he kissed her and her body stirred for the first time in a very long time. She had allowed herself to be drawn into his hunger. A long dormant stirring deep inside her had awakened, her blood pulsing with sexual arousal again.

Her hands became sweaty and she thought her heart would pound out of her chest. Her reaction surprised her most of all.

When he first started seeing her at Colonel Gannon's behest, she found herself comfortable in his company as he pursued his duty of discovery on the Cheyenne and her early life in New York. After a while, though, she realized all that was just an excuse to see her. He wanted to be with her whether he'd come to realize it or not.

Morgan sat up and folded her arms over her knees. The window was open, and a night breeze shifted the gauze curtains as it cooled the bedroom. She sighed.

A romantic involvement between them, though, was doomed. She did not have room in her heart for him. Her life was consumed by Ho'nehe and Conor and her New York relatives. Nothing else mattered but to pull the remnants of her family back together. Romance was impossible. When he came to see him next, she would tell him that.

CHAPTER FIFTEEN

"Head of the column, to the left!" Raines shouted. After the troop made a muck of it, he tried another order. "Left oblique, march!"

They tried that but again stumbled their horses about. Dust lifted off the hard pack of the parade ground. It was a scorching day, and Raines was hot and irritable. Nothing was working. Mounted in columns of four abreast, the troop was attempting close order cavalry drills with twenty new recruits recently assigned to the post among them. Many of these had never been on a horse before, and it showed. They looked ragged and disoriented.

"You are useless! A bunch of reprobates," Sergeant Reardon shouted at them, echoing Raines's thoughts. The two sat their horses, watching in gathering alarm.

Raines had been the acting company commander since Crazy Woman Creek. The previous commander, a captain, was on sick leave and not expected to return. The troop's senior lieutenant was absent on recruitment leave and not expected to return. A 2nd lieutenant had been detached as aide-de-camp to General Crook and he, too, would not return. Nearly fifty percent of the regiment's allotment of forty-three officers was missing, but as Raines had been told, not unusual at a frontier post. So, here he stood, another 2nd lieutenant commanding a company. He swore to himself not to let the chance go abegging. Last night, he had spent a couple hours reviewing Phillip St. George Cook's *Cavalry Tactics*. It was doing little good.

About to call for a right oblique, he spotted two people out on the plain walking toward the post from the Indian village, Morgan and the mixed-blood interpreter and sometime scout Lucas Gerrard. At sight of her, his stomach churned and images of the picnic the day before flashed in his mind.

Reardon said, "Are you all right, lad?"

Scowling, Raines didn't respond. The sergeant saw where he was looking and gave a easy laugh. "Ah yes, the comely Miss O'Connor. Is young Mr. Gerrard her new beau?"

That stung him, and he didn't answer. He knew Reardon had said it just to needle him, yet Raines was jealous. He doubted the interpreter had any sort of relationship with her beyond cordiality and an interest in the Cheyenne camp, but he didn't know for sure. He liked Gerrard and trusted him, more so than anyone on post except Reardon. Barely twenty, Gerrard was lean and muscular with dark features and black, curly hair. He had a Cheyenne mother and a former slave for a father. He wore leggings and a breechclout like the Cheyenne, and a checkered shirt.

One of those people who just had a knack for languages, Gerrard spoke fluent Cheyenne, Lakota and Crow along with his English, and could sign with most tribes on the plains and in the mountains. At ten, he had been captured by the Crow and lived for several years with them. Despite his unreasonable jealousy, Raines liked him and had come to rely on him.

The interpreter and Morgan parted with barely a nod. As she went past the men, they stopped to gawk, a breach of discipline that Raines allowed since he was doing the same thing. A few who knew her from the fight at Crazy Woman waved and shouted and she waved back, then caught Raines's eye and waved to him.

Reardon chuckled. "Well, wave back, lad."

He did. As she strode on, Raines saw the sun shining through the thin fabric of her dress outlining her legs clearly. My God, no undergarments again. All the men saw. Raines squirmed in the saddle.

"What are you mucks doing?" Reardon screeched. "This is not a siesta."

Getting back to training was not easy, but Raines put his mind to it.

Afterward, he went to the adjutant's office to check for mail and telegrams. The clerk had two letters—one from his older sister and one from his mother—and a telegram. He read the telegram immediately. What it said hit him with infinite sadness. He read it again.

Lieutenant Raines,

Apologies for the delay. Recently returned from East. If you are searching for a white boy that lived with Big Crow's band, I regret to inform you he died of disease several months ago. I saw this myself. He was white and bore a scar on his cheek as you describe. He was brought here by Big Crow for the post doctor to save. Alas, it was not to be. Being white, we buried him in our cemetery.

Major Winterbourne, Commanding
Rosebud Creek Depot on the Yellowstone
Montana Territory

Conor O'Connor was dead. He dreaded bringing the news to Morgan. This will crush her. She'd been through too much hardship as it was. No one should have to bear what she had been made to carry. Now this. As Raines stepped onto the colonel's porch, his throat constricted and he ran a finger through his collar. He stood without knocking for nearly a minute. A thermometer registered 98 degrees.

She appeared at the screen door and stepped outside, shutting the door behind her. A sheen of sweat beaded her forehead. "What in the world are you doing standing out here, Will? Why didn't you knock?" When he didn't immediately answer, she said, "Let's sit on the porch. It's an inferno in there. There's something we must discuss."

She led the way, and like a prisoner to the gallows he followed. He could not think of anything he would like to do less than this. She sat on the porch swing and looked up at him. "Oh, my, what a scowl. Why so serious?"

He said gently, "Morgan, I have information about your brother."

Immediately, she jumped to her feet. "What? Have you found him?"

He nodded. It would be cruel to prolong this. "Conor died last year of illness. I am sorry. I just received the telegram from the commanding officer of Rosebud Depot informing me of the fact. He was with him at the last."

The color drained from her face. A low moan escaped her and she backed up, knocking the porch swing against the side of the house. He stepped toward her, to take her in his arms, but she snapped her hands up stopping him.

Her eyes began to water. "What happened?"

"He was very ill," Raines explained. "Big Crow brought him into Rosebud Depot to see their doctor, but it was too late. Since he was white, they buried him in the post cemetery."

Her voice quivered. "He was always getting sick."

She sat back on the swing and cried for her lost brother. He sat beside her and rubbed her back. He told her he was sorry again but then fell silent. Little he could say would comfort her. He was surprised she didn't break down completely but soon the sobs stopped.

She lifted her head; her eyes bloodshot but void now of emotion. "Thank you, Will. You are a good friend. I prefer to be alone."

He hesitated. "I am so sorry, Morgan."

"Go, please," she said softly but firmly.

Not wanting to, he left as she wished. As he walked away, he could not help but be surprised, even alarmed, by the coldness of the young woman. Her brother had meant everything to her yet her response to news of his death had been hardly more than the death of a favorite horse. He supposed that the harshness of her life in the last four years had hardened her soul into ancient leather.

When he was nearly back to his own quarters, he saw her across the parade ground. She had changed into moccasins and was striding from the post toward the Cheyenne village.

***

Morgan's anguish was excruciating. She could not see how she could bear it any longer. All she could think about was Conor and the time when the two of them were younger. As a baby, he crawled everywhere exploring and she, often tasked with watching him, lost him several times. At three, he pulled Fiona's hair, and she screamed for mam. The time he stood his ground when the school bully turned out to be the teacher. These images and many others once had brought smiles to her face. Now, they brought stabs of grief; he was gone forever.

As soon as she reached Lame Deer's lodge, she collapsed and started crying uncontrollably. Ho'nehe hung back from her, frightened. Lame Deer guided her to the creek where the two mourned the loss of her brother. Several other women joined them and began wailing.

With darkness came the clouds, moving in like a shroud over the unbearable heat. Kneeling, Morgan hacked her hair short with a knife and tossed the strands in the water. Conor's death had brought back the full force of her family's slaughter, the shock of it all and the sorrow. She cried till her eyes dried up, then she cried more. A great emptiness took hold of her. She slipped her hand inside her blouse, grasped the gold cross and prayed to God for Conor's soul, held the arrowhead and prayed to the Wise One.

She did not know which one was God, or as Will suggested, they are one and the same. What she did know was cruelty drove both of them.

***

Near ten that night, Raines sat in a chair in front of his small billet to avoid the appalling heat inside. He was drunk. High-pitched wailing drifted in from the Cheyenne camp a half-mile away, loud and rhythmic. It had been going on since the afternoon. He still felt terrible for Morgan. It pained him that he could do nothing for her, she would not allow it. Reardon sat beside him, leaning his chair back on two legs against the wall and hoisting a bottle of whiskey.

"Hot as a bad day in hell," Reardon said, offering Raines the flask again.

"It is that, Sergeant." He took a quick drink and handed it back. The rotgut burned his throat and ate at his stomach. He flushed and shivered at the awful taste. "We have to leave before sunrise tomorrow. We ought to be turning in, Sergeant, instead of drinking this swill of yours. Where the hell do you get it?"

Raines had been assigned a detail to cut wood for winter, still months away. Hundreds of cords would be needed. He was taking a detachment of thirty men and ten wagons out early the next morning.

"Lord, Billy Boy, we can leave right now if you want, but leaving so early ain't going to make the assignment go any quicker. You'll get back to her soon enough." He held up the flask. "Besides, this puts hair on your chest. I suspect you need some to handle her."

"How long you estimate the assignment will last?"

"Not long. Two days, three at the most. If we don't have too many of those lazy Irish bastards with us, it should go smoothly."

"All our men are Irish. You're Irish."

The sergeant's eyes sparked with a mischievous twinkle. "Ah, well then, we might never get back." After a moment, he said as if remembering something important, "Oh, saw Nash leaving today. Just upped and rode out. Wanted to be on his way, I figure, and good riddance. Said he was going to Chicago to be an actor and become more famous than Buffalo Bill. Can you believe that horseshit? Nash an actor?"

"If I never see that man again it will be too soon." Raines took the flask for another drink. He was trying to separate out the distant Indian voices, trying to hear hers. He could see the Indian campfires in the distance. Indicating them with a wave of the hand, he asked, "How long you figure it's going to last?"

"Till morning. It means just one thing, Lieutenant."

"What's that?"

The sergeant looked at him with sympathy. "The girl is more Indian than white."

CHAPTER SIXTEEN

Just after morning mess, Raines's wood cutting detail rode out from the post in a clatter of horses' hooves and wagon wheels stirring up dust. The grey clouds that had rolled in the night before still spread from horizon to horizon, casting the world into constant twilight.

From Tall Bull's village, Morgan saw them go over the far ridge. Pushing the lieutenant from her mind, she left the Cheyenne lodges with Ho'nehe, walking unhurriedly toward the post so the three-year-old boy could keep up. She was tired of hiding him in the Indian village. With Conor dead, she had no need any longer. Morgan knew the wasicus reaction to her son would be nothing short of apoplectic, seen as a woman who committed a crime against God. She didn't care. When they came on post, people stared, curious. Morgan gave them no thought. She had no concern for screeching magpies.

As she walked through the fort toward the colonel's house, Morgan felt weak, as weak as she'd ever been, even more so than the early days in Big Crow's camp. As if dead inside. The hurt of Conor's death clawed fiercely at her soul. Sometime last night during her mourning, she had collapsed and lost consciousness, drifting in and out of lucidity. Her Seyan came again, the place of the dead, with her family in Lone Tree. What troubled her was Conor. He wasn't there. Was his shadow wandering lost?

Yet, despite the numbness and exhaustion of her body, she stood up straight, her focus clear. Too much had been taken from her. This land had killed nearly everyone she loved. It would not get her son. Staying any longer was unbearable. She needed to get Ho'nehe away before it took him as well.

On the porch of the colonel's house, the boy pulled at her dress not wanting to go in. She squeezed his hand and gave him a reassuring smile. "We'll be away from here soon," she said in Cheyenne and repeated in English.

When Morgan and Ho'nehe entered the house, Mrs. Gannon was clearing dishes off the breakfast table while Colonel Gannon stood in the drawing room in front of the china cabinet, gazing at his reflection in the glass. He smoothed down his glossy black hair, snapped his uniform jacket with colonel's epaulets into place, then adjusted a black silk cravat at his neck.

Both the colonel and his wife saw Morgan at the same time. Immediately, Mrs. Gannon set the plates down and rushed to her, hugging her. "Oh, my dear, we heard about your brother. I am so, so sorry. The good Lord is placing some hardships in your path, testing you. You must remain strong."

Colonel Gannon joined them. "Yes, my condolences, Miss O'Connor. We will do everything we can to get you back on your feet."

"I am on my feet. I plan to leave for New York as soon as possible. To find the last of my family." Both of them had to notice her short, chopped hair, but neither remarked on it.

The colonel gave her a firm nod. "Yes, that would be best." He saw the boy's head peek out from behind Morgan's skirts and knelt down to speak with him. "Well, who's this? You brought a young warrior chief to visit us, I see."

Ho'nehe buried his head against his mother's leg for a second, then looked at the colonel.

Still kneeling, Gannon glanced up at Morgan. "What strange eyes, but what a delightful child. Is he the son of a squaw friend of yours?"

"He is my son."

Mrs. Gannon's hands went to her face in shock. The colonel blinked as if he didn't understand, then stood abruptly. "This is your boy?"

"Yes," she replied without hesitation.

Glaring, he slapped his gloves into his palm, unable to speak for several seconds, then said, "You should have told us this from the beginning that you…that you—." He sucked in a deep breath. "You have betrayed our kindness. You have stayed under our roof under false pretenses. I am most disappointed."

Though her own anger rose, she remained outwardly calm, saying, "I need an additional ticket for my son and the loan of a horse so we can make for Cheyenne. With it, I will be gone today. I promise you, Colonel Gannon, I will repay you."

Frustrated and upset, he ran a hand through his black hair. "Dear God, this is the worst time for you to spring this on me. There is an important senator from Washington stopping here on his way to the Red Cloud Agency for negotiations with the Sioux. And he wants to meet the famous Captured Girl. I can't let you go, at least not yet." He focused his eyes hard on her. "If you are here to greet him, I will provide tickets for you and the boy to travel to New York. Are we understood?"

She nodded. Only a little longer. For the tickets, she would wait.

Mrs. Gannon's eyes darted back and forth between the boy and Morgan. Her face softened and even the hint of a warm smile appeared. She stepped up to Ho'nehe and caressed his hair. "I bet you're hungry."

He looked up at his mother and she nodded. Ho'nehe turned back to Mrs. Gannon and nodded.

Gannon shook his head. "No. That will not do, Francis." He glared at Morgan. "Until the senator comes, you can return to Tall Bull's camp. I'm sure you're quite at home there. You are no longer welcome here."

"Natty!" Mrs. Gannon said in shock. "She will do nothing of the kind. She is staying here as is her son. If she must go to the Indian village, then I will pack my valise and go with her and that's that."

Morgan made an effort not to smile. While Colonel Gannon commanded all the soldiers on post with an iron will, in his own house his wife was in charge. He bounced on his polished boots for several seconds, then with a slap of his gloves against his pants leg, he strode out the door.

Mrs. Gannon smiled down at Ho'nehe. "Let's get you some breakfast, young man. I bet you'd like a cinnamon roll."

Word that the Indian boy was her child spread quickly through the post. In the next couple days, Mrs. Collins led a campaign against Morgan and her "black papoose," turning most of the post women against her. The officers' wives thought her presence an affront and despite Mrs. Gannon, refused to have anything further to do with her. Some of the Irish soldiers still acted with courtesy toward her, tipping their caps, but the camaraderie of the trail was gone. The rest of the regiment, mostly German emigrant companies, behaved as if she had brought the plague into their midst.

When Raines returned with wagons loaded with cordwood, the post was still abuzz about the Captured Girl and her Cheyenne bastard. He found the news shocked him more than he thought possible. Like all Indians, people were saying, she'd been dishonest, hiding the fact that she'd been a Cheyenne's squaw all along. He told himself a baby was hardly a surprising consequence from her savage treatment by the Indians, but a squaw? He could not accept that to be true. She would not have done such a thing. He decided he must show his support and stand by her.

The next morning just after Reveille, he hurried over to the colonel's house. She sat out back on the wooden bench, watching the Indian boy playing with a fat pup. Raines was shocked by her hair, as if a drunk soldier had cut it with a sabre. When he approached, she glanced up, held his gaze a moment, then without any hint of greeting, looked back at her son.

He sat beside her, uncertain where to begin. The creek rolled lazily by. A bird in the tree chirped for several seconds then flew off. He was all too aware that as soon as the great senator came and went, she would leave, and he would never see her again. The thought struck him with the force of a hammer on his chest. He desperately didn't want that to happen.

Her voice was abrupt. "Say it, for God's sake. You're like a lidded pot with boiling water inside."

He held his hands up as if surrendering. "I'm on your side."

"So, you think."

"I am. I've struggled with this since I got back." He gestured toward the boy. "I just wanted to tell you I don't think you bear any guilt. It is unfair in the extreme to blame you."

Her eyes flared explosively. "Sir, you think my son is a fault to be apportioned? My son is not someone's fault. I bear no guilt because I feel no guilt."

"I did not mean…You had no choice."

"Oh, sir, I did. People call me a squaw. I was. I was willingly the wife of a Cheyenne warrior and bore his son. You act as if I am a beggar on the street you wish to give a small coin of your compassion. Am I to be moved by such generosity of spirit?"

He was shocked by her admission. He had been sure she was not a willing partner. The idea of it cut like a knife blade along his chest. And he was angry. "Should I ignore your situation and hope everything just magically works out? Should I not honestly present you with the consequences of your actions? I am your friend and I'm trying to help you. I came here to offer you my support."

She stood up and called for the boy, who ran to her, trailed by the puppy. She glared at Raines. "You offer your support, no doubt, against your better judgment. I do not need it or want it. And as for such friendship, I don't need that or want that either."

Hurrying away, she and the boy walked through the back door and were gone.

During training that day, thoughts of Morgan plagued him. He could not get her out of his mind. His feelings for her, her crime against morality. He had meant to support her, but hadn't, couldn't. Under the skin, was he as corrupt as Mrs. Collins? He refused to believe that about himself. Yet, perhaps, he should let Morgan go. It would not be easy to do, but perhaps for the best. For the both of them.

After cavalry drill that afternoon, he was heading to the adjutant's office when a woman's scream came from somewhere in the direction of Suds Row. He first thought that the post was under attack, but dismissed it immediately. Not enough chaos or any gunfire. Another scream came, and he rushed toward the commotion.

At Suds Row, four laundresses stood in a semi-circle facing Morgan, who was brandishing a knife. One woman sat on the ground in the water from a spilled washbasin, holding her forearm and trying to stem the flow of blood from a long gash. Raines recognized her, Big Nose Sally, one of the unmarried laundresses with whom the men used most of their wages for sporting purposes.

Pointing at Morgan, she screamed, "She cut me! The bitch cut me! I told that Irish whore she's got no business bringing that breed spawn of hers among decent folk. It ain't right. And she cut me."

Morgan's lips were drawn back in a feral grimace. "I don't care what you say about me. But I'll cut the heart out of anyone who says affronts about my boy." She took a step toward them. "Is there anyone here who thinks I won't do it?"

One of the women, Alice Reardon, the sergeant's wife, said firmly, "It's done, Miss O'Connor. No one here wants to hurt you." She was a tall, strong-boned woman with a no-nonsense demeanor.

Raines held out his hand to Morgan. "Miss O'Connor, there's no need for this. Give me the knife."

She glanced at him dismissively. "Not likely." She stepped toward Big Nose Sally, who shrieked with terror, and he was about to rush in when Morgan wiped the blade on the woman's blouse and then slipped it inside the pocket of her dress.

Raines asked what happened.

"Ain't your funeral, Lieutenant," Alice said, calmly. "We'll take care of it."

Like a three-star general, she directed two of the women to take Sally to the infirmary, then ordered Raines to escort Morgan back to the colonel's house. In an instant, he'd gone from being a company commander to being ordered around by a laundress. After a moment's hesitation, he did as he was told and gestured to Morgan."

Reluctantly, she followed. As they walked out of Suds Row, her calm deserted her and she trembled with a mixture of distress and fury. "I'll not take that. I'll not take it."

He did not respond. What could he say to her in this state? He thought this relationship with her was madness. He can't be in love with a woman who would deliberately cut another woman, no matter the provocation. A willing squaw. His parents would disown him for the very fact she was poor Irish alone. They would die of shock and embarrassment if they knew she'd given birth to an Indian child. What would they say about a girl who used a knife in ways other than kitchen use?

He spotted Gannon pacing on the porch of his house, smoking a cigar. He already knew. Certainly, he thought, there would be enough people on post, soldiers and civilians, who would race to the colonel the moment something like this happened. When he saw them coming, he furiously stubbed out the cigar on the railing and went inside.

"Don't come any farther," she said to Raines. "Please. I can deal with the colonel."

Raines didn't argue, allowing her to go on alone. He knew Gannon wanted to wash his hands of the girl and this might be the last straw. He left her to face the colonel alone.

It was the next day that the senator from the East arrived to meet the Captured Girl.

CHAPTER SEVENTEEN

Senator Hiram P. Dodd, the powerful member of the Indian Affairs committee from New York, was one of the Allison Commission sent west by President Grant to buy the sacred Black Hills from the Sioux and Cheyenne. The previous summer, Lt. Colonel George Custer led an expedition into the Black Hills ostensibly to scout suitable locations for army posts, but actually to determine prospects for mining. The United States was in the midst of a long and great depression with many people moving west to find land or instant wealth. When the report came back from Custer that two miners had panned gold out of a stream, the floodgates opened, and swarms of prospectors poured through into the Black Hills.

The Allison Commission, made up of officials from the national government and local territories, was to meet with the Sioux and Cheyenne in a great council at the Red Cloud Agency near Camp Robinson in Nebraska. Senator William B. Allison of Iowa, its chairman, had already arrived there, impatiently waiting, while General Alfred Terry, Senator Dodd and other members took their leisure to reach the site.

With a large entourage, Dodd arrived at Camp Harrison in great pomp just before noon. Supposedly, he made the detour to join a cavalry detachment that would provide security during the talks, but his primary reason was pure politics with a huge dash of curiosity. He came to meet the Captured Girl.

Nearly two months after the glorious battle of Crazy Woman Creek, newspapers in New York and Washington were still filled with sensational stories about her. Not the first female ever taken, however, this one had captured the country's imagination. Each article included lurid drawings of her with her clothes being ripped off by savages. Her pluck and determination and, most of all, her incomparable beauty had people enthralled. She had become the rage of the summer. For Dodd, having reporters accompanying him decided the matter. He made the detour. He wanted to succeed Grant as President. Meeting with the girl who had enthralled so many would do his popularity no harm.

That night, in Mrs. Gannon's living room several officers and their wives stood with wine glasses filled, engaged in deep discussion. A blue haze drifted over the room from the men's cigars. At the center of attention, Gannon held forth amid a circle of officers.

When Raines came, he searched for Morgan and felt a rush of sympathy when he saw her standing alone, ignored by the other women and officers. In his mind, he had not resolved any of the issues with her, but here tonight, she looked a revelation. The short, auburn hair had been evened out and made presentable, even to a few dangling curls on the side. Except for the coppery skin from life outdoors, there was no hint of the Captured Girl to her. She looked the belle of any ball, her body snug in an evening gown of faded olive, low cut to show off a hint of cleavage. She even had a fan in one hand.

At that moment, Senator Dodd arrived with Joseph York, the Indian Agent at the Tall Bull Agency. The colonel introduced the senator to the gathering and everyone applauded.

Dodd held his hands up as if to stop the applause, but it was clear he was enjoying it. "No speeches tonight. No speeches. I am here to enjoy myself, don't you know." He then lifted his wine glass. "Ladies and gentlemen, may I propose a toast. We who are about to sit down with the heathen savage and attempt to bring peace to this land wish to honor you tonight, you the glorious victors of Crazy Woman Creek."

A cheer rose from the guests including boisterous huzzahs from the younger officers. Lieutenant Percy, the foppish 1st lieutenant, blurted obsequiously, "Colonel, you won the battle, and you were the one who killed Running Hawk."

Gannon cocked his head and shrugged as if only receiving his just due. "We were all doing our duty, were we not, gentlemen?"

"Yes, sir!" every officer shouted at once including Raines.

Dodd said to Gannon, "I am eager to meet the Captured Girl. Is she here?"

"Indeed, Senator." Gannon waved Morgan over and introduced her.

Dodd's eyebrows rose at her hair. "Yes, yes, it is difficult, indeed, to keep up with the latest ladies hairstyles. I had not expected someone so lovely. A Helen of Troy. Surely that is apropos, is it not, gentlemen?"

Dodd hid his disappointment. Indeed, she was pretty, but not the great beauty he had expected after the reports in the *World* and the *Times*. A Helen of Troy she was not. Nowhere near. There were many, many stunning beauties in New York, and this girl would pale beside them. Still, with several newsmen in tow, it would do nicely for the senior senator from New York to attend a reception and meet the celebrity over which his city and state were swooning.

"I give you my solemn promise, my dear," he said. "I am soon bound for the Red Cloud Agency and talks with the Indians. Any redskin who does not return to the reservation will pay. We will burn every single wigwam to the ground. You shall be avenged."

She stared at him coldly. As he waited for her to respond, the moment stretched on awkwardly. Flustered, Dodd rolled on the balls of his feet, wondering if she might be addled.

At that moment, Mrs. Gannon announced, "Ladies and gentlemen, please repair to the dining room. Dinner is ready."

In the large dining room, Raines sat next to Mrs. Collins, stifling a cough at her thick perfume. He prayed she would not engage him in conversation. Being cordial with so tedious a woman would tax his loyalty to the military. He found himself glancing at Morgan, who sat beside Percy. The colonel and Mrs. Gannon sat at opposite ends of the long table. To Mrs. Gannon's left was the Indian Agent Joseph York, a thin man with neatly combed blond hair and a handlebar moustache. According to Lucas Gerrard, the interpreter, he was loved by some in the Cheyenne camp but hated by most. Gerrard put himself in the latter group.

York would be traveling with Dodd to Camp Robinson not only as a local member of the Allison Commission, but also to provide cattle and other annuities to the Indians in attendance. Raines's first week on post, he had learned that the poor man's wife and child had been captured by Cheyenne more than four years before, about the time Morgan was taken. Nothing had been heard of them since.

To the clinking sound of dinnerware, the mess sergeant and four of his men served onion soup, steak, rice, peas and yellow carrots while Mrs. Gannon attempted to direct the conversation to mundane things. During the meal, Raines was unable to avoid Mrs. Collins's constant chatter about excruciating trivia, once for five minutes she ruminated about her favorite bath soap and its heavenly lavender smell. But when the dinner was done and coffee and cognac brought out and cigars produced, the talk of the table inevitably turned to the Indian problem and the Allison Commission mandate.

Everyone listened raptly as Senator Dodd told Colonel Gannon which Indians he expected to show up for the negotiations. "We don't know how many redskins will come, but I suspect a couple thousand. It's been rumored some of the hard cases like Crazy Horse, Sitting Bull and Spotted Horse will not be there, but I'm quite certain they will." He gave a knowing smile. "We must have two thirds of the Indians present to sign the treaty for it to become law, and if they are not present, they cannot refuse to sign. Alas, more the fool they. I assure you, gentlemen and ladies, we will have all the heathen on reservations before the year is out."

"I must disagree, sir." Setting his coffee cup down, York shook his head. "The Sioux are not going to sell the Black Hills, and the wild, free roaming Indians are not ready to give up their savage ways and live on any reservation."

"You might be right, sir," Dodd replied, taking his cigar from his mouth and staring at it a moment. "But I have an answer to that. I will tell you all a parable if you don't mind. It might clarify our strategy."

He spoke of meeting General Sheridan at the Division of the Missouri headquarters in Chicago. "The general had just returned from testifying to the Texas legislature. Don't you know, hunters were trespassing on Indian lands to kill buffalo, which made the Comanche mighty upset, so the Texans planned to prohibit the hunters killing bison on reservation land to forestall any further incidents. Thought that would keep the peace, they did."

"No legislature ever won a battle," Gannon put in.

"Indeed, sir. The general felt the same way. He took them to task. Told that legislature to let the hunters kill, skin and sell the buffalo until they are exterminated." Dodd relit his cigar, then chuckled. "I guess Little Phil now thinks the only good buffalo is a dead buffalo."

The room erupted in laughter, all but Morgan. Everyone had heard General Sheridan's oft quoted remark, *the only good Indian is a dead Indian.*

Taking a satisfied puff on his cigar, Dodd turned to Morgan. "Miss O'Connor, what is your view of the matter? With so many Cheyenne villages within close proximity, one just a half-mile distance from where we now sit, it must be alarming to one such as yourself?"

"I have no view of the matter. As for the Cheyenne, I'm not bothered by their proximity. I lived with them for four years. I survived."

The room fell silent. Even the mess boys halted. In the growing stillness, Mrs. Gannon's soft voice was firm as any commander's. "Senator Dodd, ladies and gentlemen, shall we adjourn to the parlor."

As the dinner party broke up and the guests departed, Gannon ordered Raines to remain. He met with him, his wife and Morgan in the drawing room. Carefully, the colonel began to relight his cigar, but his wife cleared her throat sharply, and he put it out. Now that Dodd had gone, she would allow no more cigar smoking in her home.

The colonel stuck the unlit cigar in his mouth and turned to Raines, "Miss O'Connor will be leaving Camp Harrison for New York as soon as we can arrange it, Lieutenant. Do you have anything further you can report about her family before she leaves? I hope you can tell us some good news."

"No, sir. We seemed to have hit a dead end for now."

The colonel's eyebrows knitted in a heavy frown.

"It is no matter," Morgan said, "You need do no more, Colonel. I will be leaving tomorrow. I will find them myself."

"No, you cannot leave, not yet," Gannon said. "I have to send a troop with the commission tomorrow, so I am stretched far too thin to have you leave now. When Captain Mason returns from patrol, I will send a detachment to guide you and the boy to Cheyenne where you can take the train east. You'll have to wait till then. It should be only a day or two."

Raines knew she was far more capable in this land than any of the colonel's men, but she did not protest.

"Sir," Raines said, "request permission to lead Miss O'Connor's escort?"

"No, you are assigned to Captain Lawson and his company tomorrow. You will be going to Red Cloud Agency for the council. You being from New York, Senator Dodd has requested you personally as his aide. I believe he knows your father. I'm aware playing nursemaid to a politician is not the kind of work we soldiers prefer, but I expect you to do your duty."

"Yes, sir." Raines frowned, barely able to hide his disappointment. Turning to Morgan he took two envelopes from his pocket and handed them to her. He hoped he'd a chance to speak to her alone, give her the letters then, but that seemed unlikely now. "The first has a little money the men raised to see you through the first few weeks. You must accept it or you will both offend them and rob them of the satisfaction of doing a good deed." It was a hundred dollars of his own money but he knew she would, indeed, refuse that.

Clutching the envelope in her hand, she said, "You must thank them for me."

"I will. This second is a letter for my family attorney, Mr. Greenblatt, in New York. Among other things, it instructs him to find you proper employment. You will need to support yourself while you are there. You won't find much for a young single woman that pays anything to live by, but he has connections, and will help."

Her head bowed, she muttered, "I don't know how to thank you, Lieutenant Raines."

"No need, Miss O'Connor." His reply was formal.

Gannon then dismissed him and reluctantly, he offered his *goodnights* and left. As he stepped onto the porch, he felt an overwhelming sorrow that he would never see her again. He glanced up lost for the moment in the swell of stars scattered across the infinite black.

"Will."

He turned as she stepped onto the porch. She was upset. "You must be careful at Red Cloud. There's trouble in the lodges. The Sioux and Cheyenne are stirred up. Believe me, I know this. It could be very bad there."

His eyes widened in surprise. How would she know, but then realized, of course, she would know. She had genuine worry on her face and fear in her voice.

"Promise you won't try to be a hero," she said insistently.

"I promise." They stood awkwardly for several seconds. "Morgan, I want to apologize."

She held her hand up to stop him. "You have no need. I did not want us to part on such poor terms. I don't have any friends. It would be good to have one."

Suddenly, putting both hands on his face, she pulled him down and kissed him on the lips. The kiss shattered him. His hands went around her and he drew her body into his. The heavy weight that had been bearing down on him fell apart. All he wanted now was to stay with Morgan, to repair the breech between them, but orders had him going to the Red Cloud Agency with Senator Dodd. When he came back, she'd be gone.

She stepped back, breaking the embrace. "I'll miss you, Will."

***

Lt. Percy found it absurd that he and fifteen troopers were detailed to escort a white squaw and her Indian brat to Cheyenne. The country couldn't be more desolate if he had been in the Sahara, rolling treeless hills transected by hundreds of small streams. Following the cavalry manual, he had three men in the front, five each on the flanks and two in the rear, but it all was a complete waste of time. The Indians were going to the Red Cloud Agency and the council.

In the afternoon, another horde of Indians, with their entire existence piled onto travois, crossed their path on their way to the council. It annoyed him that their passage forced his men to pick their way through them. Not exactly military maneuvers. It was the third such nomadic assemblage they'd seen since leaving the fort. It seemed the entire population of savages was on its way to participate in the sale of the Black Hills, no doubt intent on making sure each got their share of the money.

As the soldiers passed, an Indian boy sat his pony, watching them. He wore leggings and a breechclout, his bare chest streaked with dust and sweat. He had a scar across one cheekbone and green eyes. His double braided hair was greased dark with tallow and charcoal so it could not be seen that his hair was red.

The Cheyenne called him Little Turkey, but he had once been known as Conor O'Connor. That time in his life came only in hazy images. He no longer knew that little boy. He was Cheyenne. He had seen soldiers before and no longer had any desire to run to them as he once did to tell them who he was. Now, they were the enemy.

Just as he was about to turn his horse and return, he recognized the girl sitting on the wagon and a thunderbolt shot through him. Morgan, his sister. His heart pounded with the old longing, and he hoped no one saw his reaction. Abruptly turning his horse, he guided it back among the People.

CHAPTER EIGHTEEN

A week after leaving Camp Harrison in the Dakotas, Morgan and Ho'nehe arrived at Grand Central Depot in New York City. Clutching the valise and draw purse in one hand, she held to her son with the other and made her way along with the flood of other passengers into the main concourse. Both stood in awe of its size with more people seemingly than in all of Cheyenne. Abruptly, she was jostled, and she dropped the valise. At that same moment, someone else snatched the purse from her hand and ran off. She caught a glimpse of a young boy running away through the crowd. Her money!

"Thief! Thief! Stop him," she shouted, giving chase.

People stared at her as if she were mad. There was no thief to be seen; the boy had disappeared. In frustration, she turned back and saw another boy, an older one of maybe fifteen, picking up her valise. Their eyes locked and he broke into a run toward the exit. She was quicker, cutting him off and tackling him hard to the tile floor. Several people jumped back, screaming.

On their knees, each clutched the valise. The boy bared his teeth and snarled, a feral animal of the streets, and drew a knife. Quicker even, Morgan drew out the bone-handled knife from her dress. This surprised him. He stared at her eyes as if gauging the amount of danger he was in. His face went pale, he let go of the valise and sprinted away.

Morgan stood up with the valise, and dread seized her. She couldn't see Ho'nehe among all the people. Like a mad woman, she shoved through them, but there were too many. In a high, shrieking voice, she cried out in Cheyenne, "Tosa'e! Tosa'e!"

Her words were met with an ululating half scream, half wail, and she hurried to it. He was pressed against the wall by the street exit, pushed there by the crowd. She knelt and hugged him. "You brave boy," she said in a hushed voice. "You are my brave boy."

At that moment, devastated by the loss of all her money, she looked up, saw the sign above the exit. It read: WELCOME TO NEW YORK CITY.

Outside was a world of sound and chaos. Throngs of people pushed passed, jostling them. On the street, a vast parade of carriages, cabs, drays and omnibuses clattered over cobblestones. Beyond, buildings rose up like high bluffs along the Tongue. Morgan was bewildered by it all, paralyzed.

Trembling with fear, Ho'nehe hugged her leg, but he would not weep or cry out. All his short life, he had been trained for silence when moving. An errant sound could mean death for the People. For her, it was like the time four years ago when the two Indians rode at her, screaming and waving their war clubs, and she was stuck in a palsy of fear. Now, she felt the same way. She could not fasten her mind on what to do. Her money was gone. Where were they going to sleep tonight?

She touched the letter in her pocket, comforted by it. The lawyer had to find work for her. She took out the envelope and checked the address again: Aaron Greenblatt, esquire, Equitable Life Assurance Society Building, New York City. She saw a man in a dark uniform with a shiny badge and asked if he knew Greenblatt or the building. "Never heard of this Greenblatt fellow, but the building I know. You can't miss it. It's the tallest building in the world."

When she started off with Ho'nehe on her hip and the valise in her hand, he called after her, astonished, "Here, lass, wait. It's four miles, at least. You can't be walking it."

Morgan kept going. She'd walked more than twenty miles in a day with heavier burdens. She could make four. But the trek was harder than she imagined, passed strange stone buildings, streets clogged with horses and wagons, and people always in motion like bees in a hive. She and Ho'nehe gaped at the endless city blocks. Crossing streets, they were nearly run down by carriages. Almost every block, she was accosted by men with lewd propositions despite her boy there. Blisters appeared like pebbles in her laced boots.

It took them more than three hours in the warm sun to walk the distance, but finding the building was easy. Seen from several blocks away, it indeed was a mountain. She counted seven stories. Once inside, her back and feet sore, she studied an address board. Greenblatt & Steiner on the seventh floor. She sighed. It just had to be on the seventh.

***

"Come in, Miss O'Connor," the man standing behind the large oak desk said. He was small and thin with black hair, trimmed black beard and dark, lively eyes behind spectacles. "As you might have surmised, I am Aaron Greenblatt. We had not been expecting you. It would be best in the future for you to notify us ahead of time.

"I am here," was all she could think to say.

He indicated for her to sit in the cushioned chair in front of his desk and pointed to a burly man standing near an open window. "This is Josiah Lamb of the Pinkerton Detective Agency. He happens to be working your case."

Morgan glanced at him and he nodded. With short-cropped hair and a wrinkled suit, he looked more a thug than a detective.

She handed Greenblatt Will's letter, and the lawyer set it aside on his desk. "And who is this lad?" he asked.

He is Ho'nehe of the Cheyenne, son of Spotted Horse, and she is Crow Killer, daughter of the great Running Hawk. But that was in a different world. They were deep in the white world, now. The boy needed another name, a white name. She was an O'Connor. He was an O'Connor. "He is my son," and on impulse added, "His name is Seamus. After my father Seamus O'Connor."

Greenblatt frowned. "Your son? Young William did not mention that piece of information."

"Seamus is here, too," she said flatly. He squirmed off her lap and began to explore the office.

"Indeed. Well, shall we begin?" He nodded to Lamb, who picked up a ledger from the desk, one stuffed with folded newspapers, and searched through it.

"Ah, here it is." The Pinkerton man placed a single newspaper before her.

On the front page was a lurid portrait of a young woman with three Indians ripping off her clothes. Morgan knew this was supposed to be her. In the background, a dashing cavalry officer was riding to her rescue. That would be Will. The headline read: *The Captured Girl Saved!* The date of the paper was only three days ago.

He kept thrusting it at her. She frowned. "What do you want me to do, autograph it?"

Then, noticing the subtitle, she took it from him. *Maureen O'Donnell Saved from Fate Worse Than Death.* She laughed at the absurdity. "This looks nothing like me, and that is not my name."

Greenblatt shrugged. "Maureen O'Donnell, Megan O'Dowd, even Mary Gladstone once. Just so you're young and pretty. That's all that matters to them."

Lamb tapped the newspaper with his finger. "The point is you have been on the front page of Frank Leslie's Illustrated and every other newspaper in the last month at one time or another as *the Captured Girl*, no matter what your name is."

She handed the paper back to Lamb. "How is this of benefit to me?"

Greenblatt answered, "The point is that these stories help us search for your relatives. The Captured Girl desperately seeking her family, and all that. When our men show this picture and tell people we are attempting to find your family, they are eager to help. At least, in Five Points, they are not trying to kill our men anymore."

"We have a substantial lead now, thanks to you," Lamb added. "Last week when we asked people around Bayard and Mulberry Bend if they'd heard of your family, a few did. They are no longer there, but we did learn your uncle was friends with a man named Johnny Dolan. We know Dolan."

She tried to remember the name from her childhood but couldn't. "Have you spoken with him? Does he know where my aunt and uncle are?"

Lamb gave a harsh laugh. "Dandy Johnny Dolan is not an easy man to find himself, miss. The man is a real hard case. I can speak from experience. He's chief of the Whyos. If he doesn't want to be contacted, he won't be."

"The Whyos?'

Lamb scowled. "As vicious an assortment of cutthroats, murderers and thieves as ever walked this city. Worse than the Plug Uglies or Dead Rabbits ever were."

The names had a distant familiarity for her. Great fear attached to them. "My uncle had nothing to do with crime. He was a shoemaker."

Lamb shrugged. "He still may be. Maybe Dolan's a customer. Who knows? I'll find Dandy Johnny soon enough, and we'll see."

Greenblatt picked up the letter from Will and read it, then slowly smoothed it out on the desk and shook his head. "Find you employment, he instructs. There are few working situations for young women that accords with moral society."

He glanced at Ho'nehe, who was talking in a foreign language to a pigeon on the window sill. "I might have placed you in service with a client, but I'm afraid with a child in tow, that would prove impossible. I will continue to search for something on your behalf, but you must be aware, there is little I can actually do."

"I understand."

Disheartened, she was about to ask about working situations that don't accord with moral society when Lamb said, "Perhaps, I have a solution." The Pinkerton man took the seat next to her. "My wife and I run a boarding house. We might be able to take Seamus while you are working. My two sons are out of the house now, employed by Pinkerton in Washington, but we still have our three daughters. They will dote on your boy. I assure you my wife knows how to care for young children. We would all be delighted to have him. If you went into service, you could visit on your day off. And it would cost very little."

Morgan's eyes darted back and forth from Greenblatt to Lamb, seeking, hoping there might be other suggestions. Her first instinct was to reject the offer—how could she be without her child—but realized quickly she had no choice. "How much?"

Lamb cocked his head figuring, then said, "Four dollars a month should do it."

"I would have to meet your wife, and I can't pay till I receive a salary of my own."

He gave a shrug of acceptance. "Of course."

"Then it's settled," Greenblatt said, with a clap of the hands. He took a sheet of paper from his desk drawer, dipped a pin into the inkwell and began writing.
"This letter will recommend you for a position in service to Mr. Otto Krueger. He is a client of mine.

The Kruegers are always in need of housemaids. Fair warning: working for them can be a trial. They run through servants like loaves of bread. If you're still willing, I'm sure you can speak with Mrs. Krueger this afternoon."

She nodded. "I'm willing." When he handed her the letter, she said, "Thank you. You've been very kind. Both of you have."

"You haven't got the position yet," Greenblatt said.

At a nod from him, Lamb stood up. "Shall we meet my wife, Miss O'Connor?"

The Lambs owned a two-story, red brick house on West Tenth Street with four boarders upstairs; the family lived on the first floor. When Morgan met Mrs. Lamb, she immediately felt comfortable with her. Grey-haired and tall, she reminded her of Owl Woman, both welcoming and kindhearted. While they talked over tea, the teenage daughters fussed and played with Seamus, who enjoyed the attention.

The youngest girl about thirteen beamed. "Oh, my, he's got such beautiful eyes. He's just lovely."

The only hesitation came when Mrs. Lamb said, "The boy's father is clearly Indian."

Morgan stiffened, readied herself to leave.

Mrs. Lamb smiled and held her hand out to stay her move. "I make no judgments, child. That is for the Lord to do. You see, I was raised Mennonite, and we believe in the essential goodness of all beings. If it wasn't for that big reprobate over there," she said, nodding toward her husband, "I still would be. It was just an observation."

Abruptly, Lamb rose to his feet. "Well? Have you decided, Miss O'Connor? Shall I take you to the Krueger home to meet the dragon lady?"

Morgan agreed to leave her son with the Lambs. Kissing and hugging Seamus, she told him he must be strong and brave while she was away and do as the kind lady says. She would be back to see him as soon as she could. As she left, his horrific face tore at her heart, but he did not cry out.

CHAPTER NINETEEN

Morgan sat nervously in the hallway of the Krueger mansion on Fifth Avenue, waiting to be interviewed by Mrs. Cornelia Krueger. Elegant vases and statues stood atop polished rosewood tables and portraits of stern men and women hung on the walls. She feared touching anything and kept her hands folded firmly in her lap. Despite her strong anxiety, she determined she must somehow get this position. Without it, she and Ho'nehe…Seamus…were lost. Only an hour gone, and she already missed him. When would she see him again?

On the carriage ride over with Lamb, Morgan had tried to calm her emotions, which were in chaos after leaving her son. Lamb was telling her something about the Kruegers, and she forced herself to listen. Otto Krueger, he explained, was one of the richest men in the country, along with Jay Gould, Cornelius Vanderbilt and William Backhouse Astor, none of whom she'd ever heard.

"Though you would not know they were that wealthy by the way Mrs. Krueger ran her household," Lamb added. "She is a miser who pays the help as if the family were scraping for pennies. That's just one of the reasons her servants last less time than ice on a summer day."

Leaning forward with intensity, Lamb warned her to stay out of the clutches of Mathias Krueger, the son of the family. "A drunkard and a philanderer rumored to have caused more than one maid found to be in a family way to be dismissed. But Julia, the oldest daughter, is the worst of the lot. She looks like an angel and acts like a demon. I would stay clear of her."

"She sounds like she has fangs and claws."

"She has."

The butler startled Morgan out of her reverie. "Mrs. Krueger will see you now."

She was led into the drawing room where a stout woman in her forties sat on the divan, looking like a picture Morgan had once seen of Queen Victoria with her imperious stare and double chin. She held Greenblatt's letter open on her lap. Beside the divan stood a stern, grey-haired woman in a plain, brown dress, her hands folded in front of her.

The butler bowed slightly to her. "Mrs. Krueger, this is Miss O'Connor."

"Thank you, Dawes."

When the butler left, Mrs. Krueger nodded toward a chair across the coffee table from her. On the table was a tea service with a plate of biscuits, but Morgan didn't think she would be offered any.

"So, you are ze girl Mr. Greenblatt claims as a housemaid, and you vit no experience at all," Mrs. Krueger began with a sharp clip of her syllables, German accent and stern countenance. "Vhat does Mr. Greenblatt expect? That I start a home for vaving Irish girls?"

It took Morgan a moment to piece together what she'd said, *home for waving Irish girls*. What did that mean? "I have no experience in service, ma'am, but I'm no stranger to hard work."

"Vhat kind of vork? The Jew did not say."

Tracking, killing animals, skinning them. "I grew up on a ranch. Before dawn, I was up milking cows—."

Mrs. Krueger burst out laughing. "Vee have no cows here." She glanced at the other woman. "Mrs. Stevenson, perhaps vee can keep a cow in the third floor parlor and Miss O'Connor can bring us fresh milk each morning."

Without changing expression, Mrs. Stevenson said, "Very amusing, madam."

The remark stung Morgan, but controlling her anger, said evenly, "I worked hard and did the chores right the first time. That's what I would do here."

"Ja, ja. Just off the farm." Mrs. Krueger gave a slight roll of the eyes, then fixed Morgan with a challenging gaze. "At least, you are not from Five Points like so many of your breed. Vee have two vacancies to fill. You say you can vork hard. Vee vill see. I expect a full day's labor for your pay and vill not imbibe tardiness or laziness. No servant is allowed to stay out beyond 9:00pm, even on day off. Britches of this rule are not to be occasioned."

Again, it took Morgan a moment to digest what the woman meant, *imbibe, britches*? Did she mean *breeches*?

"Pay is eight dollars a month, plus room and board." Mrs. Krueger waved her hand as if flicking away a fly. "Now, go. Mrs. Stevenson vill explain your duties."

Morgan sighed with relief. This job would keep her and her son off the streets till she found her relatives. Mrs. Stevenson led her out of the parlor and through several rooms bedecked with gold candelabras and grand chandeliers. To get to all four floors, they used the narrow backstairs, all servants did, so they never interfered with 'them.' The servants were to be seen as little as possible. Morgan never imagined there could be so many steps in a single house.

In the rooms, maids flew about doing chores, or at least seemed to be when Mrs. Stevenson appeared. In one drawing room, Morgan's leather shoes sank into the plush, wine-colored carpet. Paintings of seascapes, landscapes, and stern-looking men and women took up almost every inch of wall.

She blinked her eyes several times to gather it all in. Along the way, the housekeeper explained her duties, but awed by the luxury and sheer vastness of the place, Morgan barely heard. This could not be more alien had she been set down on the surface of the moon.

When they entered a large dining room, the third one in the mansion, a maid was polishing the gold mantel atop a massive, marble fireplace, and a footman dressed smartly in red livery was setting out flowers on the long table. The maid glanced back at Morgan and frowned, then continued with her labors.

"Is everything gold?" Morgan asked breathlessly.

"No. It's gilded."

What did that mean, she wondered, but said nothing not wanting to show her ignorance.

Stern, Mrs. Stevenson never seemed to change expression. "Much will be expected of you, Miss O'Connor. You will learn quickly or be gone."

"Yes, ma'am."

When they started down the narrow backstairs, Mrs. Stevenson turned on her abruptly, blocking the passage, her face twisted in scorn. "I know you Irish people. I have worked with your kind since I went into service. Lord knows we have enough of you on staff here. I can say without fear of contradiction that you people are prone to laziness and sometimes downright criminality. I'll not have it on my staff."

The housekeeper paused, waiting for Morgan to speak, but then giving her no chance, stuck a long, bony finger in her face. "I have found that outright lying and thievery is a way of life with you people. I will not stand for it. I will not. I warn you now, if you step out of line, Miss O'Connor, you will pay a heavy price. Have I made myself clear?"

Morgan laid on a thick Irish brogue. "I'll do me best, Mrs. Stevenson. T'is sure that I will. I would never be lying and stealing from me betters."

For a moment, the housekeeper scowled, as if uncertain whether she was being mocked. "We'll see. Come along then," she said and went on down.

In the servants' hall, Morgan sat down to tea and biscuits with the rest of the staff. Dawes introduced her to them as the new housemaid. "You will become familiar with the rest of the staff in time."

She was famished and ate her biscuit in two swift bites. Several of the servants stared at her and she said defiantly, "What are you looking at?"

With a grin, a footman answered, "I'd say you were hungry, lass."

A few chuckled. Morgan forced an awkward smile.

After servants' tea, Mrs. Stevenson took Morgan to the storeroom and issued her bedding, two brown maid's dresses, two pairs of white stockings and a single white cap. Another young maid came in. Morgan took note of her wispy, red hair that reminded her of Fiona's. Not as lustrous or tinged with gold but still attractive under her white cap. She had quick and lively brown eyes and a ready smile.

"This is Katelyn O'Neill," Mrs. Stevenson said. "She will show you to your room."

Morgan followed the young maid up the narrow backstairs to the attic. "I hope we'll be friends. We'll be sharing a room together. Morgan O'Connor is it? Irish you are then."

"Yes, part of that lying, thieving lot."

Katelyn laughed. "Aye, I see you got the talk from Old Horse Face." She led her down a short hallway. "This is the Virgins' Corridor," Katelyn said, chuckling. "That's us. The single girls. We stay up here where the male staff can't get to us." She giggled. "Or maybe they sleep in the basement so we can't get at them."

Virgin, Morgan thought sardonically. She was no virgin.

Katelyn took her into a small bedroom sparsely furnished with a single chest of drawers and two beds on opposite sides, one under the slant of the roof where it would be impossible to stand. That would be hers. She took her bedding over and bending low, placed it on the mattress and sat down. A droplet of sweat fell from her nose. The room was stiflingly hot.

"It ain't all bad, lass," Katelyn said. "The staff is pretty nice except for Stevenson and that butler Dawes. They're a mean pair, no two ways about it, but you'll learn as you go."

Morgan said there didn't seem to be many servants for such a large mansion.

"That's Mrs. Krueger. We have less than half what's needed here. Just fifteen in all. We do the work of housemaids, chambermaids and sometimes even lady's maids because that old bat is such a miser. 'Vee pay honest money for honest vork.'" Her imitation was perfect and Morgan laughed. Katelyn added, "Won't hire what she needs and won't pay the ones she's got."

"Well, I need the job."

"So do I. T'is sure."

"What do I do now?" Morgan asked, feeling lost.

"Change into one of the dresses and come down to the servants' hall. You're to meet his nibs. Mrs. Krueger likes to introduce all the new help to the lord and master. You'll also be meeting the entire family. The two girls are near our age. Miss Julia is eighteen and Miss Katherine seventeen. Both think the sun shines up their arses. Stay away from that Julia. She's a nasty one. She has a tongue sharp as a cutthroat's knife."

"So I've been told."

"Hurry, change."

A half-hour later, her hair in a neat bun, Morgan followed Mrs. Stevenson into the Music Chamber where the family had gathered. Instantly, she was struck by the strangeness of the room. Gaudy colors erupted from tapestries and paintings in vivid blues and yellows, all with scenes more appropriate for a bordello than a house, naked women being chased by men with horns and hooves. On small pedestals about the room stood strange statuettes of these same naked men copulating, raping women. Images of her own repeated rape by the Cheyenne warriors that first night after her capture flashed through her mind, and she quelled a wave of sudden nausea.

Accompanying all this was a haunting melody floating on the air. At the far end of the room behind a grand piano, a young woman played, her eyes closed and her head lolling back in reverie. She was strikingly beautiful with golden curls and a face that called up images of a sensual Madonna.

On a nearby divan, smoking a thick cigar, Otto Krueger sat beside his stolid wife, listening to the pianist raptly. He had intense dark eyes and a dark beard. Removing his cigar, he moved it gently like a smoking baton to the melody, pride illuminating his face.

Just to Morgan's left, a young man and woman sat huddled in chairs beside an unlit fireplace, whispering in hushed tones, punctuated by the girl's strident screams of laughter, which did not seem to bother the piano player. She took a piece of hard candy from a bowl and placed it in her mouth. The man had to be Mathias Krueger, the one everyone warned her to avoid, and the woman the younger sister Katherine.

When the tune came to an end, Mrs. Stevenson led Morgan to Mr. Krueger. "Sir, this is the new maid, Miss O'Connor."

The piano player clanked out a loud sour note. "Oh, dear Lord, not another mick."

From across the room, Katherine laughed. "Oh, don't be so severe on her, Julia. Give the poor thing a chance."

Mathias whispered something to her and she shrilled with laughter, slapping him playfully on the arm with a fan. Morgan didn't like the sisters Krueger already, or the brother for that matter.

Picking up a folded newspaper, Mr. Krueger began reading. Without looking at her, he said, "Welcome, Miss O'Connor. I hope you will enjoy your employment with us."

"Sing *Gretchen am Spinnrade* for us, Julia," Mrs. Krueger called to the piano player.

"Oh, all right, mutti," Julia said with feigned reluctance. It was clear she liked being the center of attention.

As the girl began to play, Mrs. Stevenson gestured for Morgan to follow her out. As Julia's beautiful soprano voice resonated in her ears, she wondered what kind of madhouse Greenblatt had sent her to.

CHAPTER TWENTY

Conor was caught up in the excitement. They had just arrived for the wasicus council and set their camp along the river next to a band of Lakota. As the women quickly erected lodges and started the cook fires, the men set their ponies to grazing in the hills and then greeted old friends.

Feeling a sense of pride, the boy stood beside his father Big Crow, staring in wonder at such a sight. More people had come to the place where Red Cloud lived than he had ever seen before. The lodges stretched endlessly along the river to the far lands of the vanishing sun. It would be a great council, remembered into the time of distant generations.

Though filled with anticipation, the boy felt oddly adrift at the same time, thinking often about the white sister he had seen not long ago. There seemed no solid ground under his feet. He lived in a halfway land between white and Indian, childhood and adult. His white reckoning put his age at twelve so he no longer played children's games, yet his father would not allow him to go out with the warriors to prove his worth. At councils, he listened to their war plans, hoping to be among them on the next raid, but he never was. Perhaps, Spotted Horse would take him. He was coming that night.

Later, Spotted Horse rode in with Little Big Man and several Lakota bad hearts. That was when the chiefs and elders, wrapped in their blankets, gathered around the fire and discussed the white commissioners who wanted to buy the Black Hills. The talk was lively; nearly fifty men spoke. Conor sat a few yards behind Big Crow, watching his broad-backed father cock his head toward each speaker. Beside him, Spotted Horse stared at the ground as if he were not listening at all. It was well known he was not much for talking.

The men were angry. The Lakota did not want to sell the Black Hills and the Cheyenne supported them. An Ogallala who had come with Little Big Man was finishing a long, fiery speech. "I tell you now, the wasicus cannot get enough of the People to touch the pen. They cannot."

He sat down with a fierce nod and Tall Bull rose. "I hear you, my brothers. You all speak truth. Nothing you say is like the coyote tricking us to do one thing when we know the other is the best way. The wasicus will never honor what they promise. Their treaties are like words on the wind. Now, they want the Black Hills and say that will be all they demand from us. Next, they will want the hunting grounds and that will be all they demand from us, then they will want the reservation land we live on and move us far off to lands fit only for dogs. And this, they will say, is all they demand from us."

As mutterings of agreement travelled about the council, he paused, staring at his audience, taking them all in. He raised his hands up as if to praise the Great Spirit. "I tell you now another true thing. I have seen the white man's cities. They are as big as the prairie itself. I have seen their people. They number more than the buffalo when I was a boy. If we do not touch the pen, the horse soldiers will take the Black Hills anyway, and we will have nothing but the sickness of the dead. I promise you. I have seen this in my visions. If we do not touch the pen, the Lakota and Cheyenne will be no more."

Angry grumbles met his words. He went on, "I want to see my sons and daughters live out their lives as the Great Spirit intended. And their children for all the generations to come. The buffalo are disappearing. If we do not touch the pen, so, too, the People will disappear."

He sat down and Little Big Man jumped to his feet, furious. He was a smaller version of Big Crow, short but broad and muscular. "We have too many Loaf-About-the-Forts who think they speak for the People. They have a taste for the white man's whiskey and the white man's food and the white man's clothes. No longer do they want the People to ride the land as free men." He raised his rifle in the air and shouted, "Hear me, my brothers, any man who touches the pen will fall like the tall grass when fire sweeps across the prairie."

A loud chorus of approval erupted from his listeners. Big Crow was nodding his head vigorously over and over. Tall Bull appeared frightened.

Slowly, Spotted Horse rose, looking across the circle at Little Big Man. Everyone quieted for him because he seldom spoke at councils. "For many seasons, the spirit of my son has been crying out to me for the blood of the wasicus. He says I will have no peace till I fill my lodge with their bones. Now, the wasicus dishonor us by sending this commission to steal the Black Hills from us. My son tells me if I kill a commissioner, I will find peace. That is what I must do."

He sat back down. Many showed their agreement with loud exclamations of assent. *Kill a commissioner.* It should be done, many said. It would show their disdain for the wasicus claiming the Black Hills. No one else spoke after that. They returned to their lodges ready to follow the course Little Big Man and Spotted Horse had set.

CHAPTER TWENTY-ONE

For Morgan, the first days of employment without Seamus seemed extraordinarily long, and the wait till her Sunday day off interminable. The Krueger work was as endless as her first months with the Cheyenne, long hours into the evening, but no beatings, only severe reprimands and threats of dismissal by Mrs. Stevenson for being lazy. That stung because she was never lazy. On Friday afternoon, Mrs. Stevenson sent her to clean Julia's private sitting room on the second floor. The elder Krueger daughter spent late nights there doing God knows what. Rumor had it among the staff that she tortured small dogs and cats even though no screams were ever heard.

As Morgan ascended the steps to the second floor carrying a broom and feather duster, a woman burst out of Julia's bedroom and collided with her. Startled, Morgan worried it was Miss Julia herself, but it was Yvette, her lady's maid, with a face scrunched in misery, crying. She looked at Morgan for a second, then turned and ran, ducking immediately into the sitting room next door.

Moments later, Julia came out scowling and raised her voice, "Where did you run off to, you buffoon? I have guests for afternoon tea. This is not the time for such silliness. Am I to fix my own hair?" Then she noticed Morgan and snapped, "What are you staring at? You look like an owl."

Morgan remembered to curtsy. “Nothing, Miss Julia.”

“Did you see where my lady’s maid went?”

“No, ma’am.”

The Krueger girl cocked her head and studied Morgan skeptically for several seconds, then went back in her bedroom, muttering, “Dumm Kopf.”

Morgan found Yvette on the divan in the sitting room, still crying, her legs tucked up under her. The French girl was pretty with lustrous black hair. As Katelyn had explained it, she was a prized possession of the Kruegers. All the great families in New York wanted a French lady’s maid and now Julia had one. Yvette had been working for her for two months, the most anyone had lasted in that position. The valuable Yvette would not be sacked unless she stole.

Morgan sat down and put a tentative hand on the French girl’s shoulder. “What happened, Yvette?”

“Merde! She is a heartless creature.” She wiped her nose. Her French accent was thick. “La petite pute. I've seen cruel things she do with her snake mouth, and laugh at the pain she causes. It is horrible. I cannot take it.”

She stood abruptly, pressed down her frilly uniform with her hands, then chin up, left the room. Morgan doubted Yvette even knew to whom she’d been talking.

Later that night in the darkness, Morgan told Katelyn about it. Exhausted, they sat in their long sleeve shifts, curled up on the seat before the open gable window, gazing down at the lights of Fifth Avenue.

“I told you,” Katelyn said. “That’s Julia.”

Their attic room was stiflingly hot and would be until near dawn. A gentle breeze feathered in through the window, cooling them. From this great height, Morgan imagined herself an eagle, perched in the high crags, peering over the Bighorn River, only this river below had street lamps and great gilded coaches.

Katelyn noticed her pensiveness. “You seem downcast, lass. Are you surviving the Kruegers?”

Morgan gave a wry smile. "Barely. I've learned to avoid Julia and Mathias, but it's not always possible."

Katelyn chuckled. "Very wise. Sometimes I think all the money in the world couldn't make me stay another day here, but I do."

"Katelyn, have you heard of a family named Raines?" Morgan asked. "They are supposed to have a home on Fifth Avenue."

Cocking her head in thought, the maid said, "I think so. The name's familiar, but I don't quite move in those circles."

A coach rolled by below, its iron-shod horses clattering on the cobblestones. The wide thoroughfare was flanked by great homes, some still with lights illuminating their windows. On the corner stood the tall spires of a massive, richly ornate church. Katelyn pointed at it. "That's where the Kruegers attend Sunday service, trying to serve both God and mammon."

It was all so strange, Morgan thought. Just a few weeks ago she was living in a Cheyenne village, looking at Cheyenne parents as her family. Now, they were dead, and she lived in New York in one of the richest mansions in the country. No parents, no family, but having her precious son and some vague notion of relatives left.

Katelyn harrumphed. "Mrs. Krueger won't even put a penny in the collection basket. Rich as they are, she is so tight, getting paid is like pulling coins out of her clinched arse."

"I don't think I'd ever want a coin that much."

They both laughed. Morgan liked Katelyn. Slightly older, she talked of her large family of nine brothers and sisters. They lived in a Five Points tenement on Bayard Street, neither parent working. "Da is a tanner, but the factories took all his work, and mam washes clothes, but everyone in the Bend washes their own clothes now. That's why I desperately need this job. If I lost it, my family would starve."

When asked about herself, Morgan merely said she'd grown up on a ranch in the West and turned the conversation elsewhere, not wanting to talk about her past. People knowing of her Indian husband and child could lead to her being sacked. She needed this job, too, and she trusted no one, not even this Irish girl at her side.

Katelyn drew her knees up and tucked her shift under them. "The Krueger house is the biggest on Fifth Avenue. Aye, just goes to show, you can have everything and still not have what you want most."

Morgan glanced at her curiously. "What could the Kruegers possibly want that they don't have already or can't buy?"

The older girl grinned as if she had the secret of the sphinx. "They want to be hobnobbing with Mrs. Astor and her friends, and they ain't never." Abruptly, she slid off the window seat and padded barefoot to the dresser and poured water from the pitcher into a basin.

Morgan swung her legs off the window seat. "With who?"

"*The* Mrs. Astor, lass. Where have you been living? In China?" she asked as she dipped a sponge into the water and began dabbing her neck and face. "That Julia and Mrs. Krueger desperately want to belong to the Four Hundred. They're New York's social elite, or think they are. There are many wealthy people in the city like the Kruegers, but the true social elite are few, only the number that could comfortably fit into Mrs. Astor's ballroom, or so people say."

Morgan said sarcastically, "You and I could fit in their ballroom."

Chuckling, Katelyn glanced over at her. "Aren't you the funny one? We couldn't get past the door. Be easier to get into the vault at the Bank of New York. No, the nobs of high society protect their little kingdom. They're always in the papers. All their grand balls and teas and soirees and socializing now with British nobility or running up to their summer homes. But, you see, the Kruegers are bounders and shoddies of the first order. They'll never make it no matter how much money they got."

She seemed to take pleasure in that. She picked up the basin and carried it to the window. Morgan ducked out of the way as Katelyn emptied the water out the gable on the roof. Taking the basin, Morgan washed up and the two women climbed into their beds, too hot for any covers. After a few seconds, Morgan asked. "Why won't they make it, the Kruegers? They've got more money than a Philadelphia lawyer."

"T'is sure they do." Katelyn chortled. "But you see, Mrs. Cornelia Krueger's father was a Munich blacksmith, and that is unforgivable."

"There are worse things to be."

"Not to the Four Hundred."

***

On Sunday morning, Morgan woke up excited for the day ahead like it was Christmas. She was seeing Seamus today. She took care washing and dressing and at exactly 9:00am went down to the servants' hall to check with Mrs. Stevenson before leaving for the Lambs' boarding house. She met the housekeeper in her office to tell her she was leaving.

"And where do you think you're going, Miss O'Connor?" Mrs. Stevenson demanded, standing behind her desk.

"It's my day off," Morgan said, her voice catching. She did not like this turn.

"Not today it isn't," the housekeeper said, emphatically. "Your work has been terribly remiss, especially Miss Julia's sitting room. She was appalled at its poor state after you had supposedly cleaned it. She asked that you be reprimanded and punished for such shoddy work and I quite agree. You owe the Kruegers and Miss Julia a good day's work. There will be no time off today. You've already taken your day off."

Morgan seethed; her fist clinched. But there was little she could do. Seamus would be wondering where she was, and she had no way to get a message to him. What message would a three-year-old boy understand for his mother not coming anyway? Julia had done this, and Morgan would not forget.

CHAPTER TWENTY-TWO

Under an icy blue sky, Raines with Lucas Gerrard, the young mixed-blood interpreter, rode out of the Red Cloud Agency stockade, sent by Senator Dodd to enlist Tall Bull's support for the new treaty. The Cheyenne chief had moved his people down from Camp Harrison yesterday for the council and set up some twelve miles away.

Outside the agency walls, the Indian camps stretched along the White River as far as the eye could see, and vast pony herds covered the grassy hills beyond. Scouts reported that some twenty thousand Sioux and Cheyenne were already here, and each day their numbers grew. They had come from agencies as far away as the upper Missouri and from wild bands in the north, all to take part in the negotiations, or to prevent them. The commission needed two of every three to sign the new treaty. But neither Sitting Bull nor Crazy Horse had made the trip, stating they would not sell the land on which the People walked.

Tensions were so high it seemed certain violence would occur. At night, dancing went on in the Indian villages into the late hours. Someone set the stores of hay at Camp Robinson ablaze. During the day, the Indians dressed up in their finery, painted themselves for war and paraded around the agency stockade with great whoops, scaring the commissioners and hangers-on inside. The four women who had come with the contractors were sure they would be scalped or worse.

For the ride to Tall Bull's camp, Raines chose to wear grey trousers, a thick flannel shirt against the chill, suspenders and a slouch hat. In the Indians' current mood, the uniform of a cavalry officer might not be the wisest outfit to wear.

"This is a bad thing," Gerrard said solemnly as they rode by one encampment after another. He had been morose ever since they had left Camp Harrison, sure he was going to die here. "Too many bad hearts. They will make much trouble."

"The senator thinks they will sign," Raines said hopefully.

"No, they will not, Lieutenant."

"You think we're on a fool's errand, then?"

The interpreter made a harsh, guttural sound that Raines took as *yes*.

"If you're right, there'll be the devil to pay," he said.

Gerrard squinted into the morning sun, fear clear in his eyes. "Maybe you and I, we pay that devil today."

An hour later, they came to Tall Bull's camp and crossed the White River into the village. A group of children followed them, screaming and chattering. Several boys darted in and touched the flanks of Raines's horse and let out wild screams as if they'd just struck down an enemy. Hard-eyed warriors stared at them.

The chief's lodge was set in a cluster of five tipis. As they came up, he was talking with two men, one of whom shouted at the boys, who scattered instantly. Something nagged at the back of Raines's mind about the Indian boys, but he was focused on his mission, and let it go.

Old with a scarred, leathery face, Tall Bull was indeed tall, six feet and erect of bearing as if a hereditary king. He wore beautifully beaded moccasins, grey annuity pants and a faded red shirt with a beaded rawhide belt. He gave a nervous glance to the two men then said to Raines, "Haahe."

"Haahe," the lieutenant replied, dismounting.

As big as the chief stood, Raines was still four inches taller, his height always garnering mutterings of amazement from Indians. He had become friends with Tall Bull, or so he thought, visiting the Indian village at Camp Harrison several times with Gerrard. Now, the chief seemed less than happy to see him.

He invited him and Gerrard into the lodge along with the two Indian men. Raines presented a pouch of tobacco as a gift, which the old chief took, nodding appreciatively. As they sat cross-legged around the fire, Tall Bull began packing the new tobacco into the red bowl of a long pipe.

It was then Raines realized something about Gerrard had changed. Always the nervous and worrying type, the interpreter now seemed near panic, his movements more like a cornered deer, his hands trembling. For the first time, Raines took notice of the two men. He had thought them other reservation Indians, but now he didn't think so. One was a giant of a man, maybe six feet but powerfully built with broad shoulders like a wrestler. The other was younger, shorter and wiry with lean muscles. The young one wore his long hair loose, not braided like most Indian men, and dressed simply with no bead or quillwork on his leggings or moccasins. Only a single eagle feather, tied with a strip of rawhide, decorated his hair. There was nothing of the reservation about him or the other Indian. They were clearly of the wild bands.

After prayers, Tall Bull passed the pipe to the left and each took a short draw. When it got to Tall Bull, he puffed and sent it back around to the right. Smoke filled the tipi. Finally, the amenities satisfied, Gerrard gave a nod to Raines, who drew out a letter written by Senator Dodd. He had been ordered to read it aloud.

Feeling this was utterly foolish, he still followed Dodd's orders and read while Gerrard translated, "First of all, be assured of the kindly intentions of the Great Father and the Government toward you. You should understand that this effort to procure a portion of your country originated solely in a desire for peace between our two peoples. Since gold is found in the Black Hills, it has been impossible to prevent white persons from entering."

He paused allowing Gerrard's translation to catch up. When he fell silent, Raines continued, "Be also assured that the Government does not wish to take any of your property without returning a fair equivalent. The government is offering six million dollars for the Black Hills. It would be beneficial to all concerned if this provision is accepted."

Raines shifted uneasily and cleared his throat. He knew what was coming next and didn't like it. Threatening the Indians would not work, and he didn't like being the one to do it.

"The treaty of 1868," he said, keeping his voice flat, "made to you an appropriation of meat and flour for a period of four years. This expired long ago, leaving the Sioux and Cheyenne Nations dependent upon the annual charity of Congress, which up till now we have been willing to provide. If this charity should be denied by Congress, you and your fellow Indians must be left to great hunger verging upon starvation, unless you attempt to supply your wants by marauding among the settlers, which would inevitably lead to conflict with the military and great bloodshed. So, in your best interests, it is only proper and right that you should cede the Black Hills to the United States government so we can allow the annuities to continue."

Raines folded the letter as Gerrard was finishing the translation in a quavering voice. Tall Bull glanced back and forth between them all, a blank expression on his face. He spoke softly, then looked to the two other Indians as if for approval.

"What did he say?" Raines asked Gerrard.

"He said the season is late and they must shoot for tipis."

Raines was baffled, but the interpreter explained, "They must kill buffalo for hides they need for winter. They worry that since the negotiations have not even started, they will be here too long and put them at risk in the cold that is coming."

Raines frowned. That was not an answer he could take back to Dodd. When he started to press the chief further, the wiry Indian stood and snatched the letter from his hand and tossed it in the fire. Raines jumped for it but it was already consumed in flames.

"Hear me, wasicus," the man said, his dark eyes ablaze, "the People not sell land to Great Father." He scooped up a handful of dirt. "Not this much." He tossed the dirt on Raines's boots and strode from the tent. He had spoken in English.

The big Indian muttered something to Tall Bull and left as well.

"We should go," Gerrard said apprehensively.

Outside, the sun had gone and twilight was deepening. Several men had gathered. They were all armed and, off to the side, the wiry Indian held a rifle, his hand on the trigger guard. Without rushing, Raines walked calmly past him to his horse, Gerrard hurrying to catch up. They mounted and rode out of the village without looking back.

Not until they were more than half a mile from the village did Raines let out a long sigh. He could not deny he was lucky to be alive. The meeting had ended with no farewells or declarations of long-lasting friendships. Clearly, the two Indians had wanted to kill him on the spot. Had it not been for Tall Bull, perhaps, they would have.

"Those two," Raines said. "Who were they?"

"Big Crow and Spotted Horse."

"Jesus," Raines muttered.

"Yes, Jesus."

"Spotted Horse spoke English straight up," Raines said. "I've never heard of a full-blood Cheyenne who could do that."

Gerrard glanced back over his shoulder at the village as if someone might overtake them, then said, "He had a white woman as a wife."

CHAPTER TWENTY-THREE

Morgan was in the servants' hall eating lunch with the rest of the staff when Katelyn entered. Glancing from Mrs. Stevenson to Morgan and back again, she said, "Madam has sent me down with a message that she and Miss Julia want to see Miss O'Connor in the first floor parlor." She gave Morgan a look of misery, as if to say she was sorry to be the bearer of such bad tidings.

Mrs. Stevenson glared at Morgan. "What's this about? What have you done?"

Morgan gave a puzzled shrug. "I don't know." But she had a good idea. Earlier that day, she had been alone in Julia's bedroom 'turning it out,' a once-a-week thorough cleaning, making the bed when Julia walked in, her golden hair dancing with each purposeful stride.

"What an ungodly mess," she said offhandedly, going directly into her closet.

Morgan had seethed for days at being prevented from seeing Seamus. At Julia's sudden appearance it resurfaced. Maids, as Mrs. Stevenson constantly instructed, were to keep their heads bowed and avoid eye contact whenever a member of the family entered a room. Morgan usually did that. She wanted no contact with any of the Kruegers. But, when Julia reappeared from the closet, Morgan was unable to keep her head bowed, eyeing her coldly.

Julia was adjusting a wide-brimmed hat with large yellow feathers in the mirror, tilting it slightly. Abruptly, she turned towards the bed and saw Morgan staring at her, glanced back at the mirror, then to Morgan again. "You're the new one. What is your name?"

"Morgan O'Connor," she answered flatly.

Julia shot back. "You say Morgan O'Connor, *Miss Julia*. You don't even know how to address me properly. And you are ogling me, O'Connor. Do you think you are here to ogle me?"

"No." She tried to keep any disrespect out of her tone but knew she failed.

"You're that inept housemaid who gave such a poor effort cleaning my sitting room." When Morgan did not shift her gaze away as expected, Julia frowned. "I know what this is. You are furious that I took away your little afternoon off. You should count yourself lucky. I can make your life more miserable than you have ever experienced."

Morgan smiled slightly without a hint of humor. "I assure you, Miss Julia, that you cannot do."

Furious, Julia blinked, then hesitated. "We shall see. I'm late. I've no time at the moment to deal with an upstart housemaid." She spun about and strode from the room.

Now, as Morgan walked down the first floor hallway toward the parlor where the Krueger women awaited her, a burning anxiety settled like acid in her stomach. She was not afraid of these people, but did not want to lose her job. When she entered the parlor, Mrs. Krueger and her two daughters sat on the divan, going over a sheet of paper on the coffee table, a list of some kind. The Krueger women drew up lists such as friends to cultivate, what dresses best fit which activities and on whom to make afternoon calls. Knowledge of these lists made the rounds of gossip in the servants' hall. The purpose of them all was to move the Kruegers higher into the social heavens. It amused the servants that they never worked.

"You wished to see me, Mrs. Krueger?" Morgan said, looking down at the floor with her hands folded in front of her as she had been taught.

The women looked up at Morgan. Mrs. Krueger said, "Vhatever happened to Julia's bedroom this morning?"

"I don't know, ma'am. I cleaned it."

Mrs. Krueger nodded as if this told her much. Morgan and Julia exchanged a glance. Mrs. Krueger set the sheet of paper down. "O'Connor, you are vell fed and given a bed on vhich to sleep, are you not?"

"Yes, ma'am."

"You are learning the value of hard vork and in return vee expect you give us a good day's labor. Or would you rather look for vork elsevhere?" she added raising an eyebrow.

This incensed Morgan. She knew the value of hard work. Her parents had taught her. These people knew nothing about hard work. But she held her resentment in. She understood what this was, a threat. Not from Mrs. Krueger, but Julia. She could be sacked at any time, at any one of Julia's many whims.

At that moment, Seamus entered her thoughts. "I will work harder, Mrs. Krueger."

Satisfied, Mrs. Kruger held her hand out and flicked her wrist as if shooing away a dog. Morgan left the parlor.

***

On Sunday, Morgan surprisingly got her day off. Either Julia had forgotten the confrontation or had something else planned for her. Likely the latter. So, at 9:00am, she set off to visit Seamus.

The atmosphere of the Lamb's dining room was lighthearted and fun, much like at her home in Lone Tree. *Do not talk loudly at the table* was the only good manner dictum her parents ignored. So, it seemed, did the Lambs. As they sat down at the table, said grace, and passed the bowls of food around, the conversation began, lively and vivid. Just after grace, Lamb
caught her eye with a nod of his head, which she read to mean, they would speak later. She returned the nod. Had he found Johnny Dolan? Did he know where her relatives were?

Along with Lamb, his wife and three teenage daughters sat their boarders, four single men, each of whom worked as bookkeepers for the A. T. Stewart Dry Goods store. The females sat toward one end, the men toward the other. The Lambs did not want to tempt fate by letting the boarders mingle with their daughters, even at the dinner table.

Seamus sat beside Morgan, propped up on several books to raise him to table level. His eyes bulged as she dished out spoonfuls of food onto his plate. He still hadn't gotten used to the amount and variety of food available here. In his life among the Cheyenne, it had been feast or famine. Life depended on hunting and following the buffalo. When game was scarce and the buffalo harder to find, they ate pemmican or dried meat. When those ran out, they had nothing. Especially in winter, starvation was seldom more than a few days away.

Here, on the Lamb table, though, food was bountiful, bowls of green beans, carrots, potatoes, rice, platters of beef and ham, bread, and small pitchers of gravy. Within the first minute, Seamus's face was smeared with more food than had entered his mouth. Morgan wiped his face with her napkin. His great burp sent the Lamb girls into fits of giggles.

"How has your first couple of weeks in service gone?" Mrs. Lamb asked her.

Morgan set her fork down and finished chewing before answering. "Tolerable, ma'am. How has my little devil been acting? Has he been behaving himself?"

"Oh, he's a delight. He wears the four of us females out and keeps Josiah busy when he comes home in the evening, but we all love him. He is a boon to us all."

"If he's ever a problem, tell me."

"Oh, he's never a problem."

She was thankful this part of her situation had worked out. She couldn't have found a better place, a better family with which to leave Seamus. That morning, she had taken him to a nearby park with a carousel, where families had gathered with children clamoring to ride it. Morgan had never seen the like of it, horses carved beautifully in vivid blues and reds and white, but other animals as well, dogs, cats, bears, tigers, lions, elephants, all to ride.

Seamus climbed up on the bear. Like the other mothers, Morgan stood beside him as the carousel spun around. He laughed in delight, and she grinned and felt for a few minutes as if she were just like everyone else.

After the dinner, Morgan played with Seamus and the teen girls—she was the same age as the oldest one—before it became time for her to leave. At eight, she put Seamus to bed, telling him a story about Wihio, the spider, and coyote the trickster, his favorite character. By the time she finished the story, Seamus was asleep. She kissed his forehead, wondering with a stab of guilt if she was a good enough mother.

It was dark when Lamb escorted her down the steps of the boarding house. "I can fetch a cab for you," he said. "I'd feel better than seeing you walk back in the darkness. You never know who might be about."

"I will be fine," she said. "What have you found out?"

"I'm to meet Johnny Dolan tomorrow. At least, it's what one of his men has said. A man I've dealt with before. He will take me to Johnny."

"Can this man be trusted?"

He shrugged. "None of them can be trusted."

"You must be careful."

Momentarily, he turned his face away to hide his apprehension, but she'd seen it. When he looked back, he smiled. "Oh, Miss O'Connor, I plan to."

CHAPTER TWENTY-FOUR

By mid-September, most of the commissioners had arrived at the Red Cloud Agency, including delegates from Dakota and Wyoming Territories, all crowding into the stockade. Only General Alfred Terry had not yet come. On a slight hill overlooking the **White River,** the agency was a sizeable complex with a large warehouse, traders store, offices, the agent James Hastings's home, **blacksmith** shop and **stables**. Four women, a wife and three daughters of a single contractor, complained of the terrible odor drifting in from the nearby Indian villages. With the wild, unruly Sioux and Cheyenne growing in ever greater numbers, everyone in the stockade became more nervous in the waiting.

To pass the time, Senator Dodd, Joseph York and three contractors sat at a corner table of the trader's store playing poker, smoking cigars and drinking whiskey. Nearby, Raines worked at a desk, cleaning his Colt single-action revolver. His days were long stretches of doing nothing, then when Dodd got a wild hair up his ass, him and Gerrard riding out among the Sioux or Cheyenne on some fool's errand.

In reality, he was far more upset by Gerrard's words the other day when they left Tall Bull's camp about Spotted Horse. *He was married to a white woman.* It still plagued him with a sense of confusion and anger. Was it Morgan?

It was eating at his insides. Who else could it be? She had been married to a Cheyenne man, though she'd never wished to talk about him. If it was Spotted Horse, that would be a hard pill to swallow. He could forgive her being used by the Indians so sordidly. That, in fact, was not his to forgive. She would have had no choice and in reality few sane persons would have acted otherwise.

But if Morgan had married an Indian of her own accord, had married Spotted Horse of all people, and given birth to his son, then that would change everything. It meant she had gone over to them heart and soul. It seemed an act of betrayal.

Unlike many of his frontier colleagues, he thought of the Cheyenne and all Indians as human, not creatures less than human. But he also considered them as savage without the same concepts of morality or mercy he knew. The shock had been seeing at Crazy Woman Creek many of the regiment tossing aside their own ideas of morality and mercy, killing wantonly anything that moved in front of them in a bloodlust. However, white savagery didn't absolve Indian savagery. Now, the possibility had presented itself that Morgan had gone over to them.

Tossing down his cleaning rag, he quickly reassembled his Colt, strapped on his holster and left the store to find Gerrard. If anyone knew the truth, it would be him. Raines found him by the blacksmiths shop, standing at an outdoor table with a large basin of water. Bare chested, he wore his leggings and breechclout, a towel draped around his neck, his usually black curly hair now filled with suds.

Raines sat in the wooden chair and drummed his fingers on the tabletop. Gerrard glanced at him. "Damn woman said all Indians got lice," he said with intensity. "She was looking straight at me. I got no lice."

The clang of the blacksmith's hammer pounding on a glowing hot horseshoe on the anvil echoed through the stockade.

"Is Morgan O'Connor the wife of Spotted Horse?"

Gerrard stopped kneading his head and dropped his hands, staring back at Raines for several seconds. "I thought you might get around to asking me that."

"Well?"

The interpreter returned to working his scalp. "She was. From what I heard they were married for a year or so, then she upped and left his lodge. In the Cheyenne way of things that means she divorced him. He could have come after her but didn't. So they're not married anymore."

Divorced or not, the actual fact of her marriage rocked him like the blow of the blacksmith's hammer. Looking to the ground, he exhaled slowly but said nothing.

Gerrard dunked his head in the basin then began drying himself with the towel. "It seems a bit unfair to me, Lieutenant, to blame a person for trying to survive and make a life in the place she found herself."

But Raines barely heard. He rose and walked purposely down to the stable, saddled his horse and rode out of the stockade. He went south away from the Indian encampments for several hours before he turned back, moving aimlessly with only a vague sense of direction. His luck when it came to love was abysmal. Was it love with Morgan O'Connor? It hurt like it.

Through Greenblatt, he'd learned that she was working for Otto Krueger as a housemaid. It would be late in New York, and she'd be ensconced in the servants' quarters of the Krueger mansion fast asleep without a care or worry. If he could, he'd wake her up and ask her why she had done it. Why had she debased herself so?

Toward evening, he passed a long line of sterile, high bluffs, whose raw sides glowed ghastly white in the sun. Traversing up the side of one and navigating through a narrow gap, he noticed a huge footprint, like he'd stumbled upon the home of the cyclops. He knew it was a grizzly ahead.

He imagined taking out his knife and facing it like one of the old mountain men, but that was far too fanciful.
He had to stop being a fool. His relationship with Morgan O'Connor was strained, if not over. He kneed the horse into a gentle gallop heading back toward the agency.

The next day, he rose early to prepare for Issue Day, when cattle purchased by Joseph York for distribution to the Indians was to be delivered. Under Dodd's orders, he had to protect Tall Bull's interests. When he arrived in the chief's camp, everything changed in his relationship with Morgan.

Because that morning he found her brother Conor.

CHAPTER TWENTY-FIVE

On Tuesday, Morgan received a message from Lamb sent by a runner. With pursed lips of disapproval, Mrs. Stevenson passed the message along and was visibly upset when Morgan didn't immediately open it. Instead, she went to the seldom-used, third floor parlor before she opened the envelope.

The message simply read: *Dolan found at the Morgue in Bowery.*

What did that mean? Was Dolan dead? He was the only one, at least as far as anyone could tell, who knew where her relatives were. Annoyed, she slipped the message back in her pocket. After asking the other servants about a Bowery morgue, she learned nothing. The Bowery didn't have a morgue, Katelyn told her. Bodies often just lay on the street till someone picked them up and buried them in Potters Field.

Then, the maid's eyes went wide with enlightenment. "I know exactly what it means. The Morgue is a Five Point's dive on the lower Bowery. You must never go there. Never! And you sure as hell don't want anything to do with Dandy Johnny Dolan."

Hearing nothing further from Lamb, Morgan attempted to contact Greenblatt, giving one of the kitchen boys a coin to take a message to him, but didn't hear back. She was beginning to feel abandoned.

Two days later, Greenblatt himself showed up. Morgan met him in the Servant's Hall alone. Mrs. Stevenson was upset again. Her normal state, it seemed. Greenblatt had recommended Morgan for this position, and the housekeeper wondered what their relationship was. A Jew and an Irish girl!

"Mrs. Krueger is not happy I've come to see you," Greenblatt said. "They seem to think I am your inamorato." His voice was shaky; his hand trembling as he ran it across his brow.

Fear shot through her. "What is it? Seamus? Is something...?"

"The boy is fine as far as I know."

"You've found my relatives? They're dead?"

He shook his head, his voice a whisper. "No. Mr. Lamb has been shot. He has been taken to Bellevue Hospital. He is not expected to survive."

His words shocked her. Lamb was such a big presence. Greenblatt went on. "He said he'd located Dandy Johnny and arranged a meeting. That's the last time anyone saw Lamb till he turned up last night in the Bowery lying unconscious in the gutter."

"I'm sorry. He sent me a message. Maybe it had something to do with it." She showed it to him: *Dolan found at the Morgue in Bowery.*

Puzzled, Greenblatt studied it for several seconds. "To my knowledge, there is no morgue in the Bowery. I don't know, Miss O'Connor."

"It's a saloon. One of the other maids has heard of it. How does this affect my situation?" she asked.

That angered him. "Your concern for Mr. Lamb is admirable," he said sarcastically. "Your situation is unchanged. I'm sure Mrs. Lamb will still care for your child. She needs the money now more than ever. As for your case, we have other Pinkertons working it. But I will not be sending any more men after Dandy Johnny Dolan. That's a dead end."

"Then I will seek out this Dolan myself," she said.

Angrily, he snatched the message from her hand, ripped it up and tossed it on the table. "Are you insane? Don't be foolish. The Whyos and Dolan are vicious thugs. Dolan is said to wear boots with axe blades and carry a metal thumb gouge to rip out eyes. That's who you're talking about. A young girl such as yourself will be easy prey for the likes of him and the thousands of other cutthroats who inhabit those regions."

His eyes widened in bewilderment when Morgan began undoing her blouse. Two buttons down from the neck, she reached in and pulled out the necklace with bear claws, arrowhead and Catholic cross.

"You see these, Mr. Greenblatt?" she said, fingering the bear claws. "Do you know what they are?"

He shook his head.

"These are the claws of a grizzly," she said, stuffing the necklace back inside her blouse and redoing the buttons. "A bear so big it can look over the top of a house. This one charged me and I killed it not ten feet from me with one shot. Believe me, sir, I have a healthy respect for the dangers of this world. I do not take Mr. Johnny Dolan lightly, but I've faced monsters before. I came here to find my relatives. If they are still living, that is what I will do."

Greenblatt was surprised at the coldness in those grey eyes and realized she was telling the truth. After all, she was the Captured Girl. She had survived marauding savages, animal predators and Indian captivity. Still, Dolan was a different sort of animal altogether. "To my knowledge, grizzly bears are not devious creatures. They won't lure you in with a smile and stab you in the back. Please, Miss O'Connor, do not go into Five Points after Johnny Dolan."

She was surprised to see his face actually show concern and made an effort to sound convincing. "All right, Mr. Greenblatt. I'll do as you ask."

Just after eleven that night, after the Kruegers and servants were finally in bed, Morgan slipped down to Otto Krueger's private office. She had cleaned it more than once and knew that he kept a small caliber .32 revolver in the top drawer. Her knife would not be enough. Morgan stuck the revolver into her dress pocket and slipped out of the house by the servants' entrance.

***

Late at night, Julia sat in her private sitting room, what she thought of as her hideaway, reading the Wilkie Collins book *The Moonstone,* a strange new form of novel called a mystery. No one knew she read such books or that she even read at all. She was entranced by intelligent eighteen-year-old Lady Rachel Verinder and the gentleman detective Franklin Blake. The pursuit of who stole the moonstone fascinated her. But finally, reluctantly, she found a place to stop for the night and closed the book. In a moment, she would ring for Yvette to prepare her bed and reprimand her when the French maid was inevitably late. Julia felt no remorse over causing her to stay up so late. It was the job of a lady's maid to attend to her mistress.

She rose, turned out the lamp, casting the room in darkness, and stepped to the window overlooking the Avenue. Across the way, she could see the Van Rijn brownstone, the light out in their third-story bedroom window. Often, late at night, Julia could see the two of them arguing, and even at times hear their muffled, angry shouts.

Two months ago, as she watched one of their epic fights, she had seen a maid slipping out of the house and hurrying down the street with a sack. She passed the sack on to a man and returned to the house. That was strange business, and the next day Julia called on the Van Rijn's and reported what she'd seen. It led to the girl's apprehension for theft. Apparently she'd been stealing items for weeks and the Van Rijn's were at a loss to find the culprit till Julia. She smiled at the memory. She was a lady detective like Franklin Blake was a gentleman one.

At that moment, she spotted a small figure exit the servant's door of her own house and hurry down the sidewalk. In the lamplight it appeared to be the new maid. What was her name? Megan, no Morgan O'Connor. What was she doing? Was she another thief? Being Irish, likely so.

***

Quickly, walking the few blocks into the red light district, already becoming known as the Tenderloin, Morgan spotted several hansom cabs and approached one. "Take me to the Bowery," she said to the driver.

"Hop in, miss."

As she was about to climb up, she heard a woman's voice behind her. "Where do you think you're going?"

She turned abruptly and saw Julia Krueger advancing on her.

CHAPTER TWENTY-SIX

On Issue Day when Raines saw Conor O'Connor, he arrived in Tall Bull's encampment with a detachment of cavalry to ensure distribution of the government's cattle went smoothly. Below a string of high buttes, a corral held twenty bawling cattle. Several Cheyenne women and children sat on the rails with knives ready to butcher them. Next to the gate, Tall Bull and York stood atop a platform made out of planks and barrels, both giving orders like ringmasters in a circus.

Joseph York, the Indian agent, was not only a member of the Allison Commission, but also the man awarded the lucrative contract to bring a thousand head of cattle to the Red Cloud Agency to feed the Indians attending the council. With the contract funds, instead of a thousand head, he bought only five hundred, pocketed the remaining money, and kicked back half his profit to government officials.

When Raines learned of it from Gerrard, he went to General Terry, who told him emphatically that it was not army business. Next he tried Senator Dodd, who waved his accusations away dismissively. "You don't know the precariousness of Indian affairs." He clapped Raines on the back and chuckled. "Don't make such a fuss, my boy."

Raines felt a bit of a fool. Of course, Dodd was part of the Indian Ring in which politicians and others made fortunes off the Indian, his own father likely one of them.

He had the urge to drive his fist into Dodd's smug face, but settled for briskly walking off.

Abruptly, scores of Cheyenne warriors on horseback appeared on the crest of a hill and swiftly descended brandishing glittering lances and screaming war cries.

"We shouldn't be here," Gerrard croaked nervously.

Raines had to agree; the sound of pounding hooves and the sight of painted warriors charging the issue site chilled him.

York gave a sharp laugh, jumped off the platform onto his horse and eased up beside Gerrard. "Don't get so worked up, boys. They won't hurt you. Wait for the show."

York nodded toward one of his tribal police, who swung the gate open and the cattle burst out, shooting between the flanks of warriors. With sharp cries, they gave chase, striking the animals with lances and arrows. Raines saw this as a parody of a buffalo hunt. These were not wild animals the Indians took down. It was then he understood the significance of the Black Hills. If they were sold, and the non-treaty Indians came onto the reservation, the old way of life was over. This would be the closest they ever came to hunting buffalo again.

Quickly, the women and children rushed in with their knives to cut up the carcasses. One calf nearby was bawling beside its dead mother. York kneed his horse forward, drew his new Winchester and shot it in the head.

Kissing the barrel of the rifle, he came back beside Raines. "This carbine is a marvel. Shoots straight and true every time. Of course, I shoot straight and true every time." He gave an easy laugh.

Raines said nothing.

"Big Crow," Gerrard said, nodding toward one of the Cheyenne.

Until the interpreter said that, Raines had not seen any cause for concern. Now he did. He did not trust Big Crow. The chief and his warriors were unpredictable.

They had gathered in groups chattering excitedly, reliving the excitement as if it had been a great hunt, not a cattle slaughter that lasted less than fifteen minutes. Beside Big Crow was a young boy laughing easily while some of the older men teased him.

Something about him struck Raines as odd. No more than twelve, he was listening to a man who seemed to be asking a question. What he answered caused them all to laugh and Big Crow to beam proudly. There was something familiar about the boy, and Raines nudged his horse toward them to get a closer look. When Big Crow saw him coming, he eased his horse out of the pack and blocked his way. At that moment, one of York's drovers rode in hard. Raines returned to see what he wanted.

"Trouble with that damn Red Cloud, Mr. York," the man declared. "These damn redskins. He's claiming Spotted Tail got more cattle than him, and he's mad as a March hare. He's threatening to ride over to Spotted Tail's station and take what's his."

"Damn!" York swore. "Those two are going to be the death of me." He turned to Raines. "Better bring your troop, Lieutenant. We may need them."

Without a word to Tall Bull, York, Raines and his detachment rode back toward the Red Cloud Agency. The conflict between the two wily old chiefs was settled without violence since York gave in and parceled out several more cattle to both men for a feast. That may have been the goal all along.

That evening, back in the campaign tent he shared with Captain Lawson, Raines felt keyed up like a wind-up toy, its band twisted to snapping. Alternately, he paced the floor and sat at the camp desk, going over the incident with Big Crow again and again. Like the other time in Tall Bull's camp, something about it was odd.

Why had the chief come out from the pack and blocked his way? What did he want to prevent Raines from seeing? It unsettled him. He had overlooked something. That was when images of the boy in the group slid into his head. Sitting his horse beside Big Crow. Laughing with the men. Telling his story of the hunt. Something nagged at Raines's mind. He sat down again and drummed his fingers on the desk.

Then it came to him.

The other men were good-naturedly teasing him about the mock hunt. He was enjoying the attention. One warrior asked him a question, and in response, his face took on an expression of exaggerated fear. He placed his hands together in a gesture of prayer and said something that made them all laugh. It was the gesture of prayer. That was of the white world, not Indian.

He shot up and hurried over to the agency office where General Terry and several of the others were meeting in the back room. Agitated, Dodd spoke first. "What is it now, William? We are quite busy, don't you see?"

Raines directed his response to the general. "Sir, I saw a white boy with Big Crow today." He explained what had happened, even lying, saying the boy had green eyes, which he thought was true, but not certain. "They're only a few miles away. Captain Lawson and I can take the troop and get him."

York erupted angrily, causing others from across the room to stare, "Are you mad? Twenty thousand or more hostile Indians around and you propose to ride into Big Crow's camp and take one of his children?"

"He is not one of his children. He is not Indian."

"So you say."

Raines ignored him, addressing General Terry. "Miss O'Connor's brother was with Big Crow. It could be him. Colonel Gannon promised…"

"Miss O'Connor's brother is dead, or haven't you heard?" York said sharply. "General, we'd be insane to send in a troop now. These negotiations are about to blow up in our faces as it is. The Indians are mad as hell right now and anything can set them off."

"Perhaps, if all the cattle allotted to them actually got to them they would not be so angry," Raines said.

York's pale blue eyes stared at him coldly. "They got all they were supposed to get." He turned to Terry. "General, there's even a rumor that a Cheyenne warrior has promised to kill a commissioner before we're done. Maybe all of us. You send a troop in now, we might none of us get out of here alive."

Senator Dodd sputtered, fear edging his voice. "Can't have it, can't have it, William. I must agree with Mr. York. We cannot jeopardize these negotiations with wild accusations and a heavy military hand. No, my boy. No. That will not do."

Gen. Terry would decide this. Neither York nor Dodd, or even the chairman Senator Allison, could order Terry one way or the other. The troops answered only to him.

"Sir, it's a captured boy," Raines said. "It's Conor O'Connor. I'm sure of it."

Frowning, the general stroked his beard, considering for a few seconds. "You have done well in bringing this to us, Lieutenant. Tomorrow will be the most important day of the council, perhaps even in the history of Indian-white relations. Word has come that all the chiefs will attend. We have a chance to settle this business once and for all. Before I send troops after the boy, I must have absolute proof he is white. Bring me that proof. But, Lieutenant, do nothing till after tomorrow. Do you understand?"

"Yes, sir," Raines replied, disappointed. What would constitute proof to General Terry?

As he left, Raines saw himself a man torn in two directions. He had a duty toward Morgan, despite or because of his broken feelings for her.

On the other hand, he could not imagine disobeying a direct order. Yet, walking back to his tent, he decided he would do exactly that. He couldn't wait. After tomorrow might be too late. With all the Indians in attendance, Big Crow especially, he would slip away from the council and rescue the boy. The general said bring him proof. The boy himself would be the proof. Then he'd be finished with his obligation to Morgan O'Connor.

CHAPTER TWENTY-SEVEN

In the light of a street lamp, Julia tapped her foot impatiently. "I said, where do you think you're going?"

Staring in shock, Morgan didn't immediately respond. Julia had on a burgundy wool cape over an elegant purple dress with ostrich feather trim, which shouted wealth. Worse, she wore gold earrings studded with diamonds.

"Are you just going to stand there like a bump too stupid to answer?"

Morgan didn't have time to escort the senseless girl back to the mansion. "I'm going to the Bowery. I have personal business."

"You can't leave after nine without permission, and I seriously doubt you have it."

"I don't, but then I suspect, neither do you."

The driver clattered the butt of his whip on his seat. "Ladies, are you going to gab all night or might you be getting aboard any time soon? I got a living to make."

Morgan climbed up. Hesitating only a second, Julia jumped in beside her. "You'll regret this," she said, then turned to the driver. "What are you waiting for? A presidential decree? Go."

He snapped the reins, and they took off.

"Take off your earrings," Morgan ordered.

"What?"

"Take them off. If you go into the Bowery with them, they'll be stolen within seconds. You should return with the driver."

"I will not." Julia lifted her chin, fierce in her determination, but a hint of fear shown in her eyes.

Morgan gave a dismayed shake of her head. The stupid girl had done something on impulse, she thought, and now found herself in a pickle, too proud to admit her mistake. But Julia undid the earrings and stuck them in her pocket. After that, the women rode in silence.

When they reached the Bowery, Morgan directed the driver to take them to the Morgue, but he refused. "Don't know exactly where it is, and if I did, I wouldn't go near it."

At Canal Street, Morgan ordered him to stop, and the two young women got out, staring in stunned awe. Even after midnight, the Bowery churned with energy. Carriages and horse carts filled the wide thoroughfare carrying people from all over the city to the notorious saloons that lined the street. Across the way, the massive Bowery Theater towered like a Greek Temple in the glare of the streetlamps, with several people in elegant evening dress climbing the steps toward its entrance. Boisterous laughter came from inside.

"What have you stolen?" Julia demanded. "I saw you sneak away from the house. You must be meeting your accomplice here."

"I'm no thief. My business is personal. So go back."

Julia shook her head like a petulant child. "I'm coming with you. You Irish. Such primitive morality. I must protect my family."

"Suit yourself."

As they walked, they passed cheap hotels, dance houses, and saloons, hurrying past the blasts of foul air coming from within. The sidewalks were packed mostly with men, but several ladies, caked in heavy make-up, stood in the hotel doorways, many of them girls barely in their teens, if that. They called out to male passersby. Several cursed Morgan and Julia for being unwanted competition.

"Toughs, thieves and fallen women," Julia said harshly. "Your people."

Morgan ignored her and hurriedly pressed on. They walked deeper into Five Points. Beyond Bayard Street the buildings became seedier, the men less well-attired and more threatening, and the prostitutes older with a worn, desperate air. Many street lamps were busted, creating pockets of deep shadows. Her face growing pale, Julia flinched at the frequent hard prods and bumps of the passing men.

Morgan admitted to herself she, too, was frightened, but knew enough not to show it. She slipped her hand inside her pocket and gripped the pistol, more for comfort than any expected use. Even to her, it seemed foolish to be looking for a notorious thug in one of the most dangerous slums in the world. More people, rumor had it, were murdered in Five Points than anywhere else in the country. This was not the kind of wilderness she knew. Here, she was a babe in the woods. But somewhere down here was a man who knew Aunt Bridget and Uncle Kevin, and her cousins Mary, Bernadette and Finn.

Finally, Morgan saw the saloon across the street, a two-story brick building in dim light. On the wall above the door in faded paint was written *The Morgue*. "There it is."

Julia's eyes opened wide in panic. "You're not going in there?"

"Go back, now," Morgan said. "It's only a few blocks up to Canal Street. You can make it and catch a cab from there."

Up the boulevard, broken lamps could be seen for several blocks with saloons, bawdy houses and men lingering outside. "No. We are safer together. Both of us must go back now."

"Sorry, no." Morgan nodded toward the saloon. "I have to find someone, and he's supposed to be in there."

In fear and rage, Julia sputtered, "You…you got me into this. You're through working for us. If anything happens, I will see you in jail. In jail."

Morgan turned and walked toward the Morgue, and Julia hurried to follow.

The first thing that assailed the two young women as they entered the dive was the overwhelming smell, which oppressed them as if it had measurable thickness, a putrid mixture of sweat, stale beer, urine and cigar smoke. The saloon was larger than Morgan expected with twenty or so men sitting at the tables or at the bar. A few women, obviously prostitutes, worked the room. Everyone had stopped what they were doing and now stared at them, shot glasses or growlers of beer suspended halfway to their open mouths.

Julia gasped, "My God."

Morgan announced, "I'm looking for Johnny Dolan. Is the man here?"

At a back table by the wall, a broad-shouldered man about thirty stood. "And what might you be paying for an answer?" He had short-cropped blond hair, cold blue eyes with a fleshy face, and large, protruding ears. Something about him struck a familiar cord in Morgan, but she couldn't place it.

"My gratitude," she answered and was met with raucous laughter.

"That and a nickel will buy you a growler of beer," the man said to more laughter.

Someone at the next table said, "Maybe she's carrying one of your little paps, Johnny. "

So that's him, she thought. Dandy Johnny Dolan, the gang boss. He turned a ruthless gaze on the man, then slapped his head hard, knocking off his bowler hat. "Stupid sap."

Morgan noticed Johnny's hobnailed boots, shiny metal on the toes, axe blades to kick his opponents. The "dandy" nickname was well earned. He had on a smart suit and cravat with a jeweled stickpin, all in the style of the uptown man. Yet, there was something seedy about it all, as if he could never clean up well enough to pass as a gentleman.

"I wish to speak with you, Mr. Dolan, about something of importance," she said, keeping her voice steady, showing no fear.

"Important to who? Me or you?"

"To me?"

For several seconds, he looked them both over. "Nothing's free, lass. If I have what you want, it will cost you. It may cost you, anyway." He gestured toward the table. "Sit down, ladies."

Two men gave up their seats, but those chairs would put their backs to the open room. A chilled bead of sweat leaked down Morgan's spine. "We prefer those." She pointed to two men on the other side, backs against the wall. Dolan nodded and the men vacated their chairs. Morgan and Julia sat down, and Dolan took the seat facing them.

"You are a real pretty lass," he said to Morgan, "but this one." He gestured a thumb toward Julia. "We can make a fortune with her. Now, she's a rare beauty. Ain't she, lads?"

A raucous cheer went up in response, and Julia trembled. "What have you gotten me into," she hissed at Morgan.

"What indeed," Dolan said. "You're not the usual colleens come in this place. Who are you?"

Morgan spoke with far more confidence than she felt. "This is Jane and my name is Mary. I am looking for someone. I've been told you might know, my uncle and his—."

He held a hand up. "No, lass, that's not the way we do things here. You first tell me what you are willing to pay, and I tell you if I accept."

Presenting herself in thought, she rubbed her hand over her chin, giving her a moment to slip her other hand into her pocket for the pistol. "There's not much I have," she answered honestly. "I have about six dollars saved."

Slapping the table top, Dolan roared with laughter as did the men in the room. "Six dollars! She's going to pay me six dollars, boys. I can buy me a mansion on the Avenue now. No, no, lass. That won't do. But don't you worry. You can work it off. You are a fine piece of leather. You can sell a little quim for me to work off payment."

Morgan noticed two men nudge in a little closer. One of them had to be at least 300 pounds, his belly drooping over his wide belt. Up front, a man shut the door and locked it. Another one, tall and emaciated, came out from behind the bar, trying to hide a shotgun at his side as he moved directly to the table.

"The point you must realize is this. You came in here," Dolan said matter-of-factly. "I don't know if you are crazy or just fools, but you are in my place now and no one can protect you here. I am the only one who can keep you alive. But, pretty girls have value. I'm not going to look a gift horse in the mouth. I can make quite a bit of money with you two."

"Tell your men to back away, Mr. Dolan," Morgan said. "We are going to leave. I'll speak with you some other time when you are more affable."

"Leave? No." He shook his head and gestured to the fat man. "You two are going upstairs with this gentleman, and he and a few others will begin your education as my dollymops, or my friend here with the shotgun, that's Declan, is going to blow your pretty heads off. So, here is the night I have planned for you. Every man will take his turn and by morning you will be expert and ready for business. We only provide first class girls to our customers."

Morgan's voice was icy calm. "That happened to me before. It will never happen again. If that beanpole with the shotgun doesn't back off, I'll put a bullet right in your back wheels. Then I'll shoot him in the head and maybe get a couple others before you get us."

He laughed. "Shoot me in the balls, eh. You are a brassy one. I'll give you that. But—."

Very distinctly from under the table came the click of a revolver hammer being pulled back. His eyes narrowed. "You have a gun. But will you use it?"

"You would not be the first bastard I've sent to hell."

He was studying her, judging her. The moment he realized she was not bluffing his tongue slipped out, and he licked his lips nervously. That's when what was familiar about him came to her. It was the oversized ears. She'd known someone like that years ago when she lived in Five Points. This was her cousin. This was Finn O'Connor.

In a low voice, she said his name, "Finn, I'm your cousin Morgan."

His jaw dropped open. His eyes darted about, not at anything in particular but seemingly in an effort to understand what she said. The silence stretched out for several seconds till it was shattered when the front door crashed in with a loud, splintering explosion. Some twenty policemen rushed in, guns drawn, screaming for hands to be raised.

A man in a bowler hat strode forward and held a badge up. "School's in, boys! I'm Joe Dorcy, precinct captain, and you Johnny Dolan are under arrest for the murder of Jimmy Noe."

"Stick your arrest up your arse," Dolan shouted, drew a pistol and fired a shot that missed. "Whyo!" he screamed.

Instantly, gunfire erupted in the bar between the Whyos and the police. Julia screamed while Dolan and several men dashed through a suddenly opened panel in the wall, an escape route. Morgan grabbed Julia's hand and started to follow just as the skinny man snuck up to Joe Dorcy, aiming his shotgun at the policeman's head. "Go to hell, you bastard. Whyo!"

But he never fired. As Dorcy looked down the barrel, Morgan shot the skinny man in the forehead. The policeman flinched then looked at Morgan as she flew through the panel, dragging Julia behind her.

Following Dolan and his men, she and Julia raced downstairs into a cellar where several people were sleeping on the floor. They awakened and scattered. Just behind the Whyos leaders, the two women raced through four more cellars, then up another set of stairs and out into an alley.

"Dolan," Morgan called as he was running toward the street. "Finn!"

He quickly came back. "What do you want with me, Morgan?"

"Mam and Da are dead. Indians got them. Patrick and Fiona and Conor now, too."

"That's nothing to me."

"I came back east to find you. To find Uncle Kevin and Aunt Bridget and the girls. To see what family I have left."

His voice was harsh. "You got none. They're dead. All of them." He gave a snappish gesture at the surroundings. "This killed them. I'm Dandy Johnny Dolan now, and I ain't your family. Be glad you got out of this alive. Now, run before the coppers come."

With that, he turned and fled down the alley. Behind them, she heard the footsteps of the officers coming up the steps and one of them calling out, "They went this way."

Morgan realized Julia was still screaming. She grabbed her hand and hissed, "Run!"

***

"You killed that man," Julia cried hysterically. In the dark of the Krueger carriage house, she was bent double, retching. "You shot him. God, you just shot him. I saw it. I could have been killed."

Her arms folded, Morgan leaned against the carriage door, unmoved. "You said that." She was upset with a sense of utter desolation closing in on her. Her journey had come to an end and the end was an abyss. Her relatives that she had come so far to find were dead, Mary, Bernadette, her aunt and uncle, all except Finn, and he the worst thug in the entire city. It left her empty, and with no sympathy for the whimpering Julia Krueger.

Julia looked up sharply. "Felons. All you Irish are felons. Pack your things and get out. I don't want you around here. You no longer work for this family."

Hesitating only a moment more, Morgan left her sobbing in the carriage house. It was near three in the morning. She first replaced the gun in Krueger's office, then exhausted and sickened by the night, went up to her room. Without waking Katelyn, she crawled into her bed and slipped quickly into a troubled sleep.

CHAPTER TWENTY-EIGHT

The morning of Thursday, September 23rd had a bite of winter in the air under a pristine, cloudless sky. After a brief lunch, the eight members of the Allison Commission and contractors rolled out of the Red Cloud Agency stockade in a line of army ambulances, open and fitted with benches. This was the day all the chiefs promised to begin negotiations. The commissioners were accompanied by several reporters including James Howard of the Chicago Tribune, who sat in the first wagon, scribbling feverishly on a sheaf of papers balanced on his knees. On the flanks of the procession, Captain Lawson's cavalry company provided the guard detail.

Lieutenant Will Raines, his long legs squeezed against the bench in front of him, sat uncomfortably behind Howard. He was keenly disappointed that the opportunity to bring home Conor O'Connor had gone awry and blamed himself. During the night, Big Crow had left, taking his band north. The lieutenant wondered if the Indian did so because he feared the army would come after the boy. Otherwise, why would he leave the council? Nothing he could do now but bide his time. Over the next few months, he hoped another chance would come.

He had to push thoughts of Conor from his mind. This morning the quartermaster at Camp Robinson reported that several boxes of ammunition had been stolen during the night and rumors surfaced that some hardline chiefs planned to disrupt the council. Perhaps, even to attack the commission. Just two years before, the Modoc Indians murdered the entire Peace Commission led by General Canby. With the open hostility of the Sioux and Cheyenne toward selling the Black Hills, Raines couldn't dismiss the possibility here.

But Dodd dismissed it all. The senator elbowed him in the ribs, barely able to control his exuberance. He pointed to the Indian horsemen in the hills, thousands of them riding toward the council site. "Look at that, William. The redskins are indeed coming as they promised. More than I'd hoped. Now, you'll see. They will all sign the treaty. Touch the pen as they say, don't you know. This will make my career, my boy, and I won't forget you. There's a presidential election next year, don't you see, and what better candidate to lead the country forward than the man who solved the Indian problem, eh, what?"

Raines didn't reply. Dodd was carrying on a steady stream of palaver and wouldn't have heard anyway. The thought of this man as president made the lieutenant choke. He'd noticed the Indians immediately. So many. They made him uneasy.

Oblivious to the danger, Senator Dodd gestured to the Indians, saying loudly to all the ambulance's occupants, "Ha! Isn't that aces, gentlemen? Mark my words, today we will set the Indian problem to rights. We will achieve the object. The Black Hills will be ours." He rubbed his hands together with glee.

Gerrard rode up beside the ambulance. "The day will be bad, very bad," he said to Raines.

Dodd hadn't heard. "Glorious day, my boy. Glorious day."

Gerrard blinked at him and rode off. He tended to be pessimistic about these things, but Raines shared his concern this time. With each turn of the wagon wheel, a powerful sense of foreboding grew.

When the ambulances finally reached Crow's Butte, site of the council, the soldiers set up a large hospital tent with stools and tables under the front canopy for the commissioners. Lawson's company of cavalry fanned out behind the tent, sitting their horses. A few minutes later, the first of the Indians began arriving.

The members of the commission stood waiting under the tent fly, General Terry and Senators Allison and Dodd in front. York, just behind Dodd, smoothed his blond hair down, as if he were expecting a camera. Fidgeting nervously, Gerrard was upfront with a couple other mixed bloods to interpret. In his full cavalry uniform, Raines stood off to the rear by one of the tables, his nerves jangling like loose coins.

As the Indians came, Senator Dodd's nervous energy got the better of him and he pranced around with a high-stepping march. "The play is about to commence. Come on, come on, Lo. Let's get this show going."

To Raines's amazement, the Indians did put on a show. Hundreds of chiefs and warriors rode down from the surrounding hills and paraded on horseback in front of the commissioners, like an army passing in review. It was not dissimilar to the one Raines had seen as a boy with his father in Washington, DC just after the War of Rebellion when the whole Grand Army passed in review down Pennsylvania Avenue. Here, instead of the dark blue uniforms, the chiefs wore feathered bonnets and scalp shirts and carried rifles or coup sticks with dangling feathers.

"Quite the display," James Howard said excitedly as he sketched hurriedly on his pad.

Raines glanced down at it. The man had ability. His charcoal drawing showed a scene of Indians in their war regalia filling the ground, the chiefs in front, facing the commissioners. What the sketch didn't show were the thousands of warriors sitting their horses in the nearby hills. At least ten thousand warriors completely surrounded the commission.

In a wild chaos of noise, Little Big Man, Spotted Horse and fifty warriors galloped hard into this makeshift arena, shouting piercing war cries and firing their rifles into the air. They reined to an abrupt stop in front of the commission. The hair on Raines's forearms rose, and he rested his hand over his sidearm. He noticed Dodd flinch and take a step back, bumping into York.

Adding to the fantastical nature of the moment, Little Big Man and Spotted Horse were utterly and completely naked. Raines studied the Cheyenne with disgust and fascination. This was Morgan's Indian husband. He wanted to draw his pistol and shoot the man. That, of course, would be suicide for him and the commission.

No longer oblivious to the danger, Senator Dodd stared aghast. "What are they doing? Are they completely mad?"

Little Big Man screamed at the commissioners and waved his rifle in the air. Spotted Horse dashed the few yards toward General Terry and screamed his war cry. General Terry stood his ground, unflinching. Calmly, Raines moved up beside him.

"Steady, Lieutenant," General Terry said. "We don't want to provoke."

Finally, after further threats, Little Big Man led his band down to the creek and rode in single file slowly for several hundred yards, then circled up the bank to the rear of the gathered Indians and melted back in among them.

Senator Dodd's stunned voice had risen an octave. "By Gad, those men had no clothes. I've never seen the like. What were they doing?"

Standing nearby, his voice unable to hide a quiver, Gerrard, said, "They are showing their contempt."

"Haw!" Senator Dodd gave a sharp snap of his coat lapels. "I am not moved by what a few savages think."

"I think the preliminaries are over," General Terry said. "Now, we can get on with it."

With Gerrard beside him to interpret, Senator Allison, a small man in his grey suit and vest, stepped out into the open ground to face the horde of seated Indians not more than thirty feet away and attempted to begin the talks, but they ignored him. He gave Terry a questioning look. "Are we to see failure before we begin, General?

"Be patient, Senator," Terry said. "They're here. They'll talk when they're ready."

Allison and Gerrard returned to the tent canopy and waited. Twenty minutes later, a gap opened in the throng of Indians, and a wagon rolled through onto the open ground between the two sides. A white man was driving with a wizened Indian sitting beside him. In his fifties, the Indian man wore annuity pants, a suit vest over a red shirt, hard boots, a wool scarf and a single eagle feather in his hair. He stepped down with the agility of a younger man. Raines recognized him. This was Red Cloud, leading man of the Oglala.

Immediately, Spotted Tail walked over to him, and the two men sat down and began talking, ignoring the commissioners, then Tall Bull and several other chiefs joined them. An Indian crier then announced in a stentorian voice the council was to begin.

With Gerrard translating, Allison got right to it. With a few opening words praising the government's actions in the past taking care of the Indians, he proposed to buy the Black Hills outright for six million dollars or lease the land for four hundred thousand a year. This was expected, but then he shocked them by saying this purchase included the vast unceded hunting lands, which took in large portions of

Wyoming and Montana Territories. The chiefs grumbled. They did not like this at all.

Next, Senator Dodd stepped to the front, grabbing the lapels of his coat as if addressing the US congress. "I have come—."

Before he could say more, Little Big Man and his warriors rode in again, this time dressed and painted for war. Dodd frantically stumbled back from them, falling over a stool. Spotted Horse sported a bandolier across his chest and red streaks down his cheeks. Instead of stopping in front of the commissioners, they moved on around the tent to face Captain Lawson's company of cavalry, spreading out in line and stopping fifteen yards from them.

Quickly, Lawson ordered, "Dismount! Stand to horses. Rifles at the ready."

The men dismounted, drawing rifles from scabbards and turning their horse to use as shields.

By the tent, Gerrard and the other mixed-blood interpreters started moving away from the commissioners, seemingly in no hurry but clearly with the purpose of escaping the coming carnage. Seeing them go, Raines realized he was about to die.

"The ball is about to commence, Lieutenant," General Terry said. "Join Captain Lawson. When the fighting starts, kill Little Big Man."

"Yes, sir."

Quickly, Raines made his way to Captain Lawson's side. As the two forces faced off, no one spoke, not a sound was made except the cock of a rifle or handgun blending with the harsh calls of blackbirds coming from down at the creek. A dust devil swept across the field and was lost among the Indians.

A few yards away, Raines caught Spotted Horse watching him. Abruptly, the Indian smiled. With barely a twitch of the lips, Raines achieved a smile of his own. It was as if they had spoken aloud. When the fighting started, the lieutenant would attempt to kill Little Big Man before Spotted Horse killed him.

That's where it stood, on the verge of a grand eruption of violence when another party of Indians arrived. Young Man Afraid of His Horses and a hundred warriors galloped in and crowded Little Big Man and his men back. The fight now was between the two Indian factions, Young Man Afraid who represented the Red Cloud, Spotted Tail and Tall Bull group against Little Big Man representing the hostile Lakota of Crazy Horse and Sitting Bull, who were not even there.

For an instant, the situation hung like a bucket of coal oil above a fire, but then as Man Afraid's men pushed, Little Big Man backed away, turned and rode off, followed by his men, all screaming their war cries. The moment was over and Raines sighed with relief. He noticed many on the grounds, Indian and white, do the same.

It took several minutes for the commission to compose themselves. Senator Allison was shaken as was Joseph York, who had drawn his pistol but now re-holstered it. Dodd sputtered with angry recriminations at no one in particular. Only General Terry seemed calm, waiting patiently till the tension played itself out. Then, almost as an afterthought, the council continued.

With Gerrard back, Allison hesitantly reiterated the proposal he'd laid out before, and each of the commissioners stood to make a speech, then it was the Indians' turn. Each chief set out what he wanted for selling the Black Hills. The price was exorbitant, one chief asking for seventy million dollars. They wanted guns and ammunition to be provided to all the warriors so they could hunt. They wanted to be paid for the gold already taken out of the ground. They wanted wagons and horses provided to each Indian. The demands went on.

Finally, Red Cloud rose to speak and the grounds fell silent; even the blackbirds stilled. "For the next seven generations, I want the Great Father to give us Texas steers for our meat. I want the government to issue for me hereafter flour and coffee, and sugar and tea, and bacon, the very best kind, cracked corn and beans, and rice and dried apples, and saleratus and tobacco, and soap, and salt and pepper for the old people."

He paused for several seconds eyeing each of the commissioners before going on. "I am an Indian and you want to make a white man out of me. Maybe you white people think I ask too much, but I think those hills extend clear to the sky. These things are what I want."

Abruptly, he turned and walked to the wagon he had come in, the white man still at the reins. He climbed aboard and they drove off back through the Indians, who were already making their way from the council site. The talks were suddenly over, and the commissioners stood agape. They now knew what the Indians wanted and none of it was acceptable. Little Big Man had won. The Black Hills would not be sold. No one had touched the pen.

As the Indians quickly emptied the field, Senator Dodd, a bit stunned, asked General Terry, "What does this mean? Surely, we make a counter proposal."

Watching the Indians move slowly away, the general didn't answer. Furious he'd been ignored, Dodd puffed himself up and heatedly repeated the question, "Sir, what does this mean?"

General Terry turned to him. "Senator, it means war, all-out war, and a lot of folks red and white are going to die."

CHAPTER TWENTY-NINE

Morgan still worked at the Krueger mansion. As she suspected—hoped—her situation with Julia was a standoff. Julia did not want it known that she'd not only slipped out of the house late at night but had been 'slumming' down in Five Points, no matter what the excuses. If word ever surfaced about her escapade in a Bowery dive, any possibility of entering the elite Four Hundred would vanish. So Morgan's position was safe for the moment.

The only mention of their little adventure came two days afterward in the garden patio with its shrubs and leafy plants. Morgan, Katelyn and Yvette, Julia's lady's maid, served the family afternoon tea. Mrs. Krueger and Katherine huddled together on the divan chattering like magpies, while Julia was subdued, and in a corner, Krueger and his son Mathias sat in wicker chairs, going through the many city newspapers.

As Morgan filled each of the women's cups, Julia shot her a look of such intense hatred her blue eyes sparked like struck flint. She was still furious, but she was always furious.

Then Otto Krueger found the story.

"Here. Listen to this," he said, snapping the newspaper open. "Whyos Hurled to Perdition in Gun Battle with Police." He shook his head in distaste. "This city is getting worse every day. Something must be done." He scanned down the story, then read aloud. "Several of the criminal element were killed and two of the police wounded. Dandy Johnny Dolan, the object of the raid, escaped through a secret panel in the establishment wall. Captain Dorcy, who led the raid, said he was looking for two women of the evening who escaped with Dandy Johnny. These fallen women, he surmised, would likely know the whereabouts of Mr. Dolan."

"Disgusting," Mrs. Krueger uttered.

Julia's eyes went wide and she exchanged a quick glance with Morgan.

"A terrible thing," Mathias said.

"Is this what we have now in our city," Krueger went on, "gang women as treacherous as men? We need a Police Commissioner who will take on the gangs. This Dorcy fellow might be just the ticket."

For the rest of the week, Morgan heard no more about the incident. As Sunday came, she suspected her day off would be cancelled again, so when that hammer did not fall, she was surprised and out the door quickly and at the Lamb boarding house twenty minutes later. She was relieved to find the Pinkerton Man home from the hospital and being fussed over by his wife and daughters. The wound to his head had left him unconscious for a full day, but now he was smiling and fighting his wife to allow him out of bed.

"Thank God, the man's got such a thick skull," Mrs. Lamb said.

Morgan thanked him profusely for his help and sided with his wife about his getting rest. After speaking with Lamb, she took picked Seamus to nearby Washington Square Park, carrying a picnic basket prepared by Mrs. Lamb.

"Aenoheso!" Seamus cried out in joy when they arrived, his short legs pumping as he chased a bird onto the lawn.

"Sparrow," Morgan called, giving him the English name.

Watching her son, she realized how dangerous it was to love someone so much, to be so vulnerable. In his rush, he fell and yelped, rubbing his knee and looking to her for sympathy. She gave none. After a moment, he jumped up and raced after another bird.

A Sunday afternoon, several families and people were enjoying the park with its stately trees, flowers and shrubs. In a grassy corner, some boys played a game with a stick and a ball Morgan had never seen before. By a fountain, two men tossed horseshoes, and a couple women with rackets hit a tiny, fluttering object back and forth.

She spread her blanket down near a family of eight. The mother had a few grey hairs and was solidly built. She held a newborn babe. The father, dressed in his best Sunday clothes with a stiff high collar, played with one of the younger boys, tickling his sides. The boy laughed and screamed in delight. Three girls, all teenagers, sat on the grass, talking and sharing a bottle of dark soda pop. A fourth girl, younger even, cooed with the baby her mother held. The two older boys, teenagers, wrestled playfully on the nearby grass. They seemed to be a loving family. Morgan hated them.

It had been a week since she killed a man and found out her family was no more and that Finn, the last of her O'Connors, was an unrepentant murderer and thug. Since the incident at the Morgue, a clammy melancholy had clung to her soul. When she thought of her family, she imagined a vast, barren prairie with nothing. Sometimes she dreamed of herself alone there, searching for Seamus. Searching for Conor and Fiona.

In her dark mood, she had not been very sociable to the rest of the staff at the Kruegers, even Katelyn, who kept asking what was wrong. She didn't want to talk about it because she didn't understand herself what was wrong. Even in the worst days with Big Crow and the Cheyenne, she had not felt so lost, so without hope. She wrapped her arms about her knees and tried not to succumb to it.

Seamus was jumping up and down in excitement, screaming and pointing to the leaf-covered ground by a nearby tree. A squirrel was burrowing under the bed of leaves.

It popped its head up, looked around, then went under again, burrowed a few feet in another direction only to pop up and look around again. It did this several times. Morgan wondered if it would ever find its way home.

"No'ee'e. See it, mommy."

She turned her full attention to him, saw his fun, his joy. He could sense her sad mood, but it didn't affect her son, always happy except when she had to leave him. He was her one point of light. Then it came to her, like sunlight piercing her soul. She and Seamus were the last of the O'Connors. Not Finn. If the O'Connors were going to be a family again, she and Seamus would make that happen.

"I see it, Seamus," she called. "No'ee'e. Squirrel."

Later, they ate Mrs. Lamb's packed picnic, sandwiches, apples and potato salad with two bottles of Cherry soda pop. After lunch, she taught him the old Irish song "Toora, Loora, Loora," one of her mother's favorites. They sang it all the to the Lamb boarding house. It had been the best day she'd had since coming to New York, but later, as always, when she returned to the Krueger Mansion, the same old emptiness at leaving him tore her apart, as if her heart had been plucked from her chest. She needed to find a way for her to be with her son.

She was met by Julia, who pulled her from the backstairs onto the second floor hallway. She shoved a newspaper at her and tapped an article in triumph. Morgan got all she needed from the headline, and wondered why Julia thought it some sort of victory for her. The headline read: *Dandy Johnny Captured!*

CHAPTER THIRTY

Hunched against a stiff wind, Raines rode beside Captain Lawson at the head of the cavalry column, glad to be away from the Red Cloud Agency and the disastrous work of the Allison Commission. Swathes of pine dotted the rolling grassland and high buttes. They were trekking northwest toward Camp Harrison, a half day behind Tall Bull's Cheyenne, who had started out before sunrise. The day was chilly and damp, and he wished he could have gotten one more cup of hot coffee before they left this morning.

Most of the commissioners had headed south to Cheyenne to catch the train for the East, while the non-treaty Sioux and Cheyenne, the ones who refused to come in to the reservation, dispersed north to set up their winter camps. Raines knew like everyone else that the Allison Commission had been an abject failure, everyone except Senators Allison and Dodd. Instead, both of them felt they'd laid the groundwork for further negotiations. Both believed bringing farming and God to the savages would prove to be the ultimate solution to the Indian problem.

In a hurry, York had left the column and rode some two miles on, lost to sight in the pines trees, ravines and hills. As he came out of a coulee, the Indian agent saw four warriors sitting their horses by a stream. He suffered a moment's alarm till he recognized them. One was Spotted Horse, a dangerous fellow, but the other three were young tribal policemen from the agency, his agency. He eased his horse up to them. "Haahe," he said with a raised hand.

"Haahe," they all said in greeting.

"You scout for white soldiers now?" Spotted Horse said in English with a chuckle.

York smiled. "I am no scout."

"You com…com…" Spotted Horse tried to say the word.

"Commissioner? Yes, I am a commissioner." He gave a shrug to suggest his high status was nothing to him. "You know this. I wanted to stop any trouble before it got started. Help my people."

"Your people?"

"Yes, the Cheyenne are my people. I take care of them."

Spotted Horse nodded. "You good friend, Agent York. Children hungry at agency but you good friend."

York caught the edge to the voice and the bite to the remark. "I try to be."

"Aieee, what is this?" Spotted Horse's eyes went wide with awe, indicating York's new rifle. He kneed his horse up next to the agent.

Uncomfortable, York edged his horse a step or two away. The Indian reached out a hand for it. "I look."

York hesitated. He wasn't afraid, especially with his tribal police there. He was just too possessive of the prized rifle to let anyone else handle it. Still, he didn't want to offend a warrior of Spotted Horse's renown. He could be a valuable ally once the Indians were all settled on reservations. He drew the Winchester out of the scabbard and handed it to him.

Exhaling a silent whistle, Spotted Horse ran his hand over the barrel.

York beamed like a proud father. "Yes, it's an amazing piece of workmanship. Better even than the model 73." He extended his hand for it back.

When Spotted Horse ignored him, York swallowed nervously and said, "I must reach the agency by nightfall. I must go."

Casually, Spotted Horse leveled the weapon and shot him through the heart.

The agent's head lolled as the body teetered for half a second, then the Cheyenne kicked him out of the saddle. Raising the rifle aloft, he let out a loud war cry as the tribal policemen leapt to the ground and struck the dead body with their clubs.

CHAPTER THIRTY-ONE

The news of Dandy Johnny's capture filled the journals, and his trial kept paperboys calling out headlines for days. During the first week, having survived his shooting, Lamb testified against him. Johnny Dolan's subsequent conviction was a sensation. Thankfully, it had long since bumped the Captured Girl from the headlines. He was awaiting execution for the murder of James Noe at the Hall of Justice, called the Tombs because of its resemblance to an Egyptian mausoleum.

Morgan did not like to take the time away from Seamus, but went to see Johnny. As heinous a creature as he was, he was still her cousin and the last member of her old family. She did not abandon family. He seemed grateful she came.

They talked about their lives, as if they had lives. She told him about her years with the Cheyenne and her marriage to Spotted Horse. She knew, of all people, he would not be judgmental, and he wasn't. He had, of course, killed Jimmy Noe in cold blood and did not deny it. They made no excuses with each other. They accepted each other for what they were, imperfect people.

Morgan laughed. "Very imperfect, Johnny." She sat across from him with the bars of his cell in between.

"Call me Finn, darlin'," he said, giving her a wan smile, then falling silent for several seconds, sadness in his eyes.

"Tell me, lass. Would you really have shot me in the balls?"

"No."

He laughed. "I knew it. Bluffing, were you?"

Her cold grey eyes fixed on him. "I would have shot you in the head, Finn, like I did that beanpole bartender of yours."

"You did that?"

"He needed it."

Finn shook his head. "You're a hard one. I'll give you that. Can't argue the mug didn't deserve what he got. Even I was a little wary of the bastard." He leaned forward, his voice a whisper. "I guess you heard they're going to hang me. It's sure now. April 21st is the day when your sweet cousin will breathe his last. Ain't but a few months."

If he was looking for sympathy, she didn't give it. She felt none, only nodding as if to say she understood the information. She looked skeptically at him. "You're saying you're sorry for what you did, Finn?"

He gave a harsh laugh. "Sorry I got caught."

He blinked a couple times, then his face sagged with a hint of gloom. Being a prisoner wore on him. He had murdered enough people and had run roughshod over Five Points long enough that if anyone deserved incarceration and hanging, he did. He was certainly the one who tried to kill Lamb. She was not going to pretend it otherwise.

To lift his spirits or perhaps her own, she told him about her family's ranch in Lone Tree, describing the snowcapped mountains standing like sentinels watching over the verdant valley, the thick forests overflowing with game and fowl, and the streams stocked with so much fish you could walk across them without getting wet.

"Sounds like an awful place," Finn said, frowning. "Why would anyone want to live where no one else lived? No people around. No one to steal from. But you, your eyes light up when you talk about it, they truly do." He studied her for a long moment. "So why are you here, lass? Why are you in New York and not there?"

With a shock, she realized she did not know the answer. She was struck with an overwhelming longing for her home along Lone Tree Creek. She saw herself in the corral helping Patrick break horses and with Fiona washing dishes. Helping mam milk cows, hunting with Da. And teaching Conor how to use the old single shot rifle. Then Fiona's bloody body appeared in her mind, lying near the well like discarded table scraps, and she flinched. She forced the image violently from her thoughts. She did not go back to Lone Tree because the memories there would kill her.

From the hall door, the guard called, telling her time was up. Grabbing the cell bars, Finn leaned forward, whispering urgently, "Will you come to my hanging, lass? Please. I know it will be a hard thing, and I don't deserve it, but I would like family there, and that's you. You're all there is of the O'Connors. I don't want to die alone."

The look he gave her took Morgan back to the days when Finn used his sisters and her for his schemes stealing from the unsuspecting, a look both of authority and pleading.

"I'll come singing a tune, Finn, like when we were kids," she said with a forced smile, not certain she would come at all.

He stared at her skeptically. Then his eyes went soft and a thin film of water glazed in them. A glimpse of the boy he had once been, Morgan thought, and quickly remembered he had been a bully even then. Seconds later, his face took on a hard expression once again. He grabbed her wrist. "I have what you came to New York for."

With a violent twist, she wrenched her hand free. "What?"

"I have what you came to New York," he repeated.

"What are you talking at, Finn?"

Glancing at the guard who had taken a step toward them, he said hurriedly, "I'll see you get it. You just be here for my send-off."

She said coldly, "I said I would."

"Time's up, miss," the guard shouted with less than friendliness. "Move it along now."

She spent the rest of the day with Seamus and the Lambs, not thinking of Finn once. The boy was growing, already nearly an inch taller by the Lamb's markings next to the doorway, and speaking English better and better. No stoic Indian he. Her son was a chatterbox and all the Lamb women encouraged it. For not the first time, Morgan realized how lucky she was to have found them.

Later, when she walked back to the Krueger Mansion, her visit with Finn settled in on her. He was such a practiced liar. *What she had come to New York for?* Not likely he had anything. Still, she would go. His violent nature troubled her, but it was not so different from her own. A heinous villain of the first rank, yet he was the last of her old family. She would go.

CHAPTER THIRTY-TWO

Morgan made it back to the Krueger Mansion in time for a late supper in the servants' hall with the staff, also returning from their days off, Katelyn among them. As was her custom, Mrs. Flanagan, the cook, had saved a meal for them all. Unlike Dawes and Mrs. Stevenson, everyone liked the cook. In fact, Morgan thought many of the staff were good people. Surprisingly, she realized she liked them. She hadn't thought she would.

As they ate, they talked about their day. Katelyn laughed at something one of the footmen had said. One of the other parlor maids told of a visit to the waterworks to gawk at its massive walls, as if they hadn't seen it before. Morgan learned that Katelyn's younger brother had been sick for a week but was now up and running around like he was full of "piss and vinegar." Everyone laughed at that, mostly due to Katelyn's use of the vulgar word *piss*.

Then the noise from upstairs interrupted them. Immediately, the harangue could be heard throughout the mansion, even down in the servants' hall. Julia was screaming at Yvette. Suddenly, from one of the hallways above, Julia's shrill voice was heard distinctly. "My flowers are not fresh, the cologne bottles not filled, my hairbrush not cleaned. You are impossible. You make me look a vagrant. You are an uneducated, empty-headed Frenchie. Why Mutti ever employed such a worm like you I cannot guess. Where are you going? I said where are you going? Come back here. Go, then. Do not come back. You'll get no letter of reference from me, French mongrel."

Five minutes later Yvette stormed into the servants' hall, wearing a coat and carrying her valise. She was crying. "I cannot stay one more day in this torture chamber." She gave a curt gesture with her hand. "Fini."

Mrs. Stevenson stopped her but not unkindly. "Where will you go? Wait till morning."

"Non, non, I am gone," the girl said. "I will stay with my cousin. She is not far."

And she left without another word.

For the next two weeks, the Kruegers attempted to hire a lady's maid for Julia, but word had long circulated how difficult working for Julia Krueger was and at such small pay. After this latest incident, only a few obvious sharpers and woefully inexperienced women applied. Even when the pay was raised to thirty dollars a month, no one suitable applied. It was known that the Astors paid fifty.

The income was far more than Morgan currently made. When she left the Kruegers, likely sometime after Finn's execution, she would need money to take care of Seamus whatever she decided to do. That morning, she went to Mrs. Stevenson and requested the job.

"Don't be absurd. You have no experience as a lady's maid," the housekeeper said dismissively. "You've been a housemaid barely two months."

"Aye, t'is true, ma'am, but I do have one important qualification."

"And what is that?"

"I am willing to do it."

Mrs. Stevenson had no ready answer. She dismissed Morgan but didn't turn her down. Later, that day, Mrs. Krueger agreed on a trial basis. Likely because there were no other takers. That was it. Morgan found herself as Julia's lady's maid, a job she hadn't the first idea how to do. Thirty dollars a month was out of the question for her. Twenty a month was offered, and though it angered her, she accepted.

And so it was, she began work for the dragon of Krueger Mansion.

Morgan took up her duties the next day. Ever skeptical, Mrs. Stevenson wrote out a list of specific tasks that lasted all day. "Before Julia rises, set out her attire for that morning. At 8:00 in the morning, wake her with a tray of tea, toast and butter. Run her bath, help her dress, do her hair. While the family breakfast, you must tidy Julia's bedrooms and arrange outdoor clothes should she choose to go riding or shopping or call upon acquaintances. You must assist her to change into her new attire. It is customary for you to accompany her if she is going out."

Do I also wipe her arse? Morgan thought, but didn't speak it aloud.

That first morning, at eight o'clock on the tick, Morgan brought the sleeping girl her tray of tea, toast and butter as directed. Also, the newspaper. "She very much likes to read," Mrs. Stevenson had said.

Morgan set the tray on the nightstand and shook the girl. "Miss Julia." She didn't stir. She said louder, "Hey, wake up."

After a moment, Julia's eyes popped open, and she saw Morgan. Horror spread across her face. "Oh, dear God, it's you. Well, don't just stand there. Go draw my bath."

Morgan stumbled through the first hours of her duties, tidying the room, cleaning the bathroom and setting out Julia's clothes. After breakfast, she helped her dress, then accompanied her in a carriage to Broadway and a two-story wood frame house with a wrap-around porch and vivid, light blue colors. Nowhere near the size of the Kruegers, but far more tasteful.

Inside, a butler escorted them to a music room where a slightly pudgy gentleman of forty-five or so with a thick grey mustache greeted Julia by taking her hand with both his, but not in an obsequious way. Usually, Julia would exert her authority when meeting anyone, but Morgan saw this man was the important one here.

He released her hand. "And who is this you brought?"

"This is nobody. O'Connor, my lady's maid," Julia said.

He raised his eyebrows. "Another one? You go through them like lemon drops. Are you ready?"

"Of course."

While he led Julia to the piano, Morgan took a seat against the far wall. Quickly, she realized this was a piano lesson. Julia played for nearly an hour, stopping only occasionally when the man had something to offer. Morgan had no idea what she was playing, only that it was alternately rousing and hauntingly beautiful.

On the carriage ride back, Morgan asked, "What was that you were playing?"

Julia glared at her, then said snappishly, "You are under the impression we are equals, and you speak to me whenever the urge moves you? We are not equals. You are my servant and as such you keep your mouth shut till I ask you to open it."

They rode in silence the rest of the way till the carriage turned in the driveway. "That was William Mason," she said reluctantly, as if grudging a child a piece of candy. "He is the most renowned pianist and composer in America, if you must know. That was one of his own pieces, Romance-etude."

"You play beautifully."

Julia stared at her for several seconds, frowned. "Now, you are a music critique."

"My mother played. She was good, very good, but you're better."

Julia shook her head as the carriage stopped and a footman opened the door. She climbed down and disappeared into the house. Morgan hurried to follow.

James Morton theatrical review in the New York World, November 14, 1875.

The Scouts of the Plains, replete with blood and thunder, savage Indians and virtuous frontiersmen, closed its one-month run at the Bowery Theater last night before a packed house, producing more scalping knives and gun powder to the square inch than any drama ever before. The star-studded combination was headlined by Buffalo Bill Cody, Texas Jack Omohundro and the Peerless Morlacchi, she the famed Italian dancer who introduced the can-can to America and whose legs are insured for $100,000, making her more valuable than the state of Kentucky. Whenever Texas Jack and Buffalo Bill appeared, two fine specimens of manly strength, the audience cheered and applauded lustily. The crowning piece of the night, which excited the audience to the wildest demonstrations of delight, occurred when the famed Mademoiselle Morlacchi, who played the lovelorn Indian maiden Dove Eye, whirled onstage to save the frontiersmen from being burned alive by Redskins.

The only moments of incongruity that brought on boos and catcalls came whenever Fearless Frank Nash took the stage. Not because he played a villain but for the infamy of his acting. Fearless on the plains he may be, but on the stage of the Bowery Theatre, he's a squeaking chicken. He spoke his part with the diffident manner of a schoolboy, fidgeting uneasily when silent, and, when in dialogue, poking out the right and then the left hand at irregular intervals, his voice barely carrying beyond the first row of seats. One could only have hoped that Dove Eye had arrived just a second too late and the execrable Mr. Nash had perished in the flames.

Crime Reporter, New York Post, November 16, 1875,

MURDER AT THE BOWERY THEATRE

In the dim, nocturnal hours on Sunday morning, murder visited the Bowery Theatre with the slaying of the theater's manager, Mr. Eustace Crawley. In addition, the blackguard absconded with the night's receipts from the last performance of Scouts of the Plains, *more than $10,000, much to the chagrin of Messrs. W. F. Cody and J. B. Omohundro, who would have shared in the boon. At present, the police have no leads or suspects, though the two Wild West scouts and actors suggest a closer look be made toward Fearless Frank Nash, who was given his walking papers that very night. After a thorough search by the New York police, Mr. Nash seems no longer to be within the precincts of the city.*

CHAPTER THIRTY-THREE

After the Allison Commission collapse, President Grant called a meeting at the White House to deal with the aftermath. He had been disappointed by the failure of the negotiations but not surprised. Too many Indian apologists had convinced him to back a peace policy in which he had little faith, and the Allison Commission was the last gasp of that policy. Now, as a former general with all his Civil War successes to draw on, he decided on a new, more direct approach, one in which he felt much more confident. He would either subdue the Indians or kill them.

On November 3rd, he brought to the White House the Secretary of War William Belknap, Secretary of the Interior Zachariah Chandler, Commanding General of the Army William Sherman, and Generals Phillip Sheridan and George Crook to go over his plan. It was simple. The government would act as if the Sioux had indeed sold the Black Hills, no longer prohibiting miners and immigrants from entering. The Interior Department would issue an edict to all non-reservation Sioux and Cheyenne that they must report to one of the many agencies on the Great Sioux Reservation by January 31st or be accounted hostiles and attacked forthwith.

***

After Raines returned from his work with the Allison Commission, Colonel Gannon sent him and several other company commanders on patrols into the Black Hills to determine the level of Indian threat. He took along Sergeant Reardon, Gerrard, who would act as scout, and a detachment of fifteen men. The Black Hills was a labyrinth of tree-cluttered canyons fit for a Minotaur. Without Gerrard, he would have been completely lost. In the weeks they were out, they found little Indian activity except, at one point, three Sioux in the distance, one carrying a stag over his horse. Raines's orders were to drive any stray Indians back onto the reservation, but he ignored them and let the three go on their way.

The afternoon light turned gold on the crests of buttes, and the creeks steamed in below-freezing weather. The winter the Indians had feared was upon them. The detachment bivouacked for the night along the creek fifteen miles from Deadwood Gulch, the new mining camp. Gerrard set out early the next morning to scout ahead. Later that day, as the detachment reached the mining camp, Raines found the place teeming with activity. Tents lined the hillsides, a few wood structured buildings were going up, and men crawled over the ground like ants.

On a nearby hillside amid the pines and cottonwoods, Lucas Gerrard sat his horse, his hands bound behind him, and twenty miners had a rope around his neck. The scout was singing his death song. Only half Cheyenne and wearing white man's clothes, he still looked all Indian with his dark leathery skin, high cheekbones and braided hair. Raines ordered his men on line, rifles at the ready.

"This man is my scout," he said firmly. "Release him."

"You got no say over us, soldier boy," an overweight man with a long flowing black beard said. Swaying slightly, he held a bottle of whiskey in one hand and the rope end in the other. "He was skulking around camp, spying on us. Look at him, General. He's a damn Sioux."

They were all drunk. Furious with the stupidity of it all, Raines dismounted and strode up to the man, placing his Colt against his forehead. "If you attempt to hang him, I'll open up a mine shaft in your head the size of Deadwood Gulch." He spoke loudly for all to hear. "Then my men will cut down the rest of you."

In an instant, the man's eyes went from belligerence to fear. "It ain't fair," the miner complained. "You're supposed to be protecting us, not these Injuns."

"Go to hell," Raines said. "Untie him."

The man did.

As they rode away, Raines shook his head, thinking he was becoming a border ruffian, threatening people with his gun. The realization that he hadn't been bluffing settled on him. He was changing, not sure for better or worse.

"Thanks, Lieutenant," Gerrard said, riding up beside him. "They would have hung me sure."

"How in the hell did you let yourself get caught by a bunch of drunken miners?"

Grinning, showing his even white teeth, Gerrard said, "I rode up to them and asked them if they've seen any Indians."

Raines pushed them hard the rest of the day and camped in a grove of trees. He left the posting of guards to Sergeant Reardon, put up his tent and started a fire, setting the coffee to boiling. The rest of the men had begun their own fires and began cooking their evening meals.

When Reardon returned, he poured himself a cup of coffee, sipped and grimaced as if catching the scent of a foul odor. "Damn, Lieutenant. You trying to kill us?"

Raines shot back, "I washed my socks in the pot to give it its spicy flavor."

Reardon turned to Gerrard. "The man's not joking."

After supper, Raines climbed into his small tent. As every night, he lay with his hands folded behind his head, unable to sleep. As usual, Morgan O'Connor resided permanently in his brain, filling his thoughts as she had since he'd learned she'd been married to Spotted Horse. He could not hate her even with his abhorrence for her actions. Did she make a conscious choice to marry him in order to survive? Or had she truly fallen in love with the murderer? Either way, it tore him apart, as if she had betrayed him personally.

But he knew himself to be a fool to think that. None of that truly mattered. He loved her. In his mind, he saw her walking across the parade grounds in her thin dress or sitting on the colonel's porch with hands folded across her lap, and his heart burst. He feared he would die from missing her. Already he had forgiven her, but then with a shock of true revelation, he realized he was in no position to judge her. She did not have to answer to him, or to anyone. He sat up and lit a candle and took out the flat piece of wood he used as a writing board. Took paper, ink bottle and pen from his saddle bags and began to write. His mind was so filled with what he wanted to say to her he wrote long into the night.

CHAPTER THIRTY-FOUR

When the postman brought the mail just after one, Morgan received a pleasant surprise, a letter from Will Raines. It was the first letter Morgan personally had ever received, and she snatched it from Mrs. Stevenson, and to the housekeeper's annoyance, hurried upstairs to read it in privacy.

Camp Harrison
October 25th, 1875

My Dearest Miss O'Connor,

Since your departure, I have wanted to write you, did so several times, destroyed the attempts and finally settled on these few lines. I hope I am not being too forward when I say I have missed you, missed our walks together, missed the glint of starlight in your beautiful eyes as we sat on the colonel's porch long after it prudent by societal standards. You must be aware of my feelings for you. I doubt I hid them well. Alas, I will refrain from saying more for fear of putting you off.

In other matters, all aspects of camp life are much the same as when you left, yet in some ways profoundly different. Immediately, upon my return, Mrs. Collins enlisted me in a production of Our American Cousin, the famous play. I could find no way to refuse since the colonel himself had a part. I found myself saying such lines as "birds of a feather gather no moss." It did generate appreciative laughter, especially unintentionally since I was playing the bumpkin American cousin. Casting to type.

I must close for I have been invited to a meal at Tall Bull's lodge again. Though I don't expect much food, I know he will provide as much as he has. From my many times eating there, I have become quite the connoisseur of dog.

If it is not too much of a burden, would you consider writing to me? Tell me if you allow my feelings for you full sway or should I restrain them? Let me know how your son is doing. I had grown quite fond of him in the times we met. Either way, you can't know how much a simple letter can help one get through the day. Tell me about your life in New York City. Greenblatt wrote that you found one of your relatives but nothing else. I hope you are well and within the bosom of your family now.

Your devoted friend,
Will Raines

P.S. You will be proud of me. I am actually learning Cheyenne. If I am fortunate enough to cross your path again, we can converse in the language.

Morgan felt a thrill by Will's protestations of love and had to admit, she liked him. At least, respected him. When he looked at Seamus, she was sure, he saw nothing but a little boy, having learned to confront his own prejudices. And when he looked at her, he saw no stain for bearing him, as others did. Respect was not an insignificant thing to feel about someone. That day, she borrowed paper and ink from Mrs. Stevenson and wrote him back.

***

In early December, darkness had already settled on Camp Harrison by the time the bugler called Retreat marking the end of the duty day. As the notes floated over the compound, Raines hurried to his quarters, excited by the letter from Morgan he had just picked up at the adjutant's office. With a blustery wind rattling the windows, he sat at his desk and feverishly opened it.

Dear Friend Will,

Why so formal calling me Miss O'Connor? I thought we threw social convention out the window long ago and used our first names. I would be more than happy to write you. I can think of no one else whom I account my friend as much as you. You express a hint of feelings for me beyond friendship and ask if I will allow them. I have no objections. You will always be someone of importance to me. I must warn you honestly, though, I can promise you nothing else. For more than four years now, I have been so preoccupied with my and my family's survival, I can allow myself nothing else.

The letter went on to explain the situation with her cousin, a cold-blooded murderer awaiting execution. She held nothing back. That forthrightness made her different. She was unlike any woman he had ever met.

He took out paper to write her back. In his first letter, he had not written anything about her brother possibly being alive for fear of causing her needless pain if it turned out not to be him. He would not add to her burden now but wait till he knew for certain whether Conor was among the living. He sent a long letter of several pages, giving full sway to his feelings.

***

In the evening by the lamp in her bedroom, Morgan took Will's new letter out and read it again. He was a strange young man, yet his words stirred something inside her.

I thought I loved you well and truly, but since those days months ago when I last saw you, I feel I love you a thousand times more now. Away from you, I am a lone wanderer in an empty desert. You have taken more than my soul; you are the one thought in my life. When Colonel Gannon sends me into the Black Hills on patrol, you accompany me. When I take a detail out to cut wood, you are with me. When I lie down at day's end, you are there. I see your lively grey eyes, your lovely auburn hair, your graceful arms and the slight swathe of freckles across the bridge of your nose. I treasure each one of them and kiss each in its turn. Oh, how I kiss you and caress you. All the beautiful young ladies in the universe might pass before me, and they would make no impression on my heart. It is irrecoverably lost to you. It is yours forever. I love you.

The thought of him kissing her and caressing her excited Morgan. Chills ran through her body and her dormant longings came alive. She had not anticipated that they would, but as she read, she began thinking of Will in a different way than she had before.

CHAPTER THIRTY-FIVE

In the subsequent weeks as Julia's lady's maid, Morgan saw how selfish and acid-tongued the young dragon truly was. Nothing governed her tongue. Part of the reason, no doubt, she had no friends. Katherine had several girlfriends visit and would often go out with them to shop. Even Mathias had his male friends. Julia seemed to have none. Morgan saw that play out vividly the day three teenage girls and an elderly aunt swung by the Krueger Mansion in their great coach to pick up Katherine for a shopping spree. To follow protocol, they came into the first floor parlor to greet Mrs. Krueger. Julia sat with her reading poetry aloud. Mostly ditties from a woman named Browning.

Morgan stood in a corner, waiting with Julia's coat. Julia had instructed her to be there because she would be going shopping that day with these girls who were, after all, known to her just as much as to Katherine. When the young women rushed in giggling and excited about the day out, they curtsied to Mrs. Krueger, each saying in unison, "Good afternoon, Mrs. Krueger."

"Going shopping, are you, girls?" the doughty woman said. "Vell, Katherine, don't spend all your father's money."

They politely laughed.

Smiling, Julia set the book of poetry down. "Shopping? Why, I could stand for an outing to the Madison Avenue shops myself."

The faces of the girls changed instantly. The smiles froze before disappearing completely to be replaced by expressions of dismay and alarm. No one wanted Julia along. Katherine's mouth remained open for several seconds as she struggled to speak, then stammered, "Are you sure you want to accompany a group of such carefree girls, Sister?" There was pleading in her voice.

No doubt, Julia heard the tone and saw it in the girls' expressions. "You are right, Sister," she said curtly. "None of you have a thought in your head worthy of the name, and I surely would not want to be seen with such a gaggle of silly twits. How could I ever live the ignominy down?" she snapped her wrist, shooing them away. "Artless clodpolls."

The girls sputtered for several seconds, knowing they had been insulted but relieved to escape. They left quickly. Morgan saw a glimpse of pain flash in Julia's eyes. Her shunting had wounded. Then, she blinked it quickly away and picked up the poetry book.

Morgan experienced a spark of sympathy for the dragon, but it lasted only a moment. It seemed even Julia, who caused so much pain in others, could have her own emotional armor dinted. Strange, indeed, that being so smart, she could not see how her viper personality kept friends away and shattered any remote chance of entering the Four Hundred, which she so wanted.

Entering the Four Hundred was what drove the women, and to a large degree, Krueger himself. Admittance into such an august social elite would be a boon to his many businesses. But no one hungered for it more than Julia, who from the first moment she awoke in the morning directed herself toward becoming a member of the elite as if that would bestow moral worth, and lacking it make her only slightly better than Five Points fishmonger.

Morgan thought it an odd thing for adults to be so concerned about. Yet, like generals before battle, the Krueger women spent hours each day plotting ways to defeat the two gatekeepers of the Four Hundred, Mrs. Astor and Ward McAllister. It reminded Morgan of Colonel Gannon and his officers leaning over a map, planning their campaign against the Cheyenne.

The immediate goal was the Astor Ball coming up in January, the most important single social event of the year. An invitation meant the acceptance they craved. They pressured Otto Krueger to call in favors, but despite his wealth, he failed. Julia even attempted to call on Mrs. Astor, but was turned away by the butler at the door as if she were selling biscuits. The night of the ball, the Kruegers stayed home in wretched misery, uninvited, and the servants dreaded going near them, any of them.

Past 9:00pm, Morgan was surprised to find Julia at her attic door dressed in the plainest dress she had, a faded velvet blue gown still more elegant than most people could afford.

"Come with me, Irish," she ordered. To Katelyn, she spoke harshly, "Say nothing, girl, or I will have your position in this household terminated."

Wearing gloves and thick coats against the cold, they slipped out of the house and hurried on foot. A light snow was falling. From way off in the distance, Morgan heard the faint jingle of horse car bells on the 42nd Street Crosstown Line before it faded, lost behind the great walls of the Croton reservoir. She couldn't guess where they were going. She asked but Julia only scowled and remained silent.

"Heavy traffic for a Monday evening," Morgan said.

"Dumm kopf, they are all headed for the ball."

As they reached 34th Street, they joined a large crowd of five or six hundred people from the nearby slums, standing across from Mrs. Astor's Fifth Avenue brownstone.

Bundled in layers of worn clothes, they watched the grand coaches roll up and release their passengers. It was a great show. The men wore top hats and black ties, and the women flowing gowns, great coiffured hair and jewels that glittered in the lamplight. The crowd cheered each one as if favorite performers.

Julia watched them with longing in her eyes, then her gaze turned dark.. "Look at them," she hissed. "Who do they think they are? They're nobodies."

"But they've been invited," Morgan said.

Julia glared at her. "You have a smart mouth, Irish. I will sack you yet."

Morgan sighed. "What tripe. All of you. You'd think this Mrs. Astor crapped gold. She's not the Queen of England."

Julia frowned. "You are not fit to talk about her. She sets the standard for good behavior and elegance. This experiment with you as my lady's maid is about at an end." Then, she blinked several times, a sudden light appearing in her eyes as if she'd just undergone a religious conversion. "Of course! That's it. You've found the pinch in the game, Irish. That's the answer. Come on. Don't dally. We must get home right away."

She rushed off as if trying to catch the crosstown bus. As they hurried back, Julia's plan spilled out in a rush. "It's simple. I'll marry a nobleman. Preferably English. Not just anyone either, not a lowly baron, but at least an earl, perhaps a marques or even a duke." She glanced at Morgan. "What do you think of that, Irish? Me a duchess. That old Astor bat will be begging *me* for invitations. I'll be higher than all of them. I told you I would climb over her."

Morgan didn't remember Julia telling her anything about Mrs. Astor. The winter cold had cut through her thin clothing, and she desired only to get back to her room and curl up under the blankets.

Suddenly, Julia stopped, clutching her arm. "You don't understand. I know what you're thinking. Why would an earl deign to marry me? But you see, the whole of English aristocracy are as impoverished as you Irish, or at least many of them are. They own these great estates that they can't keep up, and need rich wives like me to pay for them." She beamed. "They've been coming over here for years to find them, but, of course, you would know nothing of such matters."

That's true, Morgan thought. The doings of the English aristocracy had not been much discussed in the Cheyenne camps where she'd lived.

"When I marry one," Julia went on. "I will look down my nose at Mrs. Astor, Ward McAlister and every one of them, and glad to do it. As part of the English aristocracy, our social season will be in London with the Queen, not Fifth Avenue with fat Mrs. Astor." Julia paused, catching her breath. She trembled with excitement. "Our family will be received by everyone in society on both sides of the Atlantic. It is the perfect solution." Her beautiful face twisted into a grimace. "And, dear Lord, you came up with it."

CHAPTER THIRTY-SIX

Late at night, Morgan reread Will's letters. He wrote her two or three letters a week, long letters that displayed his unbridled love for her. She sensed a deep loneliness in him, situated as he was at an isolated outpost. Yet reading them also opened a wider window into his soul, and she found she liked him more and more, and that liking grew till she looked forward with anticipation to 1:45pm each day when the mail courier made his delivery on the minute. Usually, he brought something from Will.

After re-reading them, she turned out the lamp by her bed and pulled the covers up tighter around her. Katelyn was already snoring gently. As Morgan lay trying to stay warm—by morning, ice would form in the pitcher of water on the dresser—she knew deep in her bones that Will Raines was someone of character and integrity, a better person than she, and that can't be dismissed. More and more, he was taking control of her thoughts. She loved his ungainly grace and the way the cowlick of blond hair stood up in the back. The way he would almost stutter with nervousness around her, then speak with absolute confidence. And he was handsome. That was no small thing. To her infinite surprise, she began to wonder if he was someone with whom she could make a marriage, make a future, make a family.

Then she dismissed the idea angrily. Such childish meanderings. Even though he so clearly loved her, any marriage between them would be impossible. His family lived here on the Avenue. For all she knew, he might be one of the exulted Four Hundred while she was born in Five Points, grew up on a wilderness homestead and lived years as a Cheyenne. He knew the vast chasm between them as much as she did. He would never ask. It was a stupid idea, she told herself. With fury, she pounded the pillow so hard feathers burst from it.

"Are you all right?" Katelyn muttered, waking up. The light from the street lamps below cast a latticed glow through the shutters onto the ceiling.

"Yes," she snapped.

"Oh, I can surely tell you are, lass. Everyone busts open their pillows when they are feeling as calm and untroubled as you."

Morgan waited a few seconds till she had calmed down. "I am or will be fine, Katelyn. I'm always fine. I seldom have any choice but to be fine."

Then Will's letters stopped coming. At first, she thought it just the haphazard delivery of mail from the West. Or that he finally came to his senses about her. But the time stretched out over a month and she became worried. He would not just stop writing her. Not Will. If he wanted to break off their relationship, whatever it was, he would write to do it. He once said he had been a coward at Crazy Woman Creek, but he was the bravest man she knew. No, he would write her.

The last letter had been in late February, telling of the regiment heading to Fort Fetterman to begin a winter campaign with General Crook against the hostile Indians. She'd searched newspapers for any word of it, finding little. A word here or there about harsh sub-zero weather. Few details. The hint of a great battle. Her worry for him grew with each passing day, and she began to fear he might be dead.

Since Julia always napped at midday, Morgan began waiting by the servant's entrance for the mail courier to arrive, but each day, there was nothing from Will. Disheartened, she went up to her bedroom and withdrew from the drawer Will's last letters, lay down on her bed and read them again. She read the endearments to her and professions of love and the details of camp life, but found it impossible to ignore words like *Fort Fetterman, General Crook, hostile Indians.*

"Will," she whispered to herself. "You better not have gone and gotten yourself killed. I'll never forgive you."

CHAPTER THIRTY-SEVEN

In late March, Julia found the man she determined she would marry. His name was Edward Carr, the current Earl of Exeter and the only son of George Carr, the 12th Duke of Northampton. That meant when the father died, the son would become the duke, and if Julia married him, she would be a duchess. With a reputation as a great huntsman, the duke had brought his son to America for an expedition hunting bison in the American West, but everyone knew the real prey was a rich wife for young Exeter.

"They don't know it yet, but that new wife is to be our *sweet* Julia," Mrs. Flanagan, the cook, said in the servants' hall during lunch. Small and dumpy, in her forties, she always seemed to know the gossip of the house. There was a decided edge to the word *sweet*, and everyone laughed.

Worried about Will and anxiously waiting for 1:45 and the mail, Morgan did not follow the conversation with much focus.

"She'll be off to England. Can't happen soon enough," Katelyn said.

"Hold your tongue, girl," Mrs. Stevenson scolded. "She is our employer."

According to Mrs. Flanagan, the duke could no longer rub two pennies together. Nearly bankrupt, his finances were on the verge of collapse from the weight of his vast estates.

They had traveled from Charleston, South Carolina up through Virginia on to Philadelphia and now to New York City, a grand tour before the big hunt in late spring. To pay for the trip, the duke had dropped promissory notes everywhere, and they were coming due. Creditors pursued him up the coast.

"Then he's just a welcher," Tommie Blakely, a footman, said.

"We do not speak of our betters that way, Tommie," Dawes, the butler, insisted.

Tommie muttered under his breath, "He ain't my better."

With a sharp glance at Tommie, Mrs. Flanagan went on. "New York society knows nothing of these debts. Only Mr. Krueger's agents found them out. So you see, everyone still wanted the two nobles at their social events. When they arrived in New York, Mrs. Astor and Ward McAlister and the lot of them fawned all over them. He is a duke, after all, and the son is an earl."

"A real duke," Katelyn muttered dreamily. "And the son. Is he handsome? Has he found a wife yet?"

Mrs. Flanagan cocked her head in thought, drawing out the moment. "He's very handsome, they say. Young women have thrown themselves at him, but he's rebuffed them all."

"You think he's a Methodist?" Tommie asked. At Morgan's baffled look, he whispered, "A sodomite, lass." She blanched. Living in a tipi with married people, she'd seen them engaging in the sexual act unabashedly, but never had she imagined that sort of coupling. Dawes gave Tommie a raised eyebrow of warning.

"I'm sure I wouldn't know," Mrs. Flanagan huffed. "Now, may I continue? Our Mr. Krueger has a plan. Indeed, a simple one. He will hold a fancy costume ball next month, a Spring Ball, at least five hundred people, all the socially important people in the city. It will be the event of the decade. And, of course, he will invite the duke and his son."

Tommie grimaced. "Extra work for us."

Katelyn, however, was excited. "I've never seen a real duke before. Will they come?"

Mrs. Flanagan smiled. "Oh, yes, I assure you, our Mr. Krueger will see to that."

Mrs. Stevenson nodded. "With his nibs, everything is business, and he always has a plan."

Dawes stood, putting an end to the conversation. He checked his pocket watch. "It's 1:30. I'm sure we all have work to do."

With Julia always napping this time of day, Morgan waited by the servants' entrance for the mail delivery. At 1:45 exactly, when the courier came, she eagerly thanked him and took his bundle, rifling through it. Nothing from Will. Her eyes watered but she blinked any tears away. She had contacted Greenblatt, who in turn contacted the Raines family, but they had not heard anything from their son either. At least, that was a good thing, Greenblatt told her in a message. If he were dead, one would think the army would certainly notify his family.

Morgan set the bundle on the table in the servants' hall for Dawes to sort and went upstairs to wake the princess from her nap.

Finally, on April 5th, a letter came from Will. When Morgan saw it in the mail bundle, she squealed with relief and delight. Rushing inside, she tore it open right there in the servants' hall with Katelyn, Mrs. Stevenson and two of the footmen peering at her expectantly. Seeing in the first few lines he was whole and unhurt, she sighed with relief. "He's all right."

"Who?" they all asked in chorus.

She stared at them, and they stared at her. They wanted more, but she did not want to give it to them. "A friend has been ill," she said simply, then disappointed them by hurrying up the stairs to her room to finish the letter.

Fort Fetterman, Wyoming Territory
March 27th, 1876

My Dearest Morgan,

It has been weeks since I had an opportunity to write you, and I gratefully avail myself of the present moment to let you know that I am as yet among the living. I am safe again at General Crook's temporary headquarters in Fort Fetterman after going through, untouched, the most horrific and hellish campaign of this conflict with the hostiles, if brutal cold can be ascribed as hellish.

I will not give you any account of the single battle for I suppose you have read all about it in the newspapers. The campaign was a shameful calamity from beginning to end, something I never thought possible in the army of Grant, Sherman and Sheridan. I cannot bring myself to write anything about it. This summer we will surely go out again, and this time the whole country will be aflame. You and Seamus are well away from it.

I feared we'd lost Sergeant Reardon. Frostbite took two of his fingers, which had to be amputated. Afterward, he fell quite ill and was removed to Fort Fetterman, where I found him this day. With relief, I can now report he is well, and once again back to his ornery self.

Dearest of my heart, I am so overwhelmed by you. I thought of you day and night. I wanted to be with you so much I thought my heart would burst open. I hope that your heart is even a hundredth as devoted to me as I to you, for, if so, you care for me, indeed. Oh, if only I could see you now, see that fairest of faces, touch you and kiss you a thousand times. What strange enchantment you are. You surround my thoughts.

Yours Affectionately,

Will
PS Do you think we could have a life together?

Had he just asked her to marry him? The question threw her. She did not know what to think. He could mean simply, *might we be lifelong friends*. That must be it. She had already considered a future with him, and it had been an absurd thought. It would be like Mathias Krueger choosing to marry Katelyn. In that case, a donkey and a race horse with Mathias the donkey.

The bell by her door rang, Julia signaling her to come. With an annoyed sigh, Morgan folded the letter and put it into her drawer with the others to be read again and again later, then went down to the dragon's bedroom.

CHAPTER THIRTY-EIGHT

"Wonder what alley my life would have gone down had your mam and da not left all them years ago. We'd all still been one big, happy family, I bet," Finn said philosophically, leaning his face against the cell bars.

"Repairing shoes?" Morgan returned acerbically. "You weren't repairing shoes before we left."

With an angry grunt, Finn acknowledged her point and stared off into a corner where a mustachioed guard stood watching him. It was Friday, April, 14th. He was to hang in one week. With it being lunch hour at the Krueger Mansion, Morgan had time and hurried to the Tombs. As they talked, Finn slipped into long pauses in which he lost focus and attention, as he was doing now.

After a while, he sighed. "Not long now, Cousin. One week left for me on this green earth. I suppose God's going to greet me at the Pearly Gates and give me the back of his hand. 'You don't belong here, Finn O'Connor,' he will say. And off I'll go to Hell."

Giving a slight nod, Morgan offered no sympathies because she had none to give. She could hardly tell him everything would be all right or that soon he would sit with God. The man was no fool.

"On that day, find Joe Mooney," he said. "He'll be right here." With her look of confusion, he added. "He's got all my possessions in a little box." Finn smiled. "It's yours. Inside it is what you came to New York for."

That again, Morgan thought. If this Joe Mooney had Finn's in a little box, they will likely not be there by the day of the hanging.

He seemed to read her mind and grinned. "Don't be such a doubter, Cousin. Mooney's my fence. Strangely enough, he's an honest man. He's known for it." He shrugged. "Besides, he'll never get the box open and he fears me too much. He don't know who I got out there watching him."

"You've got nobody out there watching anyone," Morgan said, not easing the statement. In the time Finn had been at the Tombs, she was the only one to visit him. He'd been abandoned. When she left, both were in a somber mood.

A week later on April 21st, a large crowd had gathered in the Hall of Justice's courtyard to see the notorious criminal Johnny Dolan hang. Rain fell in a steady drizzle as Morgan slipped in among the umbrellas. A high scaffold with a single noose hanging from its beam sat back against a brick wall. When she saw it, her stomach grew queasy. She wished she had never promised Finn she would come. Hadn't she seen enough death? Hearing the chatter from the crowd, she realized most of the people, if not all, were there for the show. A man moved among them selling bags of peanuts, desperately trying to keep them dry. She might be the only one who had come just for him.

When she was a child, the child in Montana, not the one in Five Points, she had been teasingly called too emotional by her brother Patrick. Not that she cried too much or anything like that for she seldom did. But emotions seemed to explode all at once in her, exhilaration over a good kill while hunting, fierce hatred for a neighboring girl who thought herself too pretty to associate with Morgan, fury when Conor was beaten by their teacher.

That last had gotten her whacked hard on the rump by her da. Though she did not cry, it stung both on her body and in her heart. For two days she was sullen, speaking to no one beyond what was necessary to get through each hour. She had felt she'd done no wrong and still she had been punished.

One morning, her mam found her in the barn mucking out the horse stalls. They sat on the hay bales. "You are upset because your da tanned your hide," she said.

No use denying it. "I was protecting Conor, and I'd do it again."

"Do you think he punished you because you protected Conor?"

She thought about that and finally shook her head.

Mam gave her a scowl. "He should have whupped you for a month of Sundays. You nearly killed that man, Morgan. Pastor Burleigh said you would have if he hadn't dragged you off of him. Your temper, child." She shook her head. "But your da only swatted you twice and only hard enough that you'd remember."

"Remember what?"

"The violence, Morgan. You can't go after someone like that. The teacher was in the wrong, but he didn't deserve to die for it. And he would have. Your da and I want you to be a good person. Going about killing people for such things isn't exactly good. You can't do the way you did."

Morgan thought mam meant she wasn't a good person and that hurt. She hadn't meant to kill the bastard, but she guessed she could have.

Mam smiled and patted Morgan's hand. "But we are proud of you for sticking up for your brother. People wonder sometimes what the most important thing in life is, but you already know. It's family. Family is everything. Friends are good, but they come and go. When you're old, all that's left is family."

Unless they're dead before you get old, she thought. The glow of pride in her mam's eyes, though, made Morgan's eyes water, and they did now recalling it in the courtyard of the Tombs. Family was everything, so she was here for Finn. But the lesson about violence didn't stick. Because of it, by her mam's standards and her own, she had failed to become a good person.

At five minutes till noon, they brought Finn out in ragged, stripped prison clothes, his hands bound behind him, two burly police officers flanking him as if fearing he'd run. A priest and two other men followed him up the scaffold. Morgan could hear the priest speaking to him but couldn't make out the words. Visibly shaking, her cousin searched the crowd till he saw her, giving her a slight nod.

Finn was asked if he had any last words. His voice a snarl, he shouted, "Let's get it done, you sons-a-bitches, and I'll see you in hell."

The hangman dropped a cover over Finn's head, placed the noose around his neck and stepped to the lever. Morgan could see his body shaking. Silence filled the courtyard. Finn was nothing to her, she told herself again and again. The hangman threw back the lever and a loud thwack sounded as the trap door slammed open. Finn plunged down. Morgan closed her eyes and heard the snap of his neck.

The moment eternity swallowed him up her heart turned to water and drained through her bowels. Her old family was gone. All of them. Dizziness swam before her eyes. Nauseous and weak, she leaned back against the brick wall, slid down into a squat and buried her face in her hands. Her eyes filled with tears.

Now that the show was over, the crowd dispersed, ignoring her. The rain pattered on the back of her head and trickled down her neck, chilling her spine. That she reacted with such grief surprised her, made her angry with herself, yet she couldn't stop crying. She had seen death before. She had been the bringer of it many times, and truth was Finn did mean nothing to her. So why did his death hurt so much? She did not know.

"Miss O'Connor," came a man's voice.

She looked up at a tiny man who could hardly be more than five feet tall, no more than thirty.

"I'm Joe Mooney."

***

When Morgan returned to the Krueger mansion late that afternoon, she went straight to her bedroom to be alone, and if Julia rang for her, she'd just ignore it. She sat down on her bed with the box, a jewelry case, on her lap. There seemed no way to open it, no latch, no discernible place where the lid began, but it touched something familiar in her memory. It had belonged to her aunt. She slid her hand under it, found the right slat and pushed. The lid popped open.

The inside was stuffed with wadded greenbacks. She took them out and spread them out on the bed. She found a set of brass knuckles and two odd rings with steel points, the eye gougers. She set them on the bed. There was also a derringer, one so small it fit in the palm of her hand. She put that in her pocket.

It was empty. Nothing else. She gave a sardonic chuckle. Of course, Finn had lied. *What she'd come to New York for?* What a huckster. Then she spotted a small, faded daguerreotype at the bottom. She lifted the picture out, rubbed it on her blouse, and studied it. Two couples stood in front of painted trees on a canvas. With shock, she recognized a younger version of her parents, and beside them Aunt Bridget and Uncle Kevin, all dressed to the nines, the men in three-piece suits with watch fobs, and the women wearing bell-shaped dresses with high necklines. Tears welled in Morgan's eyes.

Oh, so fashionable, they were. It must have been her father's idea for the picture. Photographs cost so much money, and he was always the dreamer.

She wiped her nose with a handkerchief and stared at the daguerreotype for ten minutes at least. Look at them. So young. They weren't smiling. No one was silly enough to smile for a photograph, but you could see all four of them so full of hope, so full of life. They had the world before them and they knew they were going to conquer it. Maybe Finn wasn't lying after all. Maybe this was what she had come to New York for. To discover what things were important to her, what things would always be important to her.

CHAPTER THIRTY-NINE

"Pay attention," Julia snapped. "This one is the Queen of Hearts. Beautiful and safe. And this the Goddess Diana. I like it. Bold. Me a huntress. This one is a Helen of Troy. I'm not so sure." One by one, Julia lifted them up in front of herself, asking what Morgan thought. Why was she doing that? Morgan was a lady's maid, not a confidante.

The last one was purple with elaborate designs and golden patterns and was by far the most stunning. "That one. The Helen of Troy," Morgan said emphatically. "Wasn't she the most beautiful woman in the world? Who else would you come as?"

The household had been plunged into a swirl of excitement about the Costume Ball, and Julia burned with nervous energy. Now, the night of it, she couldn't hold still to be dressed. She nodded, accepting Morgan's logic. "You're right. Helen of Troy it is." She clutched the dress in front of her, grinning. "I wonder what he'll be like. My future husband. Dear God, I hope he's handsome. I'd hate being married to a little toad."

Eventually, Morgan was able to dress Julia, who stood in front of the long mirror, admiring herself. "Surely, something must be wrong with him," she said, glancing over her shoulder at Morgan. "Perhaps, he's demented. Otherwise, why has he not found a wife yet? Stop hurting me! Can you not fasten a necklace? You have the fingers of a lobster. What's the matter with you? You're so dreary these days? I don't need a dreary lady's maid."

Morgan didn't answer. Julia seldom listened anyway. When the costume was done, the effect was dazzling. She wore a purple toga, embroidered in gold gauze, bedecked with diamonds, her feet tucked into purple slippers, revealing a shocking glimpse of bare ankles. A bejeweled diadem sat upon her golden hair. Morgan wore a simple grey toga as befitted a slave.

"Look at my feet!" Julia wailed in desperation. "They're gargantuan. I can't bring this off."

"Don't worry so much. Helen of Troy didn't have the feet that launched a thousand ships. She had the face."

Julia glared back at her. "You are not funny."

"For God's sake, Julia, look at yourself. You *are* Helen of Troy."

Taking another glance in the mirror, Julia frowned, then nodded firmly. "I am, aren't I?"

Neither one seemed to notice the massive breach of propriety when Morgan addressed her mistress simply as *Julia*.

At the ball, the entire Krueger family stood at the entrance greeting their guests while Dawes announced each arrival and their costumed personae. Attending were at least thirty Louis the XIVs, countless Napoleons, forty or so Queen Elizabeths, numerous Catherine the Greats and King Arthurs, but only one Helen of Troy. Julia's costume was the rage of the evening. She loved being the center of attention.

By midnight, she was becoming nervous. The duke and his son had not yet arrived. With each passing hour, her exuberance faded. Soon, people would start to leave and if that happened, they might as well move to Cleveland. The night would be an utter failure.

"Where are they, papa?" she demanded. "It's after midnight."

Krueger's only bit of costume was a monocle, claiming to be Otto Von Bismarck, a leader in the new German state. "They'll be here," he said simply.

Finally, at a quarter after the hour, the Duke of Northampton and his son the Earl of Exeter arrived, wearing togas and being carried on two separate palanquins by eight black men in turbans and breechcloths. The music stopped in mid-dance while everyone gaped. When the palanquins were set down, Dawes announced to the hushed audience, "Ladies and gentlemen, Julius and Augustus Caesar."

Everyone knew who they actually were. George Carr, the 12th Duke of Northampton, was a tall man in his late forties with greying brown hair and a half-lidded, imperious gaze. His son, the earl, was shorter and stockier, in his mid-twenties, handsome with dark hair and what seemed like a permanent scowl. As the two stepped from their litters, the audience applauded. The duke bowed, but the earl stood stiffly, taking in the hall with great disdain.

Perfect match for Julia, Morgan thought.

Taking Julia's hand, the duke said, "Another Roman, I see."

She curtsied. "Helen of Troy, Caesar."

"Indeed, indeed," he responded, eyes wide, staring at her ankles, then up to her breasts and finally the lovely face. "Indeed."

With a confident smile, he drew his son in closer. "May I introduce my son, the Earl of Exeter, er, Augustus Caesar?"

Exeter gave a perfunctory nod, his face fixed in a frown. As she curtsied, he turned away and strode directly toward Morgan, who held a tray of Champaign, and snatched a flute, downing it in one great swill.

***

Well past 4:00am when all the guests had departed but the duke and his son, Krueger led the two noblemen into his office just off the ballroom to discuss marriage like two medieval families arranging a union. Morgan and the rest of the staff retreated downstairs to the servants' hall where they sat at the long table, drinking tea, nibbling on leftovers, and talking about the night, often making fun of the costumes and people. Dawes sat at the head of the table and Mrs. Stevenson at the other end.

Morgan was exhausted, but too much adrift these days she had been glad for the work to keep busy. She wanted desperately to sneak out and visit Seamus. She knew her time with the Kruegers was nearly up. She would not stay here in service living apart from her son for much longer. She had yet to find a way forward, but she felt her old confidence returning. There was a path for her and her son, she just had to find it.

"That was quite the show," Tommie Blakely said. "All them nobs and their fancy costumes. So much jewelry it nearly blinded me."

A few people chuckled. Katelyn said, "I thought it was amazing. I think I would have come as a queen, Queen Maeve."

"Well, you ain't no queen," Tommie said, more exhausted than cruel. "And never going to be."

Katelyn's face sank. Morgan pinched his arm. "Why'd you say that? There was no call to say that. No one here's a damn king or queen and I don't know who would want to be."

Tommie rubbed his shoulder. "I was only funning," he whined.

Dawes cleared his throat. "Might we please finish our tea with some decorum?"

The sound of footsteps could be heard hurrying down the stairs and everyone turned to see who it was. Julia appeared, excited, her face beaming. Dawes shot to his feet as did everyone else.

"Yes, Miss Krueger," the butler said.

She gasped for breath, waving a hand in front of her face as if fanning herself. Finally, she blurted out, "We are to hunt the buffalo. All of us. Papa is joining the duke's hunting party, and we will accompany them. I am to be married, and we are all going west."

No one said a word. At the head of the table, Dawes's jaw dropped open and he slumped down into his chair.

CHAPTER FORTY

Even in early May, winter still clung to Camp Harrison with patches of snow on the grounds and great white swathes in the nearby hills. At night, the temperature often dropped below freezing, leaving a thin layer of ice on water barrels. It had been a brutal winter, the memory of it still lay burrowed in Raines's bones. He and his men had suffered greatly in General Crook's disastrous winter campaign, ploughing through deep snowdrifts in thirty- and forty-below weather. He never thought he'd ever get warm again.

Bundled in a coat and fur cap, he leaned against the railing of the makeshift corral, watching as several of his troopers broke wild horses. The regiment had been ordered to Fort Fetterman, where Crook was reassembling his army for another campaign against the Indians, and the regiment was woefully short of horses. They were scheduled to move out the next day, and they needed several more mounts just to have a minimum compliment.

"Better for us," Reardon explained, his foot propped on a corral rail. "These wild mustangs can get by on grass. The damn horses the army brings in from the East got to have oats. Sometimes we ain't got oats."

Several soldiers and Cheyenne had gathered to take in the spectacle, even exchanging laughter and calling out encouragement to the riders. Raines thought it strange.

Many of these same Cheyenne would sneak off and join the hostiles for the fighting later this summer. These men would soon be killing each other. As many as two hundred warriors with their families had already slipped off the reservation.

"Stick your spurs in, Danny Boy," Reardon called.

The rider, Danny O'Reilly, was tossed off the horse, but furious, he bounced up, grabbed the reins and swung up on its back.

"The beast's got the devil in him, lad," the sergeant said. "Make him work."

Reardon's left hand was still bandaged where he'd lost two fingers to frostbite during the winter campaign. He was bitter about it. Not the loss of the fingers. He expected wounds far worse. He was bitter about the stupidity of it all, and Raines couldn't blame him. He too felt the same shaken faith in his leaders. The winter campaign had been an unmitigated disaster from the beginning.

By the time the Department of the Interior's decree ordering the Sioux and Cheyenne onto the reservation by January 31 reached the West, the worst winter in years had settled on the plains. Several feet of snow covered the ground, temperatures plunged below zero and blizzards swept in at regular intervals. Most chiefs didn't receive the ultimatum by the deadline, and those who did were unable to travel if they'd wanted to.

In his headquarters in Chicago, General Phillip Sheridan wasn't aware of these difficulties and ordered a three-pronged attack into the Powder River country where the hostiles were supposedly camped. Sheridan's scheme had General Crook coming up from the south and Colonel Gibbon and General Terry down from the north, enveloping the Indians within a giant claw. It seemed a good plan on paper, but in reality, it ran into trouble right off. With their posts snowed in, Terry and Gibbon hunkered down to await the thaw. Only Crook's column moved out into the heart of winter.

The general had achieved success against the Apache in Arizona and did not think the Sioux and Cheyenne would present much of a problem. As his army, which included Colonel Gannon's regiment, trekked north, the temperature dropped well below zero. For many days, blizzards made it nearly impossible to see, but still they pressed on, searching for Indian encampments to attack. Raines had never been so miserable in his life, his feet continuously numb. As he trudged through the snow, he carried Morgan with him, her letters tucked inside his shirt. As difficult as it was, each night he huddled in his small tent reading them over and over again.

Frostbite became epidemic. Lost toes and fingers plagued both the infantry and cavalry as they plowed through snow drifts four or five feet high. One morning, the regimental surgeon took two of Reardon's fingers and a day later, the sergeant came down with fever, the hand infected, and he was sent back to Ft. Fetterman.

After weeks of wandering in the snow, Crook stumbled onto an Indian camp on the Powder River. He got it into his mind he'd found Crazy Horse. While the general remained with the pack train, he sent Colonel Joseph Reynolds forward to attack what turned out to be the Cheyenne village of Old Bear and Two Moons, who were trying to reach the protection of Ft. Laramie and avoid this war.

The battle proved to be a catastrophe. It was the coldest night on the plains anyone could remember with the temperature twenty-two below. During the fight, officers ignored Crook's plan and maneuvered on their own. The Cheyenne escaped after Captain Moore decided on his own not to block the route out of the canyon. Worst of all, as several Cheyenne warriors counterattacked, Colonel Reynolds ordered withdrawal and left dead and wounded soldiers behind.

At least Reynolds captured the Indian horse herd, but he put no guard on them. The next day, several warriors drove them off. By then, the officers, including Raines, were in rebellion, calling him openly "the Great Imbecility." When General Crook came up with the pack train the next afternoon, he was furious and wanted to shoot Reynolds on the spot. Studying the shambles of his command, the general finally realized he needed to fall back to winter quarters or risk losing his entire army to the weather. Yet, as he led his retreat south, he sent dispatches to Sheridan, claiming a great victory over Crazy Horse. Now, in May, Raines did not feel great confidence as the regiment prepared again to have a go at the Indians.

O'Reilly was getting the best of the horse. It no longer bucked, walking the corral, blowing hard through its nostrils.

"Good work, Danny boy. Keep at 'em." Reardon blew on the tops of his bandaged stubs, then glanced at Raines. "That's another one. Unfortunately, only O'Reilly can ride it."

"Will we have enough mounts?" Raines asked.

The sergeant shrugged noncommittally. "Should. They'll be raw and so will the riders. No way to run an army. All just so General Crook can have another tryst with the Sioux. Wasn't his *victory* over Crazy Horse enough for him?" The word *victory* came out like a snarl.

"Summer campaign was always going to happen."

The sergeant snorted derisively. "I guess. At least it should be warmer. You think Crazy Horse knows he was in a battle yet, and lost it?"

Later, Raines spent the last hour before evening mess checking each man to ensure his pack was ready for tomorrow. One hundred cartridges per man, four days' rations, rifles cleaned and cleaned again. Then he dismissed them for mess. In darkness that evening, he was crossing the parade ground, headed to his quarters when Private Macklin, the adjutant's orderly, ran him down. He held out a packet of three letters. "I almost forgot, sir. These came up from Cheyenne today with the dispatches. They're for you."

He looked at them hurriedly. All were from Morgan. He rushed back to his quarters, lighting the oil lamp and flopping down on his bunk. He had asked her to marry him and she hadn't answered yet. Not exactly a proposal, he had to admit. A school boy stutter: Do you think we could have a life together? What was she to make of that? Had he been explicit enough? He tore open the first envelope and read slowly, cherishing each word, but nothing about his proposal. The second letter was the same. Had she misunderstood him? He should have been more direct. He would when he wrote back.

It was her third letter, the one dated April 22, which jolted him upright as if a bullet had struck his chest. She was coming west with her employers, and with a duke of all people, to hunt buffalo near the Bighorn Mountains in the Powder River country.

"Into the heart of an Indian War," he whispered desperately. "Utter madness."

Immediately, he rushed to the adjutant's office to send a telegram of warning. Drunk, Private Bauer, the telegrapher on duty, pleaded in a slurred voice, "Can't this wait till morning, Lieutenant? It's late. Most of the operators have gone off duty. I'm going off duty."

"No, Private, it can't. The morning will be too late." He wrote out his message and handed it to him. "We will both stay here till this gets through."

The private sighed. "I'll try, sir, but ain't likely no one is at their stations anymore." Sitting over his telegraph, swaying and belching occasionally, he began clicking the keys.

To Aaron Greenblatt
Equitable Life Assurance Society Building, New York City.

Imperative you warn Otto Krueger in the strongest terms not to come to the Powder River Country. Indians hostile. On warpath. Too dangerous, especially for women. Stay Southern Plains. Please warn Miss O'Connor personally. Also she should know her brother may still be alive. Saw white boy with Big Crow. Green eyes, scar on cheek. Do not want to raise hopes. Am attempting to locate. Tell her not to come till then.

Lieutenant William Raines

After an hour, Bauer sat back and relaxed. "Well, I did it, sir. I finally got the message to Cheyenne, and they're forwarding it on. It should be in New York tonight. Don't you worry, sir. This Greenblatt fellow will be able to warn them tomorrow morning."

***

The next morning, the regiment moved out for the summer campaign against the hostiles in columns of four as the band played "The Girl I Left Behind." The cavalrymen raised their voices singing loudly. The women left behind dabbed their eyes with handkerchiefs and waved. On his grey steed, a red plume in his slouch hat, Colonel Gannon led the column out.

CHAPTER FORTY-ONE

It had been there all along just under the surface like a great bull elk about to crash out of the trees, the inevitable return to Lone Tree. When Julia announced they were all going West, Morgan let it settle in her mind as if her going had been decided for months. The longing for home had built till it was a continuous ache. She just hadn't known what it was. At Julia's words, Morgan sat back down like Dawes, but unlike his stunned response, hers was an acknowledgement of relief for the path ahead, which now lay clear as the snowcapped mountains on a brilliant day.

On the day Otto Krueger's private train was to leave Grand Central Depot ten days later, Morgan ducked out of the last-minute household packing and snuck off to the Lamb boarding house to pick up Seamus. Two hours remained before the train left. She'd already told the Lambs about the departure. The women had cried. It was like a death in the family. They packed several bags with clothes and toys for Seamus, but that would not do. They could not take even a fraction of it. She quickly unpacked them and began again with a tiny child's valise. His things should have been very few but the Lambs had spoiled him, buying him clothes and toys costing far more than the four dollars a month she paid them.

Seamus sat on the floor of his tiny bedroom where his toys were now spread out in front of him. He was a big lad. In the nine months he had been in New York, he had grown dramatically, no longer a toddler, too heavy to carry any great distance. He spoke English like any other four-year-old boy, perhaps better when he chose to. Except for occasional bursts of exuberance, he was a well-mannered child. The Lambs had taught him well, Morgan thought sadly, for it hadn't been her raising him. He was a Cheyenne boy, too, and that had something to do with it. Cheyenne children did not disobey adults, mainly because adults gave them so few orders. The ones they did give had a natural force to them.

Staring at Seamus's dark, closely cropped hair and his bright, different colored eyes, a surge of warmth so strong her own eyes watered spread through her.

"You must decide, Seamus," Morgan urged him. "You can only take one. We have little room."

Before him were a wood top, a rolling hoop like the ones Cheyenne children played with, a six-inch-high wooden horse, a chariot, a wooden train, a cup and ball, wooden blocks, Noah's Ark and an odd wood and string device named a bandalore that some called a yo-yo. Morgan had become transfixed on one Sunday visit, unable to stop playing with it herself.

Finally, Seamus reached a hand out and placed it on the horse. Morgan took it and placed it in the valise with his clothes. She left his favorite sailor suit behind. "I'll make you another when we get home," she said. She stuffed in the bandalore as well.

"Are Momma and Papa Lamb coming with us?" Seamus asked, standing up.

The question stung, *Momma and Papa*, but she said gently, "No. Their home is here. Ours is in the West."

It was time to go. Mr. Lamb had gotten a hansom cab for them. Morgan hugged each of the Lambs and thanked them all, begged them to come west someday to visit.

They promised they would; each one hugged Seamus fiercely. When he and Morgan rushed down the steps to the waiting cab, she glanced back and saw the Lambs, tears streaming down their cheeks, waving, even the beefy Pinkerton man.

***

A sharp anxiety flooded Morgan as she and Seamus hurried into Grand Central Depot and made their way through the concourse to the immense terminal house. An arched glass ceiling supported by iron trusses rose high above them. None of the Kruegers or the staff, not even Katelyn, knew she had a child, a half -Cheyenne one, and she didn't believe the Kruegers were exactly tolerant people. If Seamus were seen, the two of them would not be allowed on the train, and Morgan desperately needed for them to be on that train. The hunting party planned to go within two hundred miles of Lone Tree.

As Morgan approached the platform, she saw Otto Krueger's five-car private train being loaded. She intended to sneak on at the last second and hide in the staff car till they were out of the station. Unfortunately, the party was running late, Mrs. Krueger rushing around frantically shouting for the laborers to be careful with the portmanteaus and chests. Mr. Krueger checked his pocket watch and tapped his foot impatiently.

Morgan tried to make it to the nearest steps unseen, but she heard Mrs. Krueger's piercing voice right off. "Vhere have you been?"

The doughty woman stormed over to her. "Vee are about to leave. I do not pay for lazy vorkers." Then, noticing Seamus, her eyes widened. "And who is this darky child? You are not bringing him on this train. Vee are not an emigrant train."

Legs spread apart, hands on her hips, she blocked the way. Mrs. Stevenson came up beside her and struck the exact same pose, scowling as if Morgan had broken a prized vase.

She decided a lie would not really work, and besides, she refused to even hint at disowning Seamus. "He is my son, Mrs. Krueger," she said. "I will not leave him behind."

An expression of horror spread across both women's faces. "Your child?" Mrs. Krueger bellowed.

"I said so."

Morgan sensed Seamus was upset by the big woman's screaming but he didn't show it.

"Vell, you certainly cannot bring him along," Mrs. Krueger said emphatically.

"I'm not going to leave him."

Mrs. Krueger straightened imperiously. "Then, you leave no choice. Your employment mit us is kaput."

The turmoil brought the others off the train, the Duke of Northampton, his son Exeter and Mathias Krueger, along with Julia and Katherine.

"What is all the commotion? Will we be leaving soon or not?" Mathias asked with irritation.

With a black look, Otto Krueger strode up to his wife. "What is this?"

"It's her." Mrs. Krueger pointed at Morgan. "I've dismissed her. She has brought this darky child and tried to board with it. She says it is hers. *Hers!* I von't put up mit dis."

Krueger stared in shock at Morgan. "We assumed you unmarried, Miss O'Connor. That was the terms of your employment. And certainly not the wife of someone from a dark-skinned race. With you Irish, one cannot be sure. You leave us no choice. Yes, your employment with us is terminated. Mr. Greenblatt will see to any remuneration you are due. Now, good day. I still have much to do before we can depart."

"Don't be silly, Papa," Julia said, coming up to them. "I do not intend to take this journey without a lady's maid."

"We will find one along the way," Krueger said, turning away.

Julia gave a harsh laugh. "A farmer's wife? Papa, you are so droll. No, Miss O'Connor is my lady's maid. I do not intend to go without her. If she stays in New York, I stay as well."

This surprised Morgan. Why was she doing this? Being contrary was an art with her, but this was too far for simple contrariness. Perhaps, it was just what she said. She did not want to be without a lady's maid. Yet, something niggled at Morgan that more was involved. She was happy for it. Let the girl prevail.

Krueger frowned at his daughter. Everyone knew that he was as ruthless a Robber Barron that existed in New York. Even so, his threats would not move his eldest daughter. The whole trip would be pointless without her. The marriage contract might fall apart. If that happened, he would lose his entry into European markets would be over. Julia was an endless trial for him.

His facial muscles quivered in anger, then he made a long sigh. "Fine," he snapped. "Fine. As you say, Julia, she is your maid. You are responsible for her and the child." He pointed at the boy. "Keep him from getting underfoot. Now, get on the train."

Julia kissed her father's cheek. "Thank you, Papa."

In foul moods, Mr. and Mrs. Krueger went back to supervising the loading while the others re-boarded the train, all except Lord Exeter, who stared at Julia for several seconds, then disappeared up the steps.

Julia and Morgan stood facing each other. Nothing was said for several seconds, then Julia bent down to Seamus. "Well, aren't you the handsome one." Her smile was dazzling, and unable to resist it, the boy smiled back. She stood back up and said to Morgan, "Such lovely eyes, Irish. I've never seen anything like them. So, you have a son, and you didn't tell me.

I'm hurt, but I'll forgive you." She shook her head in dismay. "You are so full of surprises. Now, you two get on board before I change my mind."

The Krueger hunting party left shortly after 4:00pm, making their way slowly out of New York City and on into Pennsylvania. To Morgan's vast relief, most of the staff accepted Seamus without a ripple of concern, in fact, cheerful at having a child among them. The few who were upset were overwhelmed by the generosity of the others.

The one who surprised her most was Dawes. In the staff car, he eyed the boy intensely for several seconds, and Morgan thought she would have to defend him again. But the austere butler's eyes glistened. "I served in India. The Bengal Cavalry. I knew a young—." He blinked several times, his eyes cleared, and then he said firmly, "You are not to shirk your duties because we have taken this lad aboard, do you hear, Miss O'Connor? When not involved with Miss Julia, you are to help the other maids. Is that understood?"

"Yes, Mr. Dawes," she said, wondering what memory had come to his mind.

In the next two hours, Morgan wasn't needed by Julia and her duties took her through the entire train. It was a stunning creation, a palace on wheels. At the rear sat a luxury parlor car appointed with gilded furnishings as glittering as any at the Krueger Mansion. Next came a dining car with the duke's French Chef in charge, brought over at the last minute, then a sleeping car with private compartments for the nobs, then the servants' car with few accoutrements beyond benches on which to sit and sleep, and then the baggage car next to the wood car and engine.

Morgan found Seamus in the staff car, sitting with Katelyn, who was silent and withdrawn. She'd been having nightmares since it was announced they'd be going west. For reasons Morgan couldn't fathom, her friend had an unreasonable fear of Indians, but then she supposed white fear of Crazy Horse and Spotted Horse, the Cheyenne and

Sioux, could never be unreasonable. Even in Five Points, it seemed, tales of Indians scalping and murdering frightened children.

Morgan sat down, taking Seamus into her lap. "I wager you'll end up liking the West, Katelyn. It has marvels the East hasn't got."

Katelyn's eyes darted toward her as if Morgan had drawn a knife. Just then Mrs. Stevenson came up. "Miss Julia is ready for you, O'Connor."

"I'll watch him," Katelyn said and took Seamus onto her lap.

Julia's private compartment featured a snug bed and a fancy table with mirror and chair. As Morgan dressed her for dinner, Julia chattered endlessly about the duke's charming patter and Lord Exeter's silence. "Perhaps, the man is dull-witted."

Once attired in a gown of blue satin, Julia patted her hair in front of the mirror. "What a mess you made of me."

Morgan shrugged. "You'd look good in a flour sack."

Julia laughed. "So I would. Still, you are the most incompetent lady's maid I've ever known."

She still couldn't understand why Julia had helped her at the station. "Then why did you help me get on the train?"

Julia shot her an amused glance in the mirror. "Oh, your face. I believe you would have died, Irish. It was just so rich."

Morgan didn't accept the explanation. Another possibility struck her. Could it be that she saw Morgan as a friend, not an equal but something akin to one? Frowning, she dismissed that as well. "Whatever the reason, I thank you. I want to take my boy home. I've been away too long and—."

Abruptly, Julia waved her hand, cutting her off. "Never mind. You can go."

That was more like it. Selfish to the core, Morgan thought as she left, Julia's actions still a mystery.

In the early afternoon two days later, the party made Chicago, where Krueger, the duke and Lord Exeter met General Phillip Sheridan at his Department of the Missouri Headquarters. The general had hunted with Northampton before, but this time excused himself from joining his old friend due to pressing business with the Indians.

"If you must go into Wyoming Territory, do not go north of Fort Fetterman," Sheridan warned. "You will find good hunting to the west I should think, but do not go north. That is travelling perilously close to our field of operations, and I do not want you caught in the midst of an Indian war. Am I understood?"

"Of course, General. You will ever be our guide on such matters," the duke said, knowing full well they intended to go much farther north than Fort Fetterman. After all, they were hunting buffalo, not rabbits and sage hens.

The party spent the night in a luxury hotel near the station, where the duke intercepted two telegrams from Aaron Greenblatt, one for Mr. Krueger and the other oddly for Morgan O'Connor, the insubordinate lady's maid. Fortunately, he'd been in the lobby with Archie MacLean, his big game hunter who had come over with the chef, when the telegrams arrived. He took them from the bellhop. He read each and showed them to MacLean.

Though small, MacLean was an imposing figure, intense like a bantam rooster, always appearing about to erupt. He had black hair and a thick moustache curled up at the ends. Famous as the best shot in all England and Scotland, he and the duke had hunted throughout the empire, tiger in India, lion and elephant in Africa and a number of odd creatures in Australia, including Aborigines. From a distance of nearly two hundred yards, MacLean had brought down fifteen in one day. Northampton had not seen the like before. The man could shoot.

Though forwarded by this Greenblatt fellow, the messages were from a Lieutenant William Raines at Camp

Harrison somewhere in Dakota Territory. The first one for Krueger was similar to the warning from Sheridan about hostile Indians.

MacLean grinned and spoke with a thick Scottish accent, "Indians, Your Grace? It looks like buffalo is not the only game we'll be hunting."

Chortling, Northampton clapped him on the back. "Indeed, Archie. Wouldn't it be marvelous to mount a few aboriginal heads on the manor walls alongside the lions and tigers?" Both men laughed.

What baffled them was why Krueger's attorney and this army officer would be sending a message to one of Krueger's servants. The O'Connor message was much the same as the first except this additional part. *I believe your brother Conor is alive. I saw him in September at Red Cloud Agency. The boy fit exactly the description, red hair, green eyes and scar. I did not mention it to you for want of raising false hopes. But, you have a right to know. I will pursue all avenues.*

"Now, what is that about?"

MacLean shrugged in answer as the duke wadded both telegrams and tossed them in the nearest wastebasket.

CHAPTER FORTY-TWO

Once the train crossed the Mississippi and the land flattened into endless plains, Katelyn changed, grew quiet, taking a seat alone at the back of the servants' car. When several people asked her what was wrong, she shook her head quickly, snapping, "Nothing is wrong."

At a small wood and water station, an old Indian man and woman with wind burned faces and wearing filthy blankets stood just outside, staring impassively at the stopped train. Tommie Blakely leaned out the window and pounded his open mouth, whooping.

Morgan slapped him hard on the buttocks, and he yelped, banging his head on the window top. "What the Sam Hill you do that for?"

"Don't be an ass, Tommie."

At the back of the car, Katelyn was whimpering, her knees pulled up under her. She was scared to death. Seamus sat beside her, uncertain what to do, while Mrs. Stevenson tried to calm her. When Morgan came up, Mrs. Stevenson said, "She won't listen. She's terrified of the Indians. I told her they're just a pair of old people, but she won't listen. She thinks they're going to attack the train and scalp her."

Morgan's heart went out to her friend. "They won't hurt you, Katelyn."

"I'm Indian," Seamus said. "I won't scalp you."

That got through to Katelyn, who reached an arm around the boy and kissed the top of his head, but then sank back into her fear, clinching her fists and bunching them in front of her.

Morgan sat down across from her and took her clinched fists in her hands and worked on them till Katelyn opened them. Morgan spoke softly, "I promise you I will not let anything happen to you. This is where I'm from, Katelyn. This is my country. You will be safe with me."

Katelyn looked up at her. Morgan could see her friend's eyes were more hopeful than reassured, but it was enough for now.

***

When Otto Krueger's private train arrived in Cheyenne, it was as if the circus had come to town. Along with several soldiers from nearby Ft. Russell, the locals had gathered to gawk at the nobs and swells. They watched as brass beds, candelabras, rolled-up rugs and ornate, cushioned chairs were unloaded onto wagons. Someone said the Queen of England was on the train. In addition, the rumor had been floating about for days that the nobs carried a queen's fortune, gold coins in a chest so heavy they needed four men to carry it and five to guard it.

One of the soldiers shouted at the four fancily dressed men huddling over a map. "Hey, Chauncey, what kind of hunting party brings along brass beds? You hunting Injun women?"

The soldiers howled with laughter and another yelled, "One that's going to lose their hair, that's what. You folks are plumb crazy going up there into that country."

Otto and Mathias Krueger, the Duke of Northampton and Archibald MacLean ignored them, studying the map Krueger tried to hold steady against a gusty breeze. The duke pointed at the map. "Sheridan says this Fort Fetterman is right about here. We should stay far to the west of it. Then, we can head north as we please and be off to the hunt. Don't want to alarm them."

MacLean nodded. "If we leave within the hour, Your Grace, we will be able to make fifteen good miles before sundown."

"Where is that guide, Mr. Krueger?" the duke demanded in his imperious voice.

The tone annoyed Krueger. A scout hired by telegraph was supposed to meet them at the station, but had not shown up yet. Despite the matrimonial agreement, the duke continuously displayed an attitude of complaint, as if put upon by the incompetence of Americans, and he, Krueger, stood as the prime example.

"He will be here, Your Grace," Krueger said sharply. He kept his temper in check but wished they could get the damn marriage done.

Mathias Krueger added eagerly, "General Sheridan said he's one of the best, an old time mountain man."

The duke ignored him, exchanging a skeptical glance with MacLean, then said, "I hope you're right, Krueger. I had Jim Bridger when Sheridan and I hunted on the Southern Plains. A disreputable fellow but a competent enough guide. Whether this man shows up or not, we will leave as soon as the wagons are loaded. It cannot be that difficult. I assume we just head northwest."

Toward the rear of the train, Morgan stepped down onto the platform with Seamus and Katelyn, gripping her elbow with a reassuring squeeze.

"I'm all right," Katelyn said, forcing a smile.

When Mrs. Stevenson waved for them to join her and the other maids, Katelyn went over but Morgan and Seamus walked to the edge of the platform to take in the town and the open country beyond. The panorama intoxicated her. The air had the strong scent of sage, grass and dust, and she felt the cool, dry air on her skin. This was her country.

"We are close to home, Seamus," she said. The boy said nothing, but she could tell he was excited to be back in the country of his birth.

Moments later when the Krueger women came down off the train in their expensive day dresses, the locals applauded as if the main event had arrived. Ignoring them, the women stared in horror at the landscape.

"What a godforsaken country," Katherine exclaimed. "Why did we have to come here, Mutti?"

Mrs. Krueger grabbed at her hat to keep the wind from dislodging it. "Your father thought it best vee support the duke in his outing. After all, his family is soon to join ours."

The girl laughed harshly. "No, that's not it. He doesn't want Lord Exeter to get too far from Julia before they are married. He might fly the coop." Then, taking in the town and the people watching them, she moaned, "Horrible. Absolutely horrible."

"Oh, don't be such a mouse," Julia said uncertainly. "It's not so bad. It's just different."

"Philadelphia is different, Sister. This is the moon."

"And you're a cretin," Julia snapped.

"Oh, you think this is Central Park?"

"Girls, mind your station. You're acting like riffer raffers," Mrs. Krueger demanded curtly.

Julia huffed and went over to stand by Morgan and Seamus at the edge of the platform. She patted the boy's head. "There's my beau."

He looked up. "Home.

She frowned. "God forbid."

They were only a few feet from a crowd of local men who stared hard at the two women, especially Julia, whose beauty left several jaws hanging slack. But, squinting against the dust stirred up by the wind, she looked past them as if they were non-existent.

Julia lowered her voice. "I would give anything if I were back in New York. Perhaps we can find a preacher in this godforsaken place and get the deed done, then I can return."

Morgan didn't reply. She noticed three riders coming out of the low hills, stirring up a dust cloud as they neared town. There was something familiar about the lead rider that constricted her throat so she could not breathe. They stopped at a saloon not thirty yards down the street, dismounted and headed for the door. Oddly, the lead man wore a theatrical costume with a bright crimson shirt, fringed buckskin pants and cross-belt holsters. Before he went inside, he paused, staring for several seconds at the huge hunting party, then followed his two compatriots inside.

It was Frank Nash.

Morgan's stomach filled with bile. What was he doing here? Then she forced herself to relax. He could not have recognized her standing among so many people.

"What's wrong with you?" Julia asked her. "You look like you've seen a ghost."

Morgan muttered. "Not a ghost."

As much as she disliked the Kruegers, she didn't want to see them or the servants harmed. Even with the duke and MacLean so sure of their prowess with a rifle, the hunting party still did not have much protection. Along with twenty or so armed freighters and muleskinners, they thought themselves able to handle any danger. She knew they were wrong. With huge war parties swarming the northern plains, this group could be swept aside in minutes.

Now, Frank Nash had shown up.

Otto Krueger approached a corporal in the crowd standing with several other soldiers. "Fellow, we are looking for the famous scout John Barnes. By any chance, have you seen him?"

There were a few guffaws from the soldiers, and the corporal jerked his thumb in the direction of the station house.

By the door, sound asleep, a nearly empty whiskey bottle cradled in his arm like a sleeping baby, lay a shaggy-haired old man in ragged clothes. He appeared not to have bathed in months. The odor of alcohol and vomit lifted off him like a thick fog.

The corporal went over and shook the man several times before he sat up blinking. "Barnes," the soldier said, "wake up. The train has come."

CHAPTER FORTY-THREE

Just below the Sweetwater River, Frank Nash and nine other men hunkered in slickers, riding through a fierce rain, following the direction the nobs and swells had taken. He estimated they were twenty miles ahead. Lightning flashed across the roiling skies, a few streaking down to the earth so close the thunderclap seemed to erupt in their chests.

Something troubled Nash. He didn't know what to think of the O'Connor girl traveling with the nobs. When Axel Grimm, who had been in the crowd at the station watching them, told him, Nash didn't believe it, but sure enough, there she sat in a carriage with her brat as the party pulled out of Cheyenne. It was surely baffling. He couldn't figure it, and what he couldn't figure worried him. The good part, though, was that when they raided the nobs, he could finally deal with the bitch. Cut off both her damn ears and feed them to her kid in front of her. Rubbing his wet hair over the nub of his ear, he savored the thought of it.

The men continued to gripe at Nash, demanding they find shelter.

"You're supposed to be an all-fired famous scout, Nash," Tyler Beck called, holding to his hat in the wind. "Can't you find us some damn shelter?"

Nash ignored him. He had known Beck for several years. Even then, the man had been outside of the law.

A former border ruffian, he carried with him a reputation for savagery from Kansas before the War. He was proud of it. He always said, "They would have called me Bloody Beck if that moniker hadn't already been taken."

Beck had brought his own men to this current enterprise and thought himself its leader, as if he were Bloody Bill Anderson himself. Can't have two leaders, Nash thought, but decided to bide his time. Beck was too deadly with his pistols and thought nothing of killing a man for little or no provocation.

Al Ferguson, the oldest among them, shouted, "I see a stand of trees up the hillside, Mr. Nash. Maybe, we can go there."

Nash wheeled his horse to face them, and they pulled up. "Shut your pans, you damn halfwits," he screamed angrily above the wind. "We need to cross the damn Sweetwater before it gets too high. Every man jack of you drops out can forget about his share."

"That so?" Beck said slowly, threateningly.

"Stay here then. It'll be a week before you get across the river and then you can find the nobs your own damn self."

When Nash turned and kicked his horse into a quick trot, they followed him. Just behind him, for no reason beyond orneriness, Beck snapped his quirt savagely on his horse's flank, causing the animal to shoot forward into a run past Nash. Nash hated men who treat horseflesh badly.

Beck looked back over his shoulder and called, "If we got to cross the damn river afore we shelter, then let's get to it."

The Sweetwater appeared a half-mile ahead, swollen over its banks, muddy from runoff, and fast, but though the crossing was treacherous, they all made it. As each came up onto the bank, they rushed into a stand of trees and dismounted to wait out the storm. After thirty more minutes, the worst passed, the lightning moved on, and under a steady drizzle, the day eased from dark to grey.

Beck announced flatly, "We camp here for the night."

Nash shrugged and tied his horse to a low-hanging limb of a cottonwood. To set up camp, they stretched a couple ponchos between trees for protection and found some wood to start a fire. It took a while but Grimm got it going and warmed up beans, slices of bacon and biscuits. He loved to cook and everyone let him. With his share, he planned to open a restaurant in Denver.

After dinner, they got drunk and talked about what they would do with the money waiting for them and joked about the women the nobs and swells had among them, fruit to be plucked. Nash only pretended to drink from the bottle passed around.

"Them pretty little society gals ain't never seen a whizzle big as mine," Beck said. "Hung like a horse, I am. They's going to squeal with delight when I plug their gaps." Several men laughed. When the rain finally stopped, Nash grabbed his canteen, sloshed it and said he'd better fill it. He arose to go to the river. Stretched out, his back leaning against his saddle, Beck studied the final contents of the bottle. "You'll be filling it with mud, pard," he said.

"I'll let it settle."

As he walked passed Beck, he pulled his colt, placed it against the back of the man's head and pulled the trigger. It blew brain matter onto two other men sitting nearby.

"What the hell!" they screamed and jumped as did the horses.

"Anyone lament Beck enough to want to avenge his sudden demise?" Nash asked calmly, a gentle smile on his lips.

A few men looked around questioningly. Axel Grimm stood opposite, a shotgun resting in the crook of his arm. No one mistook his intent. Finally, Ferguson said, "Had to be done, Mr. Nash. Now, reckon you got a plan?"

"I do," Nash said, sliding the gun into his belt. "This won't be an egg roll, gentlemen. The freighters got rifles, and those nobs are hunters. But I got a plan to make us all rich. Those rich nobs and swells had it their way long enough. It's time we took our share."

"Now, that's the kind of talk I like to hear," Ferguson said and several men nodded their heads. It seemed no one, not even Beck's own men mourned his passing.

"Get rid of this carcass," Nash ordered two men, who dragged his body to a ravine and dumped it in.

Nash walked down to the river to get away from these wretches, but Al Ferguson followed him. He came up beside Nash and started to piss into the water. He was a thin, small man who thought himself tougher than he was. He must have been in his sixties with a thick grey beard harboring a whole colony of lice. Even though he probably had no idea how to go about getting to the riches the easterners had, he desperately wanted to take charge of this outlaw gang. He'd bear watching.

"How far you figure we are behind them?" Ferguson asked.

"Twenty miles, thereabouts."

As if unconcerned, Ferguson shook his penis dry and stuffed it back in his pants. Then he picked at bits of food lodged in his yellowed teeth with his thumbnail. "Don't you think we ought to be closing the gap quickly, Mr. Nash? We still got daylight. I suspect they's still moving. We don't want to lose them."

Nash sighed. The man was an idiot. He spoke calmly as if Ferguson were an equal, "We are not going to lose them, Mr. Ferguson. They're leaving a trail as wide as Sherman's March. Rain will not wipe it out, not one that big. We don't want to get too close. They have John Barnes, and he's like an Indian. He'll know we're there if we get too close."

"Then why don't we just ride up and take them, stead of waiting till kingdom come?"

Before answering, Nash allowed his exasperation to settle. He wanted no trouble with the man till he had to kill him. Can't be taking down two men tonight. That'd unsettle the rest of the men. "Like I said, they are better armed than us and has more men. I don't like to go at a thing with those odds."

The older man gave a sharp cackle. "I noticed."

"No, it's best we let them get way up into the Bighorn area. We can take care of Barnes when he's out scouting alone. Then, you and me, we ride in and, like good Samaritans, offer to help the poor lost souls find their way."

Ferguson laughed. Instantly, he saw the wisdom in the plan, and he liked his big part in it. "I was beginning to think along those lines myself."

"Yes, I'm sure you were."

CHAPTER FORTY-FOUR

When they reached the foothills east of the Bighorn Mountains, Otto Krueger's circus with its fifteen freight wagons, four carriages and remuda of horses found no buffalo, not even small pockets of them. As they travelled farther north, the freighters grumbled about the danger of Indians, but each morning they packed up and set out. Even though there was game aplenty—the men hunted elk and deer for meat, and bear for sport. But he wanted buffalo and nothing else would do. Yet, with not a shaggy head in sight, he became more and more frustrated, snapping at the staff and berating the freighters for not moving fast enough during the day.

The Krueger sisters also grew frustrated, cooped up day after day in their carriage with their mother and sour-faced Mrs. Stevenson. Finally, they took to riding sidesaddle on their thoroughbreds, never venturing farther than fifty yards from the line of wagons for fear of running into dangerous animals or worse, wild Indians. As if they were out for a Sunday ride in Central Park, they dressed in their smartest clothes, Katherine in yellow riding habit, a perfect target for any stray Cheyenne, Morgan thought, and Julia dazzling in black with a Mandarin collar and a red felt top hat.

Two other women accompanied the hunting party, having joined in Cheyenne with their husbands to cook for the hired men. One was Jane Moore, the pretty, young wife of Caleb Moore, a muleskinner. The other was Mrs. Ida Knudsen, the wife of Eider Knudsen, the leader of the freighters. Morgan felt sorry for him. Mrs. Knudsen was a complainer, her mouth constantly yapping in a high squeaky voice about how nothing was ever right. Even a beautiful sunset only marked the end of a backbreaking day.

Katelyn quipped, "I know who wears the pants in that family." Her mood had improved a bit after the first week, though sudden sounds like the banging of a pan or a distant shot from one of the hunters could throw her into a panic.

"I feel sorry for the man," Morgan replied. Both of them laughed.

Back in Cheyenne, Morgan had bought two low-brimmed straw hats for herself and Seamus to protect against the sun and both wore their moccasins. As the days grew hotter, she dressed Seamus in a breechclout. His odd 'savage look' upset some in the party, especially Mrs. Knudson. "Does she have to flaunt her sin in front of us?"

The freighter's wife had two children of her own, a boy five and a girl nine, and neither was allowed to play with Seamus, though both did when their mother wasn't looking. From time to time Morgan snuck them rock candy from Katherine's stash.

Every evening a couple hours before sundown when the hunters returned, John Barnes circled the wagons, and the hired men put up the four large wall tents for the nobs. The Persian rugs were rolled out, the oak dressing tables and brass beds set up. The men dubbed each new camp *Little New York.*

For amusement, they competed in shooting matches while the daylight lasted. Every one of the freighters thought himself an expert marksman and entered the 'rifle frolics' as they called them. They bet their money and lost. Archibald MacLean always won. By the time they had reached the

Bighorns, many owed him what they would earn on the entire trip.

One day three weeks out from Cheyenne, a crowd gathered as usual behind a long bench to watch the evening's contest. By one of the wagons, Morgan sat with Seamus in her lap, Katelyn and Tommie Blakely alongside. She was unable to take her eyes off the rifles on the bench. After each contest she had made it a point to examine them. They were impressive weapons. MacLean's bolt action French Fusil Gras with a ten-cartridge magazine, two shiny Winchester 73s, a Sharps long rifle and a new Henry repeater. She had held one of the Winchesters and much like her earlier model, it felt like an extension of her body. She desperately wanted to shoot it.

Three chests of target plates had been brought along for practice and for shooting matches. Forty yards down range, wagons were drawn up side-by-side and a plank placed between them. Ten plates were dangled down on short fishing lines. Sunlight gleamed off them making them look to Morgan like giant suns. She could not see how anyone could miss.

Most of the men used their own rifles. Each took ten shots, and the five best scores would compete in a shoot-off of twenty targets. This night Lord Exeter had entered, but much to the duke's chagrin and Julia's disappointment, he hit only one of ten targets.

"Oh, dear," Julia muttered, standing nearby.

Oh, dear, indeed, Morgan thought. He was the worst shot she had ever seen. Many of the men had been rooting for him since, for a nob and a duke's son, he seemed a decent enough sort, always listening to them as if equals. Of the entire company, he seemed the least disappointed by his poor showing.

As the match went on, Morgan could see the Scotsman toying with the other shooters again to keep the contest close, purposely missing shots she knew he could easily make. Even though they'd lost each time, they kept coming back for more till their money ran out. They never stood a chance.

When the last contestant, Caleb Moore, missed his final shot, MacLean scooped up his winnings. "I thought Americans could shoot," he said with a sharp laugh. "Your wild west and all that. Come now, is there no one else to challenge me?"

There was a subdued silence. Morgan shifted Seamus to Katelyn's lap and stood. Absently, she brushed her skirt of dried grass and walked forward, staring at the Scotsman with a sharp glint in her grey eyes. "I'd like a go."

MacLean laughed as did several of the men, but she slapped one hundred dollars, all her savings, down on the bench. "I said I'd like a go."

"I would be taking advantage of you, miss," he said smugly.

Mrs. Krueger was aghast, but beside her Julia wore the hint of a smile. "Oh, come now, Mr. MacLean," she said. "This I would like to see. Surely, you cannot be afraid of my lady's maid?"

"I would like to see it as well," Northampton said, coming up and clapping the Scotsman on the back. His jaw had dropped open at Morgan's challenge and his ivory pipe fell from his mouth to the ground, but he decided this should be fun. "I see no reason to be impolite to her, old boy. Besides, we could all stand with a bit of amusement."

Maclean shrugged. "If a woman is to battle for American honor, Your Grace, and a house maid at that, so be it." He took out a thick roll of greenbacks and peeled off a few to match her wager.

Julia walked over to Lord Exeter, "A side wager, Your Lordship?"

He frowned, staring down into her eyes as if trying to fathom what deceitful game she played. He shook his head. "I assure you I have no love for Mr. MacLean—he is my father's man, not mine—but you cannot possibly expect a simple lady's maid to outshoot Mr. Maclean when the best shots in England have tried and failed. I will not take advantage of you, Miss Kruger." His voice carried a tone of dismissal as if she were just a silly girl, which infuriated her.

"No love for Mr. MacLean? You seem to have no love for anyone, sir," she said, her mouth tightlipped.

"Love grows out of respect, Miss Krueger. It is respect I find in so short supply."

"My, my, you are so sure of yourself. So sure Mr. MacLean will win, so sure I am just part of the rabble, and poor you, you must marry me."

When he started to speak, she turned her back on him and walked up to the two contestants. "Are you willing to accept a friendly wager, Mr. MacLean?"

An eruption of murmurings swept through the onlookers. One said loudly, "Is the lady daft?" Yet, they all took a step closer.

MacLean looked around uncertainly. Everyone turned to Krueger and he nodded. "My daughter has her own money," he said simply, gazing quizzically at her. "She spends it how she sees fit."

"You Americans do have strange ways with your women. Of course, milady," MacLean said with a slight bow. "How much?"

"Two thousand dollars."

An audible gasp escaped from the crowd. Exeter frowned heavily. Blinking in surprise, MacLean quickly regained his composure, then could not suppress a smile. "Two thousand it is."

Julia went over and stood beside her father to watch. He leaned down to her and whispered, "I hope you're sure about what you're doing?"

She glanced up at him, doubt in her eyes. "I'm not."

At the bench, MacLean picked up the French rifle. "Shall we shoot, Miss O'Connor?"

This would not take long, he thought. No reason to prolong the girl's embarrassment. He was not a cad, after all, and he was hungry, famished, in fact, looking forward to the elk he had bagged that day for the duke's chef. The smell of meat cooking over a spit was already drifting around the camp. Yes, he would make short work of the girl so they could get to the evening meal and his little flirtations with Katherine Krueger. How would that be? That weak pansy Lord Exeter marries the stuck-up Krueger shrew, and he bags the younger one. Why not? In England, there was talk he would soon receive a barony.

At the gun bench, Morgan gently took the Winchester 73 in her hands as if picking up a newborn babe, running her fingertips lovingly over the barrel. It was much like her Winchester 66. She had hunted to feed her family and could bring down birds from a hundred yards, hitting the head and leaving the meat intact, or drop scurrying rabbits, anticipating their jagged movements as if she could read their minds. For elk, deer and buffalo, she always hit the sweet spot. This would be no different.

But then a wave of doubt washed through her mind. It had been more than a year since she fired a rifle, and five years since she shot her Winchester. She had placed down all her money on impulse without thinking, her disdain for MacLean getting the better of her. All at once, she realized she'd made a terrible mistake. None of these thoughts, however, showed in her body or on her face.

"Shall we say the best of ten targets?" MacLean said. Morgan nodded. The onlookers made hush comments in anticipation.

The ammunition was laid out in small boxes. To everyone's surprise, she inserted a cartridge in the loading port and fired. The two men handling the targets downrange dove under the wagons. She seemed to have aimed at nothing and hit nothing.

"Wait, Miss O'Connor. We have not yet begun," MacLean said to general laughter.

Without a sign of emotion, she loaded ten rounds and announced, "I'm ready."

To gauge what he needed to win in one-on-one contests, he always went second, but she insisted he go first this time. He was not going to toy with her anyway, so, playing the gentleman, he acquiesced. Slamming the bolt forward on the Fusil Gras, he took careful aim, fired, slammed the bolt home again, fired again, ten times, breaking all ten plates in forty-five seconds. Several people whistled at the speed. The contest would be over in a blink.

The two target men hung ten more plates from the lines then ducked under the wagons. The plates were turning, casting glints off the waning sunlight. Morgan did not wait for them to still. Using the lever like a well pump, she rapidly fired, shattering her ten in less than fifteen seconds. Stunned, the company stood silently for a full three seconds, then burst into wild applause and cheering. Julia grinned.

Morgan did not seem to notice any of it, reloading and focusing on the two men setting up the next targets.

MacLean's brow furrowed. "Aye, so you can shoot, Miss O'Connor."

"Aye, I can shoot, Mr. MacLean."

They went on without missing through thirty more plates each, now down to the first miss to see who would win. After forty, the two wagons were moved downrange to seventy yards. Here, everyone was sure the girl would fall off the pace, but like MacLean, she hit twenty more plates without missing.

The Duke of Northampton was appalled at what was happening. National pride was at stake. MacLean had made it so with his disparaging comments about Americans. The best shot in the empire against this tiny Irish girl, this servant girl said to be from the slums of New York. She couldn't possibly win against Archie MacLean. He never lost. But Miss

O'Connor seemed unfazed by the situation as if a thousand Zulus were racing wildly for her, and she was picking them off with aplomb. An uneasy feeling began to swell in his chest.

After thirty more targets and no one had missed, Northampton seized on the pause to end the match before disaster struck. "I say, it seems we have a draw," he announced. "It will be too dark to see soon and we can't go on breaking plates all night. The girl's money shall be returned. You have done well in the match, Miss O'Connor. Let that suffice."

Murmurs of dissent ran through the crowd. Julia was about to insist they continue when Morgan spoke up, "No, I'm not quitting," she said firmly. "Unless MacLean, here, wants to back out. In that case, I win."

She was sure no one in England had ever disagreed with the duke, but his noble birth meant nothing to her. To the Duke of Northampton, it had been an affront of unparalleled proportions. This Irish trash had neither addressed him properly nor followed his directions. Furious, he began, "You upstart girl—." But immediately, he was drowned out by the uproar from the men. They all wanted the contest to continue.

Knudsen stepped forward and said he had a way to end it with one more round and also make it more interesting. "I seen it done in Denver," he explained. "Hang a plate on opposite ends of the board and at the same time set them to swinging back and forth. The one that hits their damn plate first—pardon my French, ladies—wins."

Excited about the prospect, everyone agreed, except the duke, who was still nursing his wounded vanity. MacLean nobly said he was game, but in reality he desperately wanted to end it now at a draw. The fact that she was female drove him to distraction. He could not lose to a girl and to one both Irish and American. What a terrible combination. Once they got back to England, the news of such a defeat would spread all over the country, and he would be persona non grata.

But he could do nothing except continue and redouble his concentration.

After reloading, the two combatants set their rifles on the bench in front of them to await the start signal. The two men at the wagons stood at opposite ends of the plank, drawing the plates back for their pendulum swing.

Since it was his game, Knudsen went out in front and shouted at the two target men. "Are you ready?" They waved back. He held out a handkerchief and said to the shooters, "When I drop the hanky, you may commence."

He let the tension grow, dragging out the moment. Julia noticed Morgan seemed unaffected, a deadly stillness in her small frame. She remembered her facing off Johnny Dolan without hesitation. On the other hand, MacLean constantly flexed his hands as if the rifle was too hot.

Then Knudsen dropped the handkerchief.

Seventy yards away, the two men released the plates and dove under the wagons. The pendulums began.

Both contestants snatched up their rifles simultaneously, but MacLean fired first. It was a snap shot and missed. Morgan took a fraction of a second longer, gauging the swing. Just like a rabbit scurrying to and fro. As MacLean frantically slammed the bolt home again, she fired and the plate shattered.

A great cheer exploded from the company. Before acknowledging it, Morgan scooped the money off the bench, stuffed it into her pocket, turned and gave a demure curtsy. For the first time since the challenge, she grinned.

"Congratulations, Miss O'Connor," MacLean said with a catch in his voice as if a man on the edge of a cliff. "I hope to have the opportunity for a rematch."

"You don't want that," she said flatly, infuriating him. She was quite certain she would never lose to this man. "But I'm always available."

Julia claimed her money, and announced she had placed the bet on behalf of the men and would return all the money they had lost. They cheered and called her an 'angel of mercy.' As she meticulously parceled out the cash, she glanced surreptitiously to Lord Exeter to make sure he was following the progress of her good deed.

CHAPTER FORTY-FIVE

At a canter, Raines rode through the rolling landscape of short grass with pine and cottonwood groves, Gerrard and Reardon with him. Despite being late in May, a light snow had fallen on and off throughout the day, leaving a light dusting on the ground. As they crested a rise, Raines spotted a stray buffalo on the next ridge, pawing through the snow and feeding on the grass. Raising its head, it stared for a moment at the riders, then lumbered off.

All three men wore civilian clothes, the only remnant of uniform being the sky blue cavalry trousers Raines had stuffed into his riding boots. He had on two cotton shirts, his flannel underwear, a canvas duster and dark blue slouch hat, but it did little good. He shivered in the raw weather. The temperature must have been in the forties. The cold of Crook's winter campaign clung to his bones like river leeches and may stay there for the rest of his life.

"We need to camp soon," Reardon said. "I don't want to be handling these horses in the dark tonight."

"Froze-to-Death Creek is not far," Gerrard said. "It is a good place."

"Froze-to-Death Creek?" Raines asked. "That name fits me exactly."

"Long ago, three Crow warriors camped there. Bad, bad winter," the scout explained. "Solid as trees in the morning. Even in buffalo robes."

Reardon said, "That could have been the three of us this past winter with that fool Crook."

As he had all day long, Raines searched the land, the hills mostly, for Indian sign. He knew his eyes were not as trained as Gerrard's or Reardon's, but three alert men were still better than two. Several days in Sioux and Cheyenne country and not a vestige of them had been found. Raines knew, he just knew, they were about, perhaps tracking them. Reardon had said as much the night before. "Feel them around in my bones," the sergeant had said. "Going to be hell to pay this summer for us soldiers."

With a great sense of satisfaction, Raines had written his father just before leaving Fort Fetterman that very much to his satisfaction he had been made regimental Chief of Scouts by Colonel Gannon and given an immediate assignment by General Crook to recruit Crow Indians and to search the Powder River Country for hostiles. As exciting as the responsibility and recognition were, it was tempered by real hazard; he could almost taste disaster in his mouth. Word was the Crow wanted nothing to do with this coming war. They were well out of it and wanted to stay that way. Still, his orders were to recruit a scout force.

Two days later near the old adobe ruins of Fort C. F. Smith, Raines, Reardon and Gerrard found a Crow village of some forty lodges on the far side of the Bighorn River. It was clear they had been seen as well for several mounted Indians came out in great numbers, swimming the animals across the swollen torrent and up the bank toward the three men, shrieking war cries. The lead warrior fired off a shot.

"Hold," Gerrard said.

Gerrard broke away from his companions and galloped at the lead man. Pulling up in front of him, he leapt down, as did the warrior, and they embraced. Several men recognized the scout. Raines and Reardon exchanged relieved glances.

That night about a central fire, there was singing and dancing and storytelling, but it was not till the next morning that Raines and Gerrard met in council with the camp elders in the open. Gerrard identified the chiefs present, each coming forward to vigorously shake hands with Raines, Tin Belly, Mountain Pocket, Old Onion, White Mouth, Old Crow and several others. Gerrard knew them all and they seemed to respect him.

It was still unseasonably cold, but the sky was clear, promising a warmer day. They sat around the smoldering coals of the dying fire from the night before with Reardon and at least two hundred warriors gathered close to hear. Women with children seated behind them clung to tattered blankets. Tall young men watched from any vantage point they could find. The chiefs passed a pipe from man to man in the circle, including Raines and Gerrard.

Gerrard nodded to Raines. "Go ahead, Lieutenant. They're waiting to hear what you have to say."

In his mind, Raines had written and rewritten what he would say several times. Now, he took a deep breath and rose to speak. "The Sioux are enemies of both the white people and the Crow. The white chief Crook is coming to make war on them. If the Crow want to make war on the Sioux, now is the time. If they want to drive them from their country and prevent them from murdering Crow people, now is the time. If they want revenge for the Crow that have fallen, now is the time."

He paused to allow Gerrard to interpret, then continued, "White men and red men make war in different ways. The white man goes through the country with his head down and sees nothing. The red man keeps his eyes open and sees everything. Now, I have come to ask for Crow warriors to scout for me. To use their eyes and tell me what they see. I want brave men who will be my eyes." He saw some of the chiefs exchange glances, but couldn't read their level expressions. "They will be soldiers of the US government, get soldiers' pay and soldiers' food."

When Raines sat down, White Mouth, a short, stocky man, rose. "Touch the Clouds, you speak true." Because of Raines's height, the man had given him an Indian name. *Touch the Clouds*. He liked it. "The Sioux are great enemies. The white chief Crook was already down below making war on them. Our young men went with him and he only scared a few old Cheyenne women, then ran back without doing anything. We are afraid that he will do it again."

He was right. Mention of Crook's winter campaign had the ability to sting Raines both for its humiliation and the misery of that brutal cold. He noticed Reardon showing a warrior his nub fingers and the warrior nodded with understanding.

When White Mouth took his seat, Raines jumped up again, "The white chiefs Gibbon and Terry and Custer are also coming with their armies. We have many soldiers. As long as there are Sioux and Cheyenne, we will stay. If the Crow will let us know where their enemies are, we will fight them."

Holding to his medicine pouch, Mountain Pocket stood. The news of the other armies coming had caused a stir, and he waited for it to subside. His voice was sharp and clear. "I have fought the Sioux till I am old and tired. You want to fight now, I'll let you go alone." He sat back down.

Old Crow, a small wizened man, spoke, "Touch the Clouds must listen to me. I have been to war many times. I always do what I set out to do. If you find the Sioux and don't want to fight, our young men will break loose and be killed and that would be a bad thing. You better go alone."

Raines kept his face impassive, but he was disappointed. He'd expected better support, but did not sense any at all. They were all old chiefs, the youngest middle aged, and maybe they had seen enough war. He decided to try a different tact. "I'd rather have nobody than an unwilling soldier," he said. "I want to hear from the young men. I want to hear from the fighting men, men who want to go to war."

No younger man stood up to speak; no one came forward. Instead, Old Crow took the center, pulling his blanket tighter about his small frame. "I have something to say to you and the Great Father. We are not given enough flour and beef. There are buffalo about. We must hunt the buffalo before he is gone or we will starve. I want to say this to you. You ask for our young men to go with you. If they are not willing to go, I cannot force them."

No one else spoke for a long time. They seemed to be waiting for him to reply. Raines saw that they were not well fed, especially coming out of a bad winter. He couldn't do anything about that. He had nothing to do with their annuities. He was no Indian agent and could not promise them more food. He needed to provide General Crook with the eyes and ears for a successful campaign, but looking around at the assembled warriors, he realized not one Crow wanted to scout for him.

Finally, he stood again. His voice had an unmistakable edge of anger to it. "Men usually go to war thinking they might be killed," he said. "Men who want to sleep in their tipis every night don't want to go to war. That kind of warrior wants to have his squaw and his tipi with him when he goes to war. We don't want anyone who goes to war with his squaw and tipi. I have heard several of you talk. The talk all seems to be one way. If any of you want to go to war, I want to hear from you. If not, there is an end to it."

Old Crow gave a shrug with his hands. "Be patient. Do not hurry us. You have told us what you want. Let us hold a council among ourselves and see who will go with you and who will not."

A few minutes later, Raines, Gerrard and Reardon sat silently outside of camp on the banks of the Bighorn, eating pemmican hard enough to chip a tooth. Trying to soften it, the lieutenant worked it with his teeth till his jaw was sore.

He could see how it could last for years. Back in the village, the loud harangues of the chiefs carried to the river bank. Raines was disappointed and didn't expect them to change their minds. How could he be designated Head of Scouts with Gerrard his only scout?

A young Crow with a slight limp approached. Lean and broad shouldered, his left leg was bowed, and Raines realized he had a clubfoot.

"Touch the Cloud," he said, "I am Broken Leg. I will go with you if you go where the Sioux are, but will turn back if you go the wrong way."

Raines rose to shake his hand. "We hunt the Sioux. We go where they are."

The Indian youth's arm swept to where the council continued making speeches. "All these chiefs I don't understand. I don't know what to make of such men. Maybe I can get one or two other men to go with you."

"That would be a good thing."

By the afternoon, twenty-two Crow warriors had agreed to scout for Raines, friends of Broken Leg, most of them young, except for one man, Iron Shirt, who appeared in his seventies, his face an old piece of leather. They swore on the point of a knife, a blood oath with each warrior cutting a tiny piece of skin from his arm. But Broken Leg was not done. He made Raines swear, too, that he would believe all that the scouts told him and that he would do all they told him to do concerning the Sioux and Cheyenne. He agreed and cut his own arm as they had.

Not wanting to test his good luck, he rode out with his detachment of scouts within the hour, heading south directly into Sioux and Cheyenne country.

CHAPTER FORTY-SIX

Near sundown, the young Cheyenne warrior White Antelope found the tracks of the wasicus they'd been hunting. He guessed many wagons, a large party not far ahead, and it excited him. He was fifteen on his first war party as a fighting warrior, not just along to hold the horses. More warriors than leaves on a tree had joined Spotted Horse for this raid to kill the enemies of the People, and he had volunteered to scout with the ten other warriors, ranging with them far off from the main body. The most important thing in his life was to impress Spotted Horse, and now he had found a large band of whites.

"Do not puff your chest out so," Smoke said to White Antelope, and the other men laughed. "A wasicus child could find this trail."

The air went out of the boy all at once and his shoulders sagged, but Smoke wasn't unkind. He added, "You and Bull Bear go tell Spotted Horse what you have found. Tell him to come up quickly."

White Antelope grinned but closed it down immediately. Who would want to go on a war party with a fool of a warrior who went around grinning? He swung his horse alongside Bull Bear, and the two rode off.

***

"It's been a month in this horrid wilderness without a decent bath," Julia said, inside her tent, wearing her undergarments and washing out of a porcelain basin while Morgan handed her another towel. Julia threw the cloth into the basin, splashing water onto the nightstand. "Utter madness, and I'll not stand it a moment longer. I must have a real bath! Grab the towels and soap. We're going down to the river."

On the way, Morgan picked up a Winchester from the armory, and they set out from camp, going a quarter of a mile along the stream till the shrubs and trees and curve of the creek around a small hill hid them from camp. With the sun hovering above the mountains, the ruddy glow of sky promised a glorious sunset. At their sudden presence, a huge bullfrog croaked and jumped into the water with a loud splash and a snake slithered away from the bank. Morgan propped the Winchester against a tree and set the towels and castile soap on the grassy bank.

Julia nodded toward the rifle. "I would have never guessed you could have used that thing so well. That was amazing. Everyone is looking at you now as if you had two heads." Abruptly, she laughed. "Did you see how that fool Lord Exeter raised his eyebrows when I gave the money back to the ruffians?"

Morgan placed her hands on her cheeks in mock surprise, "Why, Miss Julia, that was not out of the kindness of your heart?"

Julia laughed, and Morgan actually joined in, then pulled her dress off over her head and naked, picked up a bar of soap and waded into the water. She wore only the necklace with the arrowhead, gold cross and bear claws.

Julia snapped. "What are you doing?"

"Bathing. You coming in?"

Impatiently, Julia tapped her foot on the grass for several seconds. "We are here for my bath, not yours. You are the worst lady's maid in all creation. But I can hardly replace you out here, can I?" Quickly she divested herself of her clothing and, naked, waded in beside Morgan. The water rose to mid-thigh. "You are such a bad influence. Hurry with the soap."

Morgan lathered herself and handed it over. A week's grime and sweat loosened and lifted off her. She brought water up with her hands and doused her hair, pulling it back from her forehead. The scar where Nash had tried to scalp her was a thin pink line two inches long.

Beside her, Julia began cleaning herself. "I don't understand what the men see in all this hunting. This trip through Hades, but they are like little boys in a land of toys."

"I hope being a duchess is worth it then," Morgan said.

"It is, or will be." Julia eyed her askance. "You know when we return, you will no longer be employed with us. I do not believe anyone would hire you." Her voice trailed off noticing the purple gauges on Morgan's hip and chest. And the seven slashes on her left arm. "My God, what happened to you?"

"I was shot," Morgan said matter-of-factly, then indicated her arm. "These were part of the Sun Dance ceremony."

"Dear God, you've been shot?" the Krueger girl said incredulously.

"A couple times." She touched her forehead. "This I got from a bastard who tried to scalp me. You can see, he failed."

Julia's jaw dropped. Morgan didn't add that she thought the man who did it was somewhere close about. After a moment, Julia shook her head. "My, my, Irish, you are a revelation. Or as mutti would say, a revolution."

Both girls laughed at that. Morgan was about to say she couldn't understand Julia's mother half the time, but decided it would be pushing familiarity too far. That was when she saw a flash of light off the last ray of sun far up a steep hill a couple hundred yards away. It rose at least a thousand feet. The flash came from the trees near the top.

"What is it?" Julia asked.

Binoculars. Someone was watching them. She shuddered. Nash. Indians didn't use binoculars. But she didn't say it. "Nothing. We need to get back."

"I'll say when we go back."

"We need to get back now, Julia," Morgan said sharply, wading from the water.

"Who is the mistress and who the lady's maid?" Julia hissed petulantly, but reluctantly she followed.

That night in camp, the freighters staged a small rebellion, and the duke was furious about it. The farther north the party went, the more acrimonious the help had become. Low types all, they complained incessantly, *this was Sioux country. This was Cheyenne country. They didn't want any part of them.* After several weeks, the hunting party had not seen a buffalo track, let alone a buffalo. Nothing to do now but push on north, even though that caused greater problems with these infernal Americans. At the center of the discontent was that harridan Mrs. Knudsen. Could not these Americans handle their women? Once again this evening, she complained to her husband and he complained to Krueger.

"This is Lodge Grass Creek," Knudsen said, indicating the nearby stream. "We never signed on to go this far north." With a tremor of fear in his voice, he went on to say that thousands of Indians might be waiting just beyond the next hill. Or perhaps, he was afraid of his wife.

While Krueger was hearing the man out, the duke stepped in. "Look, fellow, you have nothing to fear from these loathsome Aboriginals. I assure you, we are well prepared to protect you. By Gad, man, MacLean and I have fought the Zulu in southern Africa, and they are a far more perilous proposition than these ragged tribesmen at which you so quake."

"Don't know them Zulu folk," Knudsen said, agitated. "But I do know Crazy Horse and Sitting Bull and Spotted Horse and a whole bunch of others, and they are not to be messed with. I'm telling you, Governor, you ain't never seen any horsemen like these Indians." He balled his fist in sudden intensity. "They will ride right in here burning and killing, and there won't be a damned thing you or your Zulu man can do about it."

At his sudden fervor, no one answered for a moment, then Krueger said coldly, "You have made your point, Mr. Knudsen. Despite your worry, we will be pressing on in the morning. You signed a contract for the duration of the hunt, and I expect you to honor it. I will hear no further discussion about the matter." He flicked his hand. "You may go now."

Hissing through his teeth, Knudsen hesitated several seconds, then spun about and strode away, fiercely angry at being so tersely dismissed.

Morgan was sympathetic with him. She had heard the exchange while helping Katelyn set the nobs' table for dinner. In this country, stupidity was deadly, and the duke and Krueger were the worst kind of ignorant, people who thought they were smart. After what she'd seen on the hill earlier, a trickle of fear rolled down her spine. She had originally planned to leave when the party reached as far north as the Bighorn River, a ways yet to go, but now, maybe it was time to take Seamus and get far away from these people. They were headed for disaster. Katelyn was the only one among them Morgan cared enough about to bring along. She did account a level of concern for the other servants and even Julia, shrew that she was, but not enough to risk her son's life by taking them with her.

When she and Katelyn were returning to the servants' section of camp, Morgan broached the subject of leaving. "Katelyn, if I left, took Seamus and left the Kruegers, would you come with us?"

Shocked, Katelyn stopped. "Are you mad? Ride off into this wilderness alone?"

"I'm not crazy, and, yes, ride off, the three of us away from these people. I want you to come with Seamus and me to Lone Tree."

With an expression of horror, the housemaid shook her head. "I can't. I would be scared out of my wits out there. I'm scared witless all the time here. I think Knudsen is right about the Indians."

"He is."

"Morgan, I've never even ridden a horse."

"I'll teach you. You'll do fine."

Katelyn shook her head more firmly. "Even if you could, I have family back in New York. I could never leave them. They count on me. Thank you for asking me, but I think it would be foolish for you to go out there alone."

Morgan was disappointed, but she understood family. She felt it pointless to explain that they would be far safer *out there* by themselves than in here with all them.

***

Morgan awoke in the dark, careful not to disturb Seamus or Katelyn, who shared their grass pallet, and slipped away. The sun would be up in another hour but morning twilight was already growing brighter. She wanted to be in the trees on the hillside before she could be seen. Quietly, she saddled one of the horses, took the Winchester from the armory and led the animal from camp. No one stopped her. The few guards Knudsen had set were likely asleep. Fifty yards out, she mounted and rode onto the wooded slope.

Morning twilight was now enough to distinguish the pine needles on the trees. She remembered Running Hawk calling this the time when Earth awakened, when little by little, light leaked out of the ground. Among the tall lodge pole pine, the spruce and aspen in full leaf, she caught glimpses of elk and deer scurrying away. Likely grizzly and black bear in here as well. Good country, like Lone Tree. She thought of home with sudden, painful longing. Not far now. Maybe no more than two hundred miles.

An hour later, skirting just inside the tree line, she saw an antelope out on a bare knoll, fat and golden in the first light of the sun, nibbling at the grass. A perfect target. She lifted her arms as if she held a rifle, took aim and pulled the imaginary trigger. But she was not here to hunt. At least not that kind of animal. She felt sure about who was watching them. If it were Cheyenne or Sioux, it would have been unlikely she would have seen them. They would not have binoculars.

A couple hundred yards from the top, she dismounted, tying the reins to a tree limb, drew the Winchester and went on foot. She wore moccasins and moved silently, soon wet with sweat. The rock outcrop where she had seen the flash the evening before was just ahead. She slowed and circled on the spot, taking each step as if even the lightest footfall might shake the earth. She came across hoof prints where a horse had disturbed the undergrowth. The horse was shod. A white man as she figured. Nash or one of his men. God, she hoped it was Nash. She saw the blood gushing from his ear and heard his screams of anguish, a sound so pleasing to her, like a beautiful Irish melody. But those images were replaced by the constant battering she took at his hands, the repeated violations. The sadistic joy that twisted his face every time he caused her pain. If it was him up here, she would kill him and ease the terrible wound in her soul.

Twenty yards away from the outcrop, she knelt hidden among the trees and watched. No one was there, but that didn't mean no one was around. Several minutes went by before she heard the stamp and wheeze of a horse somewhere to the right. She continued to wait, not moving or making a sound for a half-hour. Finally, she heard a loud belch and fart and then a heavy sigh. She moved silently to close in.

A huge man in a filthy buckskin coat stood beside a pine, binoculars thrust through branches, watching the camp far below. Ten feet behind him, she cocked the rifle loudly. He tensed and turned slowly. When their eyes met, she saw that he recognized her, and she knew him as well. She would never forget such a face. That glass eye. That tobacco-stained beard. That madness in the good eye. Axel Grimm.

His name caught in her throat. He had come to Big Crow's camp all those years ago. He and Nash had dumped her brother at Big Crow's feet and destroyed her last chance of saving him. As the thought of it flashed through her mind, her rage burst into flames.

Her voice tight. "Where's Nash?"

He grinned, showing blackened teeth. "Close. He knows you are with them. He is coming for you. Settle old scores." He laughed. "Lot of gold down there, ain't there? So, what do you think? You think—."

At point blank range, she shot him in the chest, his eyes wide in shock, and as he fell, she shot him once again in the forehead, then three more times into his lifeless body.

CHAPTER FORTY-SEVEN

Not yet dawn, Raines glanced at his pocket watch, 4:00am, a cloudless morning that promised a warm day. Last night, they had camped among the cottonwoods along the small stream whose name the Crow called Froze-to-Death Creek. Feeling exposed on foot, he was anxious to be on horseback, to get moving. Much speculation had passed between the Crow as to where the Sioux and Cheyenne were. No hard sign had been found, only occasional tracks of several small parties of three or four, once of ten. Raines sensed in his bones hostiles about in great numbers. The Crow did, too, and were edgy, which made him even more nervous.

He roused Reardon and the scouts, and no one protested the early start. Within minutes, sharing a quick breakfast of pemmican, they were out riding toward the Wolf Mountains, a set of tall hills some ten miles distant. Broken Leg and Iron shirt rode three hundred yards ahead. Two buzzards circled in the pristine sky ahead and farther on a wide-winged eagle floated on the currents, searching for its morning meal.

Raines had found no village for Crook to attack, and he would have to report back soon. Crook wouldn't like failure. "What do you think?" he asked Gerrard. "Where are our friends?"

Gerrard patted his horse, which seemed jittery, then shrugged. "I don't know. I think we will find them today."

Reardon gave a sharp laugh. "Bub and sis, that's you two. You act like children. There's no sign because they ain't here. They've seen the armies coming after them and become scared. I'm telling you they've gone back to the agencies where, under the guidance and protection of the Indian Bureau, they've been transformed from blood-thirsty savages into good, peaceable Indians." His sarcasm was bitter. "That is till the storm blows over, then mark my words, they'll take to the field again killing whites."

Gerrard frowned. "I don't think so," he said quietly. Had he argued, made more of a forceful statement, it might have had less of an impact. As it was, Reardon glanced hard at him. "You don't say."

Gerrard faced Reardon. His words were not confrontational. "You see but you don't see. I think we will find them today and I think we won't like it."

After a couple hours, they reached the tall hills and began to climb them. Just below the highest peak, Raines dismounted and moved up cautiously on foot to Broken Leg and Iron Shirt, lying on their bellies and looking into the distance. Below was a wide panoramic view of the Rosebud River from its mouth to where it disappeared in a distant haze in the north. There was no sign of smoke anywhere in the great vista that would indicate a village.

"Nothing," Raines muttered. He was disappointed. Hating the thought of failure, he was desperate to find them. Later in the day, Iron Shirt did, the first significant sign. It was so conspicuous Raines would have spotted it, a wide swathe of tracks, Indian ponies.

"About two hundred warriors," the old Crow said, his wizened face impassive. "One day ago."

"Damn," Reardon whistled.

"They follow many wagons. White people," Iron Shirt added. "Those people go to spirit world soon."

Raines's heart lurched with the sudden realization it could be Morgan. She might not have received his messages and come west with the Kruegers. They would not be the first fools to perish on the frontier. They come across miners bound for Deadwood, who had not been deterred. He doubted if Krueger would be either.

Raines and his scouts set out following the war party. His goal was to skirt them, get ahead of them and warn whomever was travelling with the wagons. God help them if the war party got to them first. God help Morgan if she were among them.

CHAPTER FORTY-EIGHT

When Morgan rode into camp, leading Grimm's horse, the freighters and nobs stood behind the wagons as if expecting an attack. They gathered around her as she dismounted.

"What happened? We heard gunfire," Knudsen said.

"Where have you been, Miss O'Connor?" Krueger called. "You can't just ride off on your own. It's far too dangerous."

Mrs. Knudsen said breathlessly, "Was that Indians out there? Those shots?"

Several other questions were shouted, but Morgan ignored them as Seamus pushed through the crowd to her. "You had breakfast yet?" she asked.

He shook his head.

"We'll see to that," she said and started to leave them.

"See here, Miss O'Connor," Kruger said, blocking her path, his face reddening with frustration. "You must tell us what is happening."

"Such as whose horse are you escorting into camp?" the duke said.

"Mine now," she answered. She knew she had to tell them of the danger Nash posed, though she wasn't sure she'd be believed or heeded. "Someone's been watching us. My guess he'd been at it for a few days. I saw a flash of metal last night and went to find out who it was."

The duke gave an incredulous laugh. "And so you a housemaid decided to investigate on your own?"

Krueger added, "Young lady, you best remember your position. We can't be having such as this."

Barnes cut him off. "Now, what she says, that's true enough."

Still early in the morning, his white hair in disarray, he wore only his pants over sweat-stained long johns, which Morgan doubted he had ever taken off. "I come across his tracks three days ago. It was clear enough someone was following us."

"Why didn't you say something?" Krueger demanded.

Barnes shrugged. "Only one man. Didn't worry me none."

Shaking his head in frustration, Krueger turned to Morgan. "So you stole his horse, Miss O'Connor? My God, is he still up there?"

"He is. But he doesn't need the horse. I shot him." Everyone fell silent in surprise, the nobs horrified. The first one to speak was Exeter. "Did he assault you?"

"No." Studying their appalled faces, she said in a reasonable voice as if explaining the mechanism of a breechloader, "He needed killing, so I killed him. His name was Axel Grimm. He rode with Frank Nash, and that alone was reason enough." She turned to Barnes. "You know Nash?"

"I know him. Not that I'd trust him."

"He's behind us, my guess with several men. Before I shot Grimm, he said there was gold down here. That's what Nash is coming for."

There was a ripple of muttering among the freighters. "Oh, dear," Mrs. Knudsen said.

Krueger shook his head. "Gold? We have no gold. I don't understand you, Miss O'Connor."

Barnes cackled, as if Krueger had just told the funniest joke he'd ever heard. He said to Morgan, "I was at Camp Harrison when you come in last year. When I seen you with this bunch in Cheyenne, I couldn't figure how you was with these codfish nobles, so I didn't say a word."

"What are you talking about?" Krueger said.

"You want me to tell them?"

Morgan shrugged. "Tell them what you want."

He gave a sharp hoot. "Well, folks, we got a real famous person among us. Yes, sir, real famous. The newspapers and even a brand new dime novel I saw in Cheyenne done called her *The Captured Girl*. Lived with them Cheyenne Indians she did, lot longer than I ever did. And after what I saw of her at Camp Harrison when she cut up a laundress who said bad things about her boy, well, if she says Grimm is dead, then the man is dead. And if she says Frank Nash is coming after us, I'd say he's coming, and it's time to worry as much about him as the Indians."

They all stood quiet, staring at her as if she had sprouted horns.

"You?" Kruger gaped. "You're the Captured Girl?"

She didn't answer, but Barnes said, "In the flesh."

"Who?" the duke asked, glancing around with confusion.

Krueger waved the duke's question away and addressed Morgan. "How in the world did you..." He sputtered over the question.

Barnes said, "You gentlemen better stop gawking at her and start thinking on Nash. He ain't going to stop till he gets what he wants."

They all stood quiet for a long time, some still staring at Morgan, others considering their situation, till Mathias cleared his throat nervously. "Father, perhaps we can entice the man to speak with us. Convince him we have no great horde of gold and show him how well-armed we are. That might end any threat."

"That won't work," Morgan said flatly. "He won't care. Anyway, I plan to shoot him on sight. But by all means, ask him to come and parlay. He'll be an easier target then."

The duke's eyebrows knitted in derision. "Do you shoot everyone you dislike, Miss O'Connor?"

"No. If I did, you wouldn't have made it out of New York."

***

Despite the warnings of thieves on their trail and Indians in the area, the nobs set off for that day's hunt and the household staff readied the Krueger women for travel. If any trouble came, the freighters were well-armed, and the hunters could rush back. Before the wagons started out, the freighters gathered in a meeting and Mrs. Knudsen lobbied for them to turn back.

"We got Injuns all around us and now this cutthroat following us," she said. "What can the nobs do if we turn back? They'd have to go along. They can't stay out here on their own." She added sarcastically, "Who would set up their tents for them?"

"We wouldn't get paid," an older man named Billings argued. "You heard what Krueger said."

"We'd have our hair, at least," Caleb Moore said, putting an arm around his wife.

"It's not our property," Billings pointed out. "We can't just leave with it. We'd be robbers."

Impatiently, Mrs. Knudsen said, "They don't want to come, we dump their stuff on the ground."

Billings shook his head. "I don't know, ma'am. I don't like backing out on my word. I signed on to this outfit. Thick or thin, figure I got to stick it out."

"More the fool you, Billings," Mrs. Knudsen snapped. "I got my own littlins to worry about."

"I say we vote on it," Knudsen said.

When the count was taken, ten voted to turn back, fifteen to continue on. Within five minutes, the wagons pulled out, rolling north once again.

CHAPTER FORTY-NINE

A morning fog was lifting from the valley floor as Raines and his Crow scouts picked their way carefully down the steep hillside and rode across Lodge Grass Creek out onto the flats. On the surrounding hills, tufts of clouds clung to trees like cotton bolls. Yesterday they had crossed the Rosebud, following the Indian and wagon tracks northwest back in the direction of abandoned Fort Smith. All day the Crow found signs of war parties; one trail extending fifty yards across. The scouts were nervous and Raines jumpy.

"Sioux or Cheyenne?" he had asked Gerrard.

Reardon answered first, "Does it matter? Both probably. They're still apt to take our hair if we ain't careful."

"I think it is Spotted Horse," Gerrard said. "Broken Leg found a Cheyenne medicine bag, and in the camps, Spotted Horse is the one the young men follow."

With twenty-five men, twenty-two of them Crow, Reardon didn't have enough to fight a pitched battle against great numbers, and pitched battles were something Indians shunned, unless the odds were overwhelmingly in their favor. The Crow would ride away first even if he were foolish enough to order a fight.

Now by Lodge Grass Creek, Raines halted his command and leaned forward in the saddle, gazing through the remaining haze at several black smudges a half-mile away.

Four Crow scouts circled them cautiously. A disquiet feeling settled in his bones.

"What is that, sergeant?" he asked.

Reardon sniffed the air. "Take a good whiff, lad. Those are the wagons we been following."

Even from this far downwind, the odor was distinct. Raines should have known. Burned out wagons. The smell of death. His heart flickered. If the Kruegers were indeed traipsing around in the middle of this war, Morgan could be lying among the mutilated bodies. He could not prepare himself for that.

They approached the killing site. Bodies lay scattered on the ground, men, women and children, all mutilated, some burned, the rest purple and rotting. Raines struggled to keep the bile from his throat, but even as he did, relief spiked through him. It was not the Kruegers. It was not Morgan, but several families traveling the Bozeman Trail.

Everyone stared at the carnage, the Crow stoically, Reardon bitterly. "Bastards," he muttered. "Bad time for folks to be on the Bozeman."

Broken Leg rode over to join them. "White families caught in open. Many warriors."

Gerrard had been checking the terrain ahead and rode back to Raines. "I found tracks for another party of whites. Looks like fifteen, twenty wagons. A larger company."

"How long ago?" Raines asked.

"A day, maybe two."

Raines was convinced if the Kruegers were indeed stumbling around out here, this would be them.

"Rider coming!" Reardon called out.

Galloping fast, a trooper was coming down the valley toward them. The sergeant recognized him. "It's O'Reilly." O'Reilly rode in swiftly and yanked his horse to a quick stop, throwing Raines a quick salute. "Followed your trail here, sir. Big as all get out." Sweaty and dust-covered, he handed over a leather pouch. "General Crook's compliments."

Raines opened the pouch and took out a single paper. He read it quickly. "Moving army out in pursuit of hostiles on the 29th of May, north toward the Tongue River. You are to hasten to my command forthwith. I need your scouting services with me."

The 29th of May. That was four days ago. The orders were not ambiguous. The army was probably somewhere forty to sixty miles to the southeast. He could meet up with it in a couple days of hard riding.

Reardon looked at him expectantly. "Where to, lieutenant?"

Raines folded the orders and stuck them in his pocket. "Northwest. We follow the wagon tracks."

CHAPTER FIFTY

When she heard the riders coming, Morgan was spreading the sleeping pallet beneath a tarpaulin for herself, Seamus and Katelyn. A full moon hung above the Bighorns, but clouds scudded across its surface and that of the stars, causing a slow kaleidoscope of pitch black and gloaming light.

A terrified male voice shouted from nearby. "Indians! I seen 'em. Indians!" Coming out of the darkness, the man, a freighter, darted between the wagons into camp.

Terrified, Katelyn shrieked and shoved in under the tarp, shaking and squeezing herself into a ball. Morgan put a hand on her shoulder and spoke gently, "It's all right. It's not hostile Indians."

Half whimpering, half snarling, Katelyn cried, "How could you possibly know that?"

Because if they were hostile, we'd already be dead, she thought but didn't say. "I went out before dark. Checked for sign. There were none, Katelyn."

Katelyn's terrified expression suggested she was unconvinced. Seamus squirmed in under the tarp and patted Katelyn's back.

"Take care of Seamus. I'll be back in a minute." Morgan picked up the Winchester and headed for the wagons. She was sure it wasn't Sioux or Cheyenne, but it could be Nash. Her blood burned with anticipation. The freighters stood at the wagons with their rifles poised, The Brits and Kruegers raced from their tents in nightclothes. Only MacLean was fully clothed as if he'd not gone to bed. He carried his Fusil.

"Vhat's happening? Vhat's happening?" Mrs. Krueger screamed, pulling her robe tighter over her nightclothes, Julia and Katherine following her.

"I seen them, governor," the man said breathlessly to Krueger. "I was out there doing my business, and I heard them. When I looked up, I was staring into the eyes of Spotted Horse hisself. Injuns. A bunch of them. Two hundred at least. No doubt about it."

When he finished with an emphatic nod, everyone went silent, listening, but the night had gone quiet. MacLean stepped to the nearest wagon and leveled his rifle. "Make ready, men. If they attack, aim for the sound of their horses. We'll show the buggers a thing or two."

The men spread across the wagon front, aiming into the darkness. In the flickering moonlight, Morgan saw the tension on their faces, men certain they would die. Mrs. Knudsen and Mrs. Moore knelt beside their husbands ready to fire their own weapons.

Finally, a call came. "Hello, the camp. We wish to approach."

Morgan recognized the voice instantly. She was surprised at how hard her heart pounded against her chest. She rushed forward and took Krueger's arm. "It's Will Raines. For God's sake, don't shoot, Mr. Krueger. You know him. You know his father. It's Will Raines."

Krueger stared at her dumbfounded. "Raines? What…how would you—."

"Identify yourself," MacLean shouted.

"Lieutenant William Raines, US Cavalry. May we approach?"

Krueger's eyes went wide. He called out, "Yes, yes, my boy, by all means."

As one, the freighters relaxed their rifles. Raising her hands skyward in relief, Mrs. Knudsen said, "Praise God, the cavalry. We are saved."

Like ghostly apparitions, two men rode out of the darkness, the light from the nearest fire flickering red and orange off worn clothes that made them look more like road agents. Raines and Reardon eased their horses into camp and dismounted while the company gathered around them shouting questions at once.

"Where's the rest of your troop?" Knudsen pressed.

Reardon answered with a smirk. "Oh, they're out there."

Krueger stepped forward, extending his hand to Will. "Welcome, my boy. This is quite a surprise, I can tell you. You and your troopers are most welcome. Did General Sheridan send you? Some of our party are worried about the Indians, but now with your protection, we can proceed with the hunt. Please, bring your men in."

Mrs. Knudsen sidled up next to Krueger. "That idiot over there, Bascom, said there were two hundred Indians out there. Like to give us all a heart attack."

"He was partly right, ma'am. I have Indian scouts with me. No soldiers but the sergeant here. We've only got twenty men, not two hundred. "

Words of distress, even anger, spread through the crowd.

Raines said, "We will camp a quarter of a mile downstream at the switch back and be off in the morning. We are on scout for General Crook's army and must rejoin him. I came only to warn you."

Finally, Knudsen shouted, incensed, "You brought Indians?"

As a few more shouted angrily, Raines cut them off. "These are Crow, blood enemies of the Sioux and Cheyenne. They've been fighting them long before any of you showed up out here." He turned back to Krueger. "We saw your tracks. I came to warn you, sir, in the most vigorous terms possible that you are in a precarious position here and must turn back immediately. We've been following a large party of Cheyenne led by Spotted Horse."

Alarm swept through the company at the mention of Spotted Horse, but the duke was unimpressed, giving a scoffing laugh. "We most certainly will not turn back. I assure you, leftenant, we are in scant need of any assistance from you or your aboriginal chappies. We are perfectly able to handle any encounter with your local heathen."

Raines couldn't hide his disgust for such obstinacy. "And you are—?"

"May I introduce the Duke of Northampton and this is his son, the Earl of Exeter," Krueger said.

Raines addressed the duke. "Sir, twenty Cheyenne warriors could ride through here and leave nothing behind but your corpses. They already did so with ten families, men, women and children about twenty miles back. This band we are following is two hundred strong, and Spotted Horse, their leader, is the worst of the worst. He doesn't just raid; he sets out to kill whites." He nodded to the Krueger women. "Sorry to speak so bluntly, ladies, but you must take this warning seriously."

"Perhaps, you are right, Lieutenant," Krueger said. "We have pushed our luck about as far as it can go. We'll start back tomorrow."

The freighters shouted their approval. Raines studied Krueger for several seconds. Had the man finally seen sense? He wasn't so sure. He nodded and turned away from him, calling out to the company, "Morgan, are you here?"

"Here, Will."

As she approached from the back, the company fell silent, parting to let her pass, gazing with curiosity as they leaned in to listen. When she stopped before him, he took her hands and gave a crooked smile. "You are a feast for these eyes, Morgan."

"Good to see you, too, Will. I've missed you."

"And I you." He leaned in to her ear, his voice so soft only she could hear. "If we weren't so public, I'd kiss you till your lips were numb."

She put her hands on his face and pulled him down to her, kissing him with longing. A few people gasped. Yet several clapped. "Good show, Lieutenant."

She released him and he stared down at her for several seconds, taking in that lovely face he once thought he'd never see again. Seamus raced up and stood beside them. Raines picked the boy up. "And who is this? It can't be Ho'nehe? This lad is so much bigger."

"In the white world he is Seamus. He's big enough to carry both names."

"That he is," Raines said.

The boy looked up at him. "I can count."

"I bet you can and do a lot more as well," Raines said, setting him down and ruffling his hair.

Morgan glanced at Reardon "I see you still have this handsome rogue with you, Lieutenant." She stepped over to the sergeant, giving him a quick hug. "Good to see you, Sergeant."

"You, too, lass. You seem to be doing all right for yourself."

"I am now. Seamus and I are going home."

"I have to get my scouts settled for the night," Raines said and suggested he and Morgan meet later. He gave his compliments to Otto Krueger, and to the company's surprise, left with Reardon, leading their horses from camp.

Later that night, it began to rain a steady drizzle that after a time soaked into everything not covered. In his shelter along the small creek, Raines could hear more than see the water coursing by just a few feet away. His Crow scouts huddled under hastily built shelters made from loose timber, shrubs and animal hides. Reardon stood watch in his slicker on the far side of the ragged stand of trees, but Raines figured no one would be prowling about in this miserable night.

He couldn't sleep, heartsick over what happened with Morgan earlier. After seeing to his own camp, he had returned to Morgan's, and she'd led him down to the creek. He placed his arm around her, and she settled into him, fitting perfectly as if a missing piece of a greater whole. In his mind was the proposal. He was going to ask her to marry him properly, but still hadn't figured out how exactly to do it now that she was beside him. Just say it, he kept telling himself. His stomach ached with nervousness. However, first he wanted to make sure she was safe and urged her to convince Krueger to leave as early as possible tomorrow.

She held the hand he draped over her shoulders. "I'm a servant, Will. These people don't listen to servants unless it's your bath is ready, ma'am. The freighters are anxious to go, though. The duke is a dangerous fool, and I think they understand that now. They may just turn back on their own."

"I will feel safer for you and Seamus when they start back."

She gave a little shake of the head. "I'm taking my boy and going on to Lone Tree no matter what these people do."

"Is that wise? With all the Indians about?"

She looked up at him. "Believe me, Will. We will be much safer on our own."

Then came the moment that tore the evening apart for him. Raines was about to propose to her but put it off again. There was one more thing he must discuss. He had already figured out that neither she nor Krueger received the telegram messages he'd sent through Greenblatt. She didn't know about Conor. She had a right to. He came directly to the point.

"Morgan, when I was at Red Cloud last year, I saw a white boy with Big Crow." She stepped back from him, frowning. He went on. "He had green eyes and a scar on his cheek just where you said it would be. I think it was Conor."

Her body stiffened abruptly. Silent for several seconds, she breathed through her mouth as if each breath took concentration. "You knew this last year and you're telling me now? All those letters and not once did you think to mention that my brother was alive? You let me spend nearly a year in agony."

"Big Crow left the talks. I wanted to find Conor first to make sure it was him before I told you."

Clinching her fists, she cut him off angrily, "You wanted to play the hero again. Will Raines to the rescue, riding in to save the damsel in distress, bringing her loved one back from the dead."

He straightened as if she'd thrust a dagger into his chest. She turned away from him and stepped down to the water. He could hear her breathing, saw her hands opening and closing. They stood like that for nearly five minutes till finally she said without looking back at him, "That was cruel of me, Will. You must know by now, I'm a cruel person."

"No, you're not."

"I should not have said that. I didn't mean it. I owe you my life."

He came up behind her and put his hands on her shoulders, but she shrugged him off violently. "Please. Leave me alone." Her voice was cold as river ice.

Shaken, he took a step back, hesitated for several seconds, then left.

Now, staring out at the blackness from his shelter, Raines couldn't believe he had found and lost the woman he loved in the same night. He resolved that whatever happened in their future, he would not leave it as it was now. In the morning, he would speak to her before leaving, try to stop the sudden bleeding of his life.

He heard movement outside his shelter and reached for his pistol.

"Are you going to shoot me, Will?" It was Morgan. She ducked in under the tarp. "Certainly, you have cause. Can you forgive me for being so awful?"

This close, he could smell the lilac scent of her in the dampness. "There's nothing to forgive. I should have handled it better."

She touched his lip and slid into his arms. The press of her body fired his blood like nothing else before; it was almost painful. He kissed her and raised his knees so her thighs parted, and she slid down over his hips. Running his fingers through her hair, he kissed her again. Then, she pulled back. "Will, you do challenge a girl."

"I hope I challenge you." He paused, then asked.

"What are you going to do?"

"This moment?"

"No, about Conor?"

"Go on to Lone Tree. I can do nothing now about Conor. He's completely Cheyenne by now. I'll have to wait."

"Wait for what?"

"Till the end. The white government wants the Indians on reservations. Someday they will all be there. Maybe they can fight a year or two more but it will not change things. The days of the free, roving bands will soon be over. You know this as well as I do."

He nodded. "I'll see what I can do. I have orders to join General Crook. We may run into Big Crow."

As he spoke, he ran his hands up and down her spine, and she groaned. She shut her eyes for a second, then opened them. "Be careful, Will," she said with concern. "This will not be like other fighting. All the Cheyenne and Lakota and Arapaho are riled. They were last year, and it can only be worse now. They are desperate."

He said with an edge of sarcasm, "I promise. I'll not be a hero."

She playfully patted his chest. "Make sure you don't."

"I love you, you know," he said. He kissed her neck and cheek and ear, and she groaned again.

Her eyes were wide. "I do know."

"Morgan, marry me."

She gave a gentle chuckle. "We are married. Didn't you know that? When I came into your lodge, even one this humble, that meant we were married. That's the way of the Cheyenne, and I was Cheyenne for four years."

"Can we also have a ceremony in a church?"

"Come to Lone tree when you can, and I'll have a preacher waiting. But make no mistake, Will. For me, if you want me, we are married from this moment."

It was not the way his parents went about marriage, but it fit Morgan, and it fit their two lives now. "I want you. It's what I've always wanted. From this moment, you are my wife."

He wrapped the blanket around her and they lay down. She whispered, "I want you inside me. I've never wanted anything so much."

With the heat of her next to him, with his whole body, skin, muscles, organs, swelling rapidly, he felt only too happy to oblige.

CHAPTER FIFTY-ONE

Next morning, when Raines and his detachment of scouts left, the parting between him and Morgan was not tearful as he had expected it to go. She was not a crying woman, and he would not show that kind of emotion in front of his Crow warriors. As for Morgan, sadness sunk deep into her soul and an overwhelming fear that he might be killed took hold. She almost asked him not to go and come to Lone Tree with her, but knew he wouldn't. She was uneasy being so close to this many Crow, but surely no one would recognize her as Crow Killer.

She embraced Will; he kissed her unabashedly as a few Crow chortled and chided him. After they stared for a long moment into each other's eyes, love crossing between them, he turned to Seamus and ruffled his hair. "Take care of your mother, lad."

"Yes, sir," the boy answered with much gravity.

The scouts mounted, ready to go. Reardon cleared his throat with exaggerated volume, and with a slight blush of his cheeks, Raines swung up into the saddle.

Morgan stepped to his horse. "Come to us when you can."

"When I get leave," he said, frowning. "I suspect it won't be for a while. It will be a busy summer."

Fighting the entire Cheyenne, Sioux and Arapaho nations, she thought with a shiver, but kept it to herself. He leaned down and with one arm lifted her to him and kissed her again. Setting her back on the ground, he said aloud, "I'll miss you, Mrs. Raines. And don't worry. I'll come back to you. We have a life to live together. You get yourself and that boy home safely."

"I promise." She gave quick goodbyes to Reardon and Gerrard, then as they rode off, walked back to the camp, trying to control the sadness tearing through her heart.

***

When she and Seamus returned to camp, she found the freighters in an uproar. After Raines's warning, they expected to begin the journey back to Cheyenne, but the nobs had no intention of leaving just yet. Krueger had ordered that the camp stay in place for now. Barnes had found buffalo tracks, and he and the other hunters were setting out to follow them. And so the camp stayed.

It took most of the day, but by evening, the men found more than just a few buffalo. A small herd of some six hundred animals grazed lazily in a box canyon not five miles from camp. Not the vast herd the duke remembered from his previous trips to America, but buffalo nonetheless. Back then, bison had spread on the plains almost from horizon to horizon. Where had they gone? Barnes said this might be the last big herd. If they were, the duke decided with a sense of pride, he would be the one to kill the last buffalo.

With twilight near, Barnes said, "They'll hold till morning. It's getting late and the light's going to be poor."

Reluctantly, everyone agreed. The duke turned to MacLean. "By gad, Archie, we will see how many of the beasts we bring down in one day. Start at sunrise. Then we have all day."

"Capital idea, Your Grace," MacLean said. "I dare say we will take down all of them."

When the hunters returned to camp, they found the freighters in mutiny. Something more than just staying another day had set them off. An hour before, a lone Indian had been seen on a nearby hillside, watching them. Mrs. Moore had screamed at the first sight and Katelyn broke into tears. A certainty of doom swept through the company, and Morgan felt this time they had got the right of it. From such a distance, she couldn't tell if he was Cheyenne or Sioux, but she did know he was unafraid. Things were getting out of hand. Time had come for her and Seamus to go. Past time for it. Tomorrow morning before sunrise.

When the hunters returned, they gathered for their evening meal already set out at the long table, Knudsen approached them backed by all the freighters and told of the Indians watching the camp. He demanded they start back first thing the following morning.

The Krueger women were alarmed. "It's true, Papa," Julia said. "We saw him, too."

"They frighten me, Papa," Katherine said.

"I will let nothing happen to you," Krueger said, then with an expression of annoyance, he glanced at Knudsen "I will let you know in the morning what I decide. Now, may we eat our meal in peace?" He waved him away with his hand.

Elbowed by his wife, Knudsen took a nervous step forward, right up to the table. "We will be going back in the morning, sir, with or without you."

Krueger was taken aback. The duke sighed. "Gentlemen, gentlemen, we are in scant threat from your Aboriginals. If ten thousand Zulus couldn't defeat Mr. MacLean and myself, I assure you, we are perfectly able to handle any encounter with a few of this rabble of red men."

Mrs. Knudsen moved up beside her husband. "His nibs ain't going to listen to you, Husband." Her eyes fixed on Krueger. "Come morning, we will be making tracks south."

A chorus of agreement rippled among the freighters. "How about it, Gov?" Knudsen asked Krueger. "You coming with us? If you stay, you stay alone."

Krueger's face became rigid and his cheeks flushed with anger. One of the richest men in America, he didn't take defiance from underlings. With the duke next to him, he was embarrassed and worried that the marriage agreement would unravel. When he spoke, it was with a hard voice of unchallenged authority. "We will be returning, Mr. Knudsen, when I say we will. We have come thousands of miles to hunt buffalo, and now that we have found them, we will not be turning back till we have accomplished what we set out to do. We will stay right here on this spot."

An eruption of protests came from the freighters. "We didn't sign on to be scalped," Mrs. Knudsen said. "The Indians know they got us in a pickle here. Any fool knows it too."

That infuriating woman! "This is what will happen, Knudsen. Tomorrow, while you maintain camp here, we will hunt. And the next day, and the next day after that if necessary, till we have concluded our purpose. If you leave, you will not be paid, and I will seek legal damages against each and every one of you. You cannot comprehend what forces I can bring down upon your ears, each and every one of you. I will not leave you with a pot to piss in. Now, there will be no further discussion. The matter is at an end."

After a moment, the freighters began trickling away, disgruntled but subdued for the moment. Mrs. Knudsen was the last to leave.

The servant staff sat silently at a small fire. Overwhelmed with terror, Katelyn's eyes blinked, trying to hold back tears. Morgan glanced at the butler and housekeeper, both bearing expressions of dismay and hopelessness. Like the freighters, they, too, believed they were on a trip of the damned. This was hardly something they understood, let alone could handle. Morgan felt a moment's sympathy for these people, but not enough to stay and risk her son.

Later, when alone with Katelyn after dinner, Morgan told her friend she and Seamus were leaving early tomorrow and
asked her to go with them, but again she refused. Sad and disappointed, Morgan told herself there was nothing she could do.

When she went to Julia's tent to help her prepare for bed, the Krueger girl, too, was frightened but desperately tried to maintain a veneer of indifference. As Morgan brushed the girl's hair, she said, "I'm leaving."

Julia's head snapped around. "Leaving?"

"Yes, before sunrise. I'm taking Seamus and heading for Lone Tree, my home."

A flicker of despair crossed Julia's face, then she straightened. "Well, you'll do what you want. You're no lady's maid, that's sure, so why tell me? I can't stop you, but you're mad to do it. Absolutely mad."

"Remember. I'm the Captured Girl. I lived with the Cheyenne. Seamus and I can survive on our own in this country, even with Indians about. If caught, no one would harm him, knowing who his father was."

"Why? Who's his father?"

"You would not understand if I told you." Morgan placed a hand on Julia's shoulders. "I would take you with us, but I know you would not leave your family."

Julia glanced up, fear deep in her eyes, then her face went impassive as she shrugged.

"You must convince your father to leave tomorrow morning, even if it ends your prospects of marriage to Lord Exeter. If you don't, you and the others will die here." She did not say that it was likely too late as is.

Julia glared at her, then blinked and swallowed as if trying to down a clump of dirt. Finally, she nodded. "I'll try to convince Papa."

CHAPTER FIFTY-TWO

A warm, moonlit night, and the mosquitoes flitted about. Morgan ignored them, swatting a few away from Seamus, who sat in front of her as they rode the horse close to the hills, avoiding open stretches and staying off the crests so their silhouette wouldn't stand out. Carrying the Winchester in a scabbard and food for several days' journey in saddlebags, she figured they could make Lone Tree in five days or so.

She guessed the time was just after 3:00am, and the hair on the back of her neck stood out. She had known Sioux and Cheyenne were around even before one had appeared in the hills watching the camp. She could feel them about tonight, could sense them in the air. At a small creek five miles from camp, Morgan dismounted to examine the bank for tracks. They would be more pronounced here where the ground was damp. Already the sky in the east had dimly lightened, beginning the long morning twilight. With the full moon, it would be bright as noon before sunrise, and that less than an hour away. She wanted to be well away before then. She knelt down to feel along the moist earth and easily found the tracks of several horses.

Seamus jumped down beside her and examined the ground. "Five?" he whispered. "Unshod."

She nodded with a spike of pride. Morgan had come across several small parties so far, and they were all headed northeast. No shod horses. She was sure Nash was staying clear. They remounted and she eased the horse northeast, considering what to do. Avoid them and continue north out of the area, or track them, assess the threat. Even with Seamus along, best to know what they faced. She decided to track them.

Twenty minutes later, Morgan saw the faint glow of flickering firelight from beyond a series of small hills. She circled to the left and rode up onto the summit of a low bluff. Near the cliff, she and Seamus dismounted and crawled to the edge. The bluff fell away in a sheer fifty-foot drop, overlooking a creek that glittered in the moonlight.

Below were a hundred and fifty warriors or more. Several campfires flickered with dying embers as warriors stood painting themselves and their horses, readying for war. She remembered how Spotted Horse always drew three red lines across his face, his chest and his horse's flanks like gashes of blood, but did not see him. Despite the warmth of the night, she shivered involuntarily. Even though Will had said there were this many around, the numbers shocked her. This many could not be turned away.

"Auntie Katelyn, Auntie Julia," Seamus whispered so low she barely heard.

She glanced at him, forcing a reassuring smile, but he knew. These warriors were going after the Krueger camp, and the whites stood no chance. Katelyn and Julia would be killed or taken, the servant staff as well, and all those freighters wiped out. Why did that weight of responsibility always fall to her? Why were they her problem? She couldn't help them. She could not risk Seamus to go back and warn them, which would do little good anyway. The words screamed in her head, *I can't go back!*

The boy read her mind. "You promise Auntie Katelyn, nahko'e," he said, using *mother* in Cheyenne. He was too smart by half, and it unsettled her. If she didn't go back, the day would come when Seamus, who loved Katelyn and Julia like family, would never forgive her. She realized for him she had to go back and warn them. If she were quick enough, there might still be a chance for them to escape all this. And she had promised. That damn promise. They backed up silently and remounted the horse.

No more than fifteen minutes later, their return was blocked. They were riding down a wide coulee covered by tall grass and scattered pine and cedar trees distinct in the growing light. Below on the flats, a small stream disappeared around a large outcropping of rock. Fat and round, it appeared like a buffalo head, Bull's Head Rock she remembered Running Hawk saying once. As they neared the bottom, Morgan heard the sound of rapidly approaching horses, and she fought a surge of panic. It was what she feared, running into a war party. She swung around and kicked her mount hard for the nearest stand of trees thirty yards away. She just barely entered the deep foliage when at least twenty-five Indians rounded the outcrop and pulled up at the edge of the stream to water their horses.

A mixture of Lakota and Cheyenne, they shouted back and forth excitedly. If the Lakota found her, Morgan's chances of saving Seamus will have dropped to near zero. They might not care who she claimed his father was. In the brightening twilight, she was able to make out some facial features, at least the ones closest to her, but recognized no one. She remained absolutely still, as did Seamus, who knew better than to flinch even a facial muscle. She held firmly to the reins and desperately hoped the horse would make no sound.

One of the Indians shouted impatiently to someone at the far end of the line of horses, "Black Shield is not here. We are at the Bull's Head. He is not. Where is he? Glory and honors await this day." He pointed to the east. "If Black Shield does not come by the time the sun stands on that ridge, I go fight the wasicus on my own."

On foot, leading his horse, the man the warrior spoke to approached. He was of modest height and lean. "Be patient, old friend," he said calmly. "He will come."

Tremors of shock and fear raced through Morgan, and she could feel Seamus stiffen. It was Spotted Horse. His face and chest painted with flame red streaks.

"Father," Seamus whispered.

The horse reacted to their sudden movement by taking a couple steps, and she pulled him up, quickly patting his neck. She sensed the tension in the beast's muscles.

Spotted Horse was now talking with the warrior too quietly for her to hear. What would he do if he captured her and Seamus? Nothing to Seamus, but her? Kill her outright? Perhaps. She had to admit he had reason to hate her. When she had left his lodge and taken his son with her, she had taken the life from him as well. To him, her actions would seem an act of betrayal.

By now, several Indians had dismounted, releasing their horses to graze, then throwing their blankets on the ground, lying down to sleep. Others sat in groups and ate pemmican, talking quietly, and waiting. With the sun nearly up, she studied her surroundings for escape. But there was none. There was no other cover for twenty yards. Too much open grass to the ridgeline. She settled in to wait.

Time passed, and they sat the horse, all remaining still without movement. It was movement that attracted the hunter to its prey. When the sun was two fingers above the far hills to the east, she estimated they'd been stuck in this copse for more than three hours. Stiff, his nerves on edge, her son had not said a word. No complaint. No crying. Twice, men had come up toward the trees to relieve themselves and gone back to their blankets. At first, she worried about the Indian ponies grazing nearby, but they ignored her horse, and he them.

As much of an evil bastard as Axel Grimm was, he did have a good horse. That, at least, said something for the man.

Suddenly, Morgan jolted to alertness. Below, Spotted Horse rose abruptly and took several steps toward the low hills to the northeast. Whatever he heard or saw, none of the others noticed. A few of them glanced his way questioningly but didn't get up to join him. That was the moment her horse gave a loud wheeze.

Spotted Horse's head snapped around, and he stared at the stand of trees. Slowly, he walked up the coulee toward it. Morgan eased her rifle up its scabbard, then slid it back in. Whatever happened here, if she died here, Seamus must survive, and if it was as Ho'nehe of the Cheyenne, then at least he would live.

Halting ten feet away, he studied the trees, close enough that she could see the intensity of his coal-dark eyes. She sat the horse, frozen, hardly breathing, and prayed the damn animal would not flicker or swish its tail or sneeze. Her husband's eyes narrowed and he leaned forward as if something had caught his attention. He took another step toward Morgan just as three Indians rounded a far hill and rode at the warriors at a fast gallop, pulling up and leaping to the ground with great shouts. The men embraced the newcomers. Abruptly, Spotted Horse turned and hurried down the coulee toward them.

CHAPTER FIFTY-THREE

Julia was awakened by the commotion outside her bedroom door. She couldn't understand who would be making such a racket so early in the morning inside her house. She would have to speak to Dawes about it. Then, when she saw the bright sunlight on the wall of her tent, she felt disorientated, and the truth fell on her like a slab of granite. She was not in New York in her beautiful, comfortable home, but on the accursed frontier.

For an instant, she feared they were under attack by Indians, but the voices were urgent, not panicky. What could possibly be happening? She glanced at Katherine on the other side of the bed and her mother on the smaller bed, both still sleeping. The men would have already gone hunting if they maintained their plan to leave early. Not a particularly avid or good hunter, Lord Exeter was going with them, wanting to see the last buffalo herd. So the women slept in.

Someone shouted right outside her tent flap. Her sister and mother woke up, looking dazed and puzzled. Irritated, Julia got out of bed, threw on her robe and stepped outside. What met her was chaos. Utter chaos.

At full gallop, Morgan and Seamus rode into camp, into the midst of madness. The freighters were frantically dumping everything of the Krueger party onto the ground.

Wearing nothing but their nightclothes, the three Krueger women stood in front of their tent in shock, Mrs. Krueger shouting orders no one listened to.

Seamus was frightened by the chaos and clutched at her hands. Morgan wrapped an arm in front of him, pulling him back to her tightly, and spoke in Cheyenne, "I need you to be a strong warrior today. You see how these wasicus are. They are like the Crazy Woman who races around the tree chasing her shadow. They are not strong. You must be."

"Heehe'e," he said, his expression suddenly impassive.

Nearby, Katelyn was throwing gear into a wagon. Reining the horse in sharply, Morgan leapt to the ground next to her. Nearly hysterical, Katelyn's words came rapidly, "We saw Indians on that hillside. Then they screamed their banshee cry and rode off. It scared everyone. Mrs. Knudsen said her family was leaving and anyone else who wants to stay could die here. Then everyone started throwing things on the ground."

Morgan took her shoulders. "We are not going with them, Katelyn."

The young woman's face shook with panic. Her mouth worked several times before she got out. "Please, why not? I want to go."

Because they are all going to die, Morgan thought but didn't say. Instead, she spoke calmly, "We need to find Krueger and the other hunters. It's safer with them." That was a lie, but it would sound better than what she now planned. "Don't worry. I know this country, and I'm not going to let anything happen to you."

Katelyn calmed a little and nodded. "The hunters, yes."

Morgan lifted her son from the horse, handing him to her. "Stay with Seamus. Pack only a few clothes and as much food as you can carry and be ready to leave in five minutes."

Before Katelyn could answer, Morgan hurried off to the Krueger women who still looked befuddled. Apparently, they hadn't seen the warriors this morning that had spooked the freighters into finally leaving.

Scowling, Julia started to speak, but Morgan cut her off. "You three get dressed in riding clothes. We're going to find Mr. Krueger and the other men."

This was too much for Mrs. Kruger, who straightened imperiously and said angrily, "Just who do you think you are, Miss O'Connor, addressing me in such a manner? Vee are staying right here. You can go on with this rubble You are dismissed from our service as of this moment."

Morgan turned to Julia and spoke with a glacial tone. "There is a band of two hundred warriors about five miles from here and they are coming. If you stay, you will die, your bodies mutilated and scalped." She took in all three now. "They are not taking captives on this raid. But before you three die, they will rape you repeatedly. Even you, Mrs. Krueger. So get yourselves ready. I will be leaving as soon as I can get horses saddled. If you are not ready, I will leave you."

The older woman's body shook, Morgan couldn't tell whether from fear or anger. "You are the most reprehensible girl I have ever had the misfortune to—."

"Mother!" Julia screamed. Terror filled her eyes now. "Enough. Hurry. We must get ready and go find papa."

Morgan left them and went to Knudsen, who had finished dumping several tables and chairs onto the ground along with chests and portmanteaus and was reloading the wagon with his own gear. He had stopped to argue with Mrs. Stevenson. Out of the corner of her eye, Morgan saw the duke's French chef climbing up into Billings's wagon, apparently fleeing with the rest. Already loaded, they began pulling out ahead of the rest. The Krueger staff was getting into other wagons, fleeing.

When Morgan came up, Mrs. Stevenson said to her, "He is throwing our things on the ground."

Fed up, Knudsen yelled, "We ain't robbers. We give them fair warning. Now, we're leaving. Got to worry about our own. Ain't taking a thing that don't belong to us. You can come with us, Miss O'Connor, if you want. All of you. We'll find the room."

"No, sir, thank you. We'll go after the hunting party."

"Suit yourself. Saw you come in. Did you see any of them out there?" he asked as he handed two kettles up to his wife.

"Cheyenne and Lakota," Morgan said. "Close to two hundred warriors. Don't spare the horses for the first couple of hours, Mr. Knudsen. Put as much distance as you can between you and them. You might outdistance them."

His face went pale. His eyes shot up to his two children in the back of the wagon. "Maybe they won't come after us at all," he said hopefully.

"Maybe they won't," she said. They both knew it was a lie.

She knew what was going to happen and so did he. God help her, she counted on it to give her time. By the tracks, the Indians would know the whites had split up, and most warriors would follow the wagons. They would run the freighters down soon enough and kill them all. In her mind, she saw all the gear and bodies strewn on the ground, the warriors searching for trophies and things of value to them. Morgan couldn't help these people.

An overwhelming guilt at abandoning them filled her insides. They were good people, but she would have to leave them to their fate. She noticed Knudsen's two terrified children on the wagon settling in for the ride. They had played with Seamus despite their mother's admonitions against it. There was nothing she could do. Nothing she could do. She could not save everyone.

"They will come after you, Mr. Knudsen," she said, finally. He deserved the truth. "It's Spotted Horse."

"Damn," Knudsen groaned, looking at his children. "It couldn't get worse, but it just did." He shouted to the others, "Hurry. We move out in five minutes and anybody not ready gets left behind."

Helping saddle the horses, Mrs. Stevenson proved handier than Morgan had anticipated. They also took a couple extra rifles and ammunition and packed a few days' supply of food on a mule. By that time, the wagons were rolling across the creek and heading south at a good pace, leaving behind the camp with tables, chairs, luggage and crates of goods scattered amid the multi-colored tents.

Getting everyone mounted was a trial that had Morgan considering shooting one or two of them. There were only two sidesaddles, one each for the sisters, and Mrs. Krueger refused to ride astride.

"Come on, Mutti," Katherine pleaded.

"Hook your leg over the saddle horn," Morgan said abruptly. "Either that or walk. I don't give a damn which."

Mrs. Krueger sputtered but couldn't speak. Mrs. Stevenson coaxed her up, then mounted her own horse. When everyone was up, Morgan swung up behind Seamus. It was quickly clear Katelyn was having trouble. The horse, usually gentle, stamped around, and the girl squeaked in terror.

"Can we get on with it?" Julia snapped, glancing around the hills. "I can feel them watching us."

"You're welcome to go ahead on your own," Morgan said sharply.

Easing her horse over to Katelyn, Morgan took her bridle to steady the horse. "Relax, Katelyn. He won't hurt you. The horse can sense if you're afraid."

"Afraid?" she said shrilly. "I'm scared to death."

"Sing," Morgan directed.

"What?" Katelyn asked incredulously.

"Oh, dear lord," Julia muttered.

"Trust me, Katelyn. Sing. It will relax you and the horse. Come on." Morgan began the haunting Irish ballad *Boolavogue* and after a few seconds Katelyn joined in.

As the two Irishwomen sang, Katelyn relaxed a bit and the horse settled as they moved slowly forward. Then, Morgan gently kneed her mare and led the women out of camp, wondering if she would have to abandon them to save Seamus afterall. But that time hadn't come yet.

CHAPTER FIFTY-FOUR

"Stay inside the tracks of the men earlier this morning," Morgan demanded as they rode in a single file over the long, dry grass. A frightened and odd group of refugees, she thought. They couldn't fight and they couldn't run. All they could do was hide and that's what she intended to do.

"Tracks?" Kathrine whined. "I don't see any tracks."

The sign was conspicuous to even a four-year-old like Seamus, bent grass, scuffed dirt, clear hoof prints. Morgan tamped down her frustration. "Then don't wander out of line," she said feigning calm.

Taking in her charges with a sharp look, she tried to tamp down a sense of growing doom. Terrified, Katelyn struggled just to stay on her horse, Katherine was in tears, Julia's fear shown in her eyes and her mother kept rattling at Mrs. Stevenson about riding in such 'a bombed' way. Not even her misuse of the language eased the tension.

"We have to go faster, Mommy," Seamus said, a hint of unease in his voice, and she kissed the top of his head.

"I know."

The boy was right. They would have to be far into the foothills soon, or they would be found and that would be the end of them. They made slow progress, though, for the first hour, riding mercifully in silence but for Katherine's sniffling and Katelyn's occasional squeal at a sudden movement of her horse. The slowness weighed heavily on Morgan, and she picked up the pace, telling Katelyn, who was bouncing in the saddle like a spring toy, to stay on as best she could. The early clouds had drifted off, opening up a wide, topaz blue sky and the promise of greater heat. Across the valley, beyond the hills, the Bighorn Mountains rose thousands of feet.

The country was familiar to Morgan. She had killed a grizzly farther up toward the mountain peaks while hunting with Spotted Horse. They had visited the ancient medicine wheel together that day. That was where she hoped to take these women.

When they came to a brook that coursed down from the foothills, Morgan abruptly turned and faced the others. "We are going upstream for a while. When we enter the water, stay in it, right in the middle. Do not get out of the water for any reason. Mrs. Stevenson, you're last. Make sure no one falls behind you."

The housekeeper, who had drag on the mule, nodded.

Mrs. Krueger looked around in alarm, her voice breaking into a squeak. "Vhat? The men are ahead, are they not?"

Morgan gazed back the way they'd come and saw no one. That was unnerving because she knew they were back there. The hairs on her neck had stood up and she never ignored her instincts. She saw the panic in the older woman's eyes and responded calmly, "Indians can read our tracks, Mrs. Krueger, like you can read print in a book. But they can't read them in water. We don't want them following us or leading them to the men. Now, we must keep moving." She entered the stream and turned her horse up against the gentle current.

The explanation seemed to satisfy Mrs. Krueger, at least enough that she followed as did the others. Morgan wrapped an arm around Seamus, hugging him, then touched her necklace. She prayed to God and Heammawihio to give her wisdom and luck and hoped she had not doomed her son by coming back for these people.

***

"Buffalo! Buffalo!" Krueger shouted.

At the call, Lord Exeter experienced a surge of excitement. Despite his dislike of killing the last of these beasts, he experienced the primitive pull of the hunt. But it was only a stumbling, old bull, roaming by himself along the side of a grassy hillside.

"This won't do at all," the duke said. "What happened to that herd, Mr. Barnes?"

"Just hold your horses. They're out there," the scout answered.

"Take him, Your Grace," MacLean urged, pointing to the bull.

The duke glanced back at the footman acting as his gun bearer. "Boyle, my rifle."

Boyle, Dawes and Tommie Blakely sat their horses uneasily. No gun bearers or outdoorsmen, they detested this barren ground so far from the mansion in New York City. The duke and Boyle dismounted, and the footman handed the nob his rifle. That's when two more of the animals appeared on the crest of the hill. MacLean called for his Fusil. Northampton knelt, took aim and with two shots dropped the old bull. MacLean shot at the two on top and they scurried out of sight.

"Good shooting, Your Grace." MacLean said.

"I believe you missed," Mathias said to MacLean.

"No, you will see, Matty chap, I always hit my target. They will soon fall."

They rode up the hill past the old buffalo carcass, leaving him where he fell. Beyond, lying on the grass were the two buffalos MacLean shot, one dead, the other struggling and groaning in its death agony. As the others went on, Lord Exeter rode over and used a bullet to end its misery.

A half-mile farther on, down in a short valley of tall grass and trees, Barnes pulled up and pointed. "There, gentlemen."

The whole basin was spotted with grazing buffalo, a thousand perhaps. At a gallop, the men approached. A couple bulls or cows looked up to stare through tangled manes, then went back to eating. Finally, a few sensed alarm and trotted away.

Cautiously, the hunters spread out almost blocking the valley and dismounted, setting up for the kill. Carrying two long rifles, Dawes followed Krueger and his son. Boyle hovered behind both the duke and Exeter, while Tommie Blakely stayed with MacLean.

The Scotsman took his rifle from Blakely. "You'll see some real shooting now, lad."

"Yes, sir."

Taking up a firm stance, MacLean waited till the duke fired first, and then he opened up. Animals began to fall. At first, it seemed none of the other buffalo understood what was happening. Some glanced up but most kept on grazing, ignoring the constant report of the rifles.

"Haw!" MacLean exclaimed, his bolt-action fusil firing steadily. "See them fall, lad. See them fall."

Finally, the buffalo broke into a thunderous stampede away from the hunters. "It's all right, Gov," Barnes shouted. "This is a box canyon. They are trapped in."

As the sound of the hooves faded, then stopped, the morning grew silent, and an eerie calm pervaded it. A gentle breeze stirred the tall grass. In no hurry now, MacLean took a deep exhilarating breath. He'd never felt so good in his life. Soon, he would have at them again and further his legend as a great hunter. His future would once again be secure.

A piercing cry shattered the stillness. A fiend out of hell, black eyes blazing, rose on horseback out of the deep grass twenty yards away and raced toward him at breathtaking speed. The creature had bloody gashes across his face and chest. He held an axe aloft preparing to strike. A palsy of dread settled into MacLean's soul. He attempted to lift his rifle. Frantically, wildly, he cried out, "Zulus," just as the war axe cleaved his forehead open.

***

It was late morning, and the heat intensified. Not used to such exertions, the women were sweating heavily and grumbling. Rebellion was coming. She didn't care. She would not fight that hard to subdue it. If they wanted to leave, they were welcome. Better for her.

But she knew they wouldn't. They would be lost the moment they left her sight, and if the others didn't know that, Julia did. Morgan was about to swing her horse about when the sound of gunfire drifted in from a long way off. For the first minutes it was rhythmic, the men hunting, and Morgan told them that.

"Why don't we go to them?" Julia asked, strain in her voice.

"We will. Soon," Morgan said.

Julia looked at her skeptically.

Then, as they pushed up the mountain still in the middle of the stream, the sound of the distant gunfire changed. The new resonance was rapid and staccato, clear enough for Morgan to pick up its terrible melody. It was no longer a hunt, but an attack. The men were fighting for their lives. With the men wiped out, as they surely would be, the warriors would come for the women.

When they had travelled upstream nearly five miles, winding around hills and up gently rising canyons, steadily gaining elevation, Morgan knew they were being followed. She had seen the hint of dust a couple miles back. Her ploy staying in the creek had not worked. Four or five Sioux or Cheyenne she guessed. If it were more, they would not have cared about being seen. A chill coursed along her spine. They weren't going to make it.

Still, she decided to stay in the water and hide their tracks as long as possible. They came to a place where the creek swung within twenty yards of a cliff. Abruptly, Julia left the water to approach its edge.

"Damn it," Morgan cursed, turning on the others. "Stay here. If anyone else leaves, I'll abandon all of you."

She urged her horse up the bank toward Julia, who was staring at something in the far distance. Angry, Morgan pulled up beside her. "What are you doing? We can't stop. They're coming after us."

Julia made no reply. Morgan then saw what she was looking at. Stretching out below them was the sweep of land with its undulations, hills and swells. Ten miles off, thick smoke rose up out of the landscape. It had to be the wagons. It had to be. So far away, nothing was distinct. The only certainty was that the freighters had not made it. The large war party had caught up with them. In front of her in the saddle, Seamus gave a small whimper.

For one moment, the guilt was overwhelming, then Morgan drove it away. Their pursuers would be gaining. Heart pounding and pulse racing, she glanced back down the creek. Had they closed up? If so, they'd be on them soon. She drew out her rifle.

Julia's head snapped around at that, and she stared at Morgan in alarm. Morgan sensed she was about to scream.

With a mixture of calm and urgency, Seamus said, "We go, Auntie Julia."

Julia stared at him a second, then exhaled, saying, "Lead on, young scout."

Another fifteen minutes with Morgan glancing behind her regularly, she halted them. The stream had grown too steep. They could go no farther in it. She kneed her horse up the bank onto dry ground where the trail cut up through the defile she remembered. No one followed her. She turned back toward them.

Mrs. Krueger's face had drained of color, and her mouth worked as if gasping for breath. Moving up beside her, Mrs. Stevenson rubbed the old woman's back, saying soothing words as if to a child. The housekeeper shot a look at Morgan and mouthed the words, *now what?*

"Can't we rest, Morgan?" Katelyn pleaded. "Please. My butt hurts bad. I can't go any farther."

"We need to keep going."

Somewhere in a nearby tree a bird cawed. A warm breeze had picked up, not a cooling one even at this elevation. No one moved. Exhausted, they sat their horses in the middle of the stream as it flowed rapidly past the mounts' ankles. None of the women were used to this kind of effort. In shock, beyond exhaustion, they stared at her as if she were speaking a foreign language.

Morgan said, "We have a little farther to go, then we'll rest. Just up this canyon."

If they could just get to the medicine wheel, not far now, she could hold off an army. That was their best hope to survive. No warrior threw himself at certain death, and she could make it certain death for them. If the risk was too great, he just left to raid and hunt somewhere else another day.

Finally, Morgan said calmly, "Julia, we must go." She turned her horse and headed up, not caring if any of them followed.

Finally, the older Krueger sister blinked, looked around as if she'd just awakened and realized where she was, snatched up her sister's reins, led her out of the water. Mrs. Stevenson followed with Mrs. Krueger. Then Katelyn.

They climbed a steep game trail and several times had to dismount and lead the horses up over fields of loose rocks, dislodging stones as they went. The women, especially Mrs. Krueger, struggled to keep up. Julia called for Morgan to stop, but she kept going, and Julia cursed her while dragging her horse upward. The trail vanished over flat rock and picked up again thirty or forty yards farther on, and then entered a long, steep defile with the creek tumbling swiftly down, careening between stone banks.

Finally, after two hundred more yards, they crested onto a large bowl of scattered spruce and pine trees and loose boulders, flanked by sheer rock walls. In the middle was the circle of rocks, the medicine wheel that she and Spotted Horse had visited several years before. This was the spot where Morgan would make her stand.

CHAPTER FIFTY-FIVE

In the late afternoon, Morgan sat at the edge of the bowl with the Winchester, watching down the defile to where it spread out onto the rolling hills below and the haze of the distant valleys beyond. It was like looking through an eyeglass. Seamus slept beside her, resting his head on her lap as she absently brushed his hair. She did not wonder what happened to the Indians who pursued them. She had to assume they were down there, perhaps waiting for dark.

She doubted all two hundred warriors would come after them, not enough glory to be spread around, but there might be a smaller party, ten or twenty. If they came, they'd have to come single file. From where she sat, she was fairly certain she could stop them, unless clouds rolled in and made it a pitch-black night. If so, they'd move back to the caves. Behind her, the women slept under the shade of the trees by the spring where they collapsed the moment they arrived. She supposed she should not blame them for being weak. After all, life in a New York City drawing room did not prepare you for life out here.

Julia did not sleep long. She came up and sat beside Morgan, brushing Seamus's cheek with her hand. "Are we safe here?"

Morgan shrugged. "For now. They don't have enough to overrun us. They'll pay dearly if they try."

Julia nodded, staring down at Seamus. "You have a beautiful boy, Morgan. I want children with Exeter someday. Does that shock you? Me, a mother. It shocks me."

"It's hard for me to picture you as a mother."

"Why not?" Julia replied, hurt. "I assure you I have all the parts." She raised her eyebrows in resignation. "I don't think he likes me though. Fortunately, he's such an honorable type he'll go through with the marriage anyway."

"Not exactly love," Morgan said.

Julia gave an exasperated sigh. "Love. Who gives a twit about love? For countless centuries, men and women married because their parents arranged it. A bargain, that's all. It works better than love. Bargains last, love fades."

Morgan didn't comment. It was of no real concern to her. Exeter might be dead anyway. Surely, the hunting party had been hit as well. She watched an eagle circle above on a warm current pushing up the gorge.

Finally, Julia asked, "What are they like, Indians?"

"Good people. Some bad. Just like us," Morgan said. "Indians don't think like whites, though. They don't make war like whites. They could pursue us to the ends of the earth or ride off to hunt buffalo. A lot has to do with their own personal medicine."

"Strange people. And you lived with them for years."

"I did. Married one. Had his child."

Julia studied her for several seconds. "You never intended to take us to my father this morning. You planned to come here all along."

It was not a question or accusation, just a statement of fact, so Morgan didn't answer.

Movement far below caught her attention, and she snatched up the Winchester. In the late afternoon haze, she saw men on horseback far beyond their narrow canyon, maybe two miles away. They disappeared again quickly. She gently shook Seamus awake, whispering, "Notse."

The boy sat up hastily and, seeing his mother's gaze, looked down the gorge.

Frightened, Julia said, "What is it?"

"Riders coming."

The Krueger girl's hand went to her throat.

"Go wake Mrs. Stevenson," Morgan commanded. "She can use a rifle."

When Julia brought Mrs. Stevenson carrying the other rifle, they all lay flat, watching below for the riders to reappear. When they did, Morgan counted four, no five, not that many. She was sure she could handle them. Too far to see clearly. Indians, or maybe Nash.

Ten minutes more they appeared down at the entrance of the defile, five riders coming slowly up the steep climb, white men she was sure. Nash then. She took aim at the first one and waited. The second in line leaned over his saddles, struggling to stay on, clearly wounded. Then, she recognized the man in front, Barnes, and eased her rifle back. "It's the hunting party."

Julia leapt to her feet and waved. "Here!" Her voice echoed off the canyon walls, and the men looked up; one waved back. She was in tears. "It's them. It's them." She stared breathlessly for several seconds, then muttered, "Where are the rest? There are only five of them."

Awakened, the rest of the women came up to the edge. With just five men below, the Krueger women had to be wondering if all their family had made it. Morgan could recognize all the riders and didn't tell her they hadn't.

In a frantic voice, Mrs. Krueger asked, "Is that Otto? Is that my boy Matty?"

No one answered her as Barnes led the remnants of the hunting party up into the bowl. With the scout were Otto Krueger, Lord Exeter, his father the duke, and Tommie Blakely, the footman. The duke was the man wounded. As the others dismounted, he was helped to the shade of the trees and placed lying down on his side, his shirt red with blood and the stub of an arrow stuck out of his lower back. As Julia placed a rolled blanket under his head, Mrs. Stevenson began to see to his injuries. Blakely was wounded also. He sat back against a tree, grimacing in pain as Katelyn tended to a large gash in his forearm.

Kneeling, Lord Exeter held his father's hand. The duke's face was pale and his eyes glassy. Morgan could see he would not survive.

Anxious, the Krueger sisters peppered their father with questions. "What happened? Where is Matty? Is he coming?"

"We were attacked," Krueger muttered. His hair was in disarray and his white shirt ripped at the sleeve. His eyes bore the wary gaze of a hunted animal.

Julia stared at her father. "Papa, where is Matty?"

Krueger's eyes clouded and he started to speak but stopped himself, blinked twice and shook his head. "He fell in the first wave of them along with MacLean and the other footman."

"Boyle was his name, sir," Mrs. Stevenson said sharply, glancing up from the duke. "Brendan Boyle."

Krueger wiped his brow with a trembling hand. "Yes. Boyle. We had no chance."

Barnes told the story. They were attacked midmorning by about fifteen Indians. "It was like they came out of the ground," he told them. "Maclean was closest and kilt outright. The footman Boyle tried to run, but it was hopeless. He was cut down like that." He snapped his fingers. "His nibs there was wounded. He's a tough old bird to make it this far."

Barnes led the survivors in among the buffalo and stampeded them. They rode the surge for miles, and in the dust and chaos managed to escape. When they came out of the herd, the Indians were gone.

Mrs. Stevenson looked up from dabbing a cloth at the duke's wound. "Mr. Dawes?" Her voice was soft, calm, but underneath was a well of emotion.

"Sorry, ma'am," Barnes said. "He had trouble with his horse and fell in the herd."

"He never could ride a horse," she said and went back to working on the duke.

Barnes went on with his story. "We rode back to camp, but you all was gone. We followed the wagons for a while. Seen them from a high ridge. Indians had got to them, and I knew we best skedaddle before they come back to finish us." He looked at Morgan. "That's when I seen your tracks and figured what you done. It took us a while to get here, and I'm afraid that done in his nibs. Right smart spot you found here."

No one spoke. Julia and Katherine held each other and cried for their brother. Mrs. Krueger sat down as if shot, her head buried in her hands, her shoulders heaving from her sobs.

In the sudden silence, the wheeze of the duke's breathing was particularly loud. "Can you do anything for him?" Exeter asked Mrs. Stevenson.

The housekeeper gave the barest shake of her head. A half-hour later, he died. They buried him at the back of the bowl by scraping out a shallow grave and piling rocks on top. Mrs. Stevenson spoke a few words over him and added a few more for Mathias, MacLean, Boyle and Dawes, and the freighters and their families. It had been an appalling harvest.

When darkness came, Barnes set up guards in pairs at the edge of the bowl to watch for Indians. The moon had risen full and illuminated the trail up the gorge as if it were an overcast day. It would be difficult for even a small party of warriors to slip up on them tonight if the watcher remained alert.

Morgan's guard came at ten with Katherine. Frightened of guns, the young Krueger girl didn't even bring a weapon. She could do nothing if an attack came except throw rocks. Grieving for her brother, she whimpered loudly followed by a fit of sniffles. Once, she fished in her pocket for a rock candy and sucked on it while going on with her annoying sniffles.

Completely worthless as a guard, Morgan thought. Maybe she should be more understanding but she wasn't. They were still in danger. "Go back and get some sleep," she said.

"I'm all right," Katherine said with exaggerated bluster. "I can do my part."

"Then do it quietly."

The girl's lower lip curled in a pout but she stopped whimpering. Morgan concentrated. She wanted nothing in the gorge to move without her either seeing it or hearing it. Even amid the gurgling plunge of the water, she could hear the sound of small animals scurrying in the trees, and the distant warble of a male mockingbird calling for its mate.

Indians don't lay siege. They will either come tonight or tomorrow, or go somewhere else. They won't wait. If her ragged band of refugees could survive the next couple of days, they'd be safe, and she could take Seamus home.

Katherine jumped at the sound of a screech and then another. "What was that?"

"Nothing. Just an owl. Quiet."

"My God," she whispered in a restrained wail. Her words encompassed more than horned owls. It took in the entire day, the entire situation, the entire nature of the world. Another fifteen minutes and Katherine was asleep, her head nestled in Morgan's lap like Seamus's had earlier. At least she didn't snore.

To the left, Exeter was leading Julia to a spot not twenty feet away for some privacy. But their voices carried likely to everyone else in the bowl, so she could not help but follow the conversation. "My father made an agreement with your father," he said formally. "I never wanted it. I hated the idea of being bartered like a bale of tea leaves, even though it would save our estate."

"I see," Julia murmured.

"But I will stand by that agreement. It has been made, and I will not vacate it."

"No," Julia said, her voice insistent. "You do not have to marry me, Edward." She used his given name for the first time. "I release you from the obligation. Unlike you, I am complicit in all this. I helped entrap you. I could not live with myself now if I forced you to go through with it." When he didn't speak, she said, "As of now, our engagement is off."

"Very generous of you, Julia," he spoke gently and for a fleeting moment sharing a familiarity and friendship Morgan doubted they could maintain. "Let's allow our engagement to remain till we return to civilization and revisit the topic."

"You seem sure we will return to civilization."

"I think we will. Barnes has sobered up for the moment, and your maid seems a rather capable sort in these wilds, so shall we wait to make a final decision?"

Several seconds passed before she responded. "As you wish, Your Grace," she said, using his title now that he was the Duke of Northampton, the moment of familiarity gone already. "So you know, I must tell you in all honesty who I am at my essential being. I am an uncommonly selfish and outspoken woman and make no apologies for it. If I were you, I'd keep that in mind."

"I knew that the moment we met."

Julia returned to the spring with the new Duke following.

At midnight Morgan and Katherine were relieved by Tommie Blakely and Krueger. She was less than confident in them as guards. An odd pairing, master and servant. Exhausted, however, when she lay down beside her son, she fell immediately asleep.

CHAPTER FIFTY-SIX

Morgan came awake. Long past midnight, the bowl was cast in heavy darkness, the full moon having sunk behind the mountains. Only the vast glitter-sweep of stars lay above. Something was wrong, and she instantly knew what it was. Seamus was gone. She sat up abruptly. He might have gotten up to relieve himself, but she didn't think so. A surge of fear and panic overwhelmed her, and she sprang up, grabbing the Winchester. She glanced around at the sleeping bodies. Furious, she saw Krueger among them. He should have been on guard.

As she slipped silently away from the spring, she studied one section of the bowl, then another, but didn't see him, nothing moving. The night animals had grown quiet. Had the Indians breached their defenses? What defenses? A wounded footman, who'd never been out of New York now the only guard? It was just as much her fault as Barnes. They both knew better.

She crept up to where Tommie was posted and made out his figure lying on the ground, asleep. That left them all vulnerable. She touched his arm, shaking him sharply, and knew instantly when he didn't respond that he was not asleep, but dead. Touching his neck for a pulse, her hand came away sticky with blood. Her heart raced, and she had to force herself to stop the surge of panic. They were not under attack, or Sioux and Cheyenne would be swarming them. This had to be the work of one man. Then, dread gripped her. Spotted Horse. He had come for Seamus. Then why wasn't she dead?

Without hiding her movement now, she worked her way around the edge of the bowl. It took only forty yards till she saw him, waiting for her, his outline faintly discernible in the darkness. He was sitting on a boulder, Seamus in his lap. She aimed her rifle in his direction.

Spotted Horse said softly in Cheyenne, "You kill your husband? I did not kill you."

"You are not my husband."

"You never told me the reason you hate me so."

"You would not understand."

She didn't want to shoot him in front of his son, but would if he tried to take him. Long ago with Running Hawk, she had learned a trick to see objects at night. If you look just off to the side, a clearer image comes into view. This she did, saw the boy was not being held against his will but rested a hand on his father's shoulder. She also saw that Spotted Horse held his rifle pointed at her.

"I remember when we came to this place," he said. "You were happy then."

"What do you want?"

"My son."

"Shoot me then. I won't let you take him."

The boy muttered something she couldn't make out but caught the edge of anxiety in it. He recognized the tone of their quick exchange. Silence followed, and Morgan slipped her finger into the trigger guard. Then, Spotted Horse set his rifle against the boulder and lifted the boy off his lap, setting him on the ground. "Go to your mother."

Seamus hurried to her as she lowered her rifle. She put an arm around him, drawing him near.

"The Wasicus armies are in our country," he said, the sweep of his arm taking in the world. "More of them than the grass. The warriors rode off to join the fight against the white chief Crook. Now, I must go kill many wasicus. I cannot take the boy with me, but I will come for him when we have driven our enemies away. I will find you and him. You know this." He picked up his rifle. "The boy must come with me then. He is Ho'nehe. He must be Cheyenne, not wasicus."

With that, he was gone, dashing over the edge of the bowl and down into the gorge.

Morgan took Seamus back to the camp and lay down with him in her arms on the thick bed of dry grass. Waking everyone up to tell them poor Tommie was dead would not raise him. Spotted Horse was gone; the Indians were gone. And Nash would have stayed far away from the war parties. At least for now, she saw no need to stand watch. Excited at seeing his father for the first time in more than a year, Seamus talked in Cheyenne and English interchangeably for nearly an hour before he fell asleep.

Morgan remained awake, her former husband's promise preying on her mind. She did not waver in her hatred for him. Fiona's scalp lock in his medicine bag would always make it so. But she had loved him once, and deep in her soul, in a scabbed over area, a part of her still did. Struggling with her thoughts, she dozed off till morning.

When dawn came, rain came with it, cold and blustery, with hailstones the size of apples. Morgan, carrying Seamus and the Winchester, led everyone in a dash for the caves. Krueger and Exeter carried Barnes, who was babbling as if the demons of hell pursued him. They made it inside and laid him by the wall where he curled up, holding his knees to his chest.

"Vhat's wrong mit him?" Mrs. Krueger asked with no sympathy.

"He's missing his alcohol," Mrs. Stevenson answered.

They huddled by the entrance as the hailstones pounded the rocks just outside.

"Where's Blakely?" Krueger asked.

Morgan said nothing.

"He was on guard last night. Surely he took cover," Exeter said.

"I'm cold," Katherine whimpered, shivering. Julia put an arm around her.

"We need a fire," Exeter said.

Ten minutes later when the hail eased up, Exeter and Krueger darted out into the rain to gather deadwood. After they returned, their exchange of dark glances suggested to Morgan that they'd found Tommie's body. She wondered if Krueger felt any guilt, but doubted it. He should be dead as well. It was his watch.

After fifteen minutes, using loose pieces of flint and quartz and a stream of greenbacks from Krueger's waistcoat, Morgan started a fire in the wet wood.

"I never would have thought that a simple fire would cost five thousand dollars," the robber baron said dryly as everyone huddled around, warming themselves.

***

Nash woke in an evil mood. It was just past dawn, and rain fell heavily on the slicker he had pulled over his head. He was cold and saw little chance of getting a hot cup of coffee this morning. With a curse, he sat up, pulling the slicker up tighter around him and shivered. He gazed at the lumps on the ground, his men sleeping under their own slickers. Grimm was not among them.

"Stupid bastard," he muttered. The glass-eyed idiot had gone out to scout and hadn't come back, either lost or run into the Sioux. Served the idiot right.

Getting up with a groan of stiffness, he stumbled past the sleeping bodies and relieved himself, wincing as he sent a long stream of piss into the creek. They were getting close to the nobs and swells. That damn O'Connor bitch had almost thrown him off the trail, with her old Injun trick up the stream. He was going to enjoy killing his old girl squaw.

Nash had known all along the nobs had no pot of gold, but they foolishly brought their women with them. Foolish but lucky for him. That was the real pot of gold. Krueger would not ransom the maids and maybe not even his old biddy of a wife, but he would pay a fortune for his two daughters. All Nash had to do was snatch them, which should be easy enough. Spare Krueger himself. Better make sure these half-wits knew that. When it all worked out, he'd be leading the good life in San Francisco.

The rain slackened as he stood by the raging creek, holding his penis, trying to empty the last of his water. He grimaced. Drip, drip, drip. Pissing burned, and he had to get up every five damn minutes during the night to do it. Finally, shaking himself dry, he stuffed himself back in his pants and returned to the men.

"Wake up, you lazy bastards," he shouted. "The gold ain't going to come to us. Any man not ready in five minutes loses his damn share."

CHAPTER FIFTY-SEVEN

When the rain slackened to a steady drizzle, the remnants of the Krueger party left the cave. A blustery wind buffeted them; clouds hung thick and grey just above. They returned to the grove of trees where the horses had been tethered and prepared to depart.

"Must we leave the warmth of the cave, Papa?" Katherine asked pleadingly. All the women but Morgan were shivering, huddling together while Exeter and Krueger saddled their horses. Their clothes became soaked. "At least, we had a fire."

In the haste to flee the day before, no one packed weather gear except Morgan, who draped a small poncho over Seamus and set him in the saddle of her horse. She gave her poncho to Katelyn, who gratefully threw it on. Morgan was cold and wet like the others but had dealt with such hardships before.

"No," Krueger snapped at Katherine, then added hastily, "Dear Katherine, we must race from here before the Indians come back. We cannot dally."

"Come back?" Julia said alarmed and the other women went pale.

Quickly, Mrs. Stevenson glanced around. "Where's Tommie?"

Again, the two men exchanged glances, then Exeter said, "We found him earlier." His handsome face a grimace, he wiped water from his forehead. "He's dead. Certainly, Indians. Why they did not come and finish us off, I could not even speculate. But Mr. Barnes says they're gone."

"We buried him near the duke," Krueger said.

Morgan said nothing. She glanced at Barnes, who was squatting at the spring, splashing water over his haggard face. He squinted up and rested his knowing eyes on her. The old bastard knew, she realized. He knew it was only one man who had come last night. Likely, he knew also who that one Indian was, but fortunately said nothing either. Morgan wanted away from here as quickly as possible, and explaining about Spotted Horse would hold them up. She no longer feared an Indian attack, but she did worry that Nash and his men were coming.

Barnes groaned, "Dear God, I need a drink."

"We should not put off leaving," Exeter said to Katherine and Julia. "We must make our way back to Cheyenne."

They packed what food they had left on one of the mules, and with Morgan leading followed the trail down the defile. With gusts of wind head on, she put Seamus behind her. They came out onto the endless series of rolling hills with great stands of juniper and pine and large swathes of green-grey grass. Barnes clung to his horse, vomiting, shaking and moaning the whole way. A bit of yellow spatter hit Mrs. Krueger's dress.

"Disgusting," Mrs. Krueger wailed. "Such a vile man."

Morgan wished she had whiskey to give him, just to shut him up. Exeter rode beside her. As they passed a timbered knoll, she caught movement below and sat bolt upright.

"Someone's coming," she said sharply.

Blurred by the drizzle and overcast dimness, she made out several riders half a mile down, coming toward them. It was Nash, she was sure. Fear mixed with a murderous rage in her. He was more threat to Seamus than the Cheyenne.

When Krueger came up, he cried excitedly, "White men. By Gad, white men. They will help us."

With Seamus clinging to her, Morgan spun the horse around. "Get to the knoll!" she shouted to everyone. Krueger grabbed her arm. "What are you saying? Help has come."

She had a knife in her hand instantly, swinging it at him with such ferocity that he flinched back, yelping in alarm. She had nicked the back of his hand and drawn blood.

"You are a mad woman," he screamed, holding his hand. "We can get those men to help us."

"That's Frank Nash and he doesn't help people. Those men will kill us."

Confused, Krueger regarded the approaching riders still several hundred yards away, but closing. She yanked his reins so he faced her. "And Mr. Krueger, if you ever touch me again without my permission, I'll cut you much more than that nick."

He blanched. The woman was scary and, indeed, mad. With Seamus hanging on, she raced up toward the sandstone knoll and to the cover behind the rocks and trees. Dismounting, she put the boy on the ground and drew the rifle from its scabbard.

"Stay here, boy. If I am killed, you run, you hide and get to your father." She ran to the top of the outcrop.

Only Barnes had followed, but instead of joining her, he collapsed to the ground in a fetal ball, moaning and talking gibberish. Seamus stared at him confused. The others, still out in the open, milled about uncertainly, the women looking at Krueger and Exeter.

Julia stared up at Morgan, then said something to Exeter, and with one final glance at the riders, she galloped to the outcrop and Exeter followed. But not Krueger and the rest of the women. Nash's men began firing at them, and without any further hesitation, they kicked their mounts toward the knoll.

Morgan shouted back to Katelyn to watch Seamus, then, lying flat, she observed the oncoming riders laboring their horses upward. If Nash won this encounter, only the Kruegers would survive. They were the only ones with money. Cold drizzle soaked her clothes, her wet blouse clinging to her back. She dismissed it from her mind and brought the rifle up, nestling it against her cheek like a favorite pillow. Another hundred yards, she told herself. Her body went calm; the feral part of her nature took hold. She had only one focus. Nash.

With a rifle, Exeter crawled up beside her. She doubted he'd be able to hit anything with it, but he might get lucky. Krueger and Julia joined them lying on the ground. He had his hunting rifle and Julia a small pistol. Her wet ringlets were stuck against the side of her face. Morgan gave her a smile. Like her sister who trembled back behind the knoll in her mother's arms, Julia was scared, but she was here.

"I owe you an apology, Miss O'Connor," Krueger said. "You were right. These men mean us no good."

Focused on the riders, she ignored him.

In alarm, Exeter asked, "What are we going to do? Can we negotiate with them?"

"No. You can't negotiate with these men." Her voice was cold and flat.

The riders closed to a hundred yards, screaming as if charging Sioux, firing steadily. Nash had no idea how well she could shoot. He was about to find out. Seventy yards. Fifty. In the steady rain, she couldn't spot which one was Nash, so she'd take them all. That's when she fired, bringing down the nearest rider. At her shot, the others opened up with their weapons, creating a din but hitting nothing. For Morgan, with the horses laboring uphill, it was a turkey shoot. She took a bead on the next man, shot him from the saddle, and moved on to the next, then a third. One of the others must have gotten lucky because another rider went down.

As one, the men raced for the nearest stand of trees some twenty yards off. Before they got to it, she shot a fifth man from his saddle. She had counted them. That now left four men.

Breathless, Exeter said, "We drove them off. By gad, we drove them off." He clapped Julia on the back. "We did it." She was trembling but forced a smile, fear and pride showing in her face.

Exeter turned his head to Morgan. "I have no illusions. You got most of them, Miss O'Connor." He paused, hesitant. "How does one so lethal become a lady's maid in New York City?"

Morgan gave him a humorless smile. "Too long a story, Your Grace."

That's when they heard Katelyn's scream. She turned instantly and saw her holding the limp body of Seamus in her lap.

Morgan cried out and ran to him, dropping to the ground beside him. She heard her own high-pitched wail. "No! No! Please, no."

Blood coursed down the right side of his face, the tip of his ear was bloody and the side of his head damp with matted blood. She saw a swelling the size of a goose egg. Everything was still and silent. The wind had stopped and the light rain made no sound. Her mind swirled with immeasurable grief and guilt. She should not be with these people. Despite her promise, she should never have tried to protect them. They meant nothing to her. Not even Katelyn or Julia. She hated them for making her be here and killing her son. She had failed in the one responsibility she had left in the world, to protect Seamus.

She could not hold back the tears. They slid down her cheeks. She took both his hands in hers and kissed them. His warm hands. The blood drained down his face still moving in trickles. His chest moved as he breathed. He was still alive. Her heart soared. He was still alive.

Mrs. Stevenson knelt beside her. "Let me look at him." With her bony fingers, she examined the side of his head.

His eyes opened, and he glanced around in confusion, then grimaced, "Ouch." His eyes watered. He was in pain. With a reassuring smile, Morgan ran a hand through his hair and leaned down to kiss his forehead.

Mrs. Stevenson sat back. "I think a bullet nicked his ear and grazed the side of his head. I'm not familiar with gunshot wounds, but I believe he'll be all right. I'll clean him up."

Morgan gave her a look of infinite thanks. The housekeeper washed and bandaged the boy's wounds with a strip of cloth wrapped about his head.

Morgan took Seamus in her lap and rocked him gently. Everyone but Barnes, who was still crunched in a ball and shivering, asked after the boy, even Mrs. Krueger. Julia and Katelyn sat down with Morgan and talked to Seamus, petting him and squeezing his hands. Morgan tried to erase another pang of guilt for disowning these women, but was not successful. Katelyn was a true friend and Julia, she didn't know quite what Julia was to her, but she did care about the young woman.

Seamus tightened his grip on his mother's hand and spoke to her in Cheyenne and she replied in the same language.

"What did he say?" Julia asked.

"He asked me if the bad men would come after him again."

"What did you say?"

Morgan's grey eyes went hard. "I told him no and that I would go kill his enemies tonight."

CHAPTER FIFTY-EIGHT

Barnes gave a loud, satisfied smack of his lips. Sporting a big grin, he sat drinking from a silver flask, exhibiting miraculous recovery from his recent ailments. Still cool, the rain had stopped, and the clouds dispersed into scudding grey islands. The day was waning, the sun already fallen behind the mountains for the long twilight.

"I gave it to him," Exeter said to the assemblage. "He was suffering from delirium tremens. The alcohol will restore him, make him useful till it runs out, which by the looks of it will be very soon."

Barnes lifted the flask in a grateful gesture. Earlier, he had roused himself enough to tell Morgan he would go after Nash and his men with her, but he was in no condition. That was when Exeter gave him the flask, and his shakes stopped.

Pushing up his courage, Exeter said to Morgan, "I will go with you also."

"No. Stay and protect the women," Morgan said, holding fiercely to a wide-eyed Seamus as if she refused ever to let him go. She didn't want the newly minted Duke of Northampton along. He wasn't capable of moving silently, and silence and surprise was all they had. At first, he had argued against anyone going out at night after these cutthroats, but she'd convinced them that if they didn't, Nash and his men would come for them, and they'd have the cover of darkness to their advantage.

She handed Seamus to Katelyn, and picking up her Winchester, turned to Barnes. "You ready?"

He finished off the flask. "Yes, ma'am."

Quickly, without another word, they moved into the trees behind the knoll and disappeared instantly. They worked their way down the flank of the hillside, the shadowy light amid the trees causing Morgan a deep unease. Nash and his men could already be coming up in the opposite direction. But her mind fully alert, she felt the old exhilaration of stalking her prey.

They pushed steadily down, Barnes ahead, panting heavily, as Morgan watched for the enemy. She didn't trust his boozy old eyes to protect them. The timber ended below the stand of thick pines and aspens where the four men had taken refuge. An open meadow stood between them. Morgan and Barnes exchanged knowing glances. Nash would not expect anyone from this direction. She was betting she had made the first move, and must not let that initiative be wasted. The distance across, thirty yards, gaped before them, endless. Primal terror welled up in the dark chambers of her mind. They would have to cross. They could not wait till night. As soon as Nash had darkness, he would attack the knoll, and then the wrong people would die. Even in the cool of the evening, sweat drained into her eyes, stinging them, and she blinked them dry. Thirty yards of open space. It was her show and no other way across. Just go, she screamed inside her head. In her heart she knew Nash sat across the meadow with his long rifle, an itch on his finger, waiting for her.

Morgan sprang up. Her legs felt like oatmeal as she sprinted into the open to a clump of scraggly shrubs and slid down into a shallow trench, crawling silently, quickly, another ten yards. She hadn't heard him, but sensed Barnes behind her. God bless him, she thought.

From the end of the trench, she saw the tree line not ten yards away, beckoning, terrifyingly so. Expecting to be shot, she dashed across the last of the meadow, fast like when she was a girl. Running like a mountain lion chasing down its prey. A bullet hit her forehead every step of the way, but she made it.

Barnes was just behind her. He collapsed to the ground, his chest heaving, breath rasping, but grinning as if he'd just made off with all the gold in California. After a few minutes when his breathing had leveled, he spit out in a harsh whisper, "God damn it, I'm getting too old."

Finally, they moved silently, deeper into the grove. Toward the center, they crested a short ridge that swept down a few feet into a tiny bowl where the creek flowed. Four horses were tethered to trees, but the men were gone. Where's Nash, she mouthed, but Barnes only shrugged. She held up a hand for Barnes to wait and disappeared back into the shadows. Rapidly, she searched the grove but found no one, no tracks.

Returning to Barnes, she shook her head and pointed below. They found the tracks of Nash and the other three men across the creek and followed them into the rocks, heading back uphill. She glanced far off to the knoll and saw no one, her people hidden. Good. Her people, she thought. That was an odd phrase for her, but they were. Seamus, Katelyn, Julia, even the Kruegers and Mrs. Stevenson. Her responsibility. Her people.

Exposed to gunfire for several seconds at a time, they moved from boulder to boulder, always up. She was quick across the open areas, he agonizingly slow. What was Nash doing, she asked herself. She didn't like this.

"This is too damn easy," Barnes said, picking up the same thing. "Nash is no babe in the woods. Why is he leaving a trail even Exeter could follow?"

"Nash wants us to follow him."

"That's clear."

"Then maybe we shouldn't."

Slowly, she considered his plan. Nash was smart like a jackal. Clearly, he planned to attack the knoll from above, but had realized she was behind him and was leading her away. Now, he would race for it, defended as it was by tenderfeet. Easy pickings. She had been a fool, an utter fool. As she realized the truth, fear overwhelmed her.

"We have to get back now," she said fiercely.

Barnes's rheumy eyes took on sudden hardness. "That bastard. I think you're right."

A grassy meadow of yellow flowers led to another stand of pine forty yards across the slope. Getting there and then moving downhill from grove to grove was the quickest way to the knoll. Returning the way they'd come would take longer. Across another open field. If anyone was among those pines, they'd be dead.

She hesitated, but Barnes sprang up and started running in his stumbling gait, so slow she could almost walk to catch up. Bent low to the ground, she followed. He was halfway there when a shot echoed from the pines, and the bullet exploded out of the old mountain man's back, spraying blood and debris on her face. Instantly, he collapsed, dead.

Morgan dived behind a swell of ground as a shot sprayed dirt and clumps of grass on her. Frantically, she wiped her face clean of Barnes's blood and brushed off the dirt. Think, she told herself. She focused on who was across the way. One shot at first meant one man. Whoever it was could shoot, though. Got Barnes, barely missed her. Nash would be making his way down to the Kruegers and her son, and she was stuck here.

And then she understood. Understood his whole plan. Nash wanted Julia and Katherine. Kidnap them. Krueger would pay a pot of gold to get them back. And he would kill her son to get at her. It was the best way for his revenge. She could not wait, pinned down here, unable to protect him, but she was dead the second she stood up. Before the thought was clearly formed, she sprang to her feet and ran.

***

In the purple twilight, several stars had already appeared in the darkening sky. Huddling together near the tree line where the horses were tethered, the women talked animatedly, Mrs. Krueger and Katherine wanting to flee as soon as it was dark. Bold for those two, Exeter thought, but then he saw the absolute terror in their eyes and understood. They wanted to run and he sympathized.

Beside him, Julia said, "We can't leave Miss O'Connor." She said it only to him for she knew they were going nowhere at night. Worried and frightened, Seamus squeezed her hand.

Holding his rifle in the crook of his arm, Krueger stood on the knoll in full view but drew no shots. He turned and went back to the others. "I think we must prepare ourselves for the night," he said.

"Can we start a fire, Papa," Katherine asked, pleadingly. "They know we're here. Why shouldn't we be warm?"

"I think not." He rubbed his cheek with his knuckles for warmth. "They will be able to see us but we won't see them."

"Right you are, Governor," a voice called from the trees. Two men walked out with handguns drawn.

Slowly, Krueger began to lift his rifle, but another voice came from the opposite side. "Now, Mr. Krueger, that would be plum foolish. Ease that rifle down to the ground. We don't want to hurt you. We don't want to hurt any of you."

Krueger did not hesitate, quickly setting it on the damp grass. The man said, "There. Now that wasn't so hard, was it? Right smart." He ordered his two men, "Bring their horses here. I don't want to waste any time."

He approached Krueger, and stood not a foot from him. "I'm Frank Nash. Maybe you've heard of me. I was with Buffalo Bill in *Scouts of the Plains* in Chicago and New York. No more famous man than me in the West."

Krueger stared at him with incredulity. At that moment, several shots echoed from up the slope somewhere, and everyone looked in that direction.

***

Within her first two strides, Morgan heard the shots whine past her ear, felt their sharp, pinprick breeze. Over and over in her terrified mind, they struck her body. The man was now out of the trees, following her, trying to run and shoot. Doing that, his accuracy was off. She plummeted on down the slope, crashing twice and rolling to her feet, bruised but running on in desperation.

Sliding to a halt on her butt, she turned and aimed. He was leaping from a rock forty yards away, and she caught him in the air with the first shot. He fell to the ground like a sack of barley, bounced once and stopped, unmoving, likely dead. She put another bullet in him to make sure.

***

At the knoll, they waited, listening, and when several seconds went by without any further gunfire, the three men visibly relaxed.

"I guess that just about caps the climax, Ferguson," Nash said to the wizened old man with him. Ferguson grinned back.

"We best be moving. Orville, get their horses," Nash ordered.

Orville, the third man, untethered five horses and brought them up to the group. "What about Bonner? Ain't we going to wait for him?"

"He can catch up." Nash's eyes went cold as he scanned his prisoners. "Where's that damn Indian boy?" He saw him by Julia, grabbed him viciously and dragged him away. When Julia came at him, Nash punched her chest, knocking her to the ground.

"See here." Exeter stepped angrily toward him but froze when all three men aimed their guns at him.

"What are you going to do with him?" Julia demanded as Exeter helped her up.

Nash held the boy by the scruff of the neck. "I ain't going to hurt him lesson you folks is uncooperative," he said coldly and then fixed on Krueger. "Now, here's the nub, rich man. I'm going to take your two daughters, and there's not a damn thing you can do about it."

At that, Exeter stepped protectively in front of Julia. "You can't do that. This is an abomination."

Ferguson viciously clubbed him to the ground with his gun barrel. The women screamed; Exeter lay unmoving.

"Shut the hell up," Nash shouted at them. "Krueger, you go back to Cheyenne and pull together enough cash for me to release them, let's say fifty thousand dollars for each. No, make it $100,000. If you don't, I'll sell them to the Sioux. After we've had a little sport with them first."

Orville laughed. Krueger said, frightened, "You can't do this. Please, where's your humanity."

Nash merely chuckled. "If you fight me, I kill one of the girls. I don't need both. Price still the same." He looked at the two sisters. "If you two fight me, I kill your mother. Are we all understood here? Good."

Katherine was crying, while Julia stood in shock. Prodded by Ferguson and Orville, the sisters mounted their horses. The two men swung up on separate horses beside them and waited for Nash. Jerking Seamus's head back by the hair, Nash drew his knife. The boy began singing in Cheyenne with a fractured, high-pitched wail.

"No!" Katelyn screamed. "Please don't."

Julia pleaded, "We'll give you no trouble. I promise. Anything you want. If you have any compassion, sir."

"You'll give me no trouble anyway," Nash said. "This boy's mother owes me. She ain't here no longer for me to collect so he's got to pay the piper. I always collect my debts."

He put the knife to Seamus's throat. "See that sky. It's the last—."

In a red mist, Frank Nash's head exploded like a melon, and he fell on his back, lifeless. The sound of the shot was followed in half a second by two more. The chests of the two men on horseback opened up, one after the other.

CHAPTER FIFTY-NINE

Travelling slowly, it took Morgan and her small band of survivors ten days to reach Ft. Fetterman. She had constructed a travois to carry Exeter, and Julia tended to him. He was up and able to ride after two days, still bearing a massive headache. Before leaving, Morgan had gathered a large remuda from the horses of the dead, ten in total, claiming them all for herself. When they arrived at Fetterman, she sold them and the saddles for a tidy sum of seven hundred dollars. She planned to stay only a day before heading for Lone Tree, but two things kept her an extra day.

The first was Sergeant Reardon. He was at the fort, and he had a tale to tell. They ran into each other at the sutler's store while she was picking up supplies for her journey home. He greeted her as if she were a long lost family member, clutching her in a great bear hug and swearing she was a sight for sore eyes, even though they'd seen each other less than two weeks before.

"I heard about what happened, lass," he said. "I'm damn glad you made it."

She was excited at the prospect of seeing Will. "Is the regiment here?"

A shadow fell across his face. "No, afraid not." He explained how General Crook was claiming he defeated the Sioux chief Crazy Horse again at a place called the Rosebud.

The general had yanked Reardon off the battlefield before the fighting ended and sent him to Fort Fetterman to make the first report by wire to General Sheridan in Chicago. The sergeant sucked in a great breath. "They ran over us, those Sioux of Crazy Horse. And your Cheyenne," Reardon said with bitterness.

Her anxiety overwhelmed her. "Is Will all right?"

"I don't know, lass. I didn't see him before I left. No reason to think he's hurt." He slapped his campaign hat against his trouser leg in disgust and said with intensity, "It was a trap. Same tactics that bamboozled poor Captain Fetterman years ago, and that damn Crook fell for it. He sent us troopers to chase the Indians from ridge to ridge, breaking us into small pockets for them to attack in great numbers. They tore into us good. They left the field at their own choosing. It was no victory of ours." His face clouded over with gloom. "Colonel Gannon is dead."

Her face went pale. "Oh, God, poor Mrs. Gannon."

"It was Spotted Horse. He and his warriors overran Gannon's position. They had no chance. Many died with him but not all. The lieutenant might still be alive. No reason to think otherwise right now."

The words were not reassuring. *Overrun.* Her stomach churned. She couldn't lose another person she loved. Her wintry grey eyes softened and teared. She blinked them away. "I'll write my condolences to Mrs. Gannon. Can you carry the letter to her, Sergeant?"

"Yes, of course, I'm on my way to Camp Harrison this afternoon."

She wrote a short letter expressing her sorrow at the loss of Mrs. Gannon's husband and thanking her for all her help. She said she hated to impose on her grief but asked whether she knew if Will Raines had survived the battle. If so, could she notify her at Lone Tree in Montana Territory?

The second thing that kept Morgan and Seamus from leaving Fetterman was the sudden marriage of Exeter and

Julia. It was contracted, and he was adamant they not wait for the inevitable circuses in New York and London that would accompany their nuptials. They could put on show weddings in both cities, but he wanted it done officially now. For Seamus's sake, Morgan stayed so they could attend. Besides, she owed Julia.

The wedding of the Duke of Northampton and Julia Krueger of New York took place in the small post chapel, presided over by the army chaplain. Besides the surviving Krueger contingent—Exeter was the only one left from the Northampton side, the commanding officer and his wife were in attendance along with several other officers and their wives, all giddy with excitement over the great event taking place at their small fort. Though a contracted marriage, the passionate kiss at the ceremony's end seemed to promise a chance of happiness.

At the reception afterward, put on by the post commander's wife, Julia couldn't hide her pleasure at becoming a duchess. It was then Morgan said goodbye to them all. Even Mrs. Krueger offered thanks for their lives, and Krueger presented her with both Winchesters. Mrs. Stevenson said she still didn't like the Irish but conceded they were a fierce race. Morgan laughed and gave the woman a hug. Exeter wished her Godspeed.

They all said goodbye to Seamus and wished him well. Katelyn cried as she hugged him for the last time, and Morgan saw tears well up in her son's eyes. Finally, he ran to the new Duchess of Northampton, and she scooped him up in her arms.

"Well, you know I am a duchess now, and you must always do what a duchess says?"

He nodded.

Julia looked past him to Morgan. "Good. Then, this is not goodbye but a temporary parting. Someday I expect you and your mother to visit the duke and me in England. That, sir, is a command. We will see the Captured Girl and her son, my own special beau, again."

When Julia set him down, she and Morgan hugged quickly. Julia frowned. "Dear God, what am I going to do without a lady's maid?"

Morgan smiled. A few minutes later, the boy and his mother were unusually silent as they rode on separate horses out of Fort Fetterman, trailing behind them two mules loaded with supplies.

***

Staying well away from Indian trouble, it took Morgan and Seamus three weeks to reach Lone Tree. The entire trip she worried about Will. As they rode slowly through Lone Tree, she noted it had grown, added a couple saloons, a large dry goods store and two law offices. The church and sawmill still operated. A few people stepped outside to watch them pass, but she ignored them. She thought they were no doubt concerned by an Indian boy riding with a white woman. The hell with them.

In another hour Morgan was home. At first sight, her heart lifted into her throat. Amid the shadows of the high Absarokas, the ranch house lay blackened and destroyed but for the stone fireplace. Next to the remnants of the corral, the barn partially stood with three sides and roofing. Weeds and tall grass covered the garden and the rest of the grounds. For a flickering moment, she saw the bodies of her Da, Patrick and Fiona scattered in the yard. Her breathing grew rapid. She had not known if she could come back to this place with all its ghost. Blood burned through her veins.

Then, the bodies were gone, yet she sensed her family's overwhelming presence. Her eyes watered. This was their Seyan, their place of the dead. They would always be here. Conor, too, would be here one day, if, as Will said, he was yet alive. She would make the place ready for him.

"What's wrong, Mommy?" Seamus asked.

"Yes, son. We are home."

Morgan dismounted and lifted him to the ground, and he ran to the well and started pumping the handle.

"Careful, son. It's a long way down," she said, and then she saw the wolf and stiffened.

It was fifty yards off studying them. Slowly, she slipped her rifle from its scabbard. With Seamus always running loose, she couldn't leave this animal around, bold as it was. As it sniffed at the air, Morgan took aim. Just before she pulled the trigger, he did the strangest thing, making her hesitate. From a standing position, it leapt nearly five feet straight in the air, yelping as if shot. But the screeching was more like uncontrollable ecstasy. He broke into a breakneck run straight at her. Her own heart swelled and pounded hard against her chest. She dropped the rifle and caught the leaping beast in her arms. He kept yelping, over and over, as he furiously licked her face.

She realized she was crying. "Bran, you old rogue. I thought you surely dead."

CHAPTER SIXTY

November 25, 1876

Frost lay heavy on the landscape the night Colonel Ranald Mackenzie's army of eleven companies entered the valley of the Red Fork. The last great Cheyenne village lay less than a mile upstream, more than 200 lodges, eight hundred warriors, perhaps a thousand old people, women and children. The Indian scouts led the way, several hundred, Pawnees led by Major Frank North, Shoshones by Lieutenant Walter Schuyler, and the largest contingent of nearly 200 Lakota, Arapaho and Cheyenne led by Lieutenant Will Raines. His Crow had gone home, not wanting to take the field beside their enemies. As usual, they wore a red strip of cloth around their upper arms to distinguish them during battle. The hostiles knew they were coming.

Things never changed, Raines thought caustically as he wrapped the wool scarf tighter around his neck. Just like General Crook's winter campaign in February and March, this night was bitterly, bitterly cold. A fat, waxing moon sat in a cloudless sky and illuminated the harshness of the surrounding bluffs and steep foothills. During the night, the entire army had painstakingly maneuvered through a treacherous labyrinth of ravines and frozen streams to reach the valley.

He rode beside Gerrard with Reardon a little ways off, frequently flexing the gloved hand with the missing fingers. Then, fumbling in his pocket, he pulled out the stub of a cheroot, stuck it in his mouth and lit it with shivering hands. He glanced at Raines. "It's cold as a witch's tit, Billy Boy. My piss froze before it hit the ground last night. I got no more fingers to give to this man's army."

Coming south from Cantonment Reno, the column had crossed Crazy Woman Creek not far from where his baptism of fire took place a year and half before. Raines thought he was no longer the shavetail caught up in a comedy of errors that made him a surprising, if fraudulent, hero. Certainly, he was still frightened, but he'd learned that only a fool wasn't. Now, he was capable of handling his emotions and confident in his soldiering abilities. He almost looked forward to the coming attack. It would not end the Indian war, but it would go a long way toward it, and that was the most important thing about it. When hostilities ended, he could go home to Lone Tree.

He hunched his shoulders against a brutal gust of wind and tugged his coat tighter still. Inside his shirt, he had the latest letter from Morgan. She was pregnant. Reading that in her last letter, his heart had about burst from his chest. He had made a new baby with her. He looked on Seamus as his son, and now another child.

In the hectic summer campaign, he could not get leave to see her, especially after the Little Bighorn debacle that had shaken them all. Then in late July, he volunteered for an assignment to pursue a deserter, which he tracked to Bozeman. There, he arrested the man and took him to the guard house at nearby Fort Ellis. On the way back to Crook's army, he made a detour to Lone Tree and his wife. It was their honeymoon in the new cabin, small but livable, and to him, more beautiful than his family's mansion on the Avenue. Short as it was, the beginning of their life together. He desperately wanted to get back to that life. But he still had three years of his army commitment left before he could resign his commission. Now, he was on the Red Fork of the Powder River, closing in on perhaps a thousand Cheyenne warriors. All he wanted to do now was his duty, survive and someday get home.

The steady clomp of horses and the creak of saddles seemed loud in the cold night air. Strangely, the Cheyenne hadn't fled; his own scouts reported they were staying to fight. All around him were his Indian scouts, bundled in their thick coats. Raines had gathered them at the Red Cloud and Tall Bull Agencies. For them to attack a Cheyenne village was something Raines could not understand.

"Why do they do it?" he asked Gerrard abruptly. "The Cheyenne? And Lakota for that matter, scouting for us, fighting their own people?"

"Each man does what his medicine leads him to do," Gerrard answered, his breath coming out in white gusts, "and every man respects that. But I am only half-Cheyenne, so I only half understand."

Raines gave a sardonic chuckle.

"Maybe, I should not tell you this," Gerrard said. "Two nights ago, Medicine Wolf, a scout from this Cheyenne village we attack today, slipped into our camp to eat with his brother Two Shields. You know Two Shields. He is one of our best scouts. The two brothers sat at our campfire, ate and laughed and enjoyed the camaraderie of their friends, then Medicine Wolf slipped back out of camp, no doubt to warn his people."

After a moment, Raines said, "This might be the end of the Cheyenne."

Known to be in the camp were all the great Cheyenne chiefs, Dull Knife, Little Wolf and Wild Hog, medicine chiefs Black Hairy Dog and Cold Bear, and war chiefs Two Moons and Big Crow. There were also the two warriors that many young men followed, Last Bull and Spotted Horse of the Kit Fox warrior society, Morgan's *other* husband. And they were standing and fighting.

"I think it might," Gerrard said somberly. In the moonlight, his expression was impassive, giving no hint to his true emotions about the coming end to the freedom of his mother's people.

***

"Many soldiers come," the herald announced as he went through the village. "Many of our brothers with them. They come with the sun."

With a couple hours of darkness yet, Dull Knife addressed the other chiefs in the Council of Forty-Four, "You hear that, my brothers. They come. I have learned during our summer of victories, at the Rosebud, the Greasy Grass against Yellow Hair Custer and countless smaller fights, that each time we are fewer but each time the white soldiers become more. Soon, after more victories like these, there will be no more Cheyenne."

A muttering of agreement met his words. "We must take the women and children north into the mountains and find Crazy Horse," he urged. "There, we can protect them. We must think only of saving the People."

Other chiefs spoke in turn also wanting to go. Near the end, Spotted Horse rose to speak. He had tugged a heavy blanket over his grey, white man's coat. "We stay here. This is where we fight the Wasicus. Heammawihio sent me a vision. It told me my medicine is strong. If we stay, we will drive the Wasicus from our land. We fight them here."

Silence met this pronouncement. After a moment, Big Crow stood and gave a long speech but ended it by saying, "We must fight the Wasicus here."

Afterward, Spotted Horse and his friend Last Bull went through camp cutting the travois cinches on the horses of those who wanted to leave and called for a scalp dance. When wood was piled high, the fire started and the dancing began.

Last Bull said to Spotted Horse, "Now, you and I, we must fight and die for the People."

"Seyan awaits us all."

***

When dawn came, Raines saw the village a half-mile ahead nestled in a grove of willows. Steam rose off the Red Fork, drifting over the village and giving the lodges an otherworldly aspect in which dim figures rushed about, their frantic voices reaching back to the advancing column. The first shot was fired from the ragged hills to the right. When it came, the Indian scouts shrieked their war cries and raced ahead.

"The ball has commenced," Reardon shouted, drawing his rifle from its scabbard and kneeing his horse into a gallop. Behind them, the cavalry dashed up on line, the pounding hooves sounding like the roar of a waterfall. Several warriors ran north out of the village, up the hillside from where the first shot had come.

"Cut them off," Raines shouted and raced his horse after them, praying that his scouts would follow.

They did, firing on the fleeing Cheyenne. As they approached a ravine, he recognized Spotted Horse and several other hostiles rise up, sending a volley back at Raines's scouts. Several fell. The two groups exchanged fire for nearly half a minute at close range. Finally, outnumbered, Spotted Horse and his men withdrew to a nearby jumble of boulders for cover.

As Raines pursued them, his horse reared at something on the ground. It was the body of an almost naked boy. He had been shot trying to reach the hills. In the subzero temperature, he could not have survived long. Blocking the image from his mind, he urged his horse passed him, up the steep slope.

Nearby, Two Shields, looking for his brother Medicine Wolf, saw Spotted Horse dashing from rock to rock. Two Shields took aim.

On the other side of the village, the Cheyenne women, children and old people fled up into the hills. So quick was their escape, many had barely dressed and carried little or no belongings. That's when the cavalry slammed into the village and rode through till they hit a jagged Cheyenne skirmish line that held them up. Fighting was close up and intense, often hand to hand. The lines of warriors fell back.

In the chaos, Last Bull searched for Spotted Horse so they could make a stand together. He saw him across the valley, wearing the grey white man's coat, dashing about among the melee. Last Bull ran across the village, dodging the individual battles and skirmishes, and gained the hillside. There, as he neared his friend, he saw a puff of debris explode from Spotted Horse's chest, saw him collapse to the ground on one knee. Then a second bullet to his head finished him. A government scout dashed in to count coup. Spotted Horse was dead.

Stunned, Last Bull returned to the village to retrieve the two most important medicine bundles, the Four Sacred Arrows and the Sacred Buffalo Hat, and raced with them to the north and into the mountains, trying to find the last of his people.

The battle had been brief and bloody. With control of the village and the pony herd, the soldiers searched the lodges where the Cheyenne had left much behind. Dried corn and meat, sacred objects like shields and pipes, clothes, blankets and buffalo robes. They also found personal and regimental items from the 7th Cavalry, Custer's regiment.

At seeing these, the men seethed, and Colonel Mackenzie was seized by fury. He ordered the village razed. "Burn every damn lodge to the ground," he ordered.

In the foothills to the north, Raines was trying to gather his scouts who had been pursuing the Cheyenne. He crested the ridge of a ravine and came upon four Cheyenne huddled behind rocks, a woman, two young children and a boy of thirteen or fourteen, holding a shotgun as if standing guard.

Remembering Crazy Woman Creek, Raines didn't want to risk his life trying to save another boy. Leveling his pistol, he plunged down the ravine, shouting in Cheyenne, "Drop the shotgun, boy. You will not be hurt."

If the boy didn't surrender, Raines would kill him. Only a few feet away now, the boy turned and lifted the weapon toward him. Raines aimed the pistol. Then, he saw the boy's green eyes and the scar on his cheek. It was Morgan's brother.

"Conor," Raines cried, easing his pistol back.

The boy fired the shotgun.

CHAPTER SIXTY-ONE

January 15th, 1877

In the late afternoon, Morgan, along with Seamus and their hired hand Miguel Garcia, a taciturn old man, went to the corral to saddle their horses. Her swollen belly showed the six months pregnancy. Bundled in thick coats against the cold, they rode out to the nearby snow-covered pasture where Morgan's fifty head of cattle fed on the hay she and Miguel had spread earlier that day. Still half-wild, these fifty cattle were all that was left of what her family had once owned. Three heifers were ready to calve, and with the temperature falling into the teens tonight, she wanted to get them back to the barn out of the weather. In cold like this, new calves could freeze if dropped in the open.

First, Morgan and Miguel went down to Lone Tree Creek, both carrying sledgehammers. The creek had been frozen for weeks, and they had to go out daily to break it open so the cattle could drink. The sun had dropped behind the snow peaks of the Absarokas an hour before. On his small pony, Seamus had already cut out the heifers from the small herd.

"I think they give birth tonight," Miguel said.

"We'll get no sleep," Morgan answered.

She got little sleep as it was. Along with the pregnancy, work and taking care of Seamus, she'd been trying to battle a poisonous despair for several weeks. Not the baby. It was fine. But she'd not heard from Will for nearly two months, and she was sure something had happened to him. It could just be the uncertainty of the mail, but with all the fighting that went on this past year, more likely he'd run into trouble. In her scabbed-over heart—it had to be, she felt certain he was not coming home to her. Finally, starting a family of her own, she was losing half her core at the beginning. For Seamus's sake, she tried to dispel her dark moods but was finding it harder and harder to do.

It took them half an hour to get the three young cows back to the barn and the stalls with straw bedding. Lone Tree ranch now had a reasonably well-constructed barn, repaired corral, bunkhouse and main cabin. When she first arrived back in June, three men came to visit that afternoon. She met them out in the tall grass of the yard. One was the pastor who she remembered and the sawmill owner who she also knew. The third man introduced himself as Frank Templeton, brother of the former owner of the Templeton Ranch.

"It *is* you," the pastor said. "Morgan O'Connor. Blessed is the Lord." His eyes watered.

Not so blessed, she thought. "Yes, Pastor Rodgers. I'm back."

They looked at Seamus as if waiting for her to introduce him or explain him or disavow him. She said nothing allowing the silence to grow. Finally, Frank Templeton said, "If you'll allow it, we'll be here tomorrow. All of us, your neighbors, our wives, to help raise a house up. Get you back on your feet."

She was taken aback by the offer. "Why would you do that?"

"We're your neighbors," the sawmill owner said simply.

Templeton took a while before he added quietly, "For my brother. For my nieces."

Nearly fifty people came the next day. The valley had filled up in the last few years, Morgan realized. A temporary cabin of rough-hewn logs was put up in a day, as well as the barn and bunkhouse. Around noon, the women came with their children, who played with Seamus without recognition of any differences between them, though some of the parents seemed disdainful of the boy and his mother. Just there to do their neighborly duty.

The women also brought food, and a great feast was had. Afterward, Morgan thanked them all for their kindness. Templeton said he and his men would come to help round up her mavericks, those that survived the cougars and wolves and rustlers. Many would have by now found their way into other herds. The ranchers figured they owed her some steers because of it and so to avoid any claims by her, they all pledged a few from their stock. In that way, she ended up with nearly sixty head to start her herd. Too many had already died in the winter.

While Miguel stayed in the barn to watch the heifers, Morgan fixed dinner. By the fireplace, Seamus did homework on his numbers that his mother had set for him. Outside, the last of daylight was waning when she heard the riders coming.

"Stay here," Morgan said, throwing on her coat and taking the rifle out onto the porch. She set it against the doorjamb.

In the last of dusk, she saw two men wearing thick winter coats approach the yard at an easy canter. One of them held back near the barn as if fearful to come any farther, while the other rode in, and Morgan didn't like that. She eased back next to the rifle, but didn't pick it up. In the fading light, she couldn't make out the features of either but noticed the one holding back was likely Indian by the single long braid dropping down from under a cap with ear flaps. The rider coming on was tall, and as he got closer, she saw he only had one arm, the coat sleeve of his left pinned at the elbow.

Then, when he rode into the light cast from the windows, she recognized the wide grin and her heart broke open. It was Will. She burst from the porch with a scream. He leapt from the horse and caught her in his one arm. They kissed fiercely over and over, and she began to cry. "Will, Will, I was so worried."

Setting her down, he patted her belly. "You are a lot heavier than I remember. You used to be a little slip of a girl."

She laughed through tears, clinging to him. "That's your fault. Where have you been? I haven't heard from you in weeks."

"Sergeant Reardon wrote to you, but clearly it never came. I spent the last few weeks in the hospital at Fort Fetterman. Not a nice place to be. A tiny little log room with a dirt floor. Then, I had a lot of paperwork to handle. I'm no longer in the army."

"Oh, Will. You so loved it."

"I love you and Seamus far more and want to be with you." He held up his stump. "Gone from the elbow, but a fair exchange to come back here." He squeezed her close to him. "Besides, as you can see, I can still do all the hugging I need with one arm."

She realized a lot of that was bravado, but she loved him for it. She squeezed him hard as if she would never release him again. Seamus came out and Will picked him up and told him he was shocked at how big he was getting.

The other man was now slowly ambling his horse into the yard, turning his head about studying the place as if it held dark shadows where danger hid. Finally, he pulled up a few feet away and dismounted. Morgan wiped her eyes so she could get a clear look at him. He was maybe thirteen or fourteen. In his face she saw the remnants of the little boy he had once been.

"Conor," she gasped. Then leapt into his arms.

THE END

Printed in Great Britain
by Amazon